These Monstrous Deeds

T.J. Hamel

This is a m/m dark romance novel with lines so blurry, you'll feel like you're reading through a kaleidoscope. It is rated explicit and intended for mature audiences only (18+).

*Though a decent amount of the scenes between the main characters (**NOT ALL**) are dubcon, some are very clearly non-consensual and classify as rape, even with the circumstances as complicated as they are.*

Due to the nature of the plot, this book contains scenes that some might find triggering and/or disturbing, as well as explicit sex scenes between the main characters. I've included the warnings I feel are the most important, but not all could be covered without giving away too much of the novel.

Resources

The National Human Trafficking Hotline is a national, toll-free hotline in the United States and is reached by calling 1-888-373-7888. Other options for help include e-mailing NHTRC@PolarisProject.org, &/or texting 'HELP' or 'INFO' to BeFree (233733). These methods help victims come in contact with a human trafficking task force, NOT law enforcement. If the danger is immediate, it is best to call 911.

For Human Trafficking Hotlines in other countries, go to: ec.europa.eu/anti-trafficking/citizens-corner-national-hotlines/national-hotlines_en

Contents

Warnings

Content Warnings: Rape/Sexual Assault, Sex Trafficking/Slavery, Non-Consensual Drug Use, Physical and Sexual Violence, Psychological Torture, Non-Consensual Sharing, Suicidal Thoughts/Ideations, Gangrape (not involving main characters), Referenced Underage Rape (not involving main characters), Depictions of Child Sex Trafficking (no scenes of child rape depicted)

Read at your own risk, and please practice self-care when reading this book.

*** **This is book 1 in a 3 book series. This series DOES end in a HAPPY ENDING if you're willing to stick around!** ***

"Whoever fights monsters should see to it that in the process he does not become a monster. And if you gaze long enough into an abyss, the abyss will gaze back into you."

-- Friedrich Nietzsche --

Chapter One

THERE WAS A POST on Tumblr once. *10 Things To Do If You're Ever Kidnapped.* Carter had skimmed it before pressing the heart icon, saving it in his likes to read more thoroughly later. He never got around to it.

He thinks there was something about kicking a headlight, but Carter isn't in a trunk. He's in a wooden crate like a package on a cargo ship. There's no possibility of him kicking his way free in this scenario either, not with the way he's bound. His body is curled up in a fetal position in order to fit in the crate, his head bent at an awkward angle. He'd never be able to kick a leg out hard enough to break anything.

He thinks maybe there was something about zip-ties, but Carter's not bound with those. Whoever captured Carter wound thick, scratchy rope around his body as a way to restrain him. His arms are bent and pressed together across the center of his back, his thighs bound without space between them, his calves tied to his thighs.

He thinks he was supposed to memorize something, too. Or multiple things. If that's the case, Carter is extra screwed. He's pretty sure his kidnappers drugged him, if the fuzzy memory of something stinging his neck a moment before he lost consciousness is any indication. By the time Carter came to, tongue heavy and head full of cotton, he had already been stripped naked, blindfolded, and bound in the rope currently keeping him in his fetal position. He could have woken up on the same street that he was taken, or half a world away. There was no way to tell. There was no time to ask any questions, either. He had been picked up by his ropes like a package and shoved violently into his new home – the wooden crate.

Carter has been kidnapped.

And he has no fucking idea what to do.

Thanks a lot Tumblr.

The most concerning part of the entire situation is that his captors had known his name. Carter specifically remembers that. One minute, he was walking down the sidewalk, backpack hitched over his shoulder, mind turning as he mentally reviewed what he'd need to know for his upcoming political science exam. The next minute, someone was calling, "Hey, Carter!" and he turned to find two men behind him. That was when the sting happened in his neck.

Considering Carter is an orphan with an older brother who is nothing but a soldier in the Army, this isn't some sort of hostage situation. No one is going to be collecting a ransom. There's a good chance that whoever took him is fully aware of his family and financial situation. If that's the case, they're planning on getting their money some other way.

Carter isn't an idiot. He knows how these things work. He's seen enough made-for-TV movies and docuseries to know how his captors plan on making a profit off of him. Carter is going to be sold, either for physical labor or for sex. Considering his nakedness and the way his captors had enjoyed touching his cock and balls while he was bound and helpless, Carter has a feeling this is headed towards the sex route. Some sick fuck is going to purchase Carter to be their sex slave.

Or worse – to rape him once and then dispose of him.

On second thought, maybe that'd be the better option.

Not that Carter is under the impression that he'll be given any sort of option moving forward.

The vehicle Carter's crate is on comes to a sudden halt, his world lurching as the box skids across the inside of the truck. It slams into something that abruptly stops it. Carter's body doesn't get the memo, still moving for a second longer before it slams against the inside of the crate.

Everything goes dark.

"Miami."

"A shitty little town in Georgia."

"Lawrence, Kansas."

"Ann Arbor, Michigan."

"Kentucky. Just outside of Louisville."

Silence.

Eyes, heavy, itchy, demanding, all locked onto Carter.

Carter curls his body tighter, almost missing his crate. He's not sure how long he spent in the wooden box, but the fetal position has become second nature at this point. Especially when he's particularly anxious.

"Where you from?" a dark-skinned guy a few years older than Carter asks, as if he thinks Carter might not have been listening to the conversation. As if he thinks Carter doesn't know it's his turn. As if Carter hasn't lost more and more hope with every location mentioned. *Are they all idiots? Don't they understand?* They were all plucked from places nowhere near each other, which means only one of them might be near home, and even that chance is low. They're probably not even in the United States anymore. That's *bad*. That means it's going to be difficult for the authorities to find them. Probably fucking impossible.

When Carter waits too long to answer, they move on without him.

"Denver."

"NYC. Was there for college."

"Yeah, me too. College, I mean. I'm actually from Mississippi."

Carter closes his eyes, leaning back against the cool cement wall. He plays a new game he made for himself. The point of the game is to create scenarios for after he's been sold, anywhere ranging from a gorgeous, gentle man purchasing him, to some overweight, sweaty asshole who puts him in a brothel and injects him with so many drugs he forgets his own name. There's never a scenario where he goes free. It's not a game Carter can win. He knows that.

He just wishes the others in the cell would figure it out too.

4

CARTER'S BEEN IN THE cell for a long time. There's no light besides the dim bulb that hangs from the ceiling of the hallway outside their barred door, and they never turn it off. There aren't any windows. Their meals aren't at all regular. His only way of telling time is paying attention to his body. He knows he's been in the cell long enough for his lips to be bleeding and his fingertips to be scratchy with dehydration. Long enough for his hunger sweats to turn to hunger shakes, sweat no longer coming from his pores. Long enough for him to forget what his test was on that he had been so focused on studying for.

He's been in the cell long enough for him to watch a myriad of boys and men come in and out, some returning, most not. Long enough to learn that the ones who are returned have been brought to a place the captors call the playroom, where they endure all sorts of things other than rape. Long enough for Carter to understand that there are worse things than being raped.

Long enough for Carter to realize that for some reason, his captors aren't going to ever bring him to the playroom.

Long enough for Carter to decide he doesn't want to find out why.

CARTER'S CLAUSTROPHOBIA IS CURRENTLY fighting with his need for warmth. He wants nothing more than to curl up in his safe little ball, but he's freezing.

He's always freezing.

The naked bodies around him are all he has for warmth these days. Any self-consciousness over lack of clothing disappeared a long time ago. Before his arrival to the cell even.

There are 15 naked bodies in the cell right now. The smallest amount so far has been 12, and the most has been 17. There's barely enough room for everyone to sit on the floor at the same time. They usually take turns, sleeping in shifts, and even then, everyone has to be curled up tight or sleep sitting up. The younger boys have the advantage of not taking up as much space as the adults. They can curl up on their side to sleep and only use as much floor as Carter would use sitting up in his tight ball.

A guard starts to walk down the hallway, his boots heavy on the concrete floor. Carter feels his heart pound to the beat of the steps. Despite his effort to keep calm, he still startles when the guard's baton hits the cell bars. The sound rings in the air around them, hauntingly familiar, a warning of danger to come. Carter makes sure not to get caught looking at the man, only glancing long enough to see which guard it is.

Scarface.

The worst of them all.

There's a single drain in the center of the cell for piss and vomit, and a bucket for everyone's shit. The bucket is only taken out once it's nearly overflowing, and the guards are never happy about it. Scarface is the guard who was in a particularly bad mood one day and decided to brighten it by tossing the contents of the bucket back into the cell, shit raining down on Carter and the others.

Scarface is the guard who likes to give them the least amount of bread possible, forcing them to share to the point of each of them barely getting more than a bite or two. He's the guard who makes sure his victims bleed when he brings them to the playroom. He's the guard who aims at their crotches and faces when he brings in the power hose to clean them, enjoying the way they gasp and shriek as they bump into each other with the hope of escaping the ice-cold water coming at them through the thick metal bars. He's the guard who likes to stay afterward with a grin on his face while they stand shivering and crying as they wait for all of the water to go down the single drain so they can rest their weary bodies on the ground again.

Scarface is also the guard who makes sure no one takes Carter to the playroom. The others come back with stories of horrific medical examinations. Of sleep deprivation. Of being waterboarded. They'd come back with bloody whip marks along their skin. Bruises shaped like fingers and fists and boots. Sprained ankles and wrists.

But never Carter. The one time a guard had reached for him, intending to take him to play, Scarface had taken Carter from the man and shoved him stumbling back into the cell.

"Not that one, you dipshit," he had growled. "That's the Beckett whore."

Carter still doesn't understand what that meant, but he knows it meant something to the guard. It meant enough to keep him safe.

At least for now.

CARTER IS STILL IN the cell with the slaves when he wakes up from a dream about freedom. For just a second, he can still smell the fresh air, the grass, and the flowers, but then the cell's thick scent drowns the memories. Everything reeks of piss and shit and vomit here. There's a little boy beside him. He's new. He must have come while Carter was napping.

The boy won't stop crying.

Minutes go by.

What must be at least an hour goes by.

Still, the boy is crying. He'll make himself sick if he doesn't calm down.

"It's okay," Carter whispers to the boy. "Everything will be okay."

It's a lie, of course. Carter might not know much about this situation they're in, but he knows that at least. This boy can't be more than 13 or 14 years old, though. Carter's gut tells him he's even younger. Maybe lying is the most humane thing to do.

Maybe it's not.

Carter has no fucking idea.

"It's going to be okay," he says again.

The boy curls into Carter's side, sobbing harder.

"What's your name?" Carter asks, trying to get the boy distracted.

"E-Elliot." The boy rubs at his face, trying to calm his breathing. "I jus' wanna go home! I want my mom!"

Carter can fucking relate. He's 22 and he wants his mom so badly it hurts. He hasn't ached with this kind of need for her since the days following her death.

"I didn't do anythin' wrong," Elliot whispers. He looks up at Carter with huge blue eyes full of tears. "Can you tell 'em that? I told 'em I'm a good boy, but they – they didn't listen!"

Carter doesn't know what the fuck to say to that. Thankfully, another guy around Carter's age sits on the other side of Elliot. The three of them have to squeeze in uncomfortably close to fit, but the boy doesn't seem to mind being sandwiched between them.

"These are the bad guys, little dude," the new guy says. "And you know what happens to the bad guys, right?"

"What?"

"They lose in the end. They always fucking lose in the end. You just have to wait long enough."

Elliot sniffles, wiping his nose with the back of his hand. "You said a bad word."

The guy laughs softly, nodding. "Yeah. Sorry."

"It's okay. My mom isn't here, so like... you don't have to pay a quarter or nothin'."

The guy laughs again. Carter joins in this time. Even Elliot smiles.

The three talk for a while. Long enough for Elliot to get sleepy. He rests his head on Carter's shoulder at some point, starting to doze. It's not long after that when the guy on the boy's other side looks over Elliot's head at Carter and says, "I'm Casey."

"Carter."

"You're new, hey?"

"I don't know." Carter shrugs. "I don't feel new. Feels like I've been here forever."

Casey nods. "Yeah, I hear ya."

Carter studies the boy, vaguely recognizing him from other moments when he accidentally paid too much attention to the horrors around him. He's thin, despite his large frame. Carter could picture him as some sort of athlete in his former life. Football player, maybe. Or hockey. Now, he just looks like a ghost of those things. "How long have you been here?"

Casey shakes his head, looking away. Someone is taking a shit in the bucket that's set over in the corner. He has a sick stomach. It's not a very pleasant thing to be witness to.

Casey never answers Carter's question. He doesn't have to. It's in the weight of his eyes. The set of his mouth. The way he sighs when he looks away. The answer is evident. *Too long.*

"He won't stay more than a night or two," Casey says after a few minutes have passed. The sick guy is trying to decide if he should waste his half-slice of bread for the day to wipe his ass free of the liquid shit lingering between his cheeks.

"Who won't stay?"

"Elliot." Casey sighs, then yells, "Hey, you!" He raises his chin and snaps his fingers towards the guy by the bucket. The guy looks up with wide eyes. "Don't be a dipshit. Eat the bread. They'll come clean us soon enough."

The sick guy curls in on himself, tears falling down his bright red face. Carter prays that's never him. He focuses on Elliot instead. He just met the kid, but his chest already aches thinking of what will happen to him after this cell. It's going to be worse. He knows it. Whatever is next for all of them, it's going to be so much worse.

"Why is Elliot not going to be around long?" Carter asks, hoping Casey doesn't judge him for the sadness in his voice.

Casey doesn't judge, but he does shrug like he's unaffected by the whole thing. Maybe he is. Maybe Carter will learn how to be like that soon. "The little ones never linger. They're in too high of demand. Harder to snatch a minor, ya know? Everyone looks for a kid."

"Maybe this time it'll be different."

"Yeah." Casey shrugs again. "Maybe."

But it's not different.

The guards come for Elliot two bread deliveries later. Him and another young boy Carter hadn't noticed before. Elliot screams and sobs, reaching out for Carter and Casey as he's dragged away. "Don't let 'em take me! Don't let 'em take me!"

Casey turns to face the wall, pressing his forehead against it, his entire body trembling. Carter tries to fight. He shoves guys out of the way, pushing forward, hands outstretched, desperately trying to get to Elliot before they take him away. He manages to get his fingers to brush Elliot's. Then a guard hits him in the temple with a baton, and everything goes fuzzy.

Suddenly, Carter feels like he's suffocating. Trapped. Bodies are pressing in, his vision not working properly, his lungs full of water instead of air, his feet and hands not obeying their orders to fucking move.

Someone grabs Carter from behind. He gasps, trying to remember how to fight. All he can think is that this is it. This is when he's going to die.

But then his eyes focus, and his lungs recognize the air they're getting, and the world tilts back to where it belongs, and Carter sees that it's Casey who has him. The young man is running his hands over Carter's skin, calming him. When Carter starts to sob, Casey pulls him in and holds him close. He lets Carter sob uncontrollably until he has nothing left inside himself. When they pull apart, he sees tears on Casey's face as well. He thought maybe he'd feel better knowing Casey isn't as unaffected as he pretends to be, but it feels even worse.

Carter goes to sleep a while later, the thought in his mind that maybe it'd be nice if he doesn't wake up again.

But Carter does wake up.

He keeps waking up.

He watches more Elliots come and go, never mastering the art of unattachment. He feels each loss like they belong to him. In a way, they feel like they do.

The one constant is Casey. Through all of the coming and going, the playroom visits, the stale bread, the shit bucket dumps, the needle-like washes from the power hose, Casey is there. Brave. Steady. Wise. Always giving part of his bread to whoever had been taken by the guards most recently, their bodies usually needing the extra boost to heal.

Casey is always reminding the boys not to be idiots and try to fight the guards – Carter being one of them, more than once. Carter learns that Casey's father is a police officer, something that immediately makes things about the young man clear. He would make his father proud. When Carter tells him that, Casey looks away and locks his jaw. It's the second time since meeting him that Carter sees Casey cry.

Casey's biggest lesson for anyone willing to listen is four phrases.

Keep calm.

Breathe.

Pay attention.

Wait for your moment.

They're his tips for survival. Carter uses the mantra often, usually when the guards are pulling boys from the cell as they scream and cry for help. *Keep calm. Breathe. Pay attention. Wait for your moment.*

Carter keeps playing his game, imagining future scenarios, but one thing has changed since Casey. When Carter plays now, he's in it to win.

When Carter plays now, he's playing for freedom.

THE GUARDS COME FOR Casey.

Carter is in the middle of helping a little boy calm down from a panic attack, rubbing circles on his back as he promises things that he knows are lies. Casey is slumped in the corner nearest to them, half-asleep as he tries to heal from his last round of playroom torture. He had just finished coughing up blood.

It's Scarface who opens the heavy metal door. Two others are behind him. One grabs a man in his late twenties, yanking him into the hallway. The other points at Casey.

Casey, who hasn't even been back in the cell long enough for bread or water.

Casey, who is still bleeding between his legs.

Casey, who can barely stand on his feet when Scarface summons him.

"No!" Carter yells, panic rising in his chest. He steps in front of Casey, ignoring his friend when he tells Carter it's not worth it. "Take me. Just – just use me. He can't take any more."

Scarface sneers at Carter. "Get out of the fucking way, Beckett."

Carter refuses. "Take. Me."

"Carter," Casey rasps, his trembling hand touching Carter's shoulder. He tries to give Carter a smile. It's weak. Maybe Carter would buy it better if Casey didn't start using Carter's body to hold himself up. "You're gonna be okay, Car."

"It's not me I'm worried about." Carter looks at the guard who had pointed at Casey, narrowing his eyes. "I won't let you take him."

The guard looks at Scarface, the both of them smirking before breaking out into awful laughter. The sound echoes in Carter's chest until he feels small and insignificant. He stands his ground, though. This is *Casey*. He won't let these men take him. Not without a goddamn fight.

"Please," Carter begs, hating the way his voice cracks. "Just take me."

Scarface comes forward, his bulging veins and wild eyes making him look like a comic book villain. Carter gulps, but he doesn't back down. When Scarface grabs Carter's bicep in a painful grip, Carter is insane enough to feel relief. He might be in for a world of torment, but at least he saved Casey from having to endure it in the state he is. That's something.

That's enough.

But then Scarface uses the grip to tug Carter off to the side so the other guard can come forward and grab Casey.

Carter panics. He forgets everything Casey taught him.

Instead, Carter fights.

He fights with everything his poor body has. He hits and kicks and screams. He catches Scarface by surprise, clawing his nails across the bastard's face hard enough to draw blood. It leaves three angry marks opposite the cheek with the deep, purplish scar. Carter finds great satisfaction in that. He takes advantage of the man's temporary shock, bringing his knee to his groin. When he doubles over with a grunt, Carter brings his knee up one more time, connecting with the asshole's nose. An awful crunching sound comes from the man as bright red blood bursts from his face and splatters all over Carter's bare skin.

Carter grins.

Then Carter is being grabbed from behind, an arm around his neck to choke him, his knees buckling with panic. He sees Casey, a third guard dragging him down the hall already. Casey looks half-asleep as he stumbles along. He sees the younger boy he had just been helping with a panic attack, now crumpled on the floor as a guard kicks him in the side. Another guard is hitting boys with a black baton, not even looking as he swings wildly.

"See what you've done?" the guard holding him growls in his ear, his arm getting tighter around Carter's throat. Cries erupt around them. Screams. Sobbed pleas. The sound of boots and hands and sticks hitting defenseless skin. "Time you learn a lesson, whore."

Carter runs out of air then, his world turning into a swirl of chaos and pain, all of it *his fault, his fault, his fault...* until everything is blissfully black.

WHEN CARTER WAKES UP, he's disoriented. Uncertain. Things are... *different*. He's not in the cell. The place is too cold. Too dark. Too quiet. There aren't bodies pressing against him, damp with either sweat or ice-cold water depending on when they last had a visit from the hose. There's no single string light bulb from the hall illuminating their hell in a sickening yellow glow. There aren't whispers or whimpers. No cries. No, "I'm scared." No, "I don't understand." No, "They can't do this to us."

It even smells too good to be the cell. Instead of the lingering scent of piss and shit and vomit, the air is only damp and musty. It smells like nothing more than an old basement.

Carter rubs at his eyes, trying to see better. It's no use. Wherever he is, it's nothing but black. Pure black. There aren't shades of the color, like when you wake up in the middle of the night and your eyes are adjusting. There aren't any shadows. It's just... *dark*. The kind of darkness that wants to swallow a person whole.

The kind of darkness Carter could get lost in.

Head pounding, thoughts muddled, Carter tries to piece things together. The guards had come. They wanted Casey. Carter had begged them to take him instead.

He had fought.

He had lost.

Someone was choking him.

He must have passed out.

Idiot, Carter hears Casey say inside of his mind, the boy's gruff voice annoyed but fond. *What did I tell you about fighting?*

Carter hadn't listened. He had acted impulsively. Recklessly. Not only did he get himself choked out and relocated, but he also didn't even manage to save Casey. In fact, he made things worse, getting all the others in the cell in trouble too. He can still hear the sounds of them as they were attacked because of him.

The cold in this new place is awful. It makes his bones ache within minutes, his teeth chattering until he worries they might break.

It isn't until Carter tries to combat the temperature by curling his body into a tight ball that he discovers something else that's new. He has a collar around his throat. Tight. Heavy. Metallic. It's colder than the air around him. Carter brings shaking hands up to touch it, feeling around until he finds a ring at the front. There's a chain link attached to it. The thick, sturdy kind of chain if Carter's fingers are telling him the truth. Stomach churning, heart in his throat, Carter uses his hands to follow the chain *down, down, down* until he finds a matching ring like the one on his collar bolted to the floor. He feels around to confirm his fear. He's chained down, with nothing more than a few feet of slack.

Carter tries to stand up.

The chain doesn't let him advance past a squatting position.

Feeling like an idiot, Carter whispers into the darkness around him. "Hello? Is... anyone there?"

Nothing.

He had figured, but that doesn't mean the confirmation doesn't hurt.

How long will he be kept here? Surely they won't leave him too long. They have to feed him. Water him. They won't let him die. Not after all of their "Beckett whore" talk. Not after Scarface keeping him safe from the playroom. There's something about Carter that means something to these men. They won't leave him here to die.

Just to suffer.

Deciding he should see if there's anything useful in here that he can reach, Carter tugs at his chain until he's as far away from the ring as he can get, then slowly begins to circle around it. He reaches his arms out as far as they'll go, taking his time so that he doesn't miss anything.

He does this twice.

There's nothing. No cracks in cement – which is what he's thinking this room is made out of, considering the feel of it. No possible weapons. No food or water bowls. No bucket to go to the bathroom in. No drain either. Carter can touch two walls with his fingertips, so he must be bolted down near a corner, but that doesn't help much. He can't even use the walls to rest his body against. They're just far enough away that the chain chokes him when he tries.

Eventually, Carter winds up back near the ring so he can relax his body. He lays down and curls himself into the tightest fetal position he can manage. Even though it's dark, he closes his eyes. At least then he can pretend like it's his choice to be blind.

As the cold bites at Carter's skin, he finds his mind drifting to his game. He had shared it with Casey a while ago. They had played together, after Casey made it very clear that he thought it was a bad idea. He thinks Casey had enjoyed it, though. He had a fantasy about being purchased by some sexy business guy who wears fancy suits and just wanted a slave for convenience, not for really fucked up or painful shit. He wants there to be a pool at the house he's brought to, and he wants his new owner to be kind enough to let him swim in it sometimes. Casey had been on his college swim team. He was good, not that he said so. Carter could tell just listening to him talk about it.

Carter hopes Casey gets his businessman with the pool.

As far as Carter's future is concerned, he'll just be happy to survive this new place he's been locked up in. Anything after that is too much to even consider.

And freedom? Freedom sounds nearly impossible at this point.

He can't believe he ever let himself dream otherwise.

AT SOME POINT, CARTER starts to claw at the floor and walls. Even when he breaks his nails. Even when they start to bleed. He claws and claws, determined to find some sort of escape.

He's desperate. Terrified. There has to be a crack somewhere. Some way to get just a sliver of light. Or sound. Or something. Just... *anything*. Any goddamn thing.

He needs some proof that he isn't trapped in a black world where only he exists.

But there's nothing.

For all Carter knows, he's dead, and this is his hell.

At least there are smells now. Familiar ones even. Carter has been in this new place long enough to shit and piss, which he did as far away from his ring as possible.

Carter's lips are cracked and bleeding. His throat is raw. Whenever he swallows, he swears he tastes blood.

He needs water at the very least. Someone has to give him some goddamn water.

"Please!" Carter cries, gasping and coughing right after as his body punishes him for the sound he forced from it. He smacks a hand against the cement floor, the movement lethargic and weak. "Please..."

Nobody comes.

He's starting to think nobody will ever come.

CARTER TOOK A LITERATURE class his freshman year of college. They had to pick a poet from the time-period they were studying and do a presentation on them. Part of this assignment was memorizing one of the poet's poems – or an excerpt from the poem, if you chose a large one – and reciting it to the class. Carter had chosen William Wordsworth. Being someone who is terrible at public speaking, Carter worked tirelessly at memorizing his poem. It was only 20% of the presentation grade, but that's not what he cared about. He cared about all the eyes on him. Heavy. Itchy. Just waiting for him to fail.

So, Carter memorized that poem.

He memorized the shit out of that poem.

He memorized that poem so well that here, now, in the freezing cold depths of darkness, his body shutting down from lack of water and nutrition, Carter can recite that poem perfectly. He does so in his mind only. This partly has to do with him having very little confidence in his ability to make sound anymore, but it's also because the poem feels intimate to him. It's all he has anymore. The one thing they can't take from him.

I wandered lonely as a cloud
That floats on high o'er vales and hills,
When all at once I saw a crowd,
A host, of golden daffodils;

Carter wonders if he should drink his own piss. It's been a long time since he's had to go, considering there's nothing left in him, so all he has is the old stuff in the corner. It's probably cold, though he's not sure if that's a positive or negative thing. He's also not sure if it's still safe to drink, or if bacteria manifests the longer it sits out. In fact, he's not sure if it's safe to drink at all, fresh or not. *Was the whole drinking your pee thing a myth?* Those survival stories where people drink their own piss could be false. It could have the same effect as seawater to thirsty sailors. Things might just get worse.

God, he's thirsty.

Beside the lake, beneath the trees,
Fluttering and dancing in the breeze.

Carter lays back down and sighs, his body thanking him for giving up before wasting any more energy. It wasn't on board with his drinking urine plan. It wants him to just stay the fuck still and try to keep warm. His fingers and toes are beginning to go numb. He hopes that doesn't mean anything too serious.

Continuous as the stars that shine
And twinkle on the milky way,
They stretched in never-ending line
Along the margin of a bay;
Ten thousand saw I at a glance,
Tossing their heads in sprightly dance.

Will Carter ever see the stars again? He's starting to think he'll never even experience light again, let alone something as magnificent as the night sky. His best hope is during transport, he supposes. If he's not blindfolded. Or dead by then.

The waves beside them danced; but they
Out-did the sparkling waves in glee:
A poet could not but be gay,
In such a jocund company:
I gazed – and gazed – but little thought
What wealth the show to me had brought:

Carter closes his eyes. He remembers figuring out in his analysis that Wordsworth was drawing all of the imagery from his memories, the man in fact lying on a couch with his eyes closed the whole time. Maybe that's what Carter's problem is. Maybe he needs to close his eyes. Maybe then he'll see what Wordsworth did.

For oft, when on my couch I lie
In vacant or in pensive mood,
They flash upon that inward eye
Which is the bliss of solitude;
And then my heart with pleasure fills,
And dances with the daffodils.

It doesn't work.

Since he has nothing better to do, Carter tries again.

I wandered lonely as a cloud...

CARTER THINKS ABOUT ELLIOT. He makes up a story for him. A happy one.

Happier, at least.

The man who bought Elliot is married to a kind woman. They can't get pregnant. They've been trying for years. The adoption agency turned them down.

Wait, no, two men married to each other. They live somewhere that doesn't allow same-sex adoption. They're desperate for a family. They know it's wrong, of course they do, but they'll be good to him. They'll make it up to him somehow.

Elliot has a huge bedroom overlooking a river. The river isn't too deep. A safe place to swim. To fish. To ice skate when it freezes over.

His new parents buy him video games. One dad plays with him all the time. The other rolls his eyes and says things about frying brain cells, but they eventually lure him to the dark side and get him hooked too. On Sundays, they have Mario Kart tournaments and cook homemade pizza together.

Elliot loves them. He's happy with them. Sometimes he misses his mom, but it gets easier. Maybe one day he'll be able to find her again. For now, he's content where he is. Safe. Untouched. Loved.

MUSCLES ACHING WHEN HE awakes, Carter rolls to his side and stretches his arms and legs as far as they can go. His toes brush something. Liquid splashes against the cold concrete. Carter holds perfectly still, unsure if he imagined it. He slowly, carefully, pulls his feet up as he pushes himself into a sitting position. He touches his foot with a finger and gasps.

It's wet.

Tentative fingers crawl along the concrete, one inch at a time, until he finds what feels like a metal dog bowl. He doesn't risk lifting the thing. Instead, he brings his face down to it. The water is warm. Slightly gritty.

It tastes like heaven.

Carter cries.

Make it last, he tells himself. *Be smart. Make it last.*

Carter puts the bowl in the corner where his two walls meet, then crawls as far away from it as his chain will allow.

Feeling confident he won't accidentally spill it, he lays back down and closes his eyes.

CARTER DREAMS OF A field of daffodils. Bright yellow against lush green. There's wind in his hair. He can smell the salt from the sea. The sun is setting. The stars will be coming out soon. Carter lifts his chin, wanting to look up at the sky so he can catch the exact moment the night takes over. But something stops him, jerking his neck painfully. He gasps.

Just as Carter grabs what seems to be a metal dog collar around his throat, not understanding why it's there, the world goes black. It's not an instant thing, though. It's slow. Torturous. Color bleeds out of the sunset first. Then out of the trees. The grass. The daffodils. The world goes black and white. Then black and grays. Then, *black, black, black.*

When Carter wakes up, he doubts if he's truly awake. *How could he tell, when his reality and the nightmare are the same?*

CARTER LICKS UP THE last of the water. He cries, but only for thirty seconds. That's all he gives himself. Thirty seconds. Then he forces himself to stop. This isn't a time where he can be wasting water. Tears are a luxury he cannot afford.

CARTER DREAMS OF THE daffodils again. They're all dying. He stands in the field of them, slowly turning in a circle to take the sight in. The bright flowers are wilting. Turning to ash. They melt into the grass, and then that's ash too. There's no flame. No cause. It all just crumbles into blackened dust right before Carter's eyes. When Carter looks at his hands, he finds his body beginning to follow.

CARTER'S THROAT IS BLEEDING.

THE WATER BOWL IS filled again. Beside it is a piece of food the size of Carter's palm. It tastes like stale bread. He prays that's what it is. He eats it either way.

He DREAMS OF THE daffodils again.

Casey's dead body rests among them.

Carter carefully lies down beside his friend, taking Casey's freezing cold hand in his own.

"It's okay," he whispers to Casey, closing his eyes and holding on tight. "I'm here now."

Chapter Two

"How may I serve you, Master?" a slave asks in that same low, subdued voice they all use. He's kneeling in the proper resting position, his chin lowered, his eyes on the floor. The sight of him makes Nathan sick.

Nathan hadn't summoned him, having just been lounging in one of the leather chairs in the entertainment room, sipping a glass of his favorite scotch while listening to his men talk amongst themselves. This particular slave has been here long enough to know better than to approach without invite, which means one of Nathan's men had encouraged the slave to come cater to him.

Nathan scans his eyes over the slave, weighing the pros and cons of dismissing him. Only one other man in the room is using a slave right now. The rest are just relaxing. Sending him off wouldn't be suspicious.

With a flick of his wrist, Nathan says, "You're not needed by me tonight. Go on."

The slave's shoulders relax ever so slightly. They always pretend they're happy to be used, but it's never the truth. Nathan sending the slave away this late at night means that, as long as the slave makes it to the basement without anyone grabbing him, he'll be finished for the night. Nathan can't imagine a life like that.

Then again, part of Nathan wishes he got to quit this job at night. He hasn't had a minute off in 8 fucking years.

"Thank you, Master," the slave says quietly, eyes averted. "Goodnight."

"Goodnight, 7."

As Nathan watches the slave crawl away from him, he thinks *Bryce. Bryce Jacobson. 19 years old. Slave for 2 years. Never graduated high school.*

Bryce Jacobson. Not 7. Not slave. *Bryce.*

Nathan closes his eyes and breathes, reminding himself why he's doing this.

This operation has been hell from the start. It's beaten Nathan down into something less than human, making him damn close to the kind of person he began hunting in the first place. But it's ending soon. They're so fucking close. This international trafficking ring will be brought down from the inside by *him*, the man he's become, the man he's replaced his true self – Travis Kenton – with; Nathan Roarke, one of the wealthiest, most ruthless, powerful men in the human trafficking underground. He may have had to spend years tearing at the foundation brick by fucking brick, but this world is finally coming down.

Nathan just hopes it doesn't take much longer. Not just for himself, but for the slaves too. He has to bring this thing down so Bryce can go back to being Bryce. So all the others can be themselves again too.

He has to bring this thing to an end before he loses the final shreds of his own true identity – of *Travis* – that he's managed to hold on to.

IT'S LATE, NEARLY 3 in the morning, when Nathan's phone begins to play the opening chords of *Stairway to Heaven*. He jerks awake. There's only one number with that as the ringtone, all others set to some generic shit instead. The number calling him is for emergencies only. To be receiving a call from it means that shit has hit the fucking fan.

To receive a call from it means life or death.

Nathan's hand trembles as he hurries to get the phone to his ear. "Maison?"

"Travis," his best friend, and operation commander, says in a thick, shaky voice that's so unlike him Nathan briefly wonders if he's dreaming. "Trav, they – fuck, man. They fucking took him. They took him!"

"Who? Who took who?"

"They fucking – I don't even - some – some son of a bitch fucking took Carter!"

Sitting up, Nathan tries to understand exactly what's going on. There's a chance he's still half-asleep because the information is not computing. Carter is Maison's little brother, but Nathan has no idea what that has to do with anything.

"Back up, buddy. You've lost me."

"Someone from your fucking world took Carter!" Maison shouts. Nathan tries not to flinch too hard at the comment about this being *his* world. He knows Maison is

30

just upset right now. "Someone I don't even fucking know. I – some shithead named Quinton?"

Nathan slides off the bed, realizing just how big this is. "Quinton. Okay. I know him. He's part of the European markets. He – you're saying he took Carter? That's what you're saying?"

"Yes!"

"Just – okay. I'm not understanding, you're saying that Quinton just... took Carter? Like by coincidence, Quinton took your brother?"

"Not fucking coincidence. He found out who I am."

This is when the world screeches to a halt. Up until now, everyone in the underground knew that a small elite group of Americans were trying to track down traffickers. They also knew the leader of this group. A man named Mathew Davis. Maison Beckett's cover.

Now Maison is saying that Scott Quinton has discovered that Mathew Davis is Maison Beckett.

Which means Scott Quinton figured out that Carter Beckett is Maison Beckett's little brother. The enemy's greatest weakness.

Shit.

Nathan takes a slow, deep breath. This could end their operation if mishandled. This could also end Carter's life. Maison has gone off the deep end, which is fucking understandable, but Nathan can't do the same. He has to be the rational one here. He needs to step up to the plate for his commander and be the man to think clearly right now. Nathan has to keep his shit together.

First things first, "How did you find out he's gone?"

"I got a fucking email from the bastard. To my regular email. Can you believe that shit? He just sent it. Plain as day. Right there with my fucking junk mail! I didn't even fucking know Carter was missing. How long has he been missing? They sent the email just now but who knows how long they've had him! They – I didn't – I can't-"

"Focus, Mais. Stay with me. What did the email say?"

"It's – it's fucking pictures, man. They sent me pictures of him. So many – just – just all of these fucking *pictures*."

Nathan closes his eyes. He can only imagine what those pictures must be like. "Forget the pictures right now, Maison. What else did the email say?"

There's an awful pause. Then, "We win.""They haven't won. They *won't*. We aren't going to let them."

"They took Carter!" Maison yells, quickly nearing hysterics. "They took my baby brother from me!"

"And I'll get him back," Nathan promises, even though that's not a promise he should be making. "I'll fucking get him back, Mais. I swear to you. On my fucking life, I swear to you that I'll get Carter back."

There's a long pause, punctuated by a hitched breath. "Find him, Travis. I need you to find him."

Nathan nods. "I'll call you when I do."

It turns out that Nathan doesn't have to look far. Scott Quinton was the man who stumbled upon a trail that led him to Maison Beckett – and therefore to Carter Beckett – but he's not one of the men Maison is after. Quinton is the premier seller of humans in the European markets. That means he's not even in Maison's top 10. As far as Maison's operation is concerned, Quinton is Europe's problem. He's barely on Maison's radar. *Would Maison*

have recognized him if he was calm and Nathan had jogged his memory? Yes. But it would be a vague recognition. A name that had been tossed around on the sidelines. Nothing more.

Quinton taking Carter wasn't personal. It was beneficial. *This means he's not keeping him as a trophy.*

He's going to sell the boy to Maison's enemies.

There's an email waiting for Nathan the moment he opens his secure account.

From Scott Quinton.

Subject line: **We Win.**

A long list of men Nathan rubs elbows with regularly also received the email. Quinton knows he's going to make a fucking fortune off of this poor young man. He's spreading the news far and wide in celebration, starting the email off with the information he recently discovered and the identity of the boy they would see pictures of below.

This was always the risk Maison ran. He knew it. They all knew it. The point of the operation was to be stealthy, which meant Maison needed to be a loud, easy target for everyone to focus on. *What better way to keep the true threat a secret than by presenting a false one loud and fucking clear right before their eyes?* No one would ever suspect the man shaking hands and laughing over scotch with them, not when Maison is out there making his cause known. But that was when Maison was Mathew Davis. Mathew Davis, who had no family. Mathew Davis, who had no ties to anyone. Mathew Davis, who had no weak spots.

Mathew Davis, who had no baby brother he sees as his entire world.

But now they've found out his true identity.

They've found his baby brother.

Nathan would never say it, especially at a time like this, but this exact situation is why men like Maison shouldn't be involved in such operations. Only true ghosts like

Nathan can really slip into the world of pretend. As Travis Kenton, Nathan was a nobody with no family, no friends, no social ties, and no weak spots. He didn't even have a home. The CIA snatched him up just weeks after his Army basic training, told him about a great opportunity where he'd make more money and have less rules, and offered him a new identity. A new *life*. He became Nathan Roarke on a windy fall morning while standing in the basement of an abandoned building in Langley, Virginia. And it was easy to make the transition. Travis was nothing. Nathan was nothing too.

Then they began to build Nathan from scratch.

They began to build him into the man he is today.

They began to build him into the man who gets emails like the one on his phone screen now.

Nathan forces himself to look at the pictures. Every single picture. Not just out of solidarity for what Maison has seen, but also because the Nathan persona he has created, the monster he has become, would look at them. The last thing he needs is one of his acquaintances making a comment about how pretty the boy looked in this or that shot and be caught off guard.

It also has the added benefit of being able to see what the boy has gone through. Carter isn't going to come with a checklist when Nathan buys him. There won't be a list of injuries and health issues. Nathan needs the clearest picture possible of what Carter has endured if he has any hope of taking care of him once he has him.

The pictures go in order.

Carter still in street clothes, lying in a trunk, wrists bound behind his back with zip ties, his eyes closed, his mouth slack, the poor boy probably drugged out of his mind.

Carter stripped naked, crammed tight into a wooden crate, his body bound in an impossible position.

Carter standing in a crude mockery of a shower room, trying to hide his genitals as a man off to the left laughs at him.

Carter in the same room, this time with his hands chained above his head, his genitals on full display.

Carter's face up close, blue eyes red-rimmed and glassy, cheeks smeared with tears, fiery defiance in his gaze as he glares at the camera.

According to the email, Carter just arrived at the place where he will be held until the auction. There's a promise for more pictures to come, as well as a *To Be Announced* as far as the date, time, and location of the auction is concerned.

Nathan has never been a patient man, but there's only one thing he can do.

He waits.

1 HOUR AND 28 minutes later, another email arrives. It's a picture of Carter in a cell packed with at least a dozen other future slaves.

The caption reads: **Home Sweet Home.**

"I DON'T LIKE IT," Nathan says for the third time. He's sitting on his bed with his back against the headboard, nursing an expensive bottle of scotch. "I don't want to do that."

"You think I want this?" Maison growls in return. "You think I like the idea of my baby brother being terrified and victimized for who knows how long?"

"Then," Nathan says through gritted teeth. "Let. Me. Tell. Him."

"It's out of my fucking hands! Director says no. He says no fucking way."

"Then tell the fucking director that I say no fucking way."

There's a long pause. Then, in a choked voice, "Are you saying you won't buy him?"

"What?" Nathan sits up, his heart beating faster. "Of course not. No, Maison. Of course, I'm going to buy him. I'm saying that I won't *lie* to him. I'm telling him as soon as he's safe with me."

Another long pause.

"He's a shit liar, Trav, and an even worse actor. Kid practically ruined his high school's production of Romeo and Juliet. It was cringe worthy." He sighs. "I can't... fuck, man. I can't fully argue with the director on this. I'm not sure if Carter could handle the truth."

"What does that even mean?"

"What happens if we tell him the truth and he begs to go free? What happens when he starts to freak the fuck out and demands you let him go? Or what happens when he makes a mistake? When he slips and calls you Travis? Hell, even if he called you *Nathan* in front of people, you'd have to punish him harshly or they'd know something is up. He can't use your name. He's a slave. He has to play the part of the slave. Can you guarantee that Carter will be able to successfully switch between slave and Carter whenever necessary? Even though you've admitted to having trouble yourself juggling your Nathan persona with your identity as Travis? Can you guarantee that when he's exhausted or hurting or in pain or whatever else he ends up feeling in moments when you're doing things to him in front of your men that he won't slip up? Even if he knew the truth, he'd still be getting traumatized every once in a while, because you have to use him in front of your men in order to keep from raising suspicion. You know even better than I do that when someone is traumatized, especially sexually assaulted like that, their minds tend to disconnect. What happens when he loses himself and calls you the wrong name, or begs you to stop in a way that isn't slave-like, or does or says something else that gives everything away?"

When Nathan doesn't say anything, Maison answers for him. "I'll tell you what happens – you get killed. Carter gets fucking killed. The operation is over. 8 years are fucking wasted. And thousands of slaves that we were *this fucking close* to saving no longer get set free."

Nathan squeezes the neck of his bottle, wishing it was Scott Quinton instead. Everything was going so fucking well before that bastard went and found Carter. Everything was under control. Now, Nathan's standing in the center of a goddamn mess.

"He deserves to know. I – I *need* him to know, Maison."

"We can't be selfish about this. It ends too bloody. I'm the worst person in the fucking world – the worst *brother*

– but I'd rather Carter live as a sex slave that's treated better than most because he's owned by a man I trust, a man I know will be as kind to him as he possibly can, than have Carter know the truth and lose him altogether because he makes a mistake. You said it yourself – this case is damn close to being done. He shouldn't be stuck there too long. It's... safest to lie."

Nathan gulps his scotch, not caring that it burns. At least with it hurting he can blame the pain for the tears stinging his eyes. "Please don't make me his monster, Maison."

Maison sniffs. He's crying again. It's not a good sign. "I'm so sorry, Travis."

Eyes falling closed, Nathan sinks into the realization that he can't get out of this. Both his director and commander are saying to lie. Carter's fucking *brother* is saying to lie. Nathan is going to have to lie. Nathan is going to have to pretend to be a fucking slave owner, even in the safety of his own bedroom.

Nathan is going to have to be Carter's monster.

DESPITE QUINTON'S PROMISE, ANOTHER picture doesn't come for 17 days. 17 long, excruciating days. It's of Carter in the same shower room as before, looking much skinnier, and far less defiant. His blue eyes are covered with a heavy black blindfold. His stomach is a concave shape. His lips are cracked and his cheeks are sunken in. He's been sprayed down, the picture a high enough quality to show the drops of water still rolling down his goose-bumped skin. His dark brown hair is overgrown, falling on his forehead in wet clumps. He looks like a miserable, abused, wet dog.

The caption reads: **24 hours. Rome.**

Nathan's best friend, second-hand man, and undercover partner for the operation, is already on the phone with the pilot Nathan keeps on standby. Benny looks at Nathan with a sharp nod. "Wheels up in 30."

WITH 3 HOURS LEFT on the countdown, the final email is sent. Nathan stops pacing his hotel room when the alert chimes. Benny snaps his head up to look at him. He's not important enough in this world to be sent things as exclusive as this. Nathan tries not to crumble beneath the weight of Benny's stare as he opens the message.

It's a picture of Carter, as always. He's naked apart from three things; the standard slave collar that Nathan knows Quinton puts on all of his boys, another black blindfold, and a cock cage. Though it's not pictured, Nathan is sure that Carter's ass is plugged as well.

Unlike the last picture, Carter looks relatively good in this one. He's been dried off, all of his body hair from the neck down removed. The messy locks of dark hair have been cut and styled. His cracked lips are blood free and shiny with what Nathan assumes must be some sort of salve.

The caption reads: **Belmont. Green Room. 11.**

NATHAN'S EYES FALL ON his target the second he's brought onto the stage with the others. Even blindfolded, Carter is easy to recognize. Not that he'll have to worry about purchasing the wrong boy tonight. Carter is the main event. He's the reason at least half of the men in attendance tonight are even here in the first place, most of them preferring the markets in the Americas instead. It'll be a production when Carter goes up for sale. Quinton will make a show of it.

Hell, he's already making a show of it. Nathan has been to two of Quinton's events before tonight. Both times, the slaves were kept locked in cages in the back, only being brought out one at a time when it was their turn to be auctioned off. Tonight, they've brought them all out to be displayed before the champagne has even been distributed.

It gives Nathan a sick feeling in his gut. He has a suspicion Carter won't be leaving that stage untouched. It won't just be his sale that's entertainment. It'll be his body too.

"Roarke." Nathan turns his face toward the sound of his name, glancing up to find one of his closer acquaintances standing there. *Todd Henley.* He internally sighs as he pastes on a smile and pushes to his feet. There are few people in this world that Nathan hates more than Todd Henley. There are also few people in this world that Nathan *needs* more than Todd Henley if he has any hope in ending this goddamn operation.

"Henley," Nathan says in greeting, offering his hand to be shaken. "Take a seat?"

"I'd love to."

Nathan returns to his chair, Henley taking the open one to his left. They're turned towards each other slightly, enough for them to engage in pleasant conversation while never having to look away from the stage. Something is happening up there. Equipment is being wheeled out from backstage.

Bile rises in Nathan's throat. He takes a large gulp of scotch to burn it away.

"You here for the Beckett boy?" Henley asks conversationally, as if he doesn't know. As if he isn't here for him too.

"Of course. When I catch that son of a bitch, I'm going to tie him up and make him watch as me and every single one of my men fuck his baby brother." Nathan smirks over the lip of his glass, eyes tracking Carter as he's yanked across the stage towards the leather padded spanking bench that's now been anchored in the center of it. They pull him along so fast that his feet can't keep up. He trips, the men letting him fall face first. Someone grabs him by the bindings on his wrists to pull him to his feet. With his arms bound behind his back as they are, the movement must be excruciatingly painful on his shoulders. Blood drips down the side of his face from a fresh gash across his forehead.

Those motherfu–

"Roarke?" Nathan blinks, looking over at Henley with a questioning brow. Henley chuckles. "I asked if you're going to kill the boy after that?"

"Ah. I apologize. The show was a bit distracting." Nathan winks before nodding his head towards the stage. He hates the way Henley grins when he sees what's happening up there. "As far as what to do with the boy once he's served his purpose, I haven't decided. We'll see how good of a fuck he is, I suppose."

Henley laughs. "And how used up he is by then, right?"

"Of course." Nathan drains his glass. He wants another, but he won't have one. Tonight isn't the night to numb his guilt. Not if it means dulling everything else as well. Nathan needs to be on his game tonight. Carter Beckett is up for sale, and the boy needs to be coming home with him.

"Man, I'm jealous. You're going to have a damn good time with that little thing up there. Look at how pretty he is." Henley whistles low, eyes narrowing on Carter like a predator catching sight of his prey.

"Can't help but notice you're acting as if I've already won the boy. Are you not putting your money in?"

"Of course I am, but do you think I'll cross you?" Henley scoffs. "No one I know will cross you. As far as most are concerned, that boy is walking out of here tonight with you holding his leash."

The words soothe something in Nathan's chest, but he doesn't allow himself to get his hopes too far up. There are still challenges in his way. As Henley said, *most* see Carter as already belonging to Nathan, but not all. There is at least one man that Nathan knows he'll be fighting tonight. Nathan might be towards the top in this world's hierarchy, but he's not *the* top. Not yet.

"Master Roarke?"Schooling his expression like he always does before having to face a victim of this cruel world, Nathan turns towards his name. It's a young slave dressed in nothing but a collar and a cock cage. He doesn't meet Nathan's eye, instead focusing on the knot of his black bowtie. Nathan arches a brow. "Can I help you?"

"Master Quinton is requesting your presence backstage."

"Now?"

"Yes, Master Roarke. If – if you're able to, Master."

Nathan eyes the young man, wondering who he belongs to. Wondering what his story is. Wondering if he will finish this operation in time to save him.

"Lead the way, then." Nathan stands, buttoning his jacket as he does. He nods at Henley. "I'll see you later?"

"Of course."

The young man leads Nathan through the crowd, pausing every time Nathan is stopped by someone. He politely stands by and waits as Nathan shakes hands and fakes grins and promises things he doesn't plan on delivering. Almost every person speaks as if Carter is going home with him tonight. The few that don't are close allies with the one man Nathan sees as his true competition. *Miller*. The man Nathan fully expects he'll be going toe to toe with when it comes time for Carter's sale.

What Miller doesn't know is that there's no chance of him winning. Nathan will be purchasing that boy tonight, no matter what it takes. If there's a chance he's not going to hell, it lies with saving Carter Beckett.

"Nathan Roarke!" Scott Quinton says with a grin, his arms outstretched in a grand gesture of presenting himself. "I am so happy you decided to join us."

It takes everything in Nathan not to roll his eyes. There's no scenario where Nathan wouldn't have attended this event. Quinton is just pushing for dramatics by making it sound like it was ever in doubt.

Carefully keeping his disdain out of his tone, Nathan forces a smile and says, "It's a pleasure, Quinton. As always."

"Good. Good. I see Miller has arrived as well."

Drama-lover status proven. Only a man who enjoys conflict would speak of Miller so openly to Nathan. It's an obvious enough crossed line that Nathan doesn't bother hiding the heat in his gaze when he levels Quinton with it. The man takes a step back, though Nathan isn't sure he's aware that he even does so.

Then Nathan catches sight of what's happening on stage, and his fury threatens to boil over. Carter is strapped down to the spanking bench now. Someone is standing back, hitting him with a riding crop over and over in brutal strokes. The bench is shaking with the force of Carter's movements as he writhes in his restraints. He's sobbing for someone to please help him, his face turning this way and that as he tries to find sanctuary despite his blindfold.

The crowd is eating it up.

The other slaves cower where they've been placed kneeling in a line along the back of the stage. All of them are blindfolded like Carter, probably wondering when it will be their turn to endure the same fate.

"Are you enjoying the show?" Quinton asks, misreading Nathan's expression apparently. "I thought since he's such a popular commodity that the crowd might enjoy some extra fun before the bidding begins. Perhaps I might open the floor to some sampling, even. Allow everyone to get a taste."

"Mmm." Nathan frowns, eyes fixed on Carter. The boy is panicking. He can barely cry, barely beg, his breathing far too erratic now. Nathan wouldn't be surprised if Carter passes out soon. "You know, I plan on buying that boy, Quinton."

Quinton grins. "I'm hoping you do, yes!"

"Not if you let anyone lay a fucking hand on him."
Quinton's eyes snap to Nathan's, widening. Before he can
ask for clarification, Nathan takes one step closer and
casually moves his arm so his suit jacket rucks up just
enough to show his gun. "That boy is already mine, Scott.
You and I both know that. Everyone out there knows that.
This auction is a formality. I've allowed it because I know
you enjoy spectacle, but this is where I draw the line.
Don't you dare open up my property to be touched by
others."

"I – you – well, there are a few others–"

"He. Is. *Mine*."

"Miller–"

Nathan takes another step, his nose less than an inch
from Quinton's temple. He pastes on a smile in case
anyone is watching them. At the same time, he draws
on every evil thought he's ever harbored and directs the
energy into his tone. "It'd be a shame if you lost this
market, wouldn't it? Perhaps Miller isn't who I should
have my sights set on after all. Europe does have a sort
of... *appeal* to it, don't you agree?"

"No!" Quinton whispers in a harsh panic. He sputters
a moment before adding, "I – I won't let anyone touch
what's yours, sir. Of course not. I – I have much respect
for you. Of course he's going home with you. Of course.
Of course, Mr. Roarke."

Nathan steps back, nodding once. "Good. I'm glad we
understand each other now."

"Yes. I – but perhaps..."

Nathan tilts his head and raises an eyebrow. "Perhaps?"

"Perhaps, when you purchase him, you could... use
him? For everyone to watch. I really would love the opportunity to give my crowd a show."

His gut reaction is to shoot the request down immediately, but his training quickly kicks in. The man he's
built himself up to be – the *monster* – would do that in a
heartbeat. Nathan Roarke would fuck that boy senseless

while the audience cheers him on. It's marking territory in the best possible way. It's a public fucking claiming, right there for all to see, especially Miller.

If Nathan's training has taught him anything at all, it's to do what Nathan Roarke would do, even if it means he loses his humanity in the process.

Maybe Carter Beckett won't be the way Nathan earns a ladder out of hell after all.

Maybe Carter Beckett will be the final nail in his coffin.

"Fine." Nathan looks away from the boy, eyes meeting Quinton's. "No one fucking lays a hand on him from here forward. No one. Leave him on that fucking bench and don't even breathe too close in his direction."

Nathan walks away without asking if Quinton understands.

Quinton does.

Chapter Three

KEEP CALM. BREATHE. PAY *attention. Wait for your moment.*

The words repeat in Carter's mind as he tries forcing his lungs to work. They're spoken in Casey's calm, steady voice. Casey, who he hasn't seen since he was sequestered in the dark. Casey, who Carter failed to save. Casey, who could be dead right now.

Keep calm. Breathe. Pay attention. Wait for your moment.

Carter's moment isn't coming for a long time. He knows that. There's a possibility that whoever buys him might make a mistake during transport, but he has to survive this next part first. The part that involves him naked and strapped down to something, giving him a sick feeling that his bare ass is on display. He's pretty sure he's going to get raped. They haven't done that to him yet, miraculously, but he's pretty sure that's what they're preparing him for.

All Carter can hope is that it'll only be one man. The man who buys him. Even though Carter is a virgin, he's lucky enough to be gay, and to have experience fucking himself with toys, so he thinks he can physically handle a man fucking him. Mentally is another story, but Carter doubts he'll be able to mentally handle anything any time soon, so he's given up on that. Physically surviving is the thing right now, and Carter isn't sure he'd physically survive a gangrape. Especially considering the current state of his body.

Honestly, if the person who buys him would just give him a bit of water and a piece of bread, he'd happily let them fuck him. Preferably on a bed. *God, Carter would give anything to lay on a bed.* Nice, warm, comfortable. Maybe his buyer will be someone who cuddles. He'd be so down for cuddles. For human contact. Comfort.

A speaker crackles and Carter jumps in his bonds. What sounds like hundreds of cruel voices break out into laughter. He knows it's directed at him. *What else could they possibly find amusing?*

"Ladies and Gentlemen, I'd like to thank you all, as always, for making the time for-" Carter tunes the person out. He shouldn't. Casey's rules make it clear that details should be paid attention to. Every bit of information Carter can soak in could be what helps save him. Carter can't, though. He can't listen to this. Can't listen to these sick, fucked up people acting as if they're selling art or antiques instead of human fucking beings. Can't listen to them talking about him like he's nothing but a pretty object to bid on.

A *pleasure slave*. That's the terminology the men had used when they got him ready for tonight. They had asked him, tauntingly of course, if he was ready to become someone's *pretty little pleasure slave*. He doesn't know why they don't just call it what it really is. They should have to own it. He's going to be a *sex slave*. Pleasure gives the wrong implications. Pleasure makes it sound like he'll enjoy it.

A *pleasure slave*.

Carter's so strung out, he nearly laughs at the thought.

A round of clapping startles Carter again. He has no idea what happened, Casey saying *I told you so* in the back of his mind. Whatever brought the applause passes and the auctioneer returns to speaking. Carter focuses on his breathing and forces himself to listen and pay attention from this point forward.

Just seconds later, a gavel comes down and the man yells into the speaker, "Sold!"

More applause.

The owner is called up. There's the sound of chain link, reminding Carter of his time in the dark. He thinks about the new collar they had secured around his throat earlier. He hadn't been able to explore it before his hands were restrained, but he has a feeling it must have one of those metal loops like the one from before. Carter's cheeks flood in humiliation as he realizes the people buying them are going to leash them like animals. That's the only explanation for the sound of the chain link.

For the first time, Carter's thankful he's blindfolded. He hated that his captors had put something over his eyes before taking him out of the darkness, had been devastated at the realization he still wouldn't get to see any light, but now, as tears form in his eyes, Carter is glad they're covered. These people don't deserve to see him cry.

The slaves go one by one. There's a surprisingly large amount of them. More than he had thought when they were corralled onto the stage earlier. Some go for just a few thousand dollars. Some go for unbelievably high prices that stun Carter speechless.

Then Carter is hearing his brother's name, and the crowd is jeering and yelling expletives. He realizes the words are all for *him*. Terrible. Taunting. Threatening. These people despise his brother for some reason, and they're more than happy to transfer that hate onto Carter.

Carter wants to shout at them. He wants to tell them his brother is just a soldier. One of the many soldiers in this country. Whoever they think Maison is, they must be mistaken. There's no other explanation.

Carter just doesn't understand.

The auctioneer starts the bidding with an impossible price. It climbs quickly.

75

100

150

200

300

600

700

800

It's then between two men, one sounding high pitched and angry, the other alarmingly low and calm. Carter's not sure who sounds like they'd be a better owner.

850

900

A long, stretched out silence. Then a meek, "950."

And a low, soft, angry chuckle. "You know what? 2 mill."

The gavel falls before the other person gets time to respond. There's clapping. Laughter. Carter hears the auctioneer speak off mic. "That was entertaining."

The same calm, low voice that had been bidding on him says, "No. This will be."

Then a hand is on Carter's left ass cheek, a warm, heavy presence settling behind him, and Carter is panicking again.

"Please don't," he whispers, praying the man will be kinder if it's just the two of them speaking. Maybe if the crowd can't hear them, he can convince this man to show mercy. To not rape him. Not yet. Not here. Not like this.

Carter gasps as fingers run from his ass cheeks up his back and down his arms, not stopping until two hands are settled over his own. The man leans forward, his body covering Carter's. His clothing feels scratchy on Carter's sore skin, but he's warm, and Carter has to say it feels very nice to be warm.

Lips brush the shell of Carter's ear as the man speaks to him, his voice surprisingly soft and kind. "Just breathe, sweetheart."

Keep calm.
Breathe.
Pay attention.
Wait.
Keep calm.
Breathe.
Pay attention.
Wait.
Just wait.

Carter whimpers when the anal plug they had put in his ass is tugged on. He starts to tremble, curling his hands into fists to try and gain some control back. The man told him to breathe, but he *can't*. He can't fucking breathe. *Oh god, he can't breathe.*

"Shhh." The man nuzzles behind Carter's ear, making him whimper again. This time it's for an embarrassing reason. That's one of the most sensitive spots on Carter's entire body. He hates himself for the way he shivers. For the way his cock twitches in the tight plastic cage they've locked it in. Bile burns his throat.

His plug is gently pulled from his hole before cool lube is drizzled over his opening. Carter jerks in his restraints, earning a round of cruel laughter from the crowd. He goes perfectly still as a finger is pushed into him.

"Come on! Fuck him hard!"

"Make him scream!"

"Ruin that ass!"

"Don't listen to them," the man orders in that same soft voice as before, his lips finding Carter's ear again as his finger stroke Carter's prostate. "Just focus on me, sweetheart. You're *mine* now. All mine. I'm going to take care of you. Breathe for me. Relax for me. Forget about them. Focus on *me*."

Not sure if he should trust this man – but also not sure if there's much of a choice – Carter listens. He takes a deep breath and forces his muscles to relax. The action earns him a low, rumbling, "Good boy."

It does things to Carter's mind, fucking him up. The man isn't supposed to be kind. He isn't supposed to care about Carter breathing and relaxing. He isn't supposed to care about Carter at all. Carter is supposed to just be an object. A possession.

What game is this man playing?

And, more importantly, how can Carter survive it?

NATHAN WATCHES THE BOY beneath him in a trance as he slides a third finger into him. Everyone in the crowd is yelling for him to get on with it. To fuck the boy. To make him scream. To make him cry. Every time a particularly angry or sinister comment is yelled out, Carter shudders and tries to curl in on himself. It takes everything in Nathan not to just free Carter from the bench and run off with him.

When one of Nathan's own men yells from the front to hurry the hell up, Nathan grins and flips him off. "I'm not going to ruin his ass! I have a nice long flight home. Need him usable, don't I?"

Everyone laughs. Carter deflates. The boy's reaction kills Nathan. Damn near destroys him.

What makes him feel even worse is that he's hard when he lubes his cock and lines it up with the boy's drenched hole. He took a pill earlier, knowing he'd need the help, but that doesn't ease his guilt. Not in the least. *How can it, when arousal is pooling hot and heavy in his gut?*

"Please," Carter whispers. He's trembling gently against the bench, his cheek resting on the padding, his blindfold soaked with tears. "P-please be – be gentle."

Nathan's chest goes tight.

"Okay, sweetheart. It's okay." Nathan smooths a hand over the boy's hip, stroking him gently. He leans forward to speak to him again. "Just breathe. It won't hurt so much if you breathe."

A sob makes its way past the boy's lips. Nathan hangs his head, closing his eyes for a second. Then he forces himself to get his shit together, his grip tightening on Carter's hips as he pushes into him slowly. The crowd roars in celebration, but it's not loud enough to drown out the wrecked sound Nathan's cock forces out of Carter.

Staring at the adorable little freckle on the small of Carter's back, Nathan zones everything else out and focuses on coming. He thinks of the last person he fucked. A guy. Willing. Eager. Pinned down beneath him moaning and writhing, begging for more.

It's over quickly, Nathan's memories driving him over the edge, but not quickly enough. He can tell as he pulls out that Carter is destroyed. His breathing is too slow. Too calm. His muscles are lax. His body is lifeless. His ears are deaf to all the calls from the men. He doesn't even twitch when Nathan slides the anal plug back in his hole.

There's a chance he broke the boy already, before ever even seeing him face to face.

There's no hope.

Nathan Roarke is going to hell, and he's taking Travis down with him.

Chapter Four

CARTER IS PULLED FROM a safe, fuzzy place inside his head when he's suddenly picked up by someone, his body apparently no longer strapped down to the bench from before. He clings to the person's shoulders as he's carried off the stage, his mind spinning as he tries to remember the man finishing with him. He decides quickly that he doesn't care enough to worry about it. He just wants to go back to being fuzzy again.

Fuzzy is safe.

Fuzzy doesn't hurt.

"Sir, would you like your slave prepared for transport?" someone asks.

"No," the man holding Carter says firmly. "I'm transporting him myself."

"Are you sure? It's been a long evening. We will deal with him for you. Clean him. Water him. Prep him. Plug him. He'll arrive in his cage at your compound in the morning."

No trace of the soft, kind man from before is left when the man speaks. His tone is cold. Dangerous. "I do not repeat myself."

"Of course! Yes. So sorry, sir. Is there anything we can do for you, then?"

"Yes. Get out of my fucking sight," the man growls. Carter sinks in on himself, burying his face in the man's neck at his anger. The man adjusts him in his arms and hushes him. "Not mad at you, sweetheart. You did so very well for me up there."

Sweetheart.

He keeps using that. *Why? Is it part of his game?*

Who the fuck is this guy? What does he want? What does he plan on doing to Carter?

Something heavy brushes Carter's bare arm, startling him. He's hushed again, the thing leaving his arm before coming back less heavy. It's not until the mystery item is spread out to cover his entire curled up body in the man's arms that he realizes what it is.

A blanket.

This man has given him a blanket.

It's warm. Soft. The sensation on his skin is so phenomenal that it brings fresh tears to his eyes beneath his blindfold. He hasn't been given a blanket once since being kidnapped. No pillows. No mattresses. No clothing. Just cold concrete.

God, he had forgotten how good it felt to be cocooned in a blanket. His entire body shudders with the pleasure of it, an appreciative sigh falling from his lips. He feels himself sinking into that fuzzy safe place again.

The man seems to notice. "That's it, sweetheart. Just rest. Let me take care-" whatever else the man planned on saying is cut off abruptly, his movements halting as well. Every muscle in his body goes tense.

Then someone says, "Roarke."

"Henley," the man holding Carter replies.

"Congratulations." The person – Henley – laughs. The man holding Carter does as well. Carter feels the rumble against his body. "I know you're leaving, but I'd love to set up a meeting for this following week. We need to discuss Miller."

"Ah, yes. *Miller.*" Carter shivers at the utter disdain in the man's voice when he says the name *Miller*. "I'll have Benny get in touch with you."

"Perfect. Enjoy yourself."

"Oh, trust me. I will."

Carter doesn't like the sound of that.

At all.

He knows he should be listening to Casey's advice now that he's being transported. He should be paying attention to every detail. He should be ready for his moment. Instead, he just wants to sleep. He's so fucking *exhausted*. It's been an eternity since he last slept well. Probably not since they drugged him when he was initially captured. Adding the blanket isn't helping. The only thing that could make this better right now would be some food to alleviate the ever-present ache in his body.

At the thought, Carter's stomach grumbles. A man laughs. There's no rumble against Carter's body, so he knows it wasn't the man holding him. He doesn't get a chance to appreciate that before Henley is saying, "Sounds like the slut is hungry."

"He'll have to beg if he thinks I'm going to feed him." Carter sags in defeat at the cruelty in the man's words. He just wants to curl up and cry for days on end. This man doesn't make any sense to Carter. He hushes him and calls him sweetheart, but he rapes him. He covers him with a soft blanket, yet he's going to make Carter beg for food.

God, Carter doesn't know if he has that in him tonight.

He's so fucking tired.

But he's so fucking hungry, too...

"Sir, the car is ready."

"Thank you," the man that's holding him – who Carter thinks is *Roarke* but he's not sure – says. Then they're moving again. A door opens. Fresh air wafts over Carter. He gasps, his eyes flying open beneath his blindfold. He jerks in the man's arms as Casey's voice yells at him to take this chance. *Scream. Fight. Run.*

But Carter's arms are tangled in the heavy blanket, and he can't see a damn thing. He opens his mouth to yell for help, but a hand clamps down on it before sound can escape. Carter is dropped so his bare feet hit the cement, the hand on his face keeping his head pinned back against the man's chest, the man's other arm holding him around the waist. Refusing to waste this moment, Carter kicks and bucks as he screams into the man's hand. The man hoists him up into what he assumes is a vehicle, shoving him forward, so his bare knees scrape against the rough carpet. The blanket falls off. Carter swallows a sob at the loss.

The door is slammed behind Carter, the sound harsh inside the small space. Carter holds very still as he waits to see what will happen to him now. He doesn't even know if the man is in the vehicle with him or if he's been abandoned.

Just as he's wondering if he should take his blindfold off, someone touches his cheek. He sucks in his breath and holds it.

Then the blindfold is being removed for him.

Carter immediately closes his eyes, suddenly unsure if he wants to see the man who just raped him on a stage in front of who knows how many people. The soft touch to his cheek comes again. He fights the urge to lean into it, refusing to embarrass himself despite his desperation for human contact.

"Open those pretty eyes for me," the man says in that same voice he had used when on stage with Carter. "Look at me, sweetheart."

Not wanting to get punished, Carter forces himself to obey. He hasn't used his eyes in so long that they hurt the moment the dim lighting in the vehicle registers. Carter hisses through his teeth, reaching up to rub the ache away. His hands tremble with fear and exhaustion, with pain and hunger. Then they're taken by two much larger, warmer ones. The man's scotch breath falls over his face. "Take your time, sweetheart. Breathe."

Carter squeezes his eyes, tears falling down his cheeks. He tries to breathe. Tries to relax. He's still trembling, but the man doesn't let him go. He just holds onto Carter and waits patiently.

Finally, Carter manages to blink his eyes open and keep them that way. It takes him a moment to get past the sudden shock of seeing things again. Then he realizes that the thing he sees right now is the man who bought him. The man he's been wondering about for a very long time now. The man he and Casey spent time fantasizing about.

They stare at each other, both holding their breath.

Carter starts to catalogue the details bombarding him, unable to help himself when some are kinder than they should be.

For example: *gorgeous.*

The man seated before Carter, staring down at him with flushed cheeks from their struggle, eyes nearly black, jaw strong and locked, dark blonde hair mussed, is fucking *gorgeous.*

He's also large. Much larger than Carter. He's not a beefcake by any means, but he fills his tailored black suit well, and he's undoubtedly a few inches over six feet. Carter will have a hard time if he ever tries to overpower him. In fact, with his situation in mind, he probably has no shot in hell overpowering him. If Carter wants to escape, he'll have to go about it differently. This isn't something he's going to be able to fight his way out of.

There's a gun in the man's waist holster. That could be an option, though Carter is so inexperienced with weapons that he'd probably end up shooting himself on accident.

The man's black bowtie is crooked. Carter wonders if that happened when they struggled. He's clean shaven, but if Carter squints, he can see a shadow along his strong jaw.

After staring down at Carter for a moment longer, the man drops Carter's hands and lifts his chin to look at the driver of the vehicle. "Benny?"

"Yeah, boss?"

"Swing through a fucking McDonalds or something."

The driver – *Benny* – chuckles. "Sure."

When the man looks at Carter again, his expression is soft. "Think of what you'd like to eat. Nothing too heavy. Your stomach will need adjusting."Carter just stares at him in confusion and awe.

McDonalds?

Carter forgot McDonalds even existed.

Could he call to the person in the drive thru window? Try to get help? Is it worth the risk? Will this man keep the food from him if he tries and fails? Does the man even plan on feeding him at all, or is this just a mind game? A tease? A punishment for trying to fight just now?

"In the meantime, come here. I'd like to take a look at you."

Uncertain if that's some sort of code for *I'm going to fuck you again*, Carter shuffles forward with caution. He stops when he's kneeling between the man's legs and forces himself to look up. The man is upset. Carter sinks in on himself, unsure what he did wrong now, but the man's hand is surprisingly gentle when he cups Carter's jaw and angles his face so he can see Carter better. His thumb brushes along the edge of where Carter fell face-first on stage earlier, when his arms were bound so he couldn't break his fall. It had been bleeding, but it's dry and tacky now. The man frowns, but says nothing.

The hand moves to Carter's shoulder next, his thumb pressing into the joint there. Carter winces, clenching his teeth to keep quiet. The man's eyes flick up to meet Carter's. "Hurts?"

Carter doesn't know the right answer. His eyes start to burn, his throat going tight. He settles for lying. The guards that kept watch over them always hated when they complained. He thinks it's safe to assume this man won't be any different. Carter shakes his head no, then holds his breath as he waits to see what will happen.

The man sighs like he's disappointed before pressing his thumb down on the opposite shoulder. He nods when Carter whimpers.

"Would you like to try that again?" he asks, one eyebrow raised in a dangerous challenge. "Do your shoulders hurt?"

Shit. Now he's going to get in trouble for lying.

"Y-yes..." Carter trails off without using a title for the man. They were taught to use Master for whoever purchased them, the guards warning that they would *not* like what happened to them if they didn't, but Carter is willing to take the risk. It's a small defiance. A way to fight back without winding up dead. Or worse...

"Don't lie to me again. I can't take care of you properly if you lie to me."

Carter nods, dropping his chin in shame. He made the man upset. The man was being kind to him, gentle even, and Carter disappointed him. *Why does that hurt so much?*

The car comes to a stop just before the driver announces, "We're here." Carter peeks out the tinted windows to see that they're parked in the farthest corner of a McDonalds parking lot. It doesn't take a genius to figure out that Carter will be staying in the vehicle while Benny goes for the food. He's not getting a chance to even get close enough to speak to anyone.

"What would you like to eat?" the man who bought him asks softly, hand nudging Carter's chin until their eyes meet.

"I-" Carter stops himself, cowering. He doesn't know the correct answer. *Is there a correct answer? Will he give his order only to have Benny return with no food for him, the men laughing at Carter for being so fucking stupid? Will he bring the food back but then make Carter beg like he'd said before? Will Carter have to do something even worse than beg to earn it?*

The man – *Roarke? Is it Roarke?* – leans forward and takes Carter's face in his hands. Carter stares up at him in fear, holding his breath. "It's not a game. Not a test. I told you to tell me the truth, remember? Just tell me the truth, sweetheart. What would you like to eat?" The man had said earlier that he didn't repeat himself, yet he just did. Carter wonders when he'll be punished for that. He wonders if this man is the kind to punish right away, or when you least expect it. He wonders if his punishment will be requesting food only for the man to deny him.

But Carter is so fucking *hungry*. He refuses to miss the chance to eat. "May I have some – some chicken nuggets, please?"

"Absolutely." The man's smile is proud. Carter doesn't know what to do with that. "Do you want dipping sauce?" Carter can't help but just blink at the man. *Dipping sauce? Did his rapist just ask him if he'd like dipping sauce with his chicken nuggets from fucking McDonalds?*

"No," Carter says incredulously. Then he remembers to soften his tone and adds, "Thank you."

The man looks up at Benny, who has been listening the entire time. "Get him a water and apple slices, too."

"Apple slices?" Benny scoffs.

"Yeah, asshole. They have them for the kid meals. Don't you pay attention?"

"Do I look like I have a fucking kid?"

"No, you're right. That's just me when I have to deal with you."

"Fuck off." Benny flips the man off. Carter wonders if they're friends. They must be. Maybe even brothers. He can't see any other way that Benny would be able to speak that way to his boss.

Then again, Carter knows nothing about this world. He's just a college student turned pleasure slave. Perhaps bosses in this fucked up alternate reality don't demand respect from their employees.

"Cup of ice as well," the man says with an amused smirk, clearly not upset with the way Benny is speaking to him.

"Aye, aye, Captain," Benny grumbles before slamming the door shut.

Any interest Carter had during the interaction goes out the window the moment he realizes he's now locked in the vehicle completely alone with his new owner. He tentatively looks at the man. When their eyes meet, the man gives him a startlingly warm smile. It doesn't match what he says next. "Come here, sweetheart. Straddle my lap."

Suddenly feeling braver now that he's not outnumbered, Carter stays where he is and asks, "Why?"The man raises an eyebrow, looking caught between anger and amusement. "Because I said so."

"You think just because you're rich that you have the right to buy human beings like fucking property? That you can order them around and fucking rape them?" Carter growls, filled with a sudden outrage at this entire situation. It feels good. Much better than the terror or grief of the past.

But then the man's amusement wins over, and he smirks at Carter, and Carter is immediately regretting the outburst. "Yes."

"Y-yes?"

"Yes," the man says again. "I do believe because I am rich that I can buy human beings like fucking property. That I can order them around and fucking rape them. Though, it takes much more than money, of course. One needs connections. Respect. Power. A man like me can have anything he wants, sweetheart. Anything in this goddamn world. The sooner you give into that reality, the easier this will all be."

"All be for who? Me or you?"

"You. I'll enjoy taking the hard way with you if that's what you choose, but I can guarantee that you will not feel the same." The man's smirk turns positively wicked.

"I bet you'll be beautiful when I finally beat this defiance out of you, though."

Carter can practically hear Casey screaming in his head, panicked and angry. He's doing everything he shouldn't. This man gave him a blanket, didn't hurt him when he tried escaping, and is getting him food. *And what is Carter doing?* Giving him the proverbial middle finger. He should be complying right now. Behaving. Biding his time.

"Final warning," the man says in a hauntingly calm voice.

Any fight left in Carter dissolves. He starts to move forward, trying to avoid touching the man as much as possible. The man doesn't have the same qualms. His hands immediately find Carter's naked hips, maneuvering him until he's settled exactly where the man wants him to be. Every spot where the man touches Carter feels like fire on his skin. Part of him worries that he'll look down to find the man's fingerprints seared into him like some sick sort of brand.

Carter's face goes red hot when the man cradles his caged cock and balls like they're nothing more than a semi-interesting piece of decoration. He skims a thumb along the curved plastic. "How long have they had this on you?"

"I – I'm not sure." Carter clears his throat, trying to think. He doesn't want the man to be upset. He wants to be able to give him *something* at least. "It wasn't too long ago, I don't think..."

"How do you figure?"

"I haven't been given water since it happened. So, it couldn't have been that long, right?"

The man's expression goes dark. Carter's breath catches, his shoulders curling forward as he realizes he said something wrong. He doesn't know what. He was just being honest. The man had *said* to be honest.

Carter waits for the man to scold him or hurt him. Instead, the man just sighs. "Right. Not too long at all. I believe it's time we remove it, though. What do you think?"

Before Carter can even worry it's a trick question, he's nodding. "Yes, please."

"Hold still, then." The man reaches into his breast pocket, pulling out a small silver key. He shifts Carter's caged cock before sliding the key into the little slot and turning it. Carter sighs in relief when he hears the soft *click*. The man is surprisingly careful as he guides the first plastic piece off Carter's cock. Carter watches in both fascination and horror as the man continues disassembling it, wondering how many of these the man has handled. Probably a few if the ease of which he slides little rods and twists tiny screws is any indication. As they're removed, the pieces of the cage are tossed to the side without care, a fragile hope fluttering in Carter's chest that this man doesn't plan on putting him in the cage again. Heart pounding, he watches as the man does the final step, pulling the plastic ring around his balls apart and twisting it. The end catches on Carter's sack, pulling at the sensitive skin. He accidentally whimpers, his hips jerking to show his dislike of the situation.

"I know, sweetheart." The man gently takes Carter's balls in his hand, massaging them. He's extra careful around any of the places where there are indents in the skin from past abuse. It feels good. Humiliatingly good. Carter closes his eyes to keep from having to watch. It thankfully only lasts a few more seconds before the man is letting him go and giving the next order. "Now lay flat with your stomach on the seat beside me, your head by the door, your ass in my lap."

Swallowing hard, Carter moves into the position as directed. It makes his sensitive cock and balls rub against the man's expensive pants. Carter bites his lip to make any sounds of pain or pleasure, hating his body for betraying him as he feels his cock fill from the simple stimulation.

The man grabs each ass cheek in a gentle but firm grip. Carter cries out before quickly hiding his face in both fear and embarrassment. One of the man's hands comes up to stroke along his spine. "I'm not going to hurt you, sweetheart. Don't you see? When you behave, I'll take such good care of you. It's when you forget your place that things will hurt. Understood?"

"Yes..."

"Yes, *sir*," the man corrects.

Carter squeezes his eyes shut to stave off the tears threatening to fall. "Yes... sir."

"Good. Now, hold still. I just need to make sure there wasn't any damage done earlier."

Doing as told, Carter focuses solely on his breathing. It works for a few seconds, but then he's losing control again, his body trembling as the man spreads his cheeks to reveal his hole. It's impossible to stay calm then. Flashes of being back on that stage, back on that bench, restrained, terrified, raped by this very man holding him, assault his mind until he's gasping for air.

The man hushes him, his hand gentle and soothing as it returns to rubbing Carter's back. But the other hand is prodding at Carter's sore hole, clearly about to remove the anal plug there, and Carter can't focus on anything else. At least the man doesn't yell at him for his reactions. He just sighs in frustration and removes the plug, working quickly and efficiently as he checks Carter out. It takes an eternity before the man finally hums softly and tells Carter he can kneel again. Carter slides off the seat in relief, settling himself between the man's legs like before. He can feel lube and cum trickling out of his hole and onto the feet he has tucked beneath him. He curls in on himself until he's a tight little ball. It helps slow his heart rate, his breaths coming easier.

"Your hole is going to be fine. And it seems that your shoulders are thankfully not dislocated. They'll be sore for a while, of course. We'll keep an eye on them. I'm concerned about your head, but with all that you've been through, I doubt we'll be able to watch you for any signs of concussion. Your poor body is already too out of whack." The man grabs the blanket from before and drapes it carefully over Carter's shoulders, not making a comment about his fetal position. "We need to set some rules now."

Feeling pried open and vulnerable, Carter grips the edges of the blanket and wraps it tightly around himself, leaving only his face free as he clasps his fabric-covered hands together. He pretends it's someone else holding his hand. Casey, maybe. Maison. His mom. *God, Carter would do anything to have five minutes with his mom right now.* He'd curl up in her lap like when he was little, letting her play with his hair as she sings him a lullaby.

"Don't cry," the man says quietly, lifting a hand to Carter's face. Carter flinches before sagging in relief when he realizes all the man is doing is wiping a tear from his cheek. He hadn't realized he started crying again. He starts and stops so often lately. "I'm not going to hurt you, sweetheart. Not if you're good."

The man pauses.

Then, "Nod if you understand me."

Carter nods.

The man sits back, spreading his legs a little wider as he peers down at Carter. Carter can't help but feel exposed, even covered in the blanket like he is. He wonders if this is how those bugs felt when he pinned them to a board for his junior year biology project. *This is the wings. This is the abdomen. This is the thorax.*

Carter wonders what labels he would be given. *This is the no longer virgin asshole. This is the bleeding lips. This is the hungry stomach.*

"Hey." Carter startles, his thoughts coming back to the present. To the vehicle. To sir. He looks up at the man, prepared to be yelled at for zoning out. Instead, he finds the man just frowning at him in concern. "Just three easy rules for now, okay? I can see how tired you are. You'll be able to rest soon, once we get something in that stomach of yours. Okay?"

"Yes, sir," Carter whispers.

This is the confusing man who buys sex slaves but treats them kindly.

This is the sad boy so starved for touch he just might beg the man for more of it.

"Rule number 1. You'll call me sir. Always. Any other name will result in punishment, understood?" Carter nods. "Use your words, sweetheart."

Carter shudders, hating how much he loves that damn pet name. It makes him feel too good. Too... un-slave like. "I understand. Always call you sir. Anything else will get me in trouble... *sir.*"

"Good." The man – *sir* – tilts his head and studies Carter for a moment. He seems to be considering something. Then, "Rule number 2. You'll always be kneeling unless explicitly told otherwise or physically moved by me. The most important part of this is the *by me.* If someone else, anyone else, tries to change your position verbally or physically, you are not to listen. Ever. Your body belongs to me, and me alone. I say what it's doing. *Always.* Understood?"

A heavy weight tugs at Carter's gut, but he forces himself to nod and say, "Yes, sir."

"Repeat the rule to me."

"I should always be kneeling unless you want me to do something else." Carter grips his hands tight enough to make them ache. "And only you can tell me to do something else, sir."

"And why is that?"

"Uh. Um." Carter's heart starts to race, sir's words replaying in his mind. "Because my – my body belongs to you, sir."

"Good. Rule number 3. You will obey me, always, and without hesitation. Understood?""Yes, sir. I will always obey you without hesitation."

Sir smiles softly and nods. "Yes. Good. Just like with the second rule, you will not obey anyone but me, either. Not a single person. You won't be disrespectful, of course, but you won't obey them when given commands. You won't stand. You won't kneel. You won't strip. You most certainly will not engage in any sort of physical contact – especially sexual. You are mine. *Mine*. Is that understood?"

Carter shivers, his stomach twisting in a strangely... *warm* sort of way at the words. "Yes, sir. I'm yours."

"Mmm. I like that. Say it again."

"I'm yours, sir."

"Yes. Yes, you are. All mine. And I'm going to take such good care of you." Sir reaches down and tilts Carter's chin up, then runs the pad of his thumb along Carter's bottom lip. When Carter gives into instinct and opens his mouth for him, sir's expression darkens. He sounds nearly breathless when he says, "Good boy."

The front car door opens, catching them both off guard. Sir looks up at Benny, dropping his hand, but Carter continues staring at sir. He's trying to process the way his body just began to melt for the man who raped and purchased him like an object.

Surely, he's only feeling the things he's feeling because the man is showing him kindness. After the terrifying and lonely past few weeks, he's just trying to soak up any sort of comfort he can get before he's hurt again. *That must be a normal human reaction, right?* He's not fucked up. This experience hasn't fucked him up.

Right?

Right.

He's perfectly normal.

And, if Carter sort of likes the way sir hand feeds him small bites of food, and the way sir smiles when he offers

Carter the plushie moose backpack clip that came with his kid's meal, and the way sir cradles him to his chest and holds the cup of ice to his forehead, and the way sir whispers praise to him for being good, then that's normal too.

Totally, perfectly, *definitely* normal.

Chapter Five

THE PLANE RIDE HOME on Nathan's private jet is nearly 13 hours long. Carter sleeps the entire time, passed out on the king bed in the rear cabin. He had lasted less than five minutes after his stomach had been full, the boy falling asleep in Nathan's arms as Nathan held ice to his head wound and told him how good he was. He hadn't even stirred when Nathan carried him from the SUV to the plane, nor when Nathan placed him in the bed and pulled the blankets over his fragile body. Besides two bathroom breaks, Nathan spent the entire flight sitting in the leather desk chair in the corner, either watching over the boy or dozing.

Carter still doesn't wake up after they've arrived at the Roarke compound, Nathan once again carrying him as they travel from the plane to Nathan's private entrance. Nathan looks at Benny in concern. "Should we be worried about a concussion?"

"Why? You gonna take him to the hospital?"

"Don't be an ass."

"He'll be okay. Kid probably hasn't slept in weeks. It probably feels fucking good to be warm. Fed. His body is just soaking up every ounce of rest it can get."

Nathan nods, thankful for the reassurance. He likes how peaceful Carter is right now. Knowing he's safe makes it even better.

Benny enters Nathan's door code and opens it for him. Nathan rests his shoulder against it to keep it from closing. "We'll be good for the night. You get some rest, man."

"You too, Nate. Seriously. Sleep."

All Nathan does is grunt. Benny accepts it, disappearing down the private hall and leaving Nathan alone with his new pleasure slave. He places the boy on his massive bed and covers him with his blanket from the plane, smiling when he catches sight of the tiny stuffed moose Carter has yet to let go of since Nathan gave it to him. After waiting a full minute to make sure Carter doesn't wake up, Nathan puts in the codes to lock his doors from the inside, flipping the manual locks after. Then he heads into his attached bathroom.

With a final peek at Carter on his bed, Nathan locks himself in the bathroom, runs the sink, and makes the phone call he's been dreading all night.

As always, there are 3 rings, then a clipped voice. "Name?"

"Eagle 2."

"Code?"

"7134."

"Hold."

Nathan peeks out at Carter again, paranoid the boy will wake up. Then he paces the bathroom as he waits to be connected. Just as he's sort of hoping Maison got called away on a mission, his best friend's voice fills his ear. "Travis?"

"The one and only," Nathan answers with a hopefully convincing confidence.

"How is he?"

Nathan glances at the bathroom door. "He's asleep right now."

There's a pause. Then, "Don't make me drag this shit out of you, man. Come on. All Benny said in his text was that you got him. I need more than that."

Knowing that's fair, Nathan sinks down to sit on the closed toilet lid and fills Maison in. "The only real competition was Miller, but I shut his ass down. Fucking Quinton decided to make a damn show of it, though."

"How so?"

"He-" Nathan runs his hand through his hair, tugging until it hurts. "I had to use him. On stage. It was a deal I made with Quinton to keep him from letting the audience come up and play with him before the sales began."

When Maison says nothing, Nathan forces himself to continue. "We left right after. I checked him over, went over some rules with him, fed him, then he passed out. He hasn't woken up yet, but I think he's just damn tired. Benny doubts it's anything serious."

"How bad is it?""All things considered? Not bad." Nathan rubs his forehead, eyes closed as he tries to picture the naked boy again. "Standard sleep deprivation, starvation, dehydration. I think he was blindfolded for quite a while. His eyes had a hard time in dim lighting when it was removed. There was a surprisingly small amount of bruising, though. And nothing's dislocated or broken. Far as I could tell, he was sexually untouched until – well, until me."

Maison grunts. "He must not have been much of a fighter. That's good. That's – that's good. Is he, uh – could you tell..."

"Just ask it, bud."

"Could you tell if he's, ya know... broken?"

This makes Nathan smile, just a little. "God no. Kid's a little fighter, even if it's just in his head. Already got some attitude from him. Don't worry."

"Thank god." Maison laughs breathlessly. "He's a spitfire, Trav. You're gonna like him."

Nathan isn't sure if that's a good thing. Spitfires earn punishments. Nathan doesn't want to punish Carter. Not in the least.

Thankfully, Maison changes the subject. "What rules did you end up giving him?"

"None you and I haven't discussed."

"Clarify."

"Call me sir. Kneel unless told otherwise. And always obey me."

"And you made it clear no one else has power over him?"

"Damn clear, but I'll make sure to continue reinforcing that. No one will touch him, bud."

Maison scoffs. "No one but *you*."

The words are like a knife in Nathan's chest. "That's not *fair*."

"I know..."

"I didn't fucking sign up for this, Mais. I knew I'd have to do some questionable things, but not this. Not rape – repeatedly fucking *rape* – and control and fucking *own* my best friend's little brother. I've never even used a slave for more than cock warming or a quick blowjob. I didn't sign up for this shit."

"I *know*," Maison says again, firmly this time.

"Tonight was the first time I've ever fucking raped someone. Do you get that? Do you understand that? I'm not fucking enjoying myself here, asshole."

"Trav, I *know*. That wasn't fair of me to say. I know you, man. I know how much this is already killing you."

Nathan sighs, pushing to his feet and walking over to the door. He glances out again at Carter. The boy has moved, curled up on his side now, but he's still asleep.

"I have no idea what I'm doing," Nathan admits when he's locked himself back in the small room. "I thought this would be easier. Not *easy*, but easier. The way he looks at me already - I'm a fucking monster to him. I'm his rapist."

"I mean... yeah. You knew that's how it'd be."

"I know. I just-" Nathan swallows. "I just wish I could tell him that he's safe."

"He can't find out the truth, Travis. He *can't*."

"I know." Nathan shakes his head. "But I don't know how mean I can be to him. I – fuck, man. I can barely get myself to touch him when I'm being *gentle*."

"Hopefully he'll behave, and all you'll have to be is gentle."

Nathan scoffs. "Behaving or not, it's still rape."

"Travis, get your shit together. If you fuck this up, you not only get your ass killed and blow our entire fucking operation, but you get my baby brother killed too."

"I know. I'm not – that's not the problem. I mean it fucking is, but I'm more concerned about him being too smart. He's going to be confused when he sees the way the other slaves are treated. He's going to see that he's different."

"He *is* different. He's a trophy."

"Still..."

After going quiet for a moment, Maison releases a deep breath. "How confident are you that you could pretend that you're falling in love with him over time?"

Nathan squints at the marbled counter of the sink. "*What?*"

"Ya know, you could pretend over time that you're falling for him. You can play the whole *villain goes soft for his lover* angle. Tell him it has to be a secret between the two of you because your men will be upset. That way, you can at least be kind to him in private, and when you are a little softer in public, he'll think it's because of that."

"So, you want me to fuck with his emotions even more than I already am?"

"I – fuck, I don't know. No. Yes? Yes. No? Fuck if I know. Whatever feels right. I trust you." Maison sighs. "Nate, this whole thing is going to work out, and the operation is going to be over soon, and I'll have you to thank for saving my baby brother."

"No pressure."

"A shit ton of pressure, but you can handle it."

Nathan isn't so sure about that. Then again, he's not so sure he has any other option *but* to handle it. Anything else results in death for him and Carter. Or much, much worse. Nathan sighs heavily, feeling a headache starting to form. "You know he's going to find out what you are now, right? I can't shield him from it. He'll hear my men talking."

Maison grunts. "Yeah. I know."

"I-" Nathan stops, looking over at the door. He swears he heard – yeah, that's definitely someone walking around the bedroom. "Shit. He's awake. I gotta go. Talk soon."

Stuffing his phone in his pocket, Nathan hurries out of the bathroom just in time to find Carter standing by the dresser. The boy moves away as if the thing just set on fire, then immediately drops to the floor and curls in on himself. He's trembling. Nathan has a feeling it's not from being cold.

"Stand up," Nathan says in what he hopes is an authoritative but non-threatening voice. When Carter obeys, he adds, "Good boy remembering to kneel for me just now. You aren't in trouble, in case you were worried. I never told you that you weren't allowed to leave the bed or look around, though from now on I don't want you leaving the bed once you're put in it, unless you're given permission or need to use the bathroom, understood?"

"Yes, sir."

"If you do need to use the bathroom, you'll immediately come back to the bed after."

"Yes, sir."

"Good."

Carter fidgets in place, clearly unsure what to do or say. He has his moose from earlier tight in his hands. The sight of it does something awful to Nathan's heart.

Nathan sweeps his eyes over the boy, then sighs. "Are you still tired? Because I'm fucking exhausted."

Carter nibbles on his bottom lip before whispering to the floor, "I need to use the bathroom, sir..."

"Go on, then. Leave the door open."

The boy's cheeks go red, but he mumbles, "Yes, sir," and does as told. Nathan starts to undress while he waits, setting his Rolex and cufflinks on the top of the dresser. He shrugs out of his jacket and removes his tie before Carter returns. On a whim, he beckons the boy forward. He needs to make use of him as often as he can. This will be an excellent way to do so without causing him any harm.

"Take my shoes off." Carter surprisingly doesn't hesitate. He just lowers himself to his knees and carefully undoes the laces on Nathan's right shoe. He slides it off and places it to the side before doing the same with the left. Then he looks up at Nathan for further instruction. "Socks."

The socks come next, Carter laying them flat on top of each other beside the shoes.

Carter remains kneeling, his eyes locked on Nathan's face. There are too many emotions in his big blue eyes. It makes it hard for Nathan to breathe.

Nathan looks away.

"If you use my weapons to kill me, my men will make you regret it. You can't escape here. Don't try." Nathan takes his gun from his holster and places it on the dresser, followed by the gun in the waistband above his ass, then the folding knife from his pocket. Then he slides his holster off his shoulders and hangs it on the hook right beside the dresser. "You'll learn this soon, but I'm the best chance you have here, sweetheart. Don't run from me."

The boy doesn't argue. He just stares at Nathan, resigned and quiet.

When Nathan curls a finger, Carter stands up. "Belt." His belt is slowly removed, coiled, and handed to him. He places it on the dresser before tugging his shirt out from his waistband and looking at the boy in front of him.

Carter reaches forward tentatively. When Nathan doesn't correct him, he begins undoing the buttons of his shirt, pushing it off Nathan's shoulders and down his arms once it's free. He folds the shirt exactly as it should be and places it on top of the neatly set shoes.

"Pants."

Carter's hands begin to shake, but he obeys without hesitation again. He's careful and methodical with his movements. That is, until he guides Nathan's feet out of his pants and sees the holster with his fixed blade on Nathan's right ankle. Nathan decides to test him. The worst that can happen is Carter stabs him somewhere once. The best that can happen is he can see that the boy has already learned his lesson that hurting Nathan will only make things worse, not better. "Remove the knife first. Hand it to me, handle forward."

The boy swallows hard. He hesitates this time. Nathan allows it. His hands curl slightly as he prepares himself for a possible fight. Then Carter is reaching forward, gently sliding the knife from its holster, and handing the weapon to Nathan with the handle forward. He meets Nathan's eye as Nathan accepts the offering. Nathan can't help but allow his lips to curve into a smile. "Good boy."

Cheeks flushing again, Carter ducks his head. He likes the praise though. It's obvious in the way his shoulders relax and his body shivers. In the way goosebumps erupt on his bare skin.

"The holster next."

Carter removes the holster carefully, his fingertips brushing along Nathan's skin. He's never been so happy to have his ankle touched. It's ridiculous. It's *wrong*.

He ignores it.

Carter hands the holster to him, Nathan biting his tongue to keep from praising him once again.

Then Nathan realizes he's come to a defining moment. All that's left on his body is underwear. Carter has noticed too if his beet red face is any indication.

Nathan knows he should sleep naked.

Hell, he knows he should probably fuck Carter once more tonight. Since that won't be happening, the least he can do is take his fucking underwear off. It's not like Carter gets to have any.

With a sigh, Nathan slips into his role of cold, uncaring owner and gestures to his boxer briefs. "They aren't going to remove themselves."

Carter flinches, but he quickly follows the implied order, hooking his fingers into Nathan's underwear and pulling it down until it's around his ankles. Nathan has to bite back a moan when his semi-hard cock bobs just inches from Carter's pretty face.

It's the pill, he promises himself. *Just the lingering effect of that fucking pill.* Self-hate bubbles up inside him when his cock hardens completely the moment Carter looks up at him from where he's kneeling on the ground. He can tell the boy is preparing himself for something sexual. He can see the way he's starting to shutter himself, his eyes going distant, his expression blank. At least Nathan's arousal wanes as he watches the reaction. That makes him feel a tad better about himself.

Nathan forces a sigh, pretending like he couldn't care less about any of this. Pretending he couldn't care less about the boy at his feet. "I'm too fucking tired to deal with you anymore tonight. Do I need to chain you to the bed, or will you behave while we sleep?" Carter looks up at him with wide eyes. "I'll behave, sir."

"Good. Because this room is perfectly decorated, and if I have to drag a dog crate in here to fuck it up just so I can sleep without worrying about you, I might just give you away to someone else instead while I rest. You wouldn't want that, right?" Nathan nearly puffs up with pride at how well he just pulled that off. He sounded like a real monster there. Very convincing.

Because you are a real monster. You've become one. Can't you see?

Nathan swallows hard, refusing to give the fleeting thought his attention.

"Right, sir," Carter finally says, his voice thick and shaky. "I promise I'll be very good."

On accident, Nathan smiles again. Since he already fucked up his supposed demeanor, he follows instinct and adds, "Good boy."

The boy has the same reaction as before to the praise. Nathan loves it far too much. He's going to have to be careful around his men.

"Come then. You've had a long day, and tomorrow will be longer. Let's get some rest."

Carter wavers for a moment, clearly unsure if he's allowed to stand or not. Nathan makes it simple by reaching down for his hand and guiding him to his feet. He gestures to the side of the bed Carter was on earlier. "This is your side."

"Y-yes, sir." Carter steels himself before forcing his body towards the bed. It's almost painful to watch. He's shaking by the time he climbs onto it, his breathing erratic. It takes two tries before he manages to get the blankets over himself.

Seeing the little moose was left on the floor, Nathan picks it up and brings it to the boy. He watches the fear in his eyes as he approaches. By the time Nathan is hovering over him at the side of his bed, he's blinking away tears. Nathan's heart aches for him. "Your moose."

Carter frowns. Then his eyes leave the threat of Nathan's looming body and focus on the tiny plush moose in Nathan's hand instead. His body relaxes at the sight of it. Even a slight smile tugs at his lips. His hand still shakes when he takes the thing from Nathan, but his voice is even, his breathing slow, when he says, "Thank you, sir."

With a sharp jerk of his head, Nathan walks around to the other side of the bed. He can feel Carter's eyes tracking his every move. He slides easily under the blankets, trying to act like none of this matters to him. Then he reaches out for the control panel on the wall above the side table and swipes his hand across it, tapping the *lights off* icon. The room immediately falls into darkness.

It takes about ten seconds for Nathan to realize something is wrong. The boy beside him is trembling so violently his body is jerking beneath the blankets. Little gasps and whimpers are being frantically swallowed, just loud enough for Nathan to catch. Nathan tentatively reaches a hand out to touch where he thinks the boy's shoulder must be. The moment their skin connects, Carter releases an awful sob.

Oh, Carter...

"Hey now," Nathan says softly. "I'm not going to hurt you. Not if you're good. Remember?"

The boy sobs harder. Nathan starts to pull his hand away, his mind racing, but he's caught by surprise when Carter latches onto him. He holds Nathan like he's drowning and Nathan is a life preserver. His shaking is so hard that Nathan feels it transferring up his own arm.

"Please don't leave me," the boy cries. His body is pressing in closer to Nathan. "Please don't leave me."

"No one is leaving you, sweetheart. I'm right here."

"Please," Carter sobs. His fingernails are digging into Nathan's skin now. "I – I don't wanna be alone. Not again. Not again."

Nathan starts to sit up. The boy doesn't allow it. He releases a frustrated sigh. "What is going on? Why are you afraid right now?"

"Please," the boy begs. "Not again. Not again."

"Not again *what*?"

"The dark!" he practically wails. "Not alone in the dark. Please!"

Nathan's heart breaks. Not again. Not alone in the dark again.

When the fuck was this boy put in the dark all alone? Nathan doesn't realize how angry he is until a growl slips past his lips. The boy immediately lets go and scrambles to the other side of the bed, sounding broken and terrified. "I'm sorry. I'm sorry, sir. I'm sorry. I'll be good. I'm sorry. I'm sorry. I'm-"

The boy's panicked apologies are cut off when Nathan reaches out for him again. He tenses, prepared for pain, Nathan's sure, but he just pulls Carter in close and holds him to his chest. It takes a few seconds of Nathan rubbing his back and whispering that he's not alone before the boy finally starts to calm. Nathan holds him for as long as it takes. Even when Carter is breathing normally again, no longer jerking or crying with panic, he continues holding him.

"You're afraid of the dark," Nathan says, not because it's a question, but because it just needs to be confirmed.

"Y-yes, sir. I'm so sorry."

Nathan has to bite his tongue to keep from telling the boy he doesn't have to apologize. "Will you feel better if I turn the light by the door on low?"

The boy nods rapidly against his chest. "Yes. Yes, sir, please. Please do that, sir."

"Okay. Go to your side of the bed, and you can hold my hand if you need to until the light is fixed, okay?"

The boy cries again, but this time it's not sad or panicked. It's relieved. He holds onto Nathan's hand and slides back to his spot. Nathan reaches over and slides the fingers of his free hand across the panel again. Just the small blue light from it is enough to have Carter relaxing his hold on him. When Nathan turns the light by the door on to 1, Carter's hand leaves. Nathan aches with the loss.

"Better?"

"Yes, sir. Th-thank you so much, sir."

Nathan lays back on the bed, fighting the urge to hold the boy again. Carter doesn't want to be touched. The only reason he did was because his fear of the dark outweighed his fear of Nathan. Nathan's no idiot. Now that the dark has been conquered, Nathan is the reigning monster again.

It hurts in a way that Nathan refuses to think about.

Chapter Six

CARTER SPENDS THE NIGHT wide awake, lying stock-still as he stares up at the crystal chandelier above the bed through the dim lighting. He wonders what it would feel like for the chandelier to fall on him. For it to shatter, cutting his skin. For it to crush the life from his lungs. He wonders if death would be worth the pain.

Carter doesn't look away from the chandelier. He can't. It feels like the room is closing in, the chandelier the one thing that's staying a safe distance away. Everything else is slowly encroaching on him.

Especially sir.

He's convinced that sir keeps getting closer, despite the fact that every time he forces himself to look over, he sees sir in the exact same position, all the way on the opposite side of the massive bed. It doesn't matter, though. Unlike the crystal chandelier, he knows sir will eventually come for him. He'll cut him. Crush him. Do whatever he pleases with him. Carter's not an idiot. They're both naked, and this man *owns* him. It's only a matter of time before sir decides to rape him again.

The thought makes Carter sick. Truly sick. He slides off the bed and stumbles to the bathroom, trying to be as quiet as possible when he shuts the door and locks it. Even though sir told him to keep the door open before, he didn't technically make it a rule. Carter is willing to risk it. If the door is closed, the bedroom can't cave in on him.

Carter immediately flips on the lights before panic can envelop him once again. Then he hurries across the small room, barely making it to the toilet in time to empty his stomach. His body purges everything it has, and then some, until he's reduced to nothing but dry heaves.

When it seems that his body has finally given up, Carter pushes to his feet on trembling legs and goes to the sink. He rinses his mouth with mouthwash before splashing some water on his face. The sight of himself in the mirror when he looks up at his reflection catches him by surprise. He looks... different. His face is hollow. The bags under his eyes are heavy and dark. His stomach is caved in.

His throat is wrapped with an industrial looking collar that has a loop on the front for a leash. Carter brings his finger up to touch the collar, pulling away quickly as if it burned him.

No longer able to look at his own twisted image, Carter turns his back to the mirror and wraps his arms around his torso as tightly as he can. That's when he sees it.

A window.

In the corner, above the whirlpool tub that's made of shiny black and gold marble, is a window. Large. 4 panes. A switch to the left of the frame to frost it over for privacy. Carter rushes over, climbing up the three stairs required to even enter the oversized tub before scrambling inside of it. He props himself up on the bench inside the basin and flips the switch. He gasps.

Outside.

Night-time. Dark. Star-filled. He presses his hand and forehead against the cool glass, wanting to be as close to it all as possible.

God, he never thought he'd see the night sky again. The stars. He remembers wasting away in the dark, thinking he'd die without ever getting the chance. He forgot how beautiful it is.

The full moon illuminates the yard, if the stretch of seemingly never-ending grass and garden and trees can be considered a *yard*.

It's high. At least three stories, though possibly more. From the size of the yard, along with the winding driveway off to the side, and the edge of what he thinks might be a pool around the corner, Carter thinks he might be in some sort of mansion. He supposes that makes sense. The man *did* spend 2 million dollars on him after all. Carter would scoff at the absurdity of it if he wasn't so fucking terrified.

It's too high to jump. Even if it wasn't, there doesn't seem to be any latches to open the window anyway. Hell, even if it was lower, and there were latches, he has no delusion that he would be able to make it anywhere before someone caught him. There's nothing but trees as far as his eyes can see. Unless there's unexpectedly a city on the opposite side of the mansion, he'd be fucked no matter what.

He *is* fucked no matter what.

Carter climbs out of the tub in defeat. The moment his feet touch the bathroom floor, his emotions unlock. They bubble up and over his self-control until he's choking on a sob. Carter drops to the floor and curls in on himself as tightly as he can, burying his face in his hands to muffle the wrecked sounds escaping him.

How is this his life? What the fuck happened?

How does Maison fit into all of this?

Is this all Maison's fault?

Does Maison know he's gone yet? If so, is Maison trying to get him back?

Does Maison even have the kind of resources it would take to attempt to get him back? Will it be too late by then?

Is sir going to kill Carter once he's bored with him? How long will that take? A week? A month? Years?

Carter doesn't know if he can survive years.

But Carter doesn't want to die.

He's too young to die.

There are so many things left to do. So much left for him to learn and see.

He's not *finished*.

Carter remains on the floor and cries his way through a myriad of overwhelming thoughts until he feels nothing but raw and empty. He lays there for a while after, just listening to the sound of his breathing. Then he forces himself to get up.

Returning to the bed with sir is one of the last things he wants to do, but Carter doesn't want to get in trouble. Things are bad enough when he's being good. Carter doesn't want to find out what a punishment would be like.

After quietly cleaning up the bathroom, Carter turns off the light and unlocks the door. It makes a clicking sound that has Carter flinching, but it at least doesn't creak when he opens it.

When Carter gets to his side of the bed, he freezes.

His heart stops.

Sir is awake.

The man is lying on his side, facing Carter's empty space on the bed. Or, more accurately, facing the bathroom that Carter had just snuck out of. He doesn't look sleepy, which means he's probably been awake for a while.

Carter stands completely still, curling his hands into fists at his sides to hide that they're shaking. Sir's eyes flit over him. They linger on his collar. Then the man looks at Carter's eyes.

"All done now?" sir asks softly, tilting his head.

Feeling on the verge of tears again, Carter clamps down on his bottom lip and slowly nods.

Sir sighs. Then he curls a finger. "Come here, sweetheart."

Feeling sick to his stomach again, Carter climbs onto the bed and settles himself on his silky black and gold striped pillow. He lies on his side to face sir. When he sees his stuffed moose is between them, he hurries to grab it, holding it tight to his chest like it can protect him somehow. It's the most absurd, childish thing, but it makes him feel better. That's worth it to him.

Carter gasps when sir suddenly reaches an arm out and grabs him. The man tugs Carter across the silky sheets easily, not stopping until Carter's head is tucked beneath sir's chin. He smells good, hints of scotch overlaying something fresh and spicy beneath.

Carter's fear melts away as he realizes the man isn't going to hurt him or use him. He's just... *holding* him.

Sir begins tracing the curve of Carter's spine. It's soothing, which blows Carter's mind. He doesn't understand this man.

He doesn't understand anything anymore.

"I own you," sir whispers in his ear. The words aren't said cruelly. It's just the man stating a fact. "You've lost all control. You exist for me now, sweetheart. That's your purpose. There's no reason to worry. No reason to lie awake all night afraid. You can't control what happens to you anymore. You're mine now. All mine. And I'm going to take care of you, I promise."

Sir presses a kiss to his temple. It's nice.

Carter hates that it's nice.

"Just let go, sweetheart. Let everything go. Give it all to me."

Carter closes his eyes, letting the words sink in. Sir is right. All of this worry and overanalyzing is stupid. It's just Carter torturing himself. If Maison is going to save him, there's nothing Carter can do to help. If sir is going to use him, there's nothing Carter can do to stop it. Maybe in the future, the circumstances will change, but not right now. Now is the time to give into sir.

Keep calm. Breathe. Pay attention. Wait for your moment.

"That's it," sir coos, running a hand through Carter's hair before returning to the bare skin of his back. "Good boy. Just relax, now. Give into it."

With a full body shiver, Carter obeys. He releases everything and allows himself to relax for the first time in... a very long time. His body seems to thank him for it. It's as if by letting go, he's slammed straight into a wall. The exhaustion overtakes him, despite all the sleep he's already gotten. He falls asleep to sir stroking his back, whispering things like, "Good boy," and, "That's it, sweetheart."

It's nice.

Pretend, of course.

Just an illusion.

A moment of peace before the storm.

But nice, all the same.

Chapter Seven

NATHAN WAKES UP SLOWLY the morning after the auction, reality taking a moment to settle in. For just a second, he's surprised that there's someone wrapped in his arms.

Then it all comes rushing back.

Carter had gotten sick last night. He had hidden in the bathroom and emptied himself of everything from vomit to sobs. When he had come back to bed, Nathan had tried to do what he thought was best. He had tried to strip Carter of the person he was so he could just fucking relax and give in for a while. Miraculously, Carter had listened to him. He had fallen asleep. Right there in Nathan's arms.

Now, here the boy is, still wrapped around Nathan, using his chest as a pillow as Nathan lies on his back, a leg thrown over one of Nathan's like he couldn't get close enough, that damn moose trapped between his stomach and Nathan's side.

Nathan has to piss, but he refuses to wake the poor boy up just yet. Instead, he lets himself relax in the bed, studying Carter's sleeping form. He's peaceful like this. He looks his age.

He looks beautiful.

The boy is all messy dark brown hair and long lash-es kissing pale skin. The elegant slope of his nose begs Nathan's finger to run along it. His cheekbones are even sharper than his old pictures, exaggerated by his hunger. The small freckle on the corner of his jaw would be the perfect place for Nathan to press a soft kiss. His lips, chapped and scabbed, are impossibly full. Once they're taken care of, Nathan bets they'll be so very warm and soft. They'll look fantastic wrapped around Nathan's-

Nathan closes his eyes, exhaling slowly through his nose. He can't fantasize about things like that. Just because he's going to get to fuck this boy's mouth and ass doesn't mean he should allow himself to revel in it. It's rape. He'll never be lucky enough for it to be anything but rape.

If this were another bed, another place, if Nathan was another person - if Nathan was allowed to be *Travis* - this morning would be a good one. He can just picture it. Him waking up in Carter's off-campus apartment just like this, the boy in his arms. They'd have sleepy morning sex, Carter giggling - Nathan has no idea if Carter is a giggler, but he likes the idea of the boy being happy enough to giggle - as he tries to convince him to skip class and stay naked in bed all day. Carter would go to class anyway - Maison says he's an excellent student. He would pout, but he'd kiss Carter goodbye anyway, proud as fuck of his boy. Maybe he would even have school of his own. Art school, like he always dreamed before realizing someone aged out of the foster system didn't have a chance in hell at something like that and went and joined the Army instead. He'd spend his day covered in chalk and paint. When Carter got home later that night, they would cook dinner in the small kitchen together. They'd eat. Talk. Then cuddle up on the couch, Carter doing his homework with his head in his lap. He'd play with the boy's soft hair with his left hand and sketch with his right. Carter would hum and smile, telling him it feels nice. Eventually they'd go to bed, neither of them obligated, no one guilty, no one staying awake all night crying. They'd make love - or maybe fuck hard, depending on how Carter wants it that night - before falling asleep tangled together beneath the sheets. Then they'd wake up and do it all over again.

That'd be their life. Simple. Easy. *Happy.*

It's a nice fantasy. More than nice, even.

But it's just that – a fantasy.

Nathan gave up the possibility of a life like that the day he became *Nathan.* That kind of life – that kind of *happiness* - was for Travis. For almost a decade now, he's known he'll never have that. He'll never be Travis again. There's no going back. No off-campus apartments. No lazy morning sex. Even when this operation is over, there will be other things to do. Hell, even once he retires, he'd never take the chance of falling in love. Ghosts will haunt him until he dies. That's just what happens when you sign up for this job.

Look at Maison. Carter is right here because of him. Nathan hates to say that, he really does, but it's the truth. Maison has family. Maison has people to lose. It makes him vulnerable. It puts the people he loves in danger. Nathan will never take that chance.

If Nathan were to have a magic button, though... if he were able to become Travis even just for a day, he'd want to start that day exactly like this. Carter in his arms. Sleepy. Safe. Not afraid of him. Not obligated to be with him.

Nathan carefully extracts himself from Carter and heads to the bathroom. He takes a long shower, trying to wash away all of the doubts and stress of the past 24 hours so he can successfully pull this shit off today. In order to do what he's been able to do over the better part of this past decade, Nathan has built himself into a ruthless, evil man. He's become a fucking monster.

Being kind to Carter in front of Benny was fine, Benny is his partner in the operation after all, but the rest of his men won't accept that. He has to figure out where to draw the line. There's wiggle room with Carter because he was so expensive, because he's seen as something valuable. Maison was right about him being a trophy, even if the concept is fucked up. Nathan can use that. He can say he doesn't want to break his trophy.

But he has to be careful. Every kindness he shows Carter, every reprieve he hands him, has to look selfish. If Nathan's men ever figure out that it's *Carter* he's doing things for, it's all over. Nathan has no fucking idea how he's going to pull it off.

Nathan knows one thing for sure though.

He's going to fight like hell to not be Carter's monster.

CARTER STARTLES AWAKE WHEN he feels someone touching his body. He gasps, trying to pull out of the person's hold as his arm swings wildly. Faster than his sleepy brain can process, his wrists are pinned above his head and a hand is holding his jaw in a firm grip. Carter freezes, looking up at sir with wide eyes.

He just threw a punch at sir.

Oh god, he's going to get punished.

"Don't fight me," sir orders, his brown eyes flashing dangerously. "You can't fight me. That's not okay. Do you understand?"

Carter nods rapidly, blinking away tears. "Yes, sir. I – I didn't mean to, sir."

"I know." Sir releases his jaw and takes a step back, standing beside the bed as he watches Carter. He's freshly showered, his hands tucked in the pockets of his navy blue suit pants, an expensive watch flashing on his wrist, every part of him perfectly in place and controlled despite them fighting just moments before. "It'll get easier. Your mind will leave fight or flight mode eventually. Once you accept this. Once you accept me."

Maybe sir means that to be comforting, but it's not. It terrifies Carter that he might become complacent like that. He doesn't want to break. He doesn't want to accept this.

With a deep sigh, sir gestures towards the bathroom. "Go use the toilet, take a shower, clean yourself. *Thoroughly*," he specifies, eyes narrowing at Carter to make it clear what he means. "Then come back in here and kneel at the foot of the bed."

Carter nods, moving off the bed cautiously in case it's the wrong thing to do. When he isn't stopped, he picks up the pace and hurries to the bathroom. Sir stops him before he can shut the door, his hand grasping the edge of it in a tight grip like he had with Carter's throat.

"You don't get privacy in this house. Leave this open. And hurry. You don't want to make me miss breakfast, trust me."

"Yes, sir," Carter whispers, letting go of the door and hurrying to the toilet. He glances over to find sir standing there watching him, and he's thankful all he has to do is pee. It's awkward and humiliating to be watched as it is. He can't imagine if he had to poop in front of the man. Hopefully whenever that time comes, sir will be distracted.

Once he's relieved himself, Carter gets in the shower. He's unable to see if sir is still in the doorway or not, but it doesn't matter. He needs to focus on cleaning himself – *thoroughly* – and hurrying to get to the foot of the bed.

Carter soaps up his hair with one hand while running his other over his chest, shoulders, and arms. Then he tries to do his back the best he can. As the water does its job rinsing his hair out, Carter gets more soap on his hands and begins cleaning his bottom half. He's hairless now, they had waxed him at the auction house, and it feels strange to soap up smooth legs and a smooth crotch. He doesn't let himself dwell on it, though. He just hurries along, making sure to get every crease and hidden place he can find.

After putting it off until the very last moment, Carter forces himself to clean the place he's sure sir was referring to when speaking about being thorough. With one shaking hand on the wall to brace himself, Carter reaches back. Tears spring to his eyes as he slips a soapy finger into his hole. He's not hurt from last night, he was lucky sir prepared him so well, but he's still sore. It doesn't help that the finger reminds him of what it felt like to be raped, and he hates the way his stomach hurts with the memory. Carter needs to pull his hand away immediately, hoping the area is clean enough for sir because he can't touch himself there anymore. It feels too... he doesn't even know. It just feels *too*.

When Carter shuts the water off and slides the fogged glass shower door open, he jumps, nearly slipping, as he comes face to face with sir. Sir just lifts an eyebrow at him, lips twitching in amusement. Carter notices he's holding a fluffy white towel. He reaches for it, a *thank you* on his lips, but stops when sir pulls the towel out of reach. "Step out on the mat here. Legs parted."

Carter does as told, his heart racing. It's impossible to miss the way sir looks at him. There's a heat in his gaze. A possessiveness. Carter holds perfectly still as the man uses the towel to dry him off. It's not long before he's relaxing, though. It's impossible not to as he watches sir methodically dry him. Every touch is so... gentle. It's that same possessiveness he felt in his gaze before, but softer now. The first type of possessiveness was a *you're mine and I'm going to take you* possessiveness. The second type is a *you're mine and I'm going to take care of you* possessiveness. It's such a subtle shift, but it feels like everything.

Then sir is drying him off by wrapping his cock in the towel's fabric, stroking it until Carter is growing hard for him, and Carter remembers that the first possessiveness is the real one. The other was an illusion. Wishful thinking. This man bought him for the purpose of fucking him. Any care he shows is just sir providing maintenance on his possession.

It hurts, but it shouldn't hurt, so Carter stuffs the pain down as low as possible. Until it's almost non-existent.

Sir finishes drying him off, stepping back and tossing the damp towel into a hamper. Carter reaches up self-consciously to run his fingers through his hair. He knows it's a mess. It's always such a mess. Especially now that it's gotten so much longer than normal, the locks falling on his forehead and curling around his ears.

Before Carter even gets a chance to tame his hair, sir is wrapping a hand around Carter's bicep and pulling him out of the bathroom. Carter forgets all about his hair and focuses instead on the rest of his orders, remembering to kneel the moment sir releases his arm.

Once he's settled at sir's feet, the man does nothing but stare at him. Even without looking up to see sir's gaze, Carter can feel the weight of it. The heat. The possessiveness from before. He realizes sir is probably going to fuck him again. Maybe not this exact moment, but soon. Very soon. The thought causes Carter to sink into himself, but sir scolds him for it. "Straighten your back and look up at me. Don't be disrespectful."

Carter wants to tell him that he was only told to kneel, there weren't any other stipulations, but he bites his tongue. Sir is in a bad mood today. Worse than last night. Carter knows he shouldn't test him. "Yes, sir. Sorry, sir."

"Good." Sir sighs, the sound surprisingly shaky, and reaches his hand out to run his fingers through Carter's hair, taming the mess a bit like Carter had been trying to do earlier. Then he reaches down and unclasps the collar around Carter's neck.

The world goes still, Carter's breath catching.

Then he sees the new collar in sir's hand, and he understands. He nearly laughs at himself for being ridiculous enough to think he wouldn't be collared like an animal. This man has purchased him to be a sex slave. Of course, he's going to collar him. Sir probably just wants his own collar on Carter instead of someone else's.

In case Carter has any doubts, sir makes the situation clear. "You're mine, now. You should wear my collar. This will never come off of you, understood? It's waterproof. Once this is locked, I'm throwing away the key. Do you understand what that means, sweetheart?"

Carter nods. "Yes, sir."

"Tell me."

Forcing himself to look up at his sir, Carter states, "It means I belong to you, sir. For – forever."

The man towering over him hums his approval but says nothing as he reaches down to wrap the collar around his neck. It's softer than the one before. Carter thinks it might even be padded. He supposes if he has to be collared for the rest of his life, it's a decent collar to be stuck with.

Once sir has the collar clasped at the back of Carter's neck, he tugs at it once, then slips a finger beneath it almost like he's testing the fit. Seeming to like where it's at, sir locks the tiny padlock at the back of Carter's neck and tilts his chin with one hand, putting the collar on display for sir to look at. All Carter can focus on as he stares up at his new owner is the echo of that padlock clicking.

Forever.

It's locked there *forever.*

Oblivious to the overwhelming moment Carter has found himself trapped in, sir moves on to his next order of business. "Now, tell me the 3 rules from last night."

Shit. Carter hurries through the scrambled thoughts in his brain, desperate to please this man. He doesn't want to be bad. He doesn't want a punishment.

"I will always call you sir. I – uh – I will always kneel unless told otherwise. And my body belongs to you. Only you. Only you can give me orders, and I have to – to obey without hesitation." Carter bites his bottom lip before quickly adding, "But I have to be respectful to everyone, sir."

"And the new rule regarding the bed?"

"I'm not allowed to leave it without permission, sir. Unless it's to use the bathroom."

He waits to be told this is good, but all he gets is a curt nod. It hurts in a way Carter didn't expect.

"Lean over. Forehead on the floor. Ass in the air."

Ice runs through Carter's veins as he forces his body into the position. This is it. Sir is going to fuck him now. Carter squeezes his eyes shut, clamping down on his bottom lip as he waits with his ass humiliatingly on display. He startles when a hand touches his hip.

Carter parts his lips, intending to apologize, but he quickly closes his mouth when he realizes he's going to cry. Instead, he curls his finger until his nails dig into his palms and keeps himself in place. Every second afterward is torture as he waits to be yelled at.

But it never happens.

The familiar sound of a lube bottle being opened makes Carter's stomach twist, but he manages to keep his body still.

Then, just like the night before, sir suddenly... *softens.* "Breathe for me, sweetheart."

Carter squeezes his eyes shut even tighter, trying to force his muscles to relax. It doesn't work so well if sir's sigh is any indication. Surprisingly, though, the sound isn't angry or frustrated. It's almost... *sad.*

Or maybe that's just Carter.

A finger rubs against Carter's hole for a few seconds before sliding into him. Carter gasps, mostly out of surprise since he's slightly open already from cleaning himself in the shower. Unfortunately, sir notices this as well and adds a second finger. Carter whimpers. If sir notices, he doesn't say anything. He just continues opening Carter, his touch cold and clinical. When sir hooks his two fingers inside Carter's rim and gently runs them along the edges to stretch him, Carter grits his teeth to stay silent.

"Relax," sir reminds him, rubbing Carter's left ass cheek with his free hand. Carter feels unshed tears soaking his lashes. He's holding his breath, which he knows is why he's so tense, but he can't change it. He's pretty sure the next breath he takes will be a sob. Sir won't like that.

Sir's two fingers slide out of Carter's hole, but Carter doesn't feel any sort of relief from it. He knows something more is coming. The man wouldn't just finger him open for no reason. Carter still flinches when something impossibly big and heavy pushes at his hole. Sir doesn't yell at him or spank him. He just runs a soothing hand along Carter's spine. "Relax, remember? Relax for me, sweetheart. It's just a plug. Slaves are meant to be plugged."

More lube is drizzled over Carter's hole. Then the plug starts pushing in. "Accept your plug, sweetheart. Be good for me."

Breathing out through his nose, Carter forces himself to obey. He at least manages to relax enough to take the plug in. But the breath required to do so comes in the form of a choked sob, just as he had worried it would. He feels the man behind him go tense. Fear spikes in Carter's chest as he tries to swallow any other sobs. He tries to ground himself by focusing on the plug in his ass instead. The burning. The aching. The pain is fading as it settles inside of him, making it uncomfortable, but no longer painful. It surprisingly helps to focus on that feeling.

Particularly focusing on the weight of the plug. There's something about its presence that's almost... *calming*.

As calming as something can be in this fucked up situation.

"Sit up."

Carter listens, quickly wiping his cheeks before sir can see. He was lucky not to be scolded for crying just now. He doesn't want to push that luck. If sir is anything like the guards, he won't want to deal with Carter's emotions. He certainly hadn't liked them last night when he caught Carter crying in the bathroom.

Sir reaches over to the dresser and grabs a leash. It's new, like the collar. They match, both the same smooth black leather. Carter can't help but flinch when he hears the click of the golden metal hook when it latches onto the ring at the front of his collar.

"Come." Sir turns his back to Carter, taking a step toward the door. "Keep up."

Carter starts to stand, only for sir to stop him with a hand on his shoulder that presses him down. Carter looks up to find the man scowling at him. "Did I say you could walk?"

"N-no, sir."

"What's rule number 2?"

"Kneel unless told otherwise, sir."

"Then *listen*. That's your one and only warning. Don't fuck up in front of my men today." Sir pauses, his eyes darting away. "They won't be as forgiving."

Swallowing a whimper, Carter forces himself to nod.

Sir tugs again. This time, Carter remains on the floor. He hurries along on his hands and knees, trying to keep up like he was told. He can feel the plug shifting inside of him with every movement. He can feel lube dripping down his left thigh.

It's awful.

Humiliating.

Things only get worse when they leave the seemingly private hallway with sir's suite and turn down a hall with an audience. The first man Carter is led past grins down at him. Carter immediately drops his head, realizing it's safer if he just watches the floor instead of looking around. He'll take the time to soak in the details of his new prison some other time. Not right now, as he's busy trying to work his way through his suffocating emotions. One thing at a time.

The longer they move, the more Carter's hands and knees ache. It's harder than he thought to crawl. Especially on hardwood flooring, at the quick pace sir is keeping. Carter tries to focus on the pain like he had in the bedroom. It works for a little while.

Then someone behind Carter touches his left ass cheek, someone who *isn't* sir because sir is in front of him still holding the leash. After that, all distractions are gone. There are people everywhere. Leering at him. Commenting on him. Calling him names. Someone says he was clearly meant to be a slave because he looks so perfect collared and leashed. Someone laughs.

Another person touches him – though it's less of a touch this time, and more of a smack. Carter scrambles closer to sir and whimpers. They all laugh at that. Carter wants to sink into the fucking floor and disappear.

"Hold still, pet," sir says in amusement. Carter can't tell what's worse, that sir is going to let these people continue to touch him, or that sir just called him *pet* like he truly is an animal.

Carter begins to violently tremble as multiple hands stroke along his body. He has to clench his jaw to stop his teeth from clacking together. All of Carter's humanity has been sucked out of him, leaving nothing but a pet. He's the new puppy in the dog park, all of the kids asking if they can pet him, eagerly running their hands along him as his owner stands by looking proud. They even speak of him like a dog.

"So well behaved already."

"So pretty."

"Such a good boy."

A hand wraps around his plug, tugging at it. That's the first time Carter sheds a tear. He turns his face into sir's leg, barely able to catch his breath as he tries not to fully cry. A hand rests on his head, fingers running through his hair. He somehow knows that it's sir.

"Do not touch my slave's hole," he hears sir say in a cold, dangerous voice.

Someone apologizes.

Carter sucks in his breath, trying to calm himself by not breathing at all for a few seconds. That's when he hears the worst of all. "Can we fuck him?"

The world spins until Carter is dizzy with fear. Sir's voice is far away when he answers, the words barely reaching Carter. "No. No one will ever fuck him except me."

Carter doesn't have time to calm down. Not when sir adds, "Until we catch his big brother, of course. Then we'll all take a turn while Maison watches."

Stop paying attention, Casey whispers in the back of Carter's mind. *Keep calm and breathe. That's all we need right now. That's what we have to focus on. Keep calm. Breathe. Just shut everything else out.*

"Will we get to touch him at all, sir?" someone asks.

"On very rare occasions, and only as a reward or gift. All of you should do your best to earn him. He'll satisfy you, I'm sure."

Carter's stomach twists. Bile burns the back of his tongue.

Shut it all out, Carter. Stop listening.

Daffodils. Carter thinks of the daffodils. An entire field of daffodils. He's lying down among them, wearing his favorite purple sweater and jeans. The sun is warm on his skin. The breeze is light and refreshing. The scent of fresh grass and flowers is filling his nostrils.

Carter is yanked out of his happy place when the collar around his neck is wrenched. He gasps, eyes blinking rapidly as his body is nearly dragged across the floor. It takes him a few seconds to catch up, crawling once again instead of sir using the leash to pull him along. They're in a dining room by the time Carter has the world figured out again. Carter can feel tears on his cheeks, but sir is walking too fast now to be able to wipe at them, so he just lets them fall. When they approach the long, beautiful table, Carter is filled with dread.

There are other slaves. Some are kneeling beside their master while their master eats. Others are under the table, keeping cocks warm with their mouths or giving full-on blowjobs. Carter knew in theory that other slaves would be around, but he hadn't fully realized how hard that would be.

Where is Elliot right now? Casey?

Are they okay?

Are they still alive?

Carter tries not to panic as the thoughts swirl. Sir takes a seat at the head of the table, maneuvering Carter beneath it and into a kneeling position between his legs. Sir pushes his chair back and ducks his head down, using the leash to tie Carter's hands behind his back now. When he pulls away, his lips part like he's about to say something. He stops when he sees Carter's face, though. When he sees the tears.

Carter swears he sees something *human* in the man's expression. Just for the briefest of moments. It's a peek into the man from last night, the man who held him close, the man who called him sweetheart. Then sir's expression goes to stone and he's unzipping his pants. Carter tries not to start crying again as he watches the man pull his cock out.

Sir clears his throat, his voice particularly rough as he orders, "Keep my cock warm while I eat. No sucking. Just rest it on your tongue and hold still."

With a sharp nod, Carter waits for sir to scoot his chair into place so he can reach the cock with his mouth. He wishes he had his hands, but sir helps him by cupping the back of his neck and guiding him forward. Carter opens his mouth and accepts sir's cock as it's guided into his mouth.

Sir is soft. Carter's thankful. He wasn't sure how to keep his hard cock warm. It's a lot to keep in his mouth. Sir is the biggest Carter has ever seen. Even soft, the man is intimidating.

Carter tentatively settles the cock inside his mouth, letting it rest heavy on his tongue like told. It's hard to find a comfortable position, but Carter manages to find a place where his neck isn't crooked too badly and the cock in his mouth isn't slipping out.

It's not long before Carter's neck is cramping, though. He's at an awkward angle, ducked beneath the table, trying to keep the soft cock in his mouth, his knees aching, his arms tied behind his back pulling on his already sore shoulders. He tries to subtly shift, hoping to find a better position. The one he ends up in is even worse than the first.

When Carter first feels sir's hand come to the back of his head, he freezes. A soft whimper of fear escapes him as he prepares for pain. Sir's hand is gentle, though. Firm, but gentle. He guides Carter until Carter's head is resting on his left thigh. It feels so much better in that position, Carter exhaling as his body finally manages to relax. Things get even better when sir begins to run his fingers through Carter's hair in a calming pattern, his voice filling the air from time to time as he talks with the other men seated at the table.

It's not long before Carter is blocking everything out again, focusing solely on the cock in his mouth and sir's hand in his hair. Carter closes his eyes and deflates against sir's thigh, giving in like sir had encouraged him to do the night before. It feels so good to just let go. To forget himself. To give himself over to sir.

At some point, Carter starts to float. He loses himself. It's such a goddamn *relief*.

Part of Carter hopes he's never forced to return.

Chapter Eight

NATHAN IS FULLY AWARE that he's going easy on Carter. Nathan prepped him well for the anal plug. He helped the boy get comfortable when he was warming Nathan's cock, even stroking his hair to calm him. He's making his men earn the opportunity to use Carter, whereas most bosses allow their men to use their slave as they please whenever the slave is not in use by the boss. Nathan doesn't even plan on letting any of his men earn such an opportunity anyway, but if for some reason there's a man who undeniably deserves the reward, he'll only allow for something simple and quick. A blowjob, or some cock warming. He had even stopped one of his men from his inner circle playing with the boy's plug.

Clearly, Nathan isn't going easy enough though. Carter was fucking crying. He's *still* crying. Nathan's not sure if Carter is even aware that he's crying anymore. The boy is out of it, floating somewhere else, somewhere his mind deems safe, silent tears trailing down his cheeks as he keeps Nathan's cock warm.

Nathan is already going through his agenda for the day, trying to think of all the ways he can be kind to Carter without others noticing. Right now is perfect. No one can see under the tables besides the other slaves, and the other slaves won't say anything. They're probably not even paying attention, too wrapped up in pleasing their current masters instead.

His day ahead is actually pretty calm. He only has one meeting. The rest of it can be spent in his office, alone with Carter. That's good. Alone is good.

"Master Roarke?" Nathan turns his head to look at the slave standing beside him. "Are you finished with your plate?"

"Yes."

"More coffee, Master?"

"Yes, and water." Nathan pulls his hand away from Carter, suddenly feeling like a spotlight is on him. "Bring some food for my slave as well."

The slave nods, then looks up as a few other men around the table ask for the same thing. Some of them don't. Apparently, their slaves aren't being fed today. At least not breakfast. Nathan's gut twists as usual, but he pastes on a smile and goes back to focusing on Carter. He starts moving his hand around, touching the boy's neck, shoulder, tear-soaked cheek, gently coaxing him back to reality. It takes a small tug on his collar for Carter to fully return to him, the boy finally blinking up at Nathan just as a slave is placing a small plate in front of him. Nathan shifts his chair back enough to see Carter better, offering him what he hopes is a comforting smile.

When Carter tries to chase him, clearly worried that Nathan's cock fell out of his mouth, Nathan stops him with a gentle hand. Nathan tucks himself away to keep the boy's attention off of his cock. He wants Carter to be able to focus on being taken care of, instead of focusing on taking care of Nathan.

Nathan grabs a grape from the little plate of fruit in front of him. Carter's eyes go wide when he sees it, lips parting in anticipation. Even the boy's chest starts to rise and fall faster. It break's Nathan's heart. He knows Carter was probably wondering when he'd be fed next. After throwing everything up last night, he must be starved.

Benny takes a seat in his designated chair to Nathan's right, eyes darting down at Carter before quickly looking away. "Morning boss."

There's so much said in those two words, a dark mass forming in Nathan's chest as he hears them. Benny is trying to tell him it's okay. He's trying to offer comfort. It doesn't help, though. It just makes Nathan feel worse.

Why can't Benny be the one that has to do this? Why couldn't Benny have been the one to become boss? Why did it have to be Nathan? Why does Nathan have to be Carter's personal monster?

"What's the plan today?" Benny asks casually, just like he would every morning.

Nathan focuses back on Carter, feeding him a slice of banana next. "I have that meeting this afternoon. I need to make a few calls and send some emails."

"The exciting life of an international criminal."

"A lot more paperwork than they tell you about, that's for sure," Nathan jokes, winking at his friend. "Who knew all the fun stuff would be over once I got the big chair?"

"Oh, come on, boss," one of his men, Jason, calls from the left. "You have the fun stuff right between your legs. Ain't that worth the paperwork alone?"

Nathan maintains his smile as he reaches for a piece of strawberry. "You got me there, Jason. This little slave is worth all the paperwork."

Someone mumbles about him being a lucky bastard, but Nathan stays focused on Carter, their eyes locked as Carter parts his lips again. He takes the strawberry and carefully chews it, looking slightly confused when Nathan doesn't pull his fingers away from his bottom lip this time. When Carter swallows, he tentatively parts his lips again. Nathan hums his approval and slips his two fingers into the boy's mouth, sliding them along his tongue.

"Suck them clean," he says quietly, giving Carter an encouraging smile. The boy does as told, hopeful blue eyes staying on Nathan as he searches for approval. For praise.

Praise. Nathan can do that. If it'll help Carter through this, he can praise him. Plenty of men in this world praise their slaves. Hell, it's a goddamn kink.

"That's it," Nathan coos. "Good boy."

Carter melts, actually chasing the fingers for a second when they're pulled away. He seems to come back to himself, realizing what he just did, and his cheeks go pink. He keeps his eyes on Nathan though. Wide. Innocent. Trusting.

Nathan rewards him with a bite of bacon. Then some water, helping the boy take his drink since his hands are bound behind his back.

Breakfast continues like this while Nathan listens to his men talk amongst themselves. The spirits in the house are high today, most likely because of Carter. Nathan doesn't mind that. It's just his men enjoying the reminder of how powerful their group is. Carter himself is more of an afterthought. He belongs to Nathan.

Thank god they're all respecting that.

For now, at least.

The next time Nathan feeds Carter a piece of strawberry, the boy sucks his fingers clean without being told. It makes Nathan's cock hard and he has to swallow a groan.

Nathan's going to hell.

He's going to hell for fucking sure.

CARTER SPENDS HIS DAY waiting for the other shoe to drop. People keep touching him and keep talking about him, and he hasn't walked on his feet since he left the bedroom, but things have been mild besides that. He kept sir's cock warm at breakfast before getting hand fed by him, getting told how good he is the whole time. Then he crawled along with sir to sir's huge office, where they've been ever since. Carter was brought to the bathroom twice, both times thankfully still to only pee. He was hand-fed a small lunch. He kept sir's cock warm some more while sir did paperwork and spoke on the phone. A man came in at one point for what seemed like a laid back sort of meeting. He had called Carter a 'stupid cocksucker.' It had hurt to hear sir laugh at that, but Carter had chastised himself for caring. Sir could be doing so much worse. Carter doesn't understand why he *hasn't* yet.

At this point, they've been in sir's office for the entire day, something Carter knows because someone just came in to announce that dinner is being served in 10 minutes. Yet, Carter still hasn't been used except for his mouth to warm sir's cock from time to time. He even dozed off for a while, his head on sir's thigh like at breakfast, sir's hand running through his hair as he did things on his computer.

Dinner is much of the same. At one point, sir gets into a heated discussion with a few of the other men, something about baseball that leaves them all laughing after. It distracts them enough for most of the slaves to get bumped away, including Carter. He sits back on his folded legs and waits for sir to need him again, sir moving around as he talks far too much for his cock to stay in place.

Taking a chance, Carter glances over at one of the slaves to his right. It's a guy around his age with bright blonde hair and a collar similar to the one around his own neck. When he sees Carter looking, he gives Carter a sad but friendly smile. Carter returns it. Then the slave is being grabbed by the hair and brought back to his master's cock. Before Carter can look around for any other slaves, sir is grabbing him too, though far more gently. He's not brought to sir's cock, either. Instead, he's brought out from under the table as sir stands up.

Carter tries not to show on his face that he's disappointed he wasn't fed dinner. He hangs his head just in case he can't control his expression, hurrying along as he crawls behind sir towards a room he has yet to be in. Through a few peeks here and there, he gathers that it's a sort of entertainment room. There's a large leather couch as well as a few armchairs. Sir sits on the armchair in the center of the room, looking directly at the large TV mounted on the opposite wall.

Someone turns a baseball game on. It's not sir, since sir has a glass of what smells like scotch in one hand and Carter's leash in the other. Since Carter is kneeling for sir, facing the man, he clearly can't see the TV. He can only listen to the announcers and try to piece things together. He finds himself wondering if he's still in the United States. It's the MLB, but he's sure those games are aired elsewhere. In fact, Carter's not even sure if the MLB is only American or not. He's never been into sports.

Maison was always the athlete growing up. He played football, basketball, and baseball. Carter used to love coming to watch all his games, not because of the sports, but because he practically hero-worshipped his brother back then. Hell, he still hero-worships him.

At least, he *did*, up until a few days ago. Now, he's not so sure. His brother is clearly involved in some dark shit. He might not be much of a hero after all.

Carter flinches when something touches his face before reminding himself to relax. He looks up to find sir watching him carefully, his big hand cupping Carter's cheek. There's something in the man's gaze that Carter can't quite place. If he didn't know any better, he'd say it's concern, but Carter knows much better than that.

Sir's lips part as if he wants to ask Carter something before they quickly seal back up. Carter watches as the man exhales heavily through his nose, the corner of his jaw twitching like he's clenching his teeth. It feels like his eyes are searching Carter for something.

"How's his ass, boss?" someone from behind Carter asks.

Sir's entire presence changes in the blink of an eye, the man growing powerful and intimidating with an icy cold gaze and an evil grin. He doesn't even look away from Carter when he answers, "*Tight.*"

Carter's face burns. He tries to look away, but sir's hand slides down to grab both sides of his jaw, keeping him in place.

"Still tight?" one of the men asks. "Haven't fucked him enough then."

"Maybe I want to *keep* him tight."

"Have you at least fucked him today?"

Sir's jaw ticks, his fingers gripping Carter's face hard enough to make him whimper. "Not yet. It's been a busy day."

"Well, what's a better time than when you're relaxing and watching the game?"

"Yeah, boss. Fuck him right here."

"Let us see what a little slut he is."

"Have I not provided enough slaves for you all to entertain yourselves?" sir asks, raising an eyebrow as his gaze finally leaves Carter to look at the men in the room. "I bought him for me, not you."

There's a beat of silence. Then, "But none of us were at the auction last night. We need to see the show everyone else got to see."

"Besides," someone else adds. "You gotta use him often."

"Yeah. Don't want him getting too comfortable, right boss?"

Sir's teeth flash in a sinister smile. "Right."

Carter's stomach twists and turns into something achy and painful. He doesn't want to do this. He *can't* do this. It being rape is bad enough. It being rape in front of people – people he can see because he doesn't have a blindfold to hide behind this time – is even worse.

He should have known it was coming.

He *did* know it was coming.

That doesn't make it any easier when sir looks down at Carter and says, "Take your plug out and come up on my lap."

With a hand that shakes hard enough to hurt, Carter fumbles with his plug until it's out of his hole. He holds it for a moment, confused about what he should do with it. Sir takes it from him and puts it on the table where his glass of scotch is now resting on a coaster. It looks obscene there, resting on the flat end, the bulb slick and glistening in the lamp light.

Carter places his hands on sir's thighs and hoists himself up, his entire body trembling now. He can't meet sir's gaze. Thankfully, sir doesn't try to make him.

Carter flinches when sir spits, looking down at sir's hard cock with wide eyes as sir spits on it a second time. Sir rubs the pad of his thumb over his glistening cock head and Carter realizes that's the lube he's going to get. That, and whatever is left in his hole from this morning's preparation. He's stretched from the plug, but not nearly enough. Sir is fucking huge. Carter must have been out of it at the auction to take that thing as easily as he had.

He doesn't realize he's hyperventilating until sir frames his face with both hands and pulls him in close, their foreheads touching.

"Breathe," sir says so softly Carter's not sure if he imagined it. He smells spices and scotch as he follows the order and breathes the man in. He shudders beneath the weight of the oxygen, but sir whispers, "Good boy. Again."

Carter obeys. This time, it's a little easier.

"Again," sir whispers.

Carter feels light-headed with relief as the air he's taking in finally registers in his system. His eyes flutter shut, his body relaxing in sir's hold.

A tap on sir's shoulder catches Carter's attention. He looks up to find the man from last night – Benny – standing beside the chair, a small packet of something in between two fingers. Sir's eyes meet Benny's for a moment, the two of them holding a surprisingly intense gaze. Then he takes the packet from him and puts the edge between his teeth, tearing it open. Carter realizes it's lube when he sees sir rub a glob of it on his fingers. Sir adjusts his position in the chair slightly before threading his hand through the opening of Carter's thighs and sliding two fingers easily inside of him.

He's going to prep Carter.

Oh, thank god.

The prep is different this time. It's not clinical like this morning when he was prepping Carter for his plug, and it's not bare minimum like the night before. This is right on the edge of foreplay, sir's fingers focused less on stretching him and more on stroking his walls in ways that Carter hates to admit feels good.

Sir tightens his grip on Carter's hip and tilts him forward, the angle of his fingers shifting. His gaze is intense on Carter's face as he crooks his fingers. One stroke.

Two. Then Carter's gasping, his body bucking forward. Sir found his prostate, and if his mischievous smirk is any indication, that was his goal.

"Oh," Carter breathes, not sure what to do with himself as sir works the sensitive spot over and over with his fingertips. He thinks he might be moving himself against sir's hand now. Riding his fingers. He thinks maybe he can't get himself to care. "Oh, *oh*."

"That's it," sir growls, his fingers speeding up, a third teasing the edge of Carter's hole. "Feel good, pet?"

The *pet* is a reminder, like ice water falling over Carter's head. He gasps for a new reason, his body seeming to screech to a halt, his muscles tensing, his breath catching, his heart sinking. Tears burn his eyes. Sir catches his gaze, the fingers in his hole pausing. They stare at each other for a beat before sir's eyes fall closed, a slow, controlled exhale pushing past his lips. The hand on Carter's hip flexes once. Then sir looks at him with a far away gaze, his face suddenly devoid of emotion.

The fingers in Carter's hole are pulled out. Lube is squeezed from the packet onto sir's cock. Then sir is speaking, his voice authoritative and icy. "Up."

Breath hitching again, Carter forces himself to lift up on his knees. Sir's free hand holds the root of his cock to keep it steady for him, his other hand remaining on Carter's hip in a bruising hold. Carter doesn't look. He *can't* look. He swallows a sob when he feels the head of sir's cock press between his cheeks. Benny is standing behind sir, watching Carter with narrowed eyes. Carter looks away quickly, a tear falling down his cheek. He squeezes his eyes shut to keep any more from spilling.

"No," he whispers, more to himself than anyone else. Maybe he can convince his mind that this isn't really happening. Maybe he can shut it off again. Float away. "No, no, no."

Sir ignores him.

Everyone does.

"*Down*," sir orders. He brings his free hand up to grab Carter's other hip, fingers digging bruises as he nudges Carter down an inch or two on his cock. "Come on. You can do it, pet."

It's almost worse, being made to do it like this. It feels like Carter is raping himself. Carter swears he can feel bile crawling up his throat.

A sharp smack against his ass cheek startles a sob out of Carter. His body jerks with the power of it, more sobs welling up in his chest like a queue of grief. He's spanked again.

"Don't touch my property!" sir growls, startling Carter more than the hits had. He's even more startled by the meaning of the words. Sir isn't who hit him. It was one of sir's men. And sir is... mad about it.

Carter doesn't know what to make of that.

"Just trying to hurry the boy up for ya, boss."

"Are you indicating that I can't handle my slave myself?"

"N-no, sir," a man says from somewhere behind Carter. "Not at all!"

"Good." Sir levels Carter with a gaze that leaves no room for argument, anger flashing in his eyes. "My men are right, though, pet. You are testing my patience. I suggest you stop."

Carter forces himself to obey, lowering himself onto the massive cock waiting for him. He whimpers when it seems to catch after another inch or so. The prep wasn't enough. Not nearly enough.

One of sir's hands on his hips comes up to cradle the back of Carter's neck. Sir pulls him in close until his face is pressed against the side of sir's throat, his lips dragging along the shell of Carter's ear. His breathing is ragged, as if he's the one getting fucked. There's a chance his hand is trembling slightly against Carter's hip, but there's also a chance that Carter has just gone crazy and is imagining things.

"I've got you," sir whispers. "It's alright, sweetheart. Just breathe. You're alright."

Carter grits his teeth to keep from snapping that he's not alright, he's being fucking *raped*. The cock trying to push into his ass is too big, and the men in this room are too cruel, and all of this is too much, and Carter is being fucked *raped*, and *nothing* is *alright*.

A sob falls from Carter's lips, the skin of sir's throat muffling the sound. It doesn't seem to upset sir. The man just continues to hold Carter close, one hand on the back of his neck, the other moving down to his left ass cheek to pull at it. The shift is enough to ease the way for sir's cock, allowing it to finally bottom out, but Carter burns in shame when the room erupts at what he's sure is a lude view of his hole. Another sob is released against sir's skin. Sir holds him tighter, not in a punishing way, but in a grounding way.

By the time sir is settled, Carter is slick with sweat and shivering uncontrollably. He refuses to open his eyes even though his face is still hidden in sir's neck. He doesn't move, either. He just sits in place and waits for instructions. The last thing he's going to do is start fucking himself on sir's cock before he's forced to. No fucking way.

Surprisingly, sir doesn't tell him to do anything. He just uses his hand on Carter's ass cheek to slowly lift him up until his cock is an inch or so inside of him before using the hand on Carter's neck to slowly push him back down it. Carter's body is moved like that over and over, sir's hips rolling every few seconds to meet him halfway. He whispers to Carter the whole time, telling him to breathe, telling him he's going to be okay, telling him he's *so good, such a very good boy, taking his cock so fucking well.*

In between praise, the man breathes ragged and heavy in Carter's ear. The sound is sinful and dirty, and Carter hates himself for thinking it's hot. He hates himself for the tiny part in the back of his mind that thinks that this would be good, if Carter had given his consent, if they didn't have an audience, if sir saw him as human.

"Come on, sweetheart," sir pants, the words quiet as if they're a secret between them. "Ride me. Make yourself feel good on sir's cock."

Carter doesn't want to, but sir is being nice, and he thinks it's better to listen so sir keeps being nice. Tentatively, Carter begins to rock back against sir, moving with him in the slow, steady pace that sir has set. It does start to feel a little good, Carter's cock twitching, but it's not enough to make up for everything else that's wrong with the situation.

When sir looks down to find Carter barely hard, he glances up to meet Carter's eyes. Another tear falls down Carter's cheek on accident. He winces when he sees the way sir's expression shutters.

Sir closes his eyes and takes a deep breath, almost like he's steeling himself. When he opens them again, Carter wants to scramble away. He swears there are monsters in the man's eyes now. Monsters that want to eat Carter alive.

Sir stands abruptly, cock slipping out of Carter's ass as he moves. He ignores the way Carter cries out in shock, just tossing Carter over the arm of the chair they were in a moment ago and yanking him by the hips so his ass is at a nearly impossible angle. He shoves into Carter again, hard and fast. Each sound Carter makes is loud and wrecked and the men in the room love it. Carter barely registers them, though. He's too focused on sir's cock, the man fucking into him like an animal now. Or, more accurately, like *Carter* is an animal.

A pet.

Or something else. Something worse. Something inanimate and there solely for sir's pleasure.

A toy.

Carter buries his face in the crook of his arm, starting to feel his mind going numb as he realizes that's *exactly*

what he is. What he's become. Just a thing for sir's pleasure. A thing for all of these men to laugh at. To maybe
fuck, if they earn it. He's a trophy. An object.

He's not even Carter anymore.

Not even human.

He's just *sir's*.

Sir's... *nothing*.

Nothing at all.

It's almost a relief, to be nothing.

Carter's not sure he'll ever forgive himself for that.

Chapter Nine

NATHAN NEARLY LOSES IT when Carter goes quiet. He knows it's bad when they stop making noise. When they stop reacting. It means they've been broken. None of the slaves around here cry anymore, having gone empty a long time ago. They just let things happen to them now. It's what Nathan had told Carter to do last night. He said to give in. To just give up.

He hadn't fucking *meant* it, though.

He had hoped that flipping Carter over like this would make things easier for the boy. Carter wouldn't have to look at his rapist. He wouldn't have to fuck himself on his rapist's cock. Instead, it seems to have made things worse.

Nathan has to squeeze his eyes shut and focus on the pleasure of a tight hole around his cock. He plays his fantasy scenario out from this morning. The reason Carter is so quiet is because he's sleepy. They just woke up. When Nathan finishes, Carter is going to roll over with a lazy grin and say, "That's a great way to start a morning."

Picturing that grin, Nathan finally reaches his orgasm. He holds Carter steady as he spills inside the boy, allowing himself one more moment of pretend before he opens his eyes and faces reality.

Carter is limp against the chair, his lips slightly parted as he takes deep, even breaths. His pretty blue eyes are glazed over and empty as he stares at the back of the chair without seeming to really see it. When Nathan pulls out of him, Carter doesn't even react. It's the same when Nathan pushes the anal plug back into his hole. He just stays loose and quiet, allowing himself to be moved around like a ragdoll.

The game is finally starting, an audience cheering on the TV. Nathan can't register it. He can't focus. Not on the game. Not on his men. Not on the persona he's made for himself.

Nathan finds Benny, meeting his eyes. He shakes his head once. Benny nods in understanding. "Sorry to ruin the fun, boss, but that *thing* we discussed this morning? I got an update on it."

Relief blooms in Nathan's chest. Enough for him to fake a dramatic sigh and turn to face his men. "I suppose this is where I leave you boys, then. Hope you enjoyed the show."

It's not rare for Nathan to be swept away for important matters. They're all used to it by now. A few of his men playfully boo, but then they're all thanking him and wishing him a very happy night, all winking and smirking and nudge-nudging each other like teenage boys.

Nathan can't get himself to respond to them. He just turns his back and gets the fuck out of the room on his jelly-like legs.

Benny doesn't say a word. He just walks beside Nathan to his personal wing of the house and stops right before his door, turning to give him a concerned look. They don't know what Carter can hear right now, so all Nathan can do is nod to acknowledge his friend's help. Benny gives him a tight smile and nods back.

Nathan can't get into his bedroom fast enough. He puts Carter on the edge of the bed, making sure he can sit up on his own, then hurries away to begin the lockdown procedures for the night. Acid bubbles in his stomach, getting worse as each second passes instead of better. Nathan's legs nearly give out as he sweeps across his suite to the bathroom, his fingers fumbling with the lock on the door. He manages to turn the faucet on to hide any sound before falling to his knees and heaving into the toilet.

He can't do this.

God, how did he ever fucking think he'd be able to do this?

The sounds Carter had made echo in his mind as his stomach twists violently, threatening him with another round of vomiting. He had thought he could help him. He had thought he could make things semi-pleasant for the boy. Nathan had played with his prostate, loving each gasp and whimper that fell from the boy's lips. Loving the way his eyes had hooded with arousal. Loving the way the tip of his cock had beaded with precum. But then something had happened, and the boy no longer wanted it. So, Nathan got on with the show, wanting it to be over as soon as possible. Just when he thought he had managed to help Carter get back to that partially-pleasurable state, he had looked up to find the boy crying.

Should he not try to make him feel good? That doesn't feel... right. The least Nathan can do is give the boy some pleasure, some relief, some fucking human contact that doesn't end in pain.

He's going to have to do that again. He's going to end up raping this boy again.

Nathan vomits, his muscles jerking in protest. He heaves again and again until they go dry. Then he gives himself 10 seconds to rest his head in his hands and throw a personal pity party before forcing himself to his feet. He gargles mouthwash while spraying bleach onto the toilet, then flushes the toilet and spits into the sink. He splashes cool water on his face before wiping it with a towel.

Then Nathan reminds himself that he is not the victim in this situation, he's the monster, and he shuts his feelings down to go tend to Carter instead.

Carter is sitting exactly where he was placed before, his toes grazing the floor, his shoulders curled inward, his eyes staring at the wall without seeming to see it. His face has dried tears streaked across it. There's the slightest tremble to his muscles, only noticeable if you're studying him as carefully as Nathan is.

"How about a bath?" Nathan suggests as he carefully scoops the boy into his arms and carries him into the bathroom. Carter doesn't answer. It could be because he didn't hear Nathan. Or because he's lost the ability to speak. Or because he knows it's not really his decision so he's not going to bother giving his opinion. All perfectly valid, Nathan supposes.

He sits Carter on the counter and unclips his leash. The boy just blinks slowly at him.

"The best thing about this bathroom is the tub." Nathan swallows hard. "Have you seen it? It's huge. You'll love it."

Carter just stares at him. Or, more accurately, he just stares right *through* him.

"Okay," Nathan whispers, more to himself than any-thing. He shrugs out of his jacket and rolls up his sleeves before kneeling on the marble steps in front of the large whirlpool tub. He turns the water on and chooses the crystal bottle full of what he hopes will be the most relaxing bath oil out of the ones he has. After, he grabs the long lighter on the shelf nearby and begins lighting candles, first the ones around the tub, then the others throughout the bathroom. Lastly, he puts two towels on the towel warmer. Then he heads back to Carter.

The boy has been watching him the whole time, his eyes quickly darting away when he's caught. It's progress. At least Carter is in the moment now. At least he's *react-ing*.

Nathan guides Carter off the counter, placing him on his feet. Carter's hands tentatively come to rest on Nathan's broad chest, his fingers pressing gently against the fabric of his dress shirt. He peeks up at Nathan through his lashes before looking down. It's adorable, and it's heartbreaking, and Nathan hates himself.

With a hand on the small of his back, Nathan leads Carter over to the tub. He helps him set his hands on one of the steps before gently pushing between his shoulder blades until Carter is bent over. Carter starts shaking again. Nathan strokes his bare hip, trying to calm him. "I'm not going to hurt you, sweetheart. I'm just removing your plug."

Carter hangs his head between his shoulders, looking defeated. He stops shaking so hard, but he still whimpers when Nathan's fingers close around the flared end of the toy. Nathan tries to be as fast and clinical as he can without hurting him. When it's removed, he tosses it in the sink to be dealt with later and tells Carter he can stand up.

Nathan tries very hard not to be distracted by the way his cum slowly slides out of Carter's hole and down his leg. Very, very hard.

He clears his throat. Twice. "Do you need to use the bathroom?"

"Yes, sir."

"Go on, then." Nathan walks over to the tub and checks the water, turning it up a notch in temperature. He keeps his back to Carter, pretending he couldn't care less about him in an attempt to give him some privacy. The rule about the bathroom door remaining open wasn't something Nathan really thought through when he made it, but he can't do anything about that now. Going back on his rules will just undermine his authority, no matter how stupid or inconvenient the rules are.

Deciding that he's probably had his back turned long enough, Nathan pivots on his foot and faces Carter again. The boy is in the middle of wiping his ass, his face beet red even though he's not looking at Nathan. He flushes while still sitting down, not standing until the toilet is finished running and he's sure the toilet bowl is empty. When he finally looks at Nathan again, his eyes are glazed with unshed tears, his cheeks still pink.

"Undress me, sweetheart," Nathan says. "Just like last night."

Silently, Carter steps forward and sinks to the floor. He winces when the marble digs into his knees, his hands trembling as they work the laces of Nathan's shoes. Following the same order as Nathan instructed the previous night, he works his way through Nathan's clothing. He needs help with Nathan's tie, his hands fumbling with the knot, but he handles the rest perfectly. When he reaches Nathan's briefs this time, he barely even hesitates before hooking his fingers into the waistband and guiding them down Nathan's legs.

When Nathan is standing naked in front of him, Carter's chin lifts up, his pretty blue eyes looking at Nathan in both fear and curiosity. Nathan can't help but give into temptation. Just for a second. Just one single second.

Nathan reaches down and pulls Carter to his feet, cupping the sides of the boy's face and leaning in before he can come to his senses. Carter gasps into the kiss, his body tensing. The reaction only lasts for a moment before Carter's melting against him, his small hands clinging to his shoulders, the front of his naked body pressing harder against Nathan's. He starts to move his lips in excitement, almost taking over. Nathan makes sure not to allow a complete shift in control, needing to maintain the illusion that he's in charge, but he lets Carter push further than he probably should. He knows the boy must be overjoyed by the intimacy.

He knows that he is at least.

Nathan forces himself to break the kiss sooner than he'd like. He has to press a hand to Carter's chest after, stopping the boy from chasing him. Carter sways in front of him, flushed and panting, his pupils blow with lust.

"I can make you feel good," Nathan says breathlessly. "I *want* to make you feel good. If you just *let* me, just *trust* me, you can feel good too. This doesn't have to be hell for you."

"It's still rape," Carter whispers. He steps back and wraps his arms around his waist, not looking at Nathan.

"If you're trying to make yourself feel less guilty, then give it up. I don't care if you manage to get me hard or make me come. It's still rape."

Nathan feels bile burning his throat again. He swallows hard. "I know. It's not about that. I don't feel guilty. I'm not a good man. But I wasn't lying before. I don't want to hurt you. That's why you only have a few simple rules instead of a long ass list that will set you up for failure. That's why I try to help you relax when I use you. I don't get off on causing pain. I get off on control."

"So, you want to control my pleasure?" Carter snaps, his eyes shooting daggers at Nathan. A burst of relief ignites in Nathan's chest. *There he is.* Nathan didn't lose him after all. "Because controlling every other aspect of my life, down to when I get to take a shit or eat a fucking meal, isn't enough for you?"

Nathan shouldn't let this slide. He needs to shut it down. Remind him of his place. Mildly threaten him.

Instead, Nathan looks him in the eye, being as honest as he's allowed to be. "I'm not going to stop using you. I'm not going to get bored of you. I can get off without you feeling pleasure, you've seen evidence of that. Is it my favorite way? No. But that really doesn't matter much. So, you fighting this? That's not hurting me. That's not sticking it to me somehow. That's not you gaining some illusion of control. That's just you being a fucking *idiot* by making your life as a slave miserable instead of bearable."

Carter looks off to the side, blinking rapidly. He opens his mouth twice, but he never says anything, seeming to be speechless.

"So," Nathan says carefully, releasing a breath he hadn't realized he'd been holding. "You think on that. Let me know what you decide.

The boy nods, once, the movement sharp. His teeth are clamped down on his bottom lip.

"Let's get you in the bath now." Nathan puts a hand on Carter's back and walks him toward the tub, surprised when the boy allows it without even flinching at his touch. He helps Carter up the marble steps, holding his hand as the boy climbs into the deep basin. Carter sits on the curved bench beneath the water's surface before looking up at Nathan, the water gently lapping at his collarbone as it settles around him.

Nathan climbs in next, choosing a spot on the bench with a little distance from Carter. He suddenly feels like he's back in high school, naked in the showers with his high school crush after gym class, trying his best not to get hard while the dude talks about fucking chicks.

Closing his eyes, Nathan shoves those memories down – shoves *Travis* down – and sinks further into his Nathan persona. Just because they're alone doesn't mean he can stop being Nathan. He can be gentle, yes, relaxed, sure, but not *Travis*. Not human. It hurts too much when he lets himself be human.

"Sir?"

Nathan opens his eyes, notching his chin to look over at Carter. The boy is staring down at the water, his hands gently playing with the bubbles, gathering them in a pile and dispersing them before doing it all over again. "Yes?"

"Sorry, I – am I allowed to do that?" Carter peeks at him through his lashes before returning his gaze to the water. "Am I allowed to talk to you first like that? I'm... not sure of the rules."

"You may talk to me, yes. Do exactly as you just did. If I ignore you, don't pester me, but most of the time I'll be happy to see what's on your mind."

Carter nods. He parts his lips twice before closing his mouth for good, his lips curling into a frown. It's clear that he has something to say but doesn't have the courage to say it.

Nathan pulls it from him. "Did you want to say something? Or maybe ask me something?"

"I – well – yes, sir." Carter releases a shaky breath, eyes firmly on the pile of bubbles now in his hands. "Are you going to let them have sex with me?"

"My men?" Carter nods. Nathan's chest goes tight. "No. Not anal sex, at least. You will perform oral on them when I deem it appropriate."

"D-do I have to?"

Somehow – he has no fucking idea *how*, but somehow – Nathan manages to make his voice cold and angry when he answers. "Yes, you have to. I own you. You'll do as I say. Isn't that a rule?"

"Yes, sir," Carter whispers, sinking further down in the water. "Sorry for asking, sir."

"Don't ask if you have to do something again, understood? I do not enjoy you questioning my judgement."

"Yes, sir."

The tension in the room is overwhelming. Nathan can feel it building in his chest, threatening to crush him. He leans back and rests his head on the edge of the tub, closing his eyes, pretending to be relaxed and uncaring despite being anything but. "Tell me about yourself, sweetheart."

There's a drawn-out silence. Then, "Like what, sir?"

"You're a college student, correct?"

"I... was, sir."

The grief in the words is nearly enough to choke Nathan. He wishes he could tell Carter that he will be again, if he wants to be. He wants to grab Carter's face and look him in the eyes, promising that he'll have a future when this is all over. Carter can't give up hope. He can't forget about what he wanted before. "Tell me about that."

"About... college, sir?"

"Yes."

Carter laughs incredulously, drawing Nathan's attention to him. He looks over to find the boy glaring down at the bubbles, his fingers curling around them like he's trying to strangle the suds. "Well, I was a Global Studies major with a Human Rights minor, so, ya know... that fucking blew up in my face."

Nathan's eyebrows raise. Before he has time to comment, Carter is backtracking in a panic. "I'm sorry, sir. I didn't – that was rude. I'm sorry. Really. So sorry, sir."

"Stop," Nathan says quietly, looking Carter in the eye. "You're right. It's fucking ironic that you studied things like that, and are now a human slave. I can appreciate the sick humor."

"I was still really disrespectful, sir..."

"Do you want me to punish you?"

"No, sir."

"Then drop it." Nathan relaxes against the tub, eyes closing again. He thinks Carter might feel more comfortable with him in that position, and Nathan would do anything to keep Carter talking. Even if the conversation is upsetting him. Maybe *especially* because it's upsetting him. This kind of upset is healthy for Carter. It keeps him human. Keeps him from breaking. Nathan has to stoke that fire inside of him – carefully, of course – until Carter gets his freedom back. He can't allow that light to go out.

"Tell me more, sweetheart. Mind your tone this time."

There's the soft sound of water sloshing as Carter shifts in the tub, followed by a tense silence. Nathan opens his eyes to find the boy staring out the window that makes up the tub's backdrop. The glass isn't frosted, something Nathan is surprised he hadn't noticed. He'll need to be more careful in the future. Anyone could have seen him kissing Carter. Coddling him. Even taking a goddamn bath with him like this, doing nothing sexual during it.

A panic in Nathan's chest has him itching to frost the glass immediately, but then he catches sight of the way Carter is looking at the night sky outside. There's so much longing in his gaze. A somber grief. It'll be a cold day in hell before Nathan takes something so simple away from the poor boy. He can look all he wants right now.

Enough time passes that Nathan believes the conversation has been dropped. He's just starting to consider if he should scold Carter for it when the boy surprises him by speaking. "It's a pretty intense major and minor combination. There's a lot that goes into it."

"How so?"

"Well, they have you pick a concentration and a region. There's so much that can be done under that umbrella of global studies and human rights. It'd be impossible to be useful at all in the real world if you don't narrow it down."

"And what concentration and region did you choose?"

"I was studying Global Peace and Conflict within the European and Russian region."

Surprised by this, Nathan asks, "Why choose those?"

This gets Carter to perk up a bit, something bright flashing in the boy's eyes. "Russia and some areas of Europe are awful as far as human rights go, especially in issues of gender and sexuality. I want to-" Carter stops then, his eyes fluttering closed. The grief from before is nothing compared to the emotion that twists his expression now. Nathan feels it echoing inside of himself just from looking at the boy. "I just – um – I *wanted* to do stuff for the lgbtq+ communities in those areas."

"That's very honorable."

Carter looks out the window again. He touches his fingertips to the glass, water droplets falling slowly down from the point of contact. "It's a great program. It ties in so many different disciplines to teach you how to pull things together to make the best possible impact. I took a law class and a journalism class, and I'm signed – I-" Carter pauses, his hand flexing against the window. A tear falls down his cheek to match the water dripping down the glass. His voice is nothing but a whisper when he speaks again. "I was signed up for a psychology class in the fall."

Nathan's so caught up with Carter's passion simmering beneath his sadness that he doesn't realize how hard his following question will be for Carter until he hears it out loud. "What did you plan on doing after graduation?"

All it takes is one look at Carter's face for Nathan to be backtracking. "Never mind. Tell me something else about you. Something I can't take away."

Carter looks at him incredulously. "Sir, you've – you've taken everything away..."

Anger ignites at the words. Nathan refuses to let Carter think that. That's not a fighter's attitude at all.

"Don't be dramatic. You have memories. You have tastes. You have a favorite color. A favorite type of music. A favorite food. You enjoy certain things and dislike others. I haven't taken your mind from you." Nathan leans forward, lowering his voice. "Be grateful for that, sweetheart. Some men like me drug their slaves so far out of their minds they forget they're human. Some men beat and rape their slaves until they're nothing but a fucking empty shell. One man I know cut his slave's tongue out. Another man hit his slave so hard, his left ear went deaf. I can take more from you if you'd like."

The look on Carter's face is a mixture of shock and terror. It's good. Nathan needs him to realize where he stands. Sure, this situation is fucked up, but Carter is lucky to have Nathan as his owner. It's important that Carter knows that. For Carter to survive this, he has to have some sore of solace, some sort of silver lining. Nathan is a monster, but he's not the worst one out there.

In a tiny, regretful voice, Carter admits, "I – I like a bit of everything, as far as music goes. It depends on my mood."

Nathan waves a hand through the air. "Elaborate."

"Well, like... sometimes I just want to listen to really mellow music and relax. Or if I'm having a bad day or I'm sad, I'll listen to depressing stuff and just sort of let myself wallow. If I'm driving in the car and it's a nice day and the windows are down, I'm definitely belting out some Taylor Swift." Carter smiles to himself, the air around them getting lighter. The difference makes Nathan giddy.

"And then there's the times where I get a shit grade on an exam, or I get into a fight with my brother and-" he stops then, eyes darting over to Nathan before returning to the window.

"Maison," Nathan specifies, unnecessarily.

"Yes, sir." Carter shrugs. "He's my only sibling."

Nathan knew that, but he doesn't bother saying so. "You may talk about him."

"I'd prefer not to, sir."

"Why?"

"I'm – I'm mad at him."

That isn't at all what Nathan had expected. He thought maybe it was just an uncomfortable topic considering the circumstances, or maybe Carter protecting Maison by refusing to give Nathan information about him, or maybe even Carter just being too sad to think about his family.

Nathan never thought it'd be because Carter is *mad* at Maison.

"Were the two of you fighting before this?"

"No, sir."

"Then why are you upset with him?"

Carter looks at Nathan like he must be playing a joke on him. "He's why I'm here."

"Ahh. Yes. I suppose he is, isn't he?" It takes everything in Nathan not to blurt out that Maison is a goddamn hero. That Maison is saving him as they speak. That Maison would do anything he could to get Carter out of this. Instead, he pours disdain into his voice. "Perhaps your brother shouldn't have stuck his nose in places it didn't belong."

"Perhaps he shouldn't have," Carter says bitterly, his face screwed up in anger.

Nathan shuts that shit down immediately, partly for Maison, and partly because the man Nathan is supposed to be would. "Get that pouty look off your face before I fuck it off."

Carter stares at him for a second, letting the words register. Then he ducks his head and whispers, "Sorry, sir."

Scoffing like he's annoyed, Nathan reaches over and snatches Carter's bicep. He pulls until the boy is straddling his lap, their stomachs pressed together. His cock reacts on its own, starting to harden. He hears Carter swallow a whimper. Nathan doesn't call him out on it.

"Earlier, I wanted to get you off on riding me." Nathan cocks his head, eyes narrowing. "Do you have any idea how rare it is for men like me to let their slaves feel pleasure? Do you have any idea how many of us keep our slave's cocks locked in cages for the rest of their lives? Some men even castrate their slaves. Is that what you want?"

Carter's breath hitches as he shakes his head furiously. "No, sir. No. Please. I'm so lucky to have you, sir. I'm s – sorry I couldn't g – get hard, sir."

The panic is sending tremors through the boy, making his body jerk uncontrollably. Nathan can see that Carter is fighting to stop it. Fighting to relax and be good. There's terror in his expression as he waits to be yelled at.

"Breathe," Nathan murmurs, running a wet hand through Carter's hair. "Just breathe, sweetheart. You're not in trouble. I just need you to *understand*. I want you to be good for me, sweetheart, and then I want to reward you by making you feel good. Okay?"

Carter nods quickly. "Yes, sir. Th – thank you, sir."

"Breathe, sweetheart. Just breathe." He pulls Carter to him, putting him in the same position as earlier in the entertainment room, minus the cock pressing into his ass. Nathan squeezes his eyes shut since Carter can't see him, taking his own turn at trying to get himself under control.

"Just breathe," Nathan says again. This time, he's not sure if he's telling himself or Carter. He's not sure it matters anymore. "Just breathe."

CARTER IS RELAXED AND sleepy by the time sir has washed and dried him. Sir sets him on the edge of the bed and steps back, running a towel along himself now. Unable to help it, Carter watches the show. He's entranced by all of the curves and dips of the man's body. The scattered scars. The tattoos. There's a broken birdcage over his heart, birds scrambling out of it across his torso down to the opposite hip. Carter wants to touch each one. He wants to whisper to them, *go, fly, be free, hurry, hurry, hu rry.*

The man is gorgeous. In fact, gorgeous doesn't even begin to describe him. But he's also dark and dangerous. A man who cages little birds. Carter can't let himself forget that.

When sir catches him looking, he lifts a corner of his mouth and asks Carter, "Like what you see?"

Not willing to risk lying – or insulting the man, for that matter – Carter is honest. "Yes, sir."

"Good." Sir tosses the towel off to the side somewhere, seeming not to care about it anymore. He stalks towards Carter with hooded eyes, his cock growing by the second. "I like what I see, too."

Carter blushes and shrugs. "I'm not much."

"That's certainly not true. You cost me 2 million dollars. You're beautiful."

"I cost 2 million dollars because of my brother, sir," Carter says quietly, aware he's once again wading into dangerous territory. "He's the only thing that makes me special."

"Are you calling me a liar, sweetheart?"

This startles Carter. He jumps straight into a frantic backpedal. "No, sir! No. Not at all, sir!"

"You sure? Because I'm saying you're beautiful and that I enjoy looking at you, and you seem to be arguing with me."

"I – I didn't mean to, sir. You're right. You're always right. I'm sorry, sir."

Sir gently pushes Carter until he's lying on his back, then grabs Carter's bare hips and shifts him to exactly where sir wants him to be.

"I'm right about what?" sir asks in a low voice that sends chills up Carter's spine.

"I'm... beautiful, sir."

Slowly crawling up Carter's body, dragging his lips along his damp skin as he goes, sir murmurs, "Say that again for me, sweetheart."

Carter shivers, the heat of sir's breath tantalizing against the dip of his pelvis. "I'm beautiful, sir."

"Again."

"I'm beautiful, sir."

Sir licks a circle around Carter's nipple before nibbling at it. Carter's back bows off the bed as he gasps out in half-surprise, half-pleasure. He's more prepared when sir does the same thing to his other nipple, but being prepared only makes it feel *better*. Carter can feel his cock hardening, his face going red in shame.

Of course, sir decides to point it out, clearly wanting to make Carter even more miserable. "There we go. That's my beautiful, good boy."

Squirming, Carter mumbles, "Thank you, sir."

Sir reaches down, running the back of his hand along Carter's length. Carter shivers at the sensation of the knuckles bumping against his cock, then moans when sir nudges just beneath the crown, right where Carter has always been most sensitive.

Chuckling, sir pushes two fingers into Carter's mouth and goes back to nibbling and licking his nipples. Carter doesn't have to be told what to do. He immediately starts to suck on the fingers, acting as if they're dirty and he's determined to get them clean. He doesn't even consider where the fingers will be heading until they're pulled from his mouth and pressed between his ass cheeks.

Sir doesn't give Carter time to react. He just pushes past Carter's loose rim and buries both fingers deep inside him. The man sucks bruises into Carter's neck as his fingers twist and turn, searching. Carter tries to prepare himself, but there's truly no way to prepare for the moment sir's fingers brush along the most sensitive part of him.

"Oooh, god!" Carter cries, his hips bucking.

"Not God, just sir." Sir chuckles at his own cheesy joke, then nips at Carter's earlobe. Carter's ears have always been sensitive, just sir breathing on them gets him going, so the bite has him moaning like a damn whore. Which, he supposes, he is one. He feels like one at least, getting hard for the man who bought him like an animal. The man who turned him into a slave. The man who raped him – multiple times now.

"Get out of your head, sweetheart." Sir brings a hand up to Carter's throat, pressing down enough to show his strength but not so much that Carter can't breathe. Their eyes lock. There's something impossibly powerful about seeing the man like he is, flushed and panting, coming apart because of Carter.

Carter is making sir feel like this.

Carter is pleasing sir, just by letting sir please him.

Sir was right. Carter *is* lucky. He should be grateful.

Taking a chance, Carter tilts his chin up and skates his lips across sir's. He stares up at sir after, trying to gauge his reaction. Sir blinks once before his eyes fill with something dangerous. His hand leaves Carter's throat and goes to his hair, taking a fistful to hold Carter in place against the mattress. Then sir fucking *devours* Carter's mouth while his fingers drive Carter crazy.

It's not long at all before Carter is whining and begging, humping up against sir to try to get some relief for his aching, untouched cock. The fingers are too much inside him, yet not enough. Not nearly enough.

"Please," Carter gasps, bucking his hips unsteadily. "Please, sir!"

"Please what?" sir asks in amusement.

"Just – I don't know." Carter shakes his head, eyes squeezed shut. He thinks he knows what he wants, but he'll *never* let himself ask for it. No way.

Sir grinds their naked cocks together, chuckling against the shell of Carter's ear when Carter moans. "Do you want me to make you feel good, sweetheart? Do you want me to show you how good it could be if you'd just let go for me?"

Carter nods without meaning to, tears burning his eyes. If sir notices them, he doesn't say.

Using his obvious strength and size difference, sir easily maneuvers them on the bed until sir is sitting up against the headboard, Carter straddling his lap like he was earlier in the entertainment room.

"Then ride me," sir says in a low, growly voice. The man watches Carter with a heady expression. Carter gets a sick thrill out of it. "Make yourself come on my cock, sweetheart."

Shivering at the juxtaposition of the pet name with sir's dark, dangerous voice, Carter lifts up and reaches back a hand to take sir's cock. Sir keeps his hands on the mattress as he watches Carter do all the work. Hoping to take advantage of how aroused and pleased the man seems to be right now, Carter asks, "Can I spit on it first, sir?"

"No." Sir fists Carter's hair and pushes him down so he's at a sharp angle, his ass in the air and his mouth against the damp crease of sir's groin. "But you can suck it first."

"Thank you, sir," Carter whispers, meaning every ounce of it. He takes sir's cock in his hand, allowing himself to admire it for just a second. It's just as big as Carter had previously thought, but it has a sort of beauty to it. It's not like those monstrous, veiny things you see in porn. It's still velvet smooth, the head nearly purple even though sir just came a little while ago.

When Carter licks sir for the first time, a part of him is almost sad when he realizes the man smells and tastes differently than usual. It's the same spicy, woodsy, rum scent that he always has from his soap, but too strong. There's none of his natural musk beneath it. None of the distinct things that make sir *sir*.

Jesus, Carter, you're fucked up.

Carter shoves away the thought, deciding to analyze it after he gets his much-deserved orgasm. Or maybe never at all. *Because sir is right, isn't he? What the hell is the point?*

"Good boy." Sir releases his grip on Carter's hair, rubbing whorls into his abused scalp as Carter messily laps at his cock and balls. The praise feels so damn good that Carter moans. The pleased hum the sound earns him from sir erases nearly all guilt Carter feels at being so happy and turned on in the moment. Any leftover guilt gets shoved into the same spot his thoughts of *Jesus, Carter, you're fucked up* were just shoved. No guilt is currently welcome. Especially not when sir continues to pet and praise him so nicely. "That's it. Good. Good fucking boy. Now come ride my cock, sweetheart. Come show me how grateful you are. Make yourself feel good."

Desperate to show sir exactly that, Carter scrambles back up to straddle him. Sir holds his cock straight for

Carter so all he has to do is sink down onto it. With his slobber all over the thing, it's much easier to take. There's still some pinching and burning, but it's more pleasure than pain this time.

Unable to help himself, Carter sighs happily when sir's cock is fully seated inside him. It feels so different than before. He doesn't know if it's the preparation, or the lack of audience, or what, but he knows he's going to take advantage of it in case it never feels like this again.

The issue, of course, is that Carter has never done this. Hell, before sir, he was a *virgin*. He has no idea what he's doing. None.

Suddenly feeling clumsy and unsure, Carter tries to lift himself up. It's much harder without sir guiding him like he had in the entertainment room. Carter's hips stutter. He flinches when sir's hands come to rest on his waist, but relaxes when he sees sir's soft smile.

"Put your hands on my shoulders." Carter follows the order, already feeling better now that he has something to hold. "Good boy."

When sir tugs at his hips, Carter lifts with him. It's still awkward, clumsy, but each roll of Carter's hips against sir gets easier. His movements grow steadier. Slow. Even. Wanting to impress sir, to show how grateful he is, Carter tightens his grip on sir's shoulders and picks up the pace. It makes sir smile. A nice smile. Not mocking or danger-ous. Warm. Kind. *Fond.*

Sir's hands leave Carter's hips, fingertips trailing along his bare skin as Carter moves more confidently. He makes Carter shiver when he touches the inside of his thighs. He makes him gasp when he thumbs his nipples. He makes him throw his head back and moan when he fondles his cock and balls.

"Look how hard you are," sir rasps. Carter can't help but notice how effected sir sounds by that, as if sir really *is* turned on even more because Carter is enjoying this. He doesn't know what that means.

He doesn't *care*.

Sir starts to stroke Carter's cock in time with his thrusts. His body feels strung out and ready to burst any second as he slams himself down on sir's cock the best he can, hoping like hell he's doing it right. It all feels amazing to Carter at least, and sir is still smiling, still looking at him with eyes soaked in lust.

A heady feeling takes over Carter's body, urging him closer to the edge. His movements go erratic as he gives into the pure instinct to chase his orgasm. He can hear the noises he's making, can feel the desperation in each push and pull, but Carter refuses to feel bad about any of it. Not yet. Not right now.

"Is my good boy going to come?" sir asks in a knowing voice.

Carter nods rapidly. "Y-yes, sir. Fuck. So good, sir."

"Good boys ask for permission to come." Sir grips the base of Carter's cock with one hand and uses his other hand to keep Carter from lifting off his lap. "Your orgasms are *mine*. You don't get to choose when you have them."

"Please!" Carter whines pathetically, trying to move against sir's hold. "Please. Please. Please."

"Please what?"

"P – please, sir?"

"Please sir, *what*?"

Carter hangs his head, tears of frustration burning his eyes. A sob racks through his chest. "I – I – don't – I – siiiiiir…"

"Shhh. Calm down." Sir releases Carter's cock, bringing his hand up to nudge beneath Carter's chin. When their eyes meet, sir asks, "What do you want to do, sweetheart?"

"Wanna come, sir."

Sir nods, one eyebrow raised. "So, *ask*."

"Oh!" Carter perks up. "Please can I come, sir?"

The smile sir gives him is brilliant. Breathtaking. "You can come once I've filled your hole. Deal?"

"Deal!" Carter grabs sir's shoulders, riding him again with a newfound enthusiasm. Sir leans back against the headboard, hands lazily settled on Carter's hips, dark blonde hair mussed, eyes half-closed, tongue darting out to lick along his bottom lip. He looks so damn sexy that Carter *almost* forgets who he is. Almost forgets what he's done.

He forgets enough to enjoy himself.

He forgets enough to lose himself in the moment.

He forgets enough to pant and moan and throw his head back. To fall forward and press his mouth to sir's collarbone, lips grazing his sweaty skin, the taste of him salty and familiar on Carter's tongue.

Sir's fingers dig into his ass cheeks, holding Carter steady as he begins to piston his hips upward. Carter clings to sir, every thrust feeling like the breath is being punched out of him. He's dizzy with need and so fucking close to coming. He squeezes his eyes shut, willing sir to fill him soon before he disobeys.

Within seconds, sir's movements are going erratic. He buries his face in Carter's neck and growls, "Holy shit," sounding absolutely *wrecked*. Then he's holding Carter down and grinding up against him, his cock pulsing as it fills Carter.

Carter whines and squirms, trying to find the mental capacity to speak real words.

Sir doesn't make him ask. He just whispers, "Come for me, sweetheart," peppering Carter's neck and shoulder with little kisses after. Carter wraps himself tighter around sir and rubs his cock against sir's belly. Once, twice, and he's falling apart.

Sir holds Carter for a long time after. He strokes Carter's bare back and tells him how good of a boy he is. He kisses Carter's cheeks and neck and shoulders. Holds him close. Cleans him with gentle hands.

At some point, sir lays them down. He pulls Carter into his chest and holds him close. Gives him his stuffed moose. Kisses his forehead. Tells him he's a good boy. Whispers goodnight. Falls asleep.

Then Carter is crashing down, reality swallowing him whole.

Oh god, what has he done?

What the fuck has Carter done?

Chapter Ten

NATHAN WAKES UP FEELING ten times better than the day before. The overwhelming guilt in his chest is just a little lighter, making it easier to breathe.

Maybe he can do this after all. Maybe he can keep Carter safe *and* keep him somewhat happy. Just like Maison had suggested, Nathan can pretend to be falling in love. He can give Carter gentle and kind as often as he can. He can make this life bearable for the sweet boy.

He rolls over on the bed, a smile on his face, only to find the mattress empty where Carter should be. Nathan pushes up on one hand and scans the room before his eyes fall on the door to the bathroom. It's open, the light turned off.

"Fuck." Nathan shoves off the bed and stumbles towards the bathroom, praying the boy is in there with the lights off for some reason. He flips the switch to turn the light on, checking the shower, the tub, the cabinets beneath the sink. Nothing. "*Fuck.*"

He gets desperate. He checks the corners of the bedroom. Behind the lounge chair. *Beneath* the fucking lounge chair. He rifles through the chest of blankets. He —

The closet.

"Oh god, please," he mutters to himself as he heads to the obvious place where he's hoping Carter went to hide.

His heart pounds in his chest as he tries to keep his hopes down. As he tries to keep his *fear* down.

If Carter isn't in the closet, he doesn't know what-

Nathan deflates in relief.

There he is. His boy. Curled up on the floor of Nathan's huge ass walk-in closet, one of Nathan's dress shirts draped over him like a blanket. The tiny stuffed moose is tucked beneath his chin.

He leans against the doorframe and tries to pull himself together. This needs to be punished. Nathan knows that. It's a rule. *Carter broke a rule.*

Why?

Why the fuck would he do that? Why the fuck is he making Nathan punish him? Wasn't last night fucking good for him?

Nathan asks himself what the true Nathan would do. The character he's built over the years. The *monster*. He hates the answer. He can't do *that*.

But he has to do *something*. Carter broke a rule. If Nathan lets that slide, he's going to break more. Nathan can't risk giving him too much rope to hang himself with. Especially if he hangs himself in front of an audience.

It's best he learns his lesson now.

One harsh punishment to make it stick, then they'll be done with this. The boy won't disobey again. He'll be safe.

How fucked up is it that Nathan has to hurt him to keep him safe?

Growling in frustration, Nathan pushes off the doorframe and walks forward, stepping into the *Nathan* mindset as he does so. He rips his shirt off Carter, the action startling the boy awake. Nathan doesn't give him time to understand what's happening, grabbing his small biceps and lifting him to his feet. Carter cries out, eyes shooting wide open as Nathan presses him against the nearest wall.

He should have *slammed* him against it.

This boy has made him weak.

"I-"

"Shut. Up." Fisting one hand in Carter's hair, Nathan uses the other to clamp down on Carter's throat. He squeezes at just the right angle to cut off Carter's air completely. He sees the moment Carter realizes it. The moment he tries to breathe and can't. His pretty blue eyes go wide, terror flashing in them. "You fucked up. Big time. Are you a fucking idiot? Did you not process the very clear, very fucking *simple* rules I gave you? Or did you disobey me on purpose?"

Nathan eases his grip just enough for Carter to suck in air. The boy coughs and sputters, crying out when Nathan tugs his hair sharply. "You can answer now, slave."

"I – I – I didn't – I couldn't-"

"Stop fucking stuttering," Nathan growls, pulling at Carter's hair again. "Answer the question. Are you an idiot, or are you disobedient?"

"D-disobedient, sir," he rasps, tears filling his pretty blue eyes. "Sor-"

Nathan squeezes his throat again, cutting off his words. "I have no interest in your apologies. *None.* I gave you a good fucking night, and you did *this*? Are you fucking kidding me?"

Carter shakes his head the best he can, tears spilling over his cheeks. Travis tries to peek out from behind the curtain Nathan uses to hide him. Travis wants to hold Carter close. To kiss him better. To whisper that it's okay, that he understands, that he knows Carter probably just got too overwhelmed, or scared, or confused, and he ran.

Nathan strangles Travis until he passes out, rolling his lifeless body back behind the curtain. Travis is going to get all of them killed if he's not careful. If he had his way, they'd be dead in a week.

Nathan meets Carter's eyes, making sure his gaze is cold. "Kneel."

The boy obeys. He's trembling with terror, his breathing ragged and panicked, but Nathan ignores it. Ignores him. It hurts more than he thought it would. He turns his back to hide his face in case he's not masking the emotion well enough.

Keeping his back to the boy, Nathan methodically dresses himself. His mind races with possible punishments. He needs something that will be bad enough to keep Carter from breaking the rules again, but something that's not so bad the boy will break. The paddle, maybe. Or a cane. Nathan probably won't be able to fuck him after hurting him, even if he medicates himself, so he'll have to do it beforehand. Maybe just a blowjob. A rough one. Then a swift punishment to bring the issue to a close.

Nathan opens his top drawer and slides his hand beneath a folded pair of underwear, grabbing the little container that holds his blue pills. He pops one in his mouth and swallows it dry. When he turns, he finds Carter on his knees with his upper body curled inward as if he's trying to make himself smaller. His hand is pressed over his mouth as he muffles his hysterical sobs.

He's fucking terrified.

Nathan can't do this.

Nathan *has* to do this.

He clips Carter's leash onto the ring of his collar and tugs once, the movement sharp but not painful. The boy gasps and rocks up onto his hands and knees, preparing to crawl. He's already struggling to keep himself in the proper position, his muscles jerking, his arms going weak.

Nathan should yell at him to hurry the fuck up. To get his shit together. Maybe even smack a hand against his ass. It's what the other men here would do.

Instead, Nathan squats down and carefully maneuvers the boy until he's in a position where Nathan can fold him over his right shoulder. He feels Carter's hands immediately grab the back of his suit jacket, his body trembling furiously against him. Each tremor makes Nathan ache like they're his own.

"Let go of my jacket," Nathan says quietly. His throat feels tight. He swallows hard. "I won't drop you. Let go."

There's the slightest hesitation, but then the boy obeys.

People know what's going on when they set eyes on the two of them. Nathan can see it in the way they look at Carter. Some of them, the softer ones, cringe and look away. Any slaves that accidentally get a peek immediately bow their head and let their eyes flutter closed in shared grief. The others – the men like Nathan – love it. They smirk. Laugh. Make comments.

"Oh no," one of his men coos. Jason. An asshole. He sing-songs his next words like a student teasing another for getting called to the principal's office. "Someone's in trouble."

Nathan just grunts in response as he takes his seat at the table and manhandles Carter down his body and onto the floor. The boy hits his head on the edge of the table, crying out in pain. Nathan immediately grabs him, cradling his face in his hands as he stares into his eyes. The words *are you okay, sweetheart?* stick to the tip of his tongue. He chokes them down and lets go of the boy, digging his fingernails into his palms to keep from reaching for him again.

"Get my cock in your mouth," he growls, not because he's mad but because his voice is rough, his throat closing in on itself.

Carter obeys, his shaking hands quickly opening Nathan's pants and pulling out his soft cock. The pill hasn't kicked in, but it won't be much longer. "You're not keeping me warm today. Get me hard."

The boy's eyes flutter closed for just a second before he looks at Nathan's cock in resignation. His hands spread across Nathan's thighs in an attempt to get a better angle. Nathan should probably smack his hands away and tell

Carter he's not allowed to touch him, but there's no way in hell he'll be able to manage something like that right now. He makes up for his weakness by grabbing Carter's hair in a slightly too-tight grip, using his other hand to guide his hardening cock between the boy's lips.

"What would you like to eat this morning, Master Roarke?" a house slave asks.

"Something quick. Easy. I won't be here long." Nathan glances at the slave, hoping his rage shows in his expression. He's pissed, and though he's not pissed at Carter, no one here needs to know that. They just need to see that he's really fucking pissed. It'll make things more believable. Especially since Nathan's grip has already loosened, his fingers rubbing Carter's scalp soothingly.

The first sound Carter makes is a choking cough, followed by a gag as he rears back. Nathan is getting too big for the boy to take all of him. Surprisingly – or maybe not surprisingly, since Nathan knows how badly Carter wants to be good – the boy doesn't give up or try to fight it. He just takes a breath and dives back down, trying his best to take all of Nathan even as Nathan continues to grow.

Nathan has to bite his tongue to keep from praising him.

A bowl of yogurt with fruit and granola is placed in front of Nathan, along with a glass of water and a mug of coffee. He does his best to ignore Carter's struggles as he quickly scoops the food into his mouth. Nathan forces his mind to wander, replaying the previous night to keep from losing his shit. It only takes a few minutes before he finally feels himself nearing the edge.

Shoving his chair back, Nathan grips the back of Carter's neck and heaves the boy straight up on his knees as he stands. The pulling of his hair forces Carter's head at an angle that brings their gazes to meet. Tears are falling down Carter's cheeks. Nathan pretends they're tears from the deepthroating. The lie helps him stay hard as he strips his cock with his fist.

"Tongue out," he growls, his body trembling with a chaotic mixture of rage and need.

Carter obeys immediately. His eyes are wide. Afraid.

"God, he cries pretty, doesn't he?" one of the men comments.

Another adds, "Pretty face full of tears."

"Gonna be prettier covered in cum," a third teases.

Nathan closes his eyes. He pictures Carter in his lap again, hands on his shoulders, Nathan gripping his slim waist. He recalls the way the boy had smiled when he finally got the hang of his movements, looking adorably proud. He recalls the way the boy had shivered beneath his touch, not out of disgust but out of arousal. The way the boy had gasped so pretty when Nathan toyed with his sensitive nipples. The way he had tossed his head back, moaning as Nathan fondled his cock and balls.

He was so fucking hard, his balls tight, his cock dripping over Nathan's fingers. Nathan had been amazed. Enamored. *Proud.*

Nathan's orgasm slams into him, his eyes snapping open as he paints Carter's face with his cum. The boy flinches when the first wave hits, his eyes squeezing shut and his body shuddering. Each glob of cum seems to physically hurt him. Nathan feels the echoes of the pain in his own chest.

"C-" Nathan pauses, clearing his throat. He hopes anyone paying attention assumes he's struggling to speak because of the intensity of his orgasm. "Clean it."

Since Nathan had managed to avoid hitting the boy's eyes, Carter is able to open them to find Nathan's cock. He quickly wraps his mouth around it and sucks it clean, licking a few extra stripes along it before allowing it to fall from his mouth again.

Nathan should yell at him. He should say that Carter doesn't get to decide when his cock leaves his mouth. He should say that Carter should suck him for as long as Nathan orders him to.

But Nathan manages to keep his hands at his sides instead of cupping the boy's face to comfort him, and he manages to swallow all of the praise he had bubbling along his tongue, so he decides to forgive himself for not scolding Carter. *You win some, you lose some, right?*

Then Nathan looks up and finds himself face to face with Benny, the man staring at him like he doesn't recognize him, and Nathan realizes maybe he's not winning anything at all.

Nathan tears his gaze away, forcing himself to focus. He grabs Carter's biceps and tugs him to his feet at the same time that he crouches down, the boy easily falling over his shoulder like before. He leaves the dining area behind without a glance, ignoring all the cheers and comments from his men. Carter doesn't seem to have the same ability. By the way he begins to tremble again, small whimpers falling from his lips, Nathan thinks the boy hears every bit of it all.

There's only one of his men in the dungeon, in the midst of fucking a slave that's strapped down to a spanking bench when Nathan walks in.

"Out!" Nathan barks, tossing Carter onto the bondage bed in the center of the room. The boy bounces, nearly falling off, before managing to stabilize himself.

"S-sir?" Carter whimpers, the boy trembling violently.

Nathan closes his eyes. He won't be able to do this if the boy keeps talking to him. "Shut up."

"But-"

"Shut. Up." Nathan glares at Carter, narrowing his eyes until the boy cowers and looks away. He watches as the boy curls in on himself. Watches as the boy accepts defeat. It's like a train wreck, painful to watch, yet impossible to look away from.

By the time Nathan turns to grab a paddle and a cane, the man and his slave from before have disappeared. He turns back to Carter and takes a deep breath, steadying himself. "Are you going to be able to take your punishment like a good boy, or do I need to tie your disobedient little ass up?"

Carter shudders. "G-gonna take it, sir."

"Mmm." Nathan reaches out to yank Carter closer to the edge of the mattress by his ankle, using the momentum to flip the boy to his stomach at the same time. "We'll see. You're getting the cane 4 times because you broke rule number 4. I can give you a cold caning without any warm-up. It'll be over much sooner, but hurt like fucking hell. Or, I can warm your ass up, take a bit longer, and the cane won't hurt as much. Your choice."

"I – um..." Carter looks over his shoulder in desperation, eyes pleading with Nathan. "I don't know sir. I – just – I don't know."

Nathan's chest goes tight. He glances around, checking that they're still alone. Then, "Let me warm you up, sweetheart. Rub your cock on the sheets if you need to. It'll help ease the pain. But don't fucking come. Things will get much worse if you come."

"O-okay, sir. But I-"

"No buts. Just shut up and take your punishment. Once-" Nathan chokes on the reassuring words he had planned on giving the boy about how once the punishment is over, he'll be forgiven, his head whipping around at the sound of the dungeon door opening. His stomach drops as he watches his men start to file in. They're loud and boisterous and clapping already, clearly excited to watch the show.

Fuck.

Fuck, fuck, fuck.

Nathan hurries to turn back to Carter, squeezing his eyes shut. He focuses on the feel of his expensive suit wrapped around his body. The weight of the jacket. The silky material of his dress shirt. The cinch of his tie. The fabric that cups his ass. The buttery soft leather shoes that are perfectly molded to his feet. The cool metal of his watch.

His suit.

His armor.

His costume.

Travis isn't here right now. Travis no longer exists. It's just Nathan Roarke. Ruthless. Evil. Monster.

Nathan pictures taking Carter by the hand and leading him away behind the curtain, handing him off to Travis. No, not a curtain. A door. A heavy metal door, with industrial locks. He pictures himself sliding each lock into place, the metal soundproof, the occupants behind it already forgotten. He pictures himself turning to face a replica of the boy, one that he doesn't care about, one that is meant to be hurt and used. A slave without a name. Nathan's slave. Nathan's disobedient slave.

He opens his eyes.

A disobedient slave is in front of him.

"Ass in the air," he orders, his voice entirely Nathan Roarke's and no one else's. "Present yourself for punishment, slave."

The slave squirms, his face twisting in pain. "Sir, I have to-"

"Shut!" Nathan swings the heavy wooden paddle, catching both ass cheeks at once. "Up!" He hits the spot again.

The slave starts crying.

He hits the slave again.

The slave's eyes flutter closed in resignation before he presses his face against the bed and raises his ass higher for further abuse. Nathan swings the paddle again. The sounds that fall from the slave's lips are bordering on sobs.

Nathan's men laugh.

Nathan's chest vibrates as he swings the paddle again.

He's laughing, too.

He hadn't noticed.

He hits the slave again and again, the intensity rising in layers as Nathan works him over. He covers the slave in red blotches from his thighs to his ass until he's sobbing and writhing and screaming, *he's sorry, he's so sorry, please, he's so so sorry!*

"*Are* you sorry?" Nathan asks conversationally. His men snort and laugh. They tell Nathan they don't think the slave is sorry at all. Nathan agrees. "I feel like you're not sorry. Not yet."

The slave is humping the sheets.

Nathan sneers. "Look at this fucking slut." He steps forward, grabbing the slave's hips and forcing him to grind even harder against the silky sheets. His men laugh. He laughs.

The slave sobs.

"Sir, please!" the slave begs, squirming and fighting Nathan's hold. "Too much. I have to – I have to go-"

"Christ," Nathan growls, smacking both his hands against the boy's abused ass before stepping away to grab the paddle again. "Shut the hell up before this gets worse for you, slave!"

Nathan catches the eye of Benny, his second-hand man. He grins at Benny. His best friend looks away from him, disgust twisting his expression, his eyebrows pulling in. Something pings in the back of Nathan's mind. A voice that feels strangely familiar. Words that make him ache. *You're mine now. All mine. And I'm going to take care of you, I promise.*

The voice is coming from the door in his mind. Nathan conjures a version of Benny in his mind and slams him into the metal door until he crumples to the floor, knocked out cold.

The voice stops.

Nathan doesn't lift his gaze from the slave, wanting to avoid seeing any other version of Benny that may be lurking nearby.

"I'm sorry, sir! Please!" The slave thrashes his head in a panic as Nathan hits him harder. "Please, please, please!"

"Tell me the rule you broke," Nathan orders in a low voice as he trades his paddle for the cane.

"Don't 1 – leave bed with – without permission," the slave gasps. Then, "Sir!"

"What rule was that? What number?"

"F-four, sir?"

"Are you asking?" Nathan asks, tapping the cane like a threat against the boy's bright red ass. "Or are you telling?"

The slave sniffles. "T-telling, sir."

"Good. You're correct." Nathan adjusts his grip on the cane. "So, you'll take this cane 4 times. After each hit, you will tell me the rule you broke, and you will apologize. Is that understood?"

"Yes, sir," the slave whispers, his shoulders hunching.

Nathan acknowledges the words with a flick of his wrist, the cane hitting the slave right below the cups of his ass cheeks. Panic slams into the slave, sending him scrambling away from Nathan. He grabs the slave by his ankle just as the slave wraps his arms around the bedpost. His men step forward to help, but Nathan shakes his head. He will handle this disobedient little brat himself.

"Let go," he orders. "Let go *now*."

The slave gasps and shudders, but he obeys. He lets go.

Just let go, sweetheart. Let everything go. Give it all to me.

Nathan blinks. *When did he say that?*

Who... who did he say that too?

"Hit him again, boss!"

Nathan blinks. There is a boy on the bed in front of him. A boy he recognizes. Carter.

This is a boy named Carter.

Oh, Carter...

"Boss!"

"He has to apologize first," Benny says from the left. "Apologize, slave."

"I – I fo – forgot – no, I broke – broke rule – the bed rule. Four."

Carter.

This is *Carter.*

Nathan knows him.

Nathan... very much *likes* him...

His wrist flicks the cane on its own, most likely out of self-preservation.

Carter sobs out an apology.

Nathan bites his tongue until it bleeds. Iron soaks his taste buds; It tastes a lot like guilt and grief.

Nathan hits Carter a third time. The boy's body gives out, deflating against the mattress. A sound rips its way out of him. Something anguished and awful. Then piss is soaking the sheets, running between his legs in rivulets, pooling in the dip of his thighs. Carter clings to the sheets with trembling hands and says his apology in a single breath, his voice growing more distant and cold the longer he speaks. "Broke rule four, got'ow bed 'n I'm so – so sorry, sir. I'm really, really sorry, sir. Please. I'm sorry."

"Did he just fucking piss?" Jason asks.

"He fucking did."

"What the fuck, slave, that's our property you just pissed all over!"

"We should fucking make you suck the sheets clean you filthy slut."

"We should make you sleep in a fucking dog cage with these sheets since you can't be bothered to enjoy your master's bed."

"We should–"

"*We,*" Nathan says quietly, his voice dangerous, his eyes narrowing. The room falls silent. "Are not who owns this slave. I am. And I think you've all gotten to see enough. Goodbye."

The men all look at each other. It's Jason who has the courage to ask, "Can't we watch the ending, sir? It's just one more hit."

"Do *you* want to be hit?" Nathan asks, tilting his head in curiosity. "Because that could be a show as well, Jason."

Jason blanches. A few of Nathan's men step back. "Sir, I didn't mean to offend or overstep."

"Then leave before you do it again."

"Yes, sir." Jason ducks his head, backing away. "Sorry, sir."

He hurries out with his metaphorical tail tucked between his legs. The others follow suit. Benny is the only one who stays.

"Go," Nathan says quietly, his eyes never leaving Carter's abused body where it lies lifeless in a puddle of urine. "Please."

"Nate, let me h-"

"Go." Nathan meets his best friend's eyes, knowing his own are filling with tears. "Just fucking leave me alone."

Benny swallows hard, his eyes darting to Carter. Then he nods and steps away. Nathan hears the metal door's industrial locks sliding into place.

Then it's just Nathan and Carter.

"Last one," Nathan whispers to the boy. He forces himself to breathe. To relax. He forces his hand to stop shaking. One hit at the wrong angle could hurt Carter much worse than he'd like. Much worse than the boy deserves. It was bad enough that Nathan escaped into his head and wasn't careful earlier. He refuses to allow any further mistreatment. Hell, if Carter hadn't turned his head to watch all of the men walk out, proving he's still coherent, Nathan would have skipped the fourth hit and pretended he had administered it.

Maybe it's a good thing Carter is still with him mentally, though.

Maybe it means he's not broken.

The hit can barely be considered a hit. The cane taps against the skin, still enough to draw a gasp from the boy considering the state of his ass, but not enough to make him scream or sob.

"Come on," Nathan encourages, dropping the cane and walking forward to rest his hands on Carter's hips. Carter jolts at the touch before pushing back against it, desperate for comfort, for praise. "Just say your apology, sweetheart."

The pet name causes Carter to cry harder, but he still manages to spill out his final apology, the words running together, an added sorry for pissing himself as if it's his fault and not Nathan's that he wasn't allowed to piss this morning. The boy had tried to fucking *warn* him.

Nathan breaks. "You did so well, sweetheart. Such a good fucking boy. You took that so well. That made sir very happy."

All the tension seems to seep out of Carter's body at the words, his hands relaxing where they had been clinging to the sheets. His face is covered in tears, and snot, and dried cum. His body is soaked in piss and sweat.

He's beautiful, and so very *strong*.

It physically hurts Nathan to look at him.

He can't look away.

"I need to plug you," Nathan realizes out loud, noticing the empty space between the reddened cheeks on display before him. There are two universal rules when it comes to a slave's preparation in this world, the rest of the rules being left up to the owners. A slave should always be collared, and a slave should always be plugged.

Carter says nothing. Nathan supposes that makes sense. *What is there to say?* Nathan is going to do whatever he wants regardless.

He has to borrow a plug from the dungeon. None of them are as small as the plug Carter always wears, and the disinfectant available is a harsh one. His poor hole is going to probably be irritated, if not in pain.

At least there's decent lube.

Nathan preps Carter carefully. Quickly. Clinically. He focuses on stretching the rim, not bothering to fuck into him or mess with his prostate. The scent of bodily fluids is thick in the air. Nathan is nearly gagging on it. He uses a liberal amount of lube when he presses the plug into the boy's hole. Carter whimpers before going limp once again.

"Come here." Nathan gently pulls Carter closer, turning him over. The boy hisses when his ass rubs against the soaked sheets, but he doesn't fight Nathan. In fact, he doesn't look like he could if he even wanted to. He's too deflated. Almost... empty.

Oh god, please don't be empty.

"Why would you do this?" Nathan asks, unable to stop how helpless he sounds. How *hurt* he sounds. "After last night, why would you do this?"

Carter blinks slowly, his face far too calm for what he just endured. "I'm sorry, sir," he whispers in a voice void of emotion.

He's lax and empty, staring up at Nathan like Nathan is his God. Nathan gets the distinct impression that he could order Carter to do anything right now, and Carter would obey without hesitation. It terrifies him.

"Okay," Nathan whispers, more to himself than to Carter. "Okay. It's – it's okay.

He takes the boy's hands in his and guides him off the bed. It takes Carter a moment before he's steady on his feet. Nathan waits a few more seconds after feeling him stabilize before actually letting go of him. He wishes he could carry the boy, but everyone would be floored if they saw a man like Nathan Roarke willingly ruining a bespoke Armani by carrying a useless slave covered in piss. If this was another life, Nathan wouldn't give a fucking shit about scraps of clothing or people's opinions. He would hold Carter close for hours. Days. Forever.

Then again, if this was another life, Carter wouldn't be hurt in the first place.

Nathan grabs some wet wipes from the table beside the bondage bed, running one up the insides of Carter's thighs. He almost smiles when the boy squirms and flushes red. It's not a reaction of pain, it's a reaction of embarrassment. That means Carter is still in there somewhere. He's just hiding right now. It's a fucking relief.

When Carter is clean enough for Nathan not to have to worry about him dripping piss on the floors upstairs, he takes the end of the boy's leash and walks him out of the dungeon.

The first house slave Nathan passes gets the order to go clean up after them. They walk through the main area of the house soon after. Not many of his men are around. They probably assume Nathan isn't in a good mood and want to stay out of his way. Benny is there, though. He falls into step beside Nathan the moment Nathan passes him. He looks at Carter for just a second before his eyes rebel against the sight. Then his nose wrinkles. Twisted anguish appears on Benny's face, reflecting Nathan's own hidden emotions.

Nathan wants to defend himself. He wants to explain what happened, and his reasoning behind it all. He wants to admit to the metal door in his mind. To the selfishness of it. To the way he had run and hid like a child instead of staying present and facing his own monstrous deeds. He wants to tell Benny that he's destroyed right now. He wants to tell Benny that he's terrified he may no longer be fixable.

Nathan wants to tell Benny that he can't breathe. That he hasn't been able to breathe. Not since he first got the order from Maison to buy Carter as his personal pleasure slave.

That's all Nathan wants. He just wants to breathe.

He needs to fucking *breathe*.

But Nathan isn't the victim here, he's the villain.

So, he says nothing at all.

Chapter Eleven

CARTER HAS LOST HIS mind. He can't get himself to care about anything but *sir*. There's no reason for thought or processing, unless it's processing an order from sir. The only words he needs are the ones sir pours into his mouth. The only thing he needs to care about is making sir happy.

It's almost... nice.

Carter's muscles ache, his ass and the back of his thighs burning, but it's okay because it reminds him of sir. Every shift of his weight is like sir touching him again, sir hurting him again, even if sir isn't. Even if sir hasn't touched him since the scary dungeon. Even if sir wants nothing to do with Carter anymore.

After Carter's punishment, sir had led Carter to his office, pushed him down to his knees in the corner instead of under his desk like usual, and told Carter to stay. Sir hasn't looked at him since. He hasn't talked to him. He hasn't touched him. He just ignores Carter all day as Carter sits in the corner like a bad puppy, still covered in bodily fluids. He's starving. The plug in his ass is heavy and uncomfortable. His knees are aching. His face is itchy from the dried cum, sweat, and tears. He's exhausted. He's sad.

So very fucking sad.

But none of that matters because none of that has to do with pleasing sir. Sir wants him to stay, so Carter stays.

Even when sir leaves the room. Even when sir eats lunch at his desk, ignoring Carter's grumbling stomach. Even when sir has people come in for meetings. Even when sir's men run their hands all over him, touching his cock and balls, pressing firmly against his injuries. Even when sir and his friends make fun of him for pissing himself, commenting on him being a filthy animal. Through it all, Carter stays quiet and still, staring at the floor because that's what sir wants.

It's freeing. Carter doesn't have to care about hunger or pain or thirst, he doesn't have to care about emotion, if he's focused solely on pleasing sir.

Nothing else matters but *sir*.

Sir hangs up the phone with a louder than usual bang, making Carter jump. He quickly settles back in place and hangs his head, hoping he won't get yelled at. Sir just continues to ignore him. It hurts, but Carter swallows it down because the pain doesn't matter. None of it matters. Nothing but sir.

When sir leaves the room once again, he's gone for a long time. A long enough time for Carter to start feeling afraid.

Would sir forget about him?

Is sir mad enough to just leave him here?

Is he supposed to stay in place?

Would sir rather him pass out, or leave to go find water and food?

Is this where Carter is sleeping tonight? Should he lay down? Curl up like a puppy? Or should he try to sleep sitting up? Is he allowed to sleep at all? Does sir want him to stay awake?

The office door opens and closes again, sending a twist of anxiety through Carter's chest. He peeks up through his lashes to find sir walking towards him. Wanting to please sir, Carter makes sure to keep every muscle still, his back straight, his chin down, his eyes on the floor.

Sir stops when the toes of his expensive leather shoes are in Carter's line of sight. Carter focuses on keeping his breathing steady and slow, not wanting to upset sir by reacting without permission.

After releasing a slow breath that sounds more tired than angry, sir says, "Time for bed. Up."

Sir takes the end of Carter's leash and tugs. Anxious and eager to please, Carter scrambles up to his feet. He immediately drops back to his hands and knees when he remembers he isn't supposed to walk. He had been told to get up, but maybe that's not what sir meant.

"Your knees must be killing you," sir says softly. "You may walk."

Swallowing hard, Carter once again rises to his feet. It hurts to stand, his muscles trembling under the weight of his body, his knees locking, the skin of his ass and thighs on fire as the air kisses them. Sir begins to walk, going slow as Carter desperately tries to force his body to move properly. He only stumbles once, and he's the luckiest slave in the world because sir doesn't yell at him for it.

They walk past the dining area and kitchen, the scent of dinner still thick in the air despite no food being in sight. Carter's stomach grumbles, but he ignores it, and so does sir. They walk past men who reach out and slap Carter's bruised ass as he walks by. Carter bites down on his bottom lip hard enough to draw blood in order to keep quiet.

By the time they get to sir's bedroom, Carter is bone-tired and a little light-headed. He's trying to come up with the best way to apologize to sir a final time to gain the privilege of going straight to sleep tonight when they step through the bedroom door. Carter's breath catches as his gaze falls on a new addition to the room.

There is a metal cage at the foot of sir's bed.

The cage is all black, from the bars and lock to the leather padded bottom and restraints in the corners. It's too small. He'll have to curl up tight to fit in it.

Carter sways on his feet, feeling dizzy and untethered. He should have expected this. *Sir had mentioned a cage, hadn't he?* He had mentioned giving Carter away to someone else at night too. At least he chose the cage instead of that. Carter's not sure he would have survived that.

"Use the bathroom if you need to," sir says with a flick of his wrist. He doesn't bother looking at Carter, just dropping his leash and walking towards his closet. Uninterested. Uncaring. "Fucking shower, too. You reek."

A painful lump forms at the base of Carter's throat, but he doesn't dare try to clear it away. He just pads softly to the bathroom, his chin tucked, his eyes on the floor, the end of his leash dragging on the ground between his feet.

Carter relieves himself, though barely any pee comes out. Then he slides into the shower to wash up. The water is cold at first, but he doesn't wait to let it warm, already lathering his body with soap. He sobs when he scrubs his ass and the back of his thighs, but he forces himself to endure it. There are a few places on his skin that look like they may have bled a bit, and the last thing he needs is an infection.

After peeking through the glass shower door that has yet to fog, and finding sir nowhere in sight, Carter tilts his head back and gulps down some water. It's a little too warm and not all that refreshing, but his body still sings in relief.

A sharp knock on the open bathroom door causes him to startle, Carter almost slipping. "Hurry up!"

Heart pounding, Carter hurries to turn the faucet off and steps out of the shower. Sir isn't there with a towel, and one hasn't been set on the counter either. Carter stands on the mat dripping for a few seconds before deciding to grab a hand towel from the wall between sinks and use it to dry himself the best he can, only gently patting his ass and thighs to avoid as much pain as possible. His body protests, but he also squats down to wipe up the stray drops of water on the floor not protected by the mat.

It isn't until he's walking back into the bedroom and sees the dog cage again that Carter remembers. His stomach plummets, his throat tight.

Sir is halfway through undressing, but when Carter steps forward to help, sir lifts his chin and gives him a sharp enough look that sends Carter dropping to his knees. His body curls in on itself until he's in the closest thing possible to a fetal position while still kneeling for sir. Sir makes an indignant sound before turning his back to Carter and continuing to undress.

Hot tears of rejection sting Carter's eyes. He dips his chin even lower, not wanting sir to see him crying. He understands that sir doesn't want him, and he respects that. Whatever makes sir happy. Sir's happiness is all that matters.

But Carter is just so... *lonely*. So empty. So useless. He wants to do something for sir. He wants to please sir. He wants sir to hold him in his arms and praise him. He wants sir to forgive him now. He wants sir to make him feel good again. He wants to make *sir* feel good again.

Carter wants to prove to sir that he can be a good boy. That this was just a mistake. That it won't ever happen again.

He'll happily choke on a cock, or take more spankings, or offer his ass up to be fucked. Whatever sir wants. Whatever will make sir happy. Carter just wants to be a part of it. He *needs* to be a part of it.

Stripped down to nothing but his tight black boxer briefs, sir takes a seat on the cushioned top of the cage and snaps his fingers between his legs. Carter has seen people do the same with dogs, getting them to come forward and sit, so he makes the assumption that's what sir wants him to do. He crawls until he's between sir's knees before settling with his ass resting on his heels, his eyes trained on his bruising knees as he tries to control his fear of what's to come.

Honestly, Carter isn't sure what he's more afraid of; the idea that sir might hurt him again, or the idea that sir won't even touch him before locking him away.

The second fear is abated when sir reaches out, running a gentle hand through Carter's hair. It's one movement, his fingers not even touching Carter's actual skin, but it's enough for Carter to shudder through a dry sob of relief.

"Shhh." Sir moves his hand down to Carter's chin, encouraging him to lift it so they can look into each other's eyes. Sir's brown eyes flick from left to right across Carter's expression, his eyebrows pulling in. Carter is filled with the sudden feeling that sir is looking for something from him. *Expecting* something. A panic beats inside his chest as he tries to figure out what it is sir wants. He'd give him anything, gladly, all sir has to do is ask.

Sir drops his hands, leaving Carter cold and lonely all over again. He's in the middle of overanalyzing the situation when something warm brushes his left cheek. Caught off guard, he startles and pulls away from the thing. Sir doesn't yell at him. He just hushes Carter, fingers moving back to Carter's hair while he drags his thumb over Carter's cheek again. He's wiping Carter's tears away.

Carter hadn't even realized he'd begun to cry.

Sir takes his time, touching Carter all over even though his tears surely only managed to get on his cheeks and possibly his jaw. He touches Carter's forehead. The shell of his ear. The arch of his brow. He touches Carter's shoulders. His throat. His sternum. He touches Carter like he can't stop himself, as if he had missed touching Carter as much as Carter had missed being touched by him.

With sir so focused on his fingers gliding over Carter's body, Carter is free to openly watch the man. He studies him, memorizing the way his forehead wrinkles slightly, the way his lips hover close together without touching, the way his jaw darkens with a 5 o'clock shadow. There's a very small scar at the corner of his left eyebrow that Carter had never noticed before, and a similarly new discovery of a freckle on the shell of his right ear.

After a very long time, or perhaps no time at all, sir drags his thumb along Carter's cheekbone a final time and whispers, "You're so fucking beautiful."

Carter blinks, his eyes meeting sir's. The compliment is genuine. He can see it in the way sir is looking at him. His stomach flips. "Thank you, sir. So are you."

"Mmm." Sir's lips twitch. Then, "Turn around and press your forehead to the floor, ass in the air."

Flushing, Carter hurries to obey, hoping sir is about to remove the plug from his ass. Or, at the very least, add some lube so it's more comfortable inside him.

A whimper accidentally passes through Carter's lips the first time sir touches his plug. He cowers against the floor, biting down on his lip to keep any other noises from escaping. Sir doesn't chastise him. Carter's not sure if it's because sir doesn't feel like it right now, or if it's because his night is already going to be bad enough without sir feeling the need to add to it.

"You're okay," sir whispers as he gently adjusts the plug in him. Bile burns Carter's stomach because it's not okay. None of this is okay. His hole hurts, and his heart is breaking, and he just wants sir to *hold him*.

But sir says it's okay, and sir is law, so it has to be okay.

"Just breathe, sweetheart."

Breathe. Carter can do that, at least. He breathes nice and slow, keeping himself calm as sir removes his plug. He manages to swallow a pained gasp when his rim catches on the toy. He's proud of himself for staying so quiet, even if it meant digging his nails into his palms until they drew blood, squeezing his eyes shut until they ached, and biting down on his lip enough to make it bleed once more.

Sir mumbles something under his breath that Carter can't quite hear before standing up and stepping over Carter to walk away. Carter turns his head just enough to peek up at sir as the man disappears into the bathroom. He returns just seconds later, his hands empty, his lips twitching when his gaze locks with Carter's.

Before Carter can look away and apologize, sir curls his finger. "Back in your kneeling position."

Once Carter has situated himself properly, sir tilts his head and asks, "What rule did you break today, sweetheart?"

Self-hate burns through Carter's veins.

"Rule 4, sir. I got out of bed without permission." Carter swallows hard, trying not to cry. "And I'm really, *really* sorry, sir. I'm so sorry."

"Mmm." Sir passes in front of him, entering his walk-in closet. Carter can't tear his eyes away from the tensing and twitching of the man's ass and thighs. It's unfair how attractive he is. Men like him should have to look like the monsters they are. It's only right.

When sir returns from the closet, he's holding something in his hands. He puts it behind his back before Carter can see what it is. "Are you ready to tell me why you broke the rule yet?"

Carter sinks in on himself, feeling both empty and overfull.

"Because I'm *bad*, sir," he admits, his voice cracking in grief. He clears his throat and forces himself to repeat the truth. "I'm really, *really* bad, sir."

The sound sir makes is pained and broken, but Carter reminds himself it surely can't be regarding him. Sir probably saw a text, or maybe he's remembering how truly bad Carter is and debating what to do with him.

Or maybe Carter has gone insane and sir didn't make an abnormal sound at all.

"Look at me, sweetheart," sir encourages, his fingers nudging below Carter's chin. Carter tilts his head back to meet sir's gaze. He looks different than he had a moment ago. Haunted, somehow.

Unless Carter is going insane, which he has already decided could very well be a thing, sir's voice even has a slight tremble to it when he speaks again. "You're not bad, sweetheart. Not at all. You acted bad. You made a mistake. When your punishment is over, you'll be forgiven. You'll be my good boy again. That's how this works. Understood?"

Carter nods, sniffling as he fights back tears of relief. Sir's fingertips dance across his cheekbone, making him shiver before sir lowers himself to one knee. It feels wrong to be at the same level as sir, but Carter would never dare say so. It's not like his opinion matters anyway.

Sir presses his forehead against Carter's, his eyes falling closed. "Why'd you do it, sweetheart? Why'd you leave me?"

Carter's chest constricts at sir's words. He's not asking why Carter left the bed, not really. He's asking why Carter left *him*. It should be such a small difference, but it's not. It's everything.

"I was so afraid, sir..."

Sir opens his eyes, keeping his forehead against Carter's as he peers into Carter's eyes. The position forces sir's breath to fan across Carter's face. He smells like scotch tonight. Carter could inhale him forever.

"You were afraid of me?"

"Yes," Carter admits in a whisper, feeling as if they're sharing secrets. Very big secrets. *Maybe they are.* "I was terrified, sir."

"That I'd hurt you?"

"No. I – I was terrified that I'd want you..." Carter presses his forehead harder against sir's, desperate for him to understand. He *needs* sir to understand. His voice shakes as he forces the truth out. "You made me feel so good, sir. You – you made me *want* you. I don't want to want you."

Sir cradles the left side of Carter's face in his big palm. Carter can't help but lean into the touch, his nose tracing the lines in his skin. It feels good. So very good.

"Don't run from me again." Carter can't help but feel like the words aren't an order. They sound so much more like a desperate plea. "Let yourself feel good, sweetheart. Let yourself want me. Lord knows I want you." Sir laughs, the sound breathy and frustrated. "I want you so much I'm going fucking crazy."

"It's... wrong."

"Who cares? You're mine now. Forever. You won't get away. Your idiot brother isn't coming to save you. Trust me, I don't let my possessions go until I want to, and I don't plan on ever wanting that with you." Sir runs a thumb along Carter's bottom lip, pulling his head back just enough to meet Carter's gaze. "So, stop fighting me. Stop making yourself miserable, making yourself guilty. Let it feel good. Let yourself like it. Let yourself *want* it. Want *me*. Because it's going to happen to you either way, sweetheart."

Carter's eyes burn, but he nods. Sir is right. It would be so much easier to just give in. To find every ounce of silver lining in his situation and milk it for all it's worth.

"I'm sorry, sir," Carter whispers, wiping a tear from his cheek. "I – I won't run again. I promise."

"Good." Sir sighs. "Because I really fucking hate hurting you."

Before Carter can wrap his mind around that, sir leans forward to press his lips against Carter's. Carter gasps, caught by surprise, and sir takes advantage of the opportunity by sliding his tongue between Carter's parted lips. He licks his way into Carter's mouth, then carefully pulls his tongue back with a flick to Carter's, almost like he's tagging him. Carter chases, tasting scotch in sir's mouth as he mirrors his movements. Sir smiles into the kiss, their teeth clacking. Then he grabs Carter's head in a tight grip and holds him perfectly still as he takes complete control of the interaction.

Sir doesn't pull away until Carter is breathless.

"I have something for you," the man says quietly, seeming to be unfairly unaffected by the kiss that just spun Carter's whole world. When Carter looks at the hand sir lifts between them, he can't help but smile. Grin even.

His moose.

Carter had left the small stuffed animal in the closet this morning, having been unable to grab it when sir woke him so violently. Part of him had worried that sir got rid of it as an extra punishment. But he didn't. It's still here.

"Go ahead." Sir nudges Carter's hand. "Take it."

Carter takes the moose with his trembling hand, pulling it close to his chest right away. He blinks rapidly so he doesn't start to cry again. "Thank you, sir. I – thank you."

Sir inhales deeply through his nose, his eyes going dark enough for his pupils to blend in. Emotions seem to battle their way through his expression. Rage. Grief. Lust. Something... else. Something Carter can't quite place. Or, maybe, something Carter's too afraid to place.

He realizes what's going on in sir's head when the man's eyes slide closed and he rasps, "I don't want you in that cage tonight." He opens his eyes, a sudden desperation in his gaze. "I fucking *hate* the thought of you in that cage."

Carter nibbles on his lip, looking down at his moose. *Is this a test?* "I... deserve it, sir. I was bad."

"You were." Sir curls a finger beneath Carter's chin, gently lifting until their eyes are locked. "But I think you've learned your lesson. Haven't you sweetheart?"

"I *have*, sir." Carter nods rapidly. "I have. Never again. I'll never run from you again. And I'll try so hard to not break any other rules, sir. Really hard."

Unless he's going fucking crazy, Carter swears he sees relief in sir's expression. "Then, no point in the cage, wouldn't you say?"

"Yes, sir."

"Good." Sir cups Carter's face with his big hands again, looking at Carter like... like Carter doesn't even *know*. Not like a monster, that's for sure. "You'll sleep in my bed tonight. Right beside me. Where you belong. How does that sound?"

Carter doesn't bother to bite his smile back. "So good, sir. Thank you."

"Mmm." Sir runs his thumb along the curve of Carter's mouth before standing up. "Climb up on the bed. Lay on your stomach in the center. I'll be right back."

Carter's stomach swoops, but he obeys without hesitation. Honestly, there's a part of him – a shamefully large part – that would be okay if sir wants him to do this so he can fuck him. It'll hurt his sore hole, and probably the abused skin of his backside, but he's desperate to be touched, desperate for sir to pay attention to him, desperate to be forgiven.

By the time sir returns, Carter has himself hyped up for sex. To be used by sir. Maybe even hurt by him some more.

Instead, sir urges him to prop himself up on his elbows and hands him a water with a straw. He tells Carter to take slow sips before moving toward Carter's ass, beginning to apply a cool gel over his skin in slow strokes. Carter drops his head between his shoulders, humming in pleasure at the heavenly relief on his injured bottom. Sir chuckles, the sound almost... *fond*. It does strange things to Carter's mind. In fact, everything regarding sir seems to be doing that tonight.

"Sir?" Carter gets the courage to ask, praying he's not about to fuck everything up.

"Yes, sweetheart?"

"Are you going to... use me?"

Sir's hand pauses in the center of Carter's left ass cheek, a heavy silence falling around them. Carter squeezes his eyes shut. *Idiot, idiot, idiot.*

"Do you want me to use you?"

"I-" Carter stops himself, unsure of what he wants. He knows one thing at least. "I just want to be better for you, sir. I want you to forgive me."

A soft hum comes from sir. Then his hand returns to smoothing the gel over Carter's hot skin. Carter assumes the subject is dropped. That's why he's surprised when sir gently parts his ass cheeks and touches a wet thumb to Carter's hole. "You're too sore for me to use you tonight, sweetheart. I didn't prep you well enough in the dungeon, and that plug is shit. You're all red back here."

Just days ago, Carter would have felt a deep, burning humiliation at a man talking about his hole like that. It barely even registers now. "I can take it, sir. I can be strong for you."

Sir's sigh is almost wistful. "I have no doubt that you can. But you don't need to. Now hold still. I'm going to put some gel on your pretty hole to make it feel better."

Carter shivers, cheeks burning at the words of... praise? It sounds like praise. Dirty praise, but praise nonetheless. *Having a pretty hole as a pleasure slave is surely a good thing, right?*

The gel feels strange on his hole. Soothing, but also a tiny bit stingy as it starts to dry. When he whimpers, sir hushes him softly, peppering soft kisses to his abused ass cheeks until he's melting into the mattress.

"You're so good for me, sweetheart," sir mumbles as he shifts over Carter's body to kiss the dimples above his ass. "You're so good." He kisses up the curve of Carter's spine. "That's why I was so shocked this morning." He takes the water from Carter, placing it on the table beside the bed. "I was afraid I lost you." He settles his weight against Carter, his erection hot and heavy against Carter's abused ass cheeks. His lips skate along his shoulder blades. First the left. Then the right. "No doing that again, okay, sweetheart?" He kisses the nape of Carter's neck. The side of his throat. "Be a good boy for me." He kisses below Carter's right ear. Behind it. The shell of it. The lobe. "You can do that, can't you, sweetheart? Hmmm?" He kisses Carter's temple, his hips rolling, Carter gasping as he feels precum spread across his burning skin. "Can you be my good boy?"

"Yes," Carter gasps, over and over, moaning and trembling beneath him. "Yes, yes, yes. Sir, sir, please. *Please.*"

"Please?" sir rasps, his voice hoarse for some reason.

"Let me make you feel good. Please. Please sir, can I make you feel good?"

Sir shudders above him. Then, "No. No, you've – you've done enough. You took your punishment so well for me, sweetheart. You don't have to do anything else."

"No," Carter whines, desperation tightening his throat. "Sir, *please.*"

"Sweetheart..."

"You – you ignored me all day. I just want – please. Please touch me. Please, sir. Please let me be with you."

With a shaky exhale, sir tucks his head in the dip between Carter's throat and shoulder. His lips press against the skin there before he jerks away like Carter has burned him. Sir moans, the sound low and frustrated. Then he's pressing back against Carter, grinding with a sudden urgency. "Okay. Fuck. Okay, you can do that, sweetheart. Fuck, of course you can be with me."

Sir nudges Carter's legs apart until his cock is sliding through the apex of his thighs. The gel he had collected from rubbing himself on Carter's ass is enough to make sir slick as he begins to thrust between his legs. Carter can't help the soft sigh that falls from his lips as he relaxes into the mattress in relief. Each movement stings, but it's the kind of sting like before in sir's office, the sting that was welcome because it was a reminder of sir. He's hurting for sir. He's making sir feel good. He's being touched and kissed and used. Sir *needs* him.

"Fuck. I-" sir groans, his teeth scraping over Carter's shoulder. "I can't believe how good you are."

"*Sir.*"

"Shhh. That's it, sweetheart. That's my good boy." He glides his tongue over the places where he just bit Carter moments before, soothing the pain. "Is this what you wanted from me? What you needed? For sir to use you?"

"Yes!" Carter feels tears falling down his cheeks. He can't stop smiling. "Yes. Yes, sir. Thank you, sir."

"Fuck. Fucking hell." Sir hooks his arm around Carter's waist, tugging him up to his hands and knees. He puts a hand to Carter's mouth and orders, "Make this wet."

Wanting to keep being sir's good boy, he hurries to slobber all over the man's palm and fingers, even sucking on them greedily when sir presses them into his mouth. Sir groans before pulling his hand away.

Carter jerks in surprise when he feels the hand wrap around his hard cock that he had been trying his best to ignore. He gasps, his heart racing. "*Sir!*"

"Hush. Let me make you feel good." Sir tightens his hold on Carter's cock. "We're practicing, sweetheart."

"P-practicing, sir?"

"You obeying me. Your pleasure is mine. Remember?"

"Yes, sir!"

"So, if I want to make you feel good, you're going to fucking feel good, and you're not going to run away from me after. Understood?"

Carter nods rapidly, warmth pooling in his lower stomach. "Yes. Yes, sir. Yes!"

"Good boy. Now move for me." Sir wraps a hand around Carter's hip and guides him so he's rocking back and forth, fucking into sir's hand before stroking sir's cock between his thighs. He sets Carter up with a nice, even pace before letting him move on his own, planting a hand on the mattress to steady himself while his other hand continues to stroke and squeeze Carter's cock. Every movement makes Carter's ass burn and his sore muscles ache. The pain pools in his gut, fuel to the fire of his arousal.

"Oh god, sir. *Sir.*"

"It feels good, doesn't it, sweetheart?"

"So good, sir," Carter cries. "So good. So good."

"Are you going to come for me?"

Carter moves faster, starting to lose his rhythm. Remembering last night, he asks, "C-can I, sir? Oh, please. Please, can I?"

"Not yet." Sir kisses the curve of his shoulder before trailing more up his neck. He nibbles on Carter's earlobe. "Tell me how good it feels again."

"Sir, so good. So, so good."

"You want it? You like being used by me?"

"Sir," he whispers, hanging his head between his shoulders. "Yes, sir... wanna – wanna make you happy, sir. Wanna be your good boy."

The man behind him moans, his movements stuttering as he grips Carter's hip again and holds him steady. It hurts when his thrusts get harsh enough to slap against Carter's sore ass cheeks. He sobs, squirming and trembling, but he's still achingly hard and desperate for release. It's so good. So, so good.

It should be awful. It should feel like rape. But – but – it just – and Carter can't – and - "Oh god, sir!" Carter whimpers. "*Please.*"

"Fuck." Sir grunts, his hips snapping forward once, twice, then, "I'm gonna come. Fuck. Come with me, sweetheart. Show me how good you feel."

Carter sobs a loud, "Sir!" before his back arches and his cock spills. He can barely feel sir's hot, sticky cum coating the insides of his thighs as his mind soars up and away. He can barely hear sir's soft, whispered praise. But he knows it's all there, distantly, in the back of his mind, and it makes Carter feel... *something.*

Something he's not going to run away from this time.

Chapter Twelve

Within the first 60 seconds of interacting with Carter, it becomes clear to Nathan that the boy didn't sleep well. In fact, it seems he may not have slept at all. It's unlike him. Since they finally got on the same page the other night, Carter's been the perfect slave. He's quiet and obedient, no longer hesitating, no longer crying. They haven't had sex since then, though Carter gave him a fantastic blowjob when Nathan had accidentally gotten hard while he was warming Nathan's cock after dinner. A blowjob that Carter had – after making eye contact and arching an eyebrow in question – initiated himself. They've even found a rhythm together when alone at night, talking about nothing important with a particular ease as they take baths or lay side by side in bed.

Carter not sleeping is different.

Carter not sleeping isn't good.

"Sweetheart?" Nathan says for a second time, snapping his fingers in front of the boy's face.

Carter blinks rapidly, his head lolling on his neck. "Yes, sir?"

"I told you to go use the bathroom."

"Oh." Carter rubs the back of his fist against his right eye, nodding. "M'kay... be right back, sir."

Instead of walking like he usually does, Carter just crawls into the bathroom. His movements are slow, his poor knees slapping against the floor clumsily. Usually he hurries, and perhaps he is, but it still takes him a long time to return to the bedroom. Nathan is almost fully dressed by the time Carter is settled in front of him.

"Want help, sir?" he slurs, blinking sleepily up at Nathan.

"Come here." Nathan offers his hand, smiling when Carter takes it. He helps the boy stand up, wanting to give his knees a break. Carter is weak on his legs, but he seems strong enough for Nathan to let go. There's a slight waver to his stance, probably from exhaustion. "Button my shirt."

Nodding, Carter lazily lifts his arms and begins to work on Nathan's shirt. He gets halfway through before an adorable frown pulls at his lips. With a little huff, Carter undoes the buttons and restarts, having been off by one. Nathan pretends not to notice because he doesn't want to have to scold him at all.

When the shirt is finally buttoned properly, Carter's hands linger at Nathan's collar. "Do you need a tie, sir?"

Nathan smiles. "Sure. Socks too. Why don't you pick them out for me from my closet?"

This makes Carter smile. He seems to like helping, something Nathan makes sure to keep in mind.

Nathan gets his belt and watch on while Carter is gone, then lets the boy wrap a navy-blue tie around his neck. When Carter ducks down to put his socks on, Nathan tweaks the tie to fix the absolutely awful knot, smiling to himself. Then he shrugs his suit jacket on while Carter helps him into his shoes. He tries to be as quick as possible when prepping Carter for his plug, not wanting the boy to fall asleep on the damn floor while Nathan works him open. Carter is still awake when the plug settles inside him, but just barely.

Their trip from the bedroom to the dining area is twice as long as usual. Nathan pretends it's his fault, scrolling through his phone as if he's distracted reading something. People dart out of his way and don't question the slow pace. He's the most important person in the house. It makes perfect sense for him to be too busy to look up during transit.

When they sit down, Nathan carefully maneuvers Carter to his usual spot on the floor between his legs. He wishes no one was around so he could put a cushion down for him. Maybe he'll do it in his office whenever they're alone today. That's not too soft. Surely men like him do that for their slaves sometimes.

"What would you like this morning, sir?" a house slave asks.

"A little bit of everything today. Two waters, one with a straw, and a coffee."

The slave hurries off, Nathan's focus returning to Carter. He gently drags his knuckles along Carter's right cheek. There are so many things he wants to say to the boy. So many things he wants to do with him.

But everyone at the table is getting their cock warmed or sucked, and Nathan should be doing the same. He pulls himself from his pants and guides Carter's head to his lap. The boy's eyes are barely open, but he parts his lips and accepts the soft cock that Nathan gently nudges into his mouth. Nathan watches him pathetically try to keep his head up on his neck before cupping the back of it and pressing him down so he's resting on Nathan's thigh. The boy sighs in content, eyes blinking slowly a few times before they finally fall shut for good.

The food is brought out just seconds later. It breaks Nathan's heart to see the way Carter perks up at the smell, eyes flying open. He starts to move closer to Nathan as if he wants to climb up and eat, deflating right away when he remembers his place. Nathan's not sure what the issue is. He's been fed properly the past few days, not a meal skipped. He takes note of the reaction to be dealt with later, deciding to feed the boy now instead of making him wait like other slaves.

Slipping his thumb into Carter's mouth, Nathan tugs his bottom lip down and lets his cock fall out. He casually takes a small piece of scrambled egg between his fingers, making sure he doesn't look suspicious. Hopefully he won't get caught, but if one of his men does happen to see that he's sharing his actual breakfast with his slave, Nathan needs to look bored with it. Like he has too much to do today to deal with a second meal after this.

Carter stares up at him with wide eyes when the egg is placed on his tongue. He waits for Nathan to give him an encouraging nod before closing his mouth and carefully chewing it. Nathan takes the chance to have his own bite. They go back and forth for a while with the eggs before Nathan switches to his bacon. Carter's eyes light up bright as the flavor hits his tongue. He makes a small humming sound and grins up at Nathan, reminding him of a happy puppy.

Nathan doesn't take a single bite of bacon, letting Carter have it all. He lets Carter have all of the strawberries too. Though, he'll admit that's partly because he really enjoys watching Carter suck his fingers clean.

In between bites, Nathan makes sure to give his boy some water, angling the bendy straw so Carter barely has to lift his head from Nathan's thigh to drink. The more he eats, the sleepier he gets. By the time they finish, he's stopped bothering opening his eyes at all, just parting his lips whenever food or a straw is pressed to them.

He's asleep by the time Nathan's ready to leave for his office. Pretending to be annoyed for the benefit of his men, Nathan shoves his chair back and puts Carter over his shoulder before standing up. People laugh when the sleepy boy jolts awake with a cry. Jason slaps his barely-healed ass and winks at Nathan. "Looks like you tired him out last night, boss."

Mica gives Carter a patronizing pat and says, "Don't worry, boy. Your master'll wake you up real good."

Carter winds up clinging to Nathan by the end of the walk down the hall, his fingers holding the back of his suit jacket in a death grip. His poor, tired body is shaking non-stop. He's clearly freaked out by the hits and comments. Nathan doesn't blame him.

When they get to his office, Nathan sits Carter on the center of his desk where there are no papers or files and kisses his forehead. "You're not in trouble, sweetheart. My men don't decide when you're in trouble."

The boy nods, relaxing a little. He rubs at his eyes like a sleepy toddler and yawns.

"Did you not sleep last night?" When Carter cowers, Nathan hurries to remind him, "You're not in trouble. I just want to know."

"I – I had a really bad dream," Carter says quietly, his hands squeezing each other where they rest in his lap. "I woke up feeling sick, and then I couldn't really fall back asleep after."

"Mmm." Nathan studies Carter, wanting so badly to ask about the dream. It was obviously upsetting, though, and if he wants the boy to rest now it won't help to bring it up. Instead, he kisses his forehead and says, "I'm sorry to hear that, sweetheart. Next time you can wake me up, okay? Sir wants to take care of you when things like that happen."

Carter eyes him, skeptical, but he nods.

Nathan takes his suit jacket off, loosens his tie, and rolls his sleeves. He places the jacket beside Carter on the desk and takes a seat on his large leather desk chair. Watching Carter watch him, Nathan unbuckles his belt and very slowly pulls it from the loops of his pants. Carter licks his lips, looking at him with heavy-lidded eyes.

"Sir?" he slurs in slight confusion.

There's no fear, though.

Nathan loves that there's no fear.

"You're going to keep my cock warm with your ass today." Nathan leans forward, taking a bottle of lube out of the top right drawer on his desk. He stands, placing his hands on either side of his boy, and ducks his head to kiss him. Once he feels Carter relax, Nathan pulls away and smiles. "Lay back for me, sweetheart."

Yawning, Carter slowly lowers himself until he's lying on his back, his feet flat on the desk. Nathan spreads the boy's legs and brings each foot to rest on the arms of his chair, bracketing himself with his face just inches from Carter's ass. Mindful of Carter's injuries, Nathan guides him until his ass cheeks are right on the edge of the desk.

"Sir?" Carter asks again, sounding more awake but also more confused this time.

"I'm just going to prepare your pretty hole," Nathan explains as he gently slides the plug out of his ass. "We want you to be comfortable, right, sweetheart?"

Carter only hesitates for a second, which is a testament to how well their practicing has been going regarding Carter accepting good things when Nathan gives them to him. "Yes, sir."

"That's right. Good boy." Nathan starts trailing kisses down the inside of Carter's leg, traveling from his knee to the crease right beside his groin. He makes sure to ghost his breath over Carter's half-hard cock before starting at the opposite crease and working back down toward the other knee. The boy starts to shiver, his teeth clacking a little. Nathan pulls back, heart pounding. "You okay, sweetheart?"

Carter nods, giving him a dopey grin. "'M great, sir."

Relieved, Nathan nuzzles the inside of Carter's right knee and pours lube on his fingers. He takes his time rubbing slow, gentle circles on his boy's hole until he has Carter gyrating his hips in a silent plea for more.

"What?" Nathan smirks. "Does someone want to be filled?"

Face bright red, Carter peeks at Nathan through his lashes and nods shyly. He bites his bottom lip and lifts his hips as if to ask. Nathan doesn't mess with him, just sliding two fingers into his hole. He flicks his gaze up to check in on Carter, grinning to himself when he sees the boy sprawled out on his back, arms lazily above his head, eyes closed, pretty pink mouth open in a gasp. Nathan wants to slam straight into him and fuck him until he's sobbing with pleasure.

Instead, he takes his time. He slowly works the boy open, using a generous amount of lube, making sure he's so stretched that his cock will barely bother him. Carter's half-asleep and lust drunk by the time Nathan guides him off the desk and into his lap. He presses a kiss to the boy's temple while lining his cock with his hole and pressing Carter down on it. Carter moans, his head falling forward to rest on Nathan's shoulder.

"Feel good, sweetheart?"

Carter mumbles something unintelligible, nodding his head. Nathan smiles. He presses more kisses to the side of Carter's face before settling back in his chair. Once he's in a comfortable position, he takes his suit jacket and drapes it over the boy's shoulder as a make-shift blanket. This is why Nathan did this, instead of putting the boy on the floor. He wants Carter to rest comfortably. The only way that'll be acceptable for people to witness is if Nathan is using him as a warmer like this. Not that Nathan is exactly complaining. He's becoming quite a fan of having Carter pressed close to him.

"Now you just relax and warm sir's cock, okay?"

"Mmm, yessir."

"Go ahead and sleep, sweet boy. Get some rest."

With a happy little sigh, Carter deflates against Nathan, his head lolling until it's perfectly nestled in the crook of Nathan's neck.

He's asleep within seconds.

Carter spends his day drifting in and out of consciousness, caught up in the swirl of blissful moments when he's awake, and dreaming peacefully when he's asleep. He's sometimes shifted a little to the left or the right. Sir spends time with his hands beneath the suit jacket covering him, just rubbing soothing circles against his skin. There's no way he can be doing anything productive during these times, but Carter doesn't dare point that out. Sir has him use a bathroom at some point before placing him on the edge of his desk to share bites of a cheesy chicken quesadilla. He even gets a few sips of sir's soda, in between all the water sir forces him to drink. After that, he was pulled back onto sir's cock, suit jacket covering him again, so he could take another nice little nap.

One of the times he wakes up in sir's lap, Carter hears him on the phone. His chest rumbles against Carter's as he speaks in a low, smooth voice to whoever is on the other end of the call. Carter tries to keep still and quiet. He doesn't want sir to know he's awake.

"I see your point, of course, but I disagree. He has far too much information for a normal hit."

There's a pause as sir listens to the other person. He's getting annoyed. Frustrated. Carter doesn't know how he already knows that, but he does. Sir isn't happy with this phone call.

"No, I want him delivered to me alive," sir says casually, as if he's not discussing someone's life. "I'll kill him when I'm finished with him."

Carter's body shudders without his permission. He feels sir tense against him and holds his breath, waiting to be punished for eavesdropping.

Sir gently moves Carter's upper body so they can look each other in the eye while Carter stays in his lap. Carter bites down on his bottom lip to keep from apologizing. He doubts sir wants him to interrupt his phone call. That'll just make things worse.

Maintaining eye contact with Carter, sir continues his conversation. "That'll be fine. Payment will be wired upon his delivery."

Taking Carter by surprise, sir reaches out and touches his soft cock. Carter swallows a gasp, eyes wide, hips bucking. The smirk sir gives him is full of dirty promises. That alone has Carter's cock growing thick and heavy.

"Yes, I spoke with him briefly yesterday regarding that." Sir wraps his long fingers around Carter's cock. He just holds it. Nothing else. It's enough to have Carter panting softly. "Have the drugs been transported yet?"

Sir rubs his thumb over Carter's slit.

"He's the perfect choice." Sir's fingers whisper their way down Carter's cock until he can cup Carter's sack in his hand. "I couldn't agree more."

Sir rolls one of Carter's balls gently between his fingers.

"Absolutely. We'll need to track that, of course."

Sir rolls the other ball.

"Hanson."

Sir tucks his fingers beneath Carter's sack and presses against his taint. Carter's back bows but he somehow, miraculously, doesn't make any sound. He can taste the blood on his bottom lip from how hard he's biting it, but that's totally worth it. The feeling of sir's hard cock pressing into him from inside while sir's controlling fingers press into him from the outside is out of this world. He's strung out on it.

Sir's fingers make their way back up Carter's cock, his thumb once again rubbing at his slit. Carter's leaking now. He feels his cheeks burn when he realizes it. Then his whole body is burning, both in shame and arousal, when sir's thumb pushes into his mouth. All sir has to do is lift one eyebrow, a silent order, and Carter is sucking on the digit covered in his own precum.

"Good," sir says in a low, gravelly voice. His eyes are boring into Carter's. He looks very pleased. Carter isn't sure if the one word was meant for him or not, but he takes it anyway. He's a sucker for praise.

Sir pulls his hand back from Carter's mouth before putting a finger to his own lips. He slowly stands, tipping Carter backwards so he's laid out over the desk. The cool, solid wood against his overheated skin makes Carter shiver. There's a piece of paper crinkling beneath his left ass cheek, and Carter can't help but let himself take a moment to think about that. To think about the fact that sir is willing to ruin what could be an important paper, just so he could have Carter like this.

It sends Carter into a mini power trip.

Straightening his posture, sir holds his phone to his ear and stares down at Carter where he lies impaled on sir's cock, Carter's erection bobbing in the air, precum dripping onto his belly. Sir licks his lips, smirking when the action makes Carter's hole clench.

Putting his finger to his lips one more time, sir places his cell phone down on the desk beside Carter's bare hip and puts it on speakerphone. Carter's eyes flick down to it. The man is still talking. Something about a quota.

His attention is once again back on sir almost immediately. He can't help it. There's something about the man when he's like this that's addicting. It's dangerous. Wrong.

Carter can't fight it.

Sir collects Carter's hands, bringing them into the space between their bodies. He lets go, Carter's hands dangling willingly in the air, wrists pressed together, palms open like an offering. The end of his leash is wrapped around them once, twice, then knotted off. Sir guides his arms back down to the desk so they're pointing above Carter's head.

"I'm not sure," sir says with a sexy smirk. "Do you have the intel to back that?"

"I have-"

Carter stops listening again, all of his focus on the way sir's fingers deftly work his tie free. The look sir gives him is predatory as he tugs the fabric from his neck.

Sir skims his fingers along Carter's leaking slit to collect more precum. He leans forward, raising an eyebrow in expectation. It's all the prompting Carter needs to part his lips. There's no more shame left in him, Carter sucking greedily on sir's fingers, overwhelmed by how dirty he is in the moment. Sir pulls his fingers out too soon, smearing Carter's lips with his own spit. He grins like a cat that just caught the mouse.

Then, as he says matter-of-factly, "He can die, then. I have no use for him," sir shoves the bunched-up fabric of his tie into Carter's mouth.

Carter startles, but settles quickly under sir's gentle hand. It had just caught him by surprise. It's not like the gag means much of anything. Sir could fuck him hard on this desk until Carter screams at the top of his lungs for someone to help him. Nothing would happen. No one would come. Sir didn't take any ability away from Carter by gagging him. Not really. Sir is simply being polite to whoever is on the phone.

Sir leans forward and presses a kiss to Carter's earlobe. Then he whispers, "Good boy. Sir is going to fuck you now. Feel free to come."

And without any extra warning, without even a second to process the words, sir is putting his phone to his ear again and Carter is being fucked as promised. It's fast and hard, but sir is pinning him down with a hand on his throat so he can't go anywhere. Not an inch. He's just forced to take it, sir's cock relentless.

"Absolutely not," sir says in a surprisingly steady voice. "I'd much rather you handle that particular endeavor."

Sir shifts, Carter's leg bumping up to a different angle. His next thrust hits right on that sweet spot only sir has ever been able to find. It makes Carter nearly giddy with pleasure, his hips jerking to get more of sir. Sir digs his fingers into Carter's throat, a warning look on his face as he tells the person on the phone, "I really appreciate all of this. I owe you."

Carter can feel bruises blooming where sir is holding him. The pain just heightens the pleasure, pushing Carter higher and higher until he's dizzy with it all.

"Absolutely," he hears sir say from far away. "Forward his info to Benny."

Sir reaches between them and grips Carter's cock. There's no need to squeeze or stroke. Just the feel of sir's fingers, and Carter's orgasm is slamming into him. He bites down on the tie so hard he worries he may rip it.

"I'll see you then."

Sir ends the call. Then his phone is being tossed to the side, both of his hands grabbing Carter so he can manhandle him closer. Sir puts one hand on Carter's hip, keeping the other on his throat, and continues fucking into him like nothing happened. Carter is helpless. All he's able to manage is to lie there, tiny whimpers and sated sighs muffled by the expensive silk between his lips.

"So fucking good for me," sir growls, pounding into Carter hard enough to make his breath catch. "You should see yourself, sweetheart. Fuck. You're beautiful like this. You look fucking *wrecked*."

Sir's fingernails scrape along Carter's thighs as he stills inside him, spilling his load. He stares at Carter with heavy-lidded eyes, still coming as he pants, "I made you look like this."

Carter nods, his eyes wet with something very far away from pain or sadness. The moment sir tugs the ruined tie out of his mouth, Carter is admitting things he shouldn't. "Only one, sir. Only person to ever make me feel like this."

The look sir gives him is caught between predatory and loving, if such a thing exists. Before Carter can process, sir is sitting back in his chair, taking Carter with him. He drags Carter as close as he possibly can, one hand gripping Carter's hair and the other cradling his cheek as he brings him in for a scalding kiss. Carter swears he feels the thing in his toes.

When sir eventually pulls back, his smile is soft. Fond.

"Want to know a secret, sweetheart?" Carter barely nods, not wanting to jostle sir's hands from where they remain on his head. "You're the only person to ever make me feel like this too."

Chapter Thirteen

Something shifts in Carter after Nathan's confession, something Nathan should be nervous about, but can't get himself to be. It's a subtle shift. Less fear, more trust. Less panic, more calm. Less weight on his shoulders, more easy breaths. Nathan just hopes like hell no one can sense it when they look at him.

Nathan puts Carter in his usual place for dinner, having him keep his cock warm like the rest of the slaves. The men are nearly all at the table already, house slaves beginning to bring the meal in.

"Hey boss, you hear about Miller?" Jason asks from his spot to Nathan's left, 2 chairs down.

"Is there recent news on Miller?" Nathan asks.

"He's attending the event this weekend."

Nathan internally rolls his eyes while keeping his outward expression impassive. As *if he wouldn't know that.* "Yes, he is."

"Are we planning something?"

"Not as of now." Nathan crooks a finger at the closest house slave, saying he wants his usual night drink. He looks down at Carter next, not bothering to meet Jason's eye. "All of you will be informed if that changes."

Nathan raises his gaze, scanning the entire table now as he declares in a cold, dangerous voice, "No one will provoke or initiate any sort of action unless specifically told, understood?"

The men nod vigorously, some giving him verbal confirmation.

Thankfully, Benny shows up before Nathan has to deal with the idiots any longer. He slides into his seat directly to the right of Nathan's and passes Nathan a small slip of paper without looking at him. Nathan brings the paper to his lap, tilting it away from Carter's view, and reads it.

Check-in by 2200.

Nathan squeezes the paper in his hand and stuffs it into his pocket, giving Benny a slight nod. He skipped his check-in last night with Maison, wanting to avoid the topic of a meeting that's happening tomorrow, and he knows Maison's probably pissed. It's not the first check-in he's missed, it's not until 3 in a row are missed that anyone panics, but it's different now that Carter's in the picture. Funny thing is, Carter's the whole reason Nathan hadn't wanted to check-in.

Todd Henley is coming for a visit tomorrow.

Just the thought of it makes Nathan sick to his stomach.

Carter's hand cups the back of Nathan's calf, giving it a gentle squeeze. Nathan looks down at him in question, watching as the boy gives him a comforting smile around his soft cock, as if he knows the paper bothered Nathan and he wants to make it better. It should be concerning. Nathan should shut that shit down. It's not good for the boy to be able to read him so well, and it's certainly not okay for the boy to act like they're lovers or some shit like that.

Yet, that little smile makes Nathan's chest feel lighter, air filling his lungs for the first time in far too long, and Nathan can't get himself to stop that. With everything he's dealing with, surely he can give himself this one thing, right? A guilty pleasure of sorts. Carter feeling safe, Carter being *happy*, will be Nathan's guilty pleasure.

As long as he keeps it in check, of course.

After finishing his dinner and feeding Carter the slave's meal, sir brings Carter to the bedroom. Despite his naps, Carter is still wrung out and exhausted. He can't help but perk up when they get close to the bed, deflating when sir walks him right past it.

Sir chuckles. "Thought you were going to bed, sweetheart?"

"Yes, sir." Carter looks at sir sheepishly. "Sorry, sir."

"Don't be sorry. You'll be able to sleep soon." Sir pauses, turning to face him. He cups Carter's face in his big hands, giving Carter a soft smile as his thumbs stroke along his cheekbones. "I'd just like to clean you up first."

Carter blushes as he takes stock of his body, realizing cum is dried on his stomach, he's sticky between his ass cheeks, and sir's cum has dripped down his thighs from around his plug. If sir notices his sudden shyness, he doesn't point it out. He just guides Carter into the bathroom, instructs him to use the toilet, and begins running a bath. Carter can smell the oils he puts in, humming in appreciation. They're something else today, not the same as before, but they smell just as divine.

When they get in the tub, sir pulls Carter close right away, pasting Carter's back to his chest, their legs and arms tangling. It feels strangely intimate.

It feels *nice*.

"Tell me something about yourself," sir requests, just like he had last time when they had argued about Carter being lucky despite his circumstances.

Carter echoes the past as well, asking, "Like what, sir?"

"Mmm." Sir runs the tip of his nose along the shell of Carter's ear before nuzzling the sensitive spot behind it. "Something happy."

"*Happy*." Carter frowns at sir's right hand, which is drawing slow, steady circles against Carter's forearm. Carter isn't sure if he remembers *happy*. It feels like it's been a lifetime since *happy*.

"A memory, perhaps," sir prompts. "A favorite book. A trip you took. A football game you attended. Something that made you happy."

Carter can't help but sink in on himself a bit. *Can't sir tell how much it hurts to talk about those things? To think about his old life at all?* There are already tears in Carter's eyes as he says the first thing to come to mind. "I like fireworks."

"Oh?"

"A lot." Carter swallows, hoping sir can't hear the way his voice is trembling. "My mom – I grew up with a single mom, my dad died when I was young – she loved fireworks. She always got so excited for the 4th of July. We'd go to the big tent sales and splurge, and then we'd throw a huge party on the 3rd for everyone to come hangout. We'd cook and play yard games. We'd drink. Listen to music. When it got dark enough, we'd do the fireworks."

Sir stays quiet for a moment or two longer than Carter would like before asking, "Is it the fireworks you love or that time together with your mom?"

"Both, I guess." Carter shrugs. "I mean, when she died, we still kept doing it. Maison..." Carter trails off, shaking his head slightly.

"*Maison...*" sir prompts, his tone far too casual.

Swallowing hard, Carter forces the lump in his throat down to his belly, letting it sit there instead so sir can't hear the pain in his voice. "Maison always tries - *tried* - to make it home for the party. It wasn't really the same, though. Even when he did manage to sneak away, the party was at my mom's best friend's house instead- they're who took me in and finished raising me. They were like sisters. We've called her auntie ever since I can remember. But it was different. The people. The music. The games. The food, even. But the fireworks were never different. They were constant. I guess... I don't know. I guess I liked that."

Carter squeezes his eyes shut when sir says nothing. "That's stupid. I'm-"

"Hush, now. That's not stupid." Sir presses a kiss to his temple, making Carter shiver. "I was just processing the information."

Carter wants to ask if he's processing the information to see if he can use any of it against Maison, but he's too afraid of the punishment it'd probably earn him. He remains silent instead.

"How old were you when your mom died?"

That wasn't what Carter was expecting, the question catching him off guard. "14."

"And Maison was already in the military?"

"Yes, sir." Carter presses harder against sir, needing comfort even if it's from the man hurting him. Sir tightens his hold and starts stroking Carter's arm again. Carter hadn't realized he had stopped. He hadn't realized how much he had missed it, either. "Maison said he'd get out for me, but he had just gotten this big promotion, and I could tell he didn't want to do it. He wanted to stay in and follow his dream. I couldn't be the one to hold him back from that, you know?"

"Mmm." Sir nuzzles the side of Carter's throat. "But the family you stayed with – they were good to you?"

Carter nods. "Very. Aunt Lisa couldn't get pregnant, and they never adopted for some reason, I don't know, maybe because they didn't have a lot of money... but yeah. They were happy to have me."

Sudden panic seizes Carter's chest. He tries to sit up, but sir fights him, sending water sloshing over the sides of the tub. When he pulls again, sir lets him go, looking at him in confusion when Carter turns to face him.

"Don't hurt them," Carter begs, hating the way his voice gives out in desperation. "P-please, sir. Do whatever you want to me, but don't hurt them. Please don't hurt them. They're – they're good people, and they're all Maison has left and-"

Carter stops himself, hanging his head. He laughs dryly under his breath.

"-and I can't believe I just told you that. The only family Maison has left, and I just fucking handed them to you." Carter looks at sir incredulously, another laugh puffing from him. He's nearing hysterics, though he's not sure if it'll be hysterical laughter or sobs at this point. "You hate Maison. Of course you're going to go after his family that he has left. You're – fuck. I – I can't believe I'm such a fucking *idiot*."

Something seems to crack in sir, emotions pouring into his eyes that Carter has never seen in him before. He seals it quickly, but not fast enough. Carter saw. There's a human somewhere inside the monster.

Carter has no fucking idea what to do with that.

"Sweetheart, breathe." Sir takes Carter's face in his big hands, the grip tight enough to comfort and ground him without causing pain. "From the sounds of things, hurting them would hurt you more than it would Maison. I'm uninterested in hurting you in that way."

In that way. Such a lovely reminder that this man *is* interested in hurting him, he's just picky about his methods.

Carter can't believe this is his life now. He can't believe he's found himself in this position. He truly can't. Maybe if he just understood better...

"Sir?"

"Yes?"

"Can I ask a question about... Maison?"

Sir inhales deeply before blowing it out nice and slow. It's a calming technique. Carter hates that he made sir need one of those. He doesn't like upsetting sir. Mostly because upsetting sir makes his life harder and more miserable, but also because... well... it's nice, in a way, to be sir's good boy. To *please* him.

"Shouldn't I be the one asking you about your brother?" sir finally asks in dry amusement.

"I know stupid stuff. You know the big stuff."

"Like?"

Carter shrugs.

"Like, I know he puts ketchup on his scrambled eggs and he's never been able to stand the color orange for some reason. You know what he does. Who he really is." Carter stares down at the bubbles that are slowly dissolving before him. "You know why I'm here."

"I suppose you have a point there. Is that what your question is? Who he really is? What he does? Why you're here?"

"They're all my question, yeah."

"I'll answer one."

Carter supposes that's fair. *But what one?*

"Who is he really, sir?" Carter decides to ask. "Because he's clearly not some cookie cutter soldier, right? I mean, those guys, they don't get caught up in things like..."

"Like...?"

"This," Carter whispers, his voice carrying a slight tremble. "Things like *this.*"

Sir gathers some bubbles in his hands and begins to drag his fingers along Carter's chest and shoulders, covering him with suds. "Your brother works for an elite unit that your government will never even admit exists. To us, until recently, he was Mathew Davis from Hershey, Pennsylvania. Grew up in the foster system. No family. No collateral. No attachments. A ghost."

"But you found out the truth...?" Carter is fishing, pushing his boundaries on the question, but he can't help it.

Sir indulges him. "He made a mistake. He visited baby brother, not covering his tracks like he must have whenever he came to see you before. It didn't take long at all after that. We traced you and found some pictures of your brother Maison who looked slightly younger than our own Mathew Davis. When we called him and told him we knew, he tried to deny it. The moment your name was mentioned, he flew off the rails. That's how we knew for sure."

Carter closes his eyes. "I was hurt."

"What?"

"The reason he came to see me. The reason he blew his cover. They found his emergency number on a slip of paper in my wallet."

"How did you get hurt?"

Carter shrugs. "It doesn't matter."

"It does to me," sir says in a slightly terrifying voice. "This never showed in your report."

Trying hard not to think about how sir has a 'report' on him, Carter says, "Some guy tried to – well, he–" Carter closes his eyes, suddenly able to feel the gritty cement of the alleyway beneath his cheek and taste vodka and blood on his tongue and hear the grunted insults from the man wrestling with him in a demand to submit. *How is it possible that it's so hard to think about when it was nothing compared to his life now? Is it harder because that happened to the Carter from* before, *instead of this version of Carter?*

"He...?" sir prompts.

"I was outside of a club – a gay club – and he – this guy – he... grabbed me. Tried to... ya know." Carter stares down at the bubbles, his eyes burning. He won't cry. He's tired of fucking crying. "He tried to rape me, or whatever. In an alley near the club."

Sir's voice is startlingly dark and calm as he asks, "Did he succeed?"

"In raping me?"

"Yes," sir growls, his grip suddenly bruise-worthy where he holds Carter.

"No. He didn't." Carter runs a fingertip along the surface of the water. "I fought him. He beat the shit out of me, but he must have realized too much time had passed by the time he had me under control, or maybe he just didn't want to risk it, or he sobered up, or I don't know. Whatever. It doesn't really matter. There were no signs of sexual assault at the hospital."

"You don't remember all of it?"

Carter shakes his head. "No. He knocked me out. I never would have called Maison, even if I had been... *raped.*" Carter's tongue twists at the end of his sentence, finding *rape* such an inadequate word for what it really is.

Then again, there really is no word that could possibly encompass what the act itself does to a person.

"I knew that number was for life-or-death emergencies. But I woke up in the hospital, and they had already called him." Carter shakes his head. "I shouldn't have kept it in my wallet."

Sir sits with the information for a long time.

Feeling uneasy, Carter adds, "He begged me to come stay with him for a while. He threatened to drag me with him, but I told him it was fine. There was no way that bastard was going to come after me again, and I still had finals to take. I told him I'd be more careful. No more staying out late and drinking. No more shortcuts through alleys."

It's not until that moment, when the words are dissipating in the muggy air around them, that Carter realizes it.

His eyes fall closed, his heart sinking. "That's how you found me, isn't it?"

The tension that ripples through sir's body is answer enough. "I'm not who found you, Scott Quinton did. But yes, he used that initial call as his starter point."

"Guess I can't be mad at Maison after all."

Sir dips his hands in the water, cupping the warm liquid in his palms. He raises them over Carter's chest and gently pours until the bubbles on Carter's skin are washed away. "It wasn't your fault, sweetheart."

"Yes, it was."

"With the resources your brother has at his disposal, he could have forced you against your will to leave campus. He knew he had been compromised with that phone call. There's no way he didn't know. He took a calculated risk and let you stay where you were. You didn't get to take a calculated risk, because you weren't given the information to calculate. That's not on you."

Carter stares down at the water. With the bubbles fading, he can see their legs wound together beneath the surface. He can see his soft cock. His bruised knees.

"I'm glad the man didn't rape you," sir says softly.

A sudden flash of anger pushes Carter to snap, "Why? Because you wouldn't have been able to take my virginity in front of a cheering crowd otherwise?"

Sir's fingers dig into Carter's skin for just a second before relaxing. He clears his throat twice. When he speaks, his voice is husky and low. "You were a virgin? Before I – before the auction, you were a virgin?"

Suddenly feeling vulnerable and exposed, Carter shrugs. Then he nods.

"Christ," sir rasps, the words so soft Carter's not entirely sure if he didn't imagine them entirely.

Carter gasps when sir turns him without warning, easily manhandling Carter until he's straddling sir's lap. Carter tries to hold completely still, waiting for the pain to come. He pissed sir off. *Of course* he did. He didn't address him properly. He wasn't respectful. He snapped at him. Carter deserves to be punished.

Except... sir doesn't hurt him. He doesn't yell at him. He doesn't even glare at him. No, all sir does is lift Carter's chin with his fingers, forcing Carter to look into his warm brown eyes. "I'm sorry this happened to you. I'm sorry that I happened to you. None of this was fair. It wasn't right. I am so sorry, sweetheart."

"Then why?" Carter chokes, desperate to understand. "If you feel that way, then why would you do it? Why buy me? Rape me? Keep me?"

"Because if not me, someone else would." Sir strokes Carter's cheek, almost looking... *sad.*

In case Carter was still doubting himself, he's sure now. He's absolutely going crazy.

"You could let me go," Carter suggests, knowing it's no use.

Sir smiles, chuckling softly. It's not a mean response. It's not even angry. It's just a fact. A sad acceptance. Defeat. "As much as I'm willing to admit here, with you, in private, that this situation sucks for you and I wish your life could be different, I would never risk my status in this world for you. I'm not a good man, sweetheart. You're valuable to me. A symbol of power. A fuck you to your brother. A gift to offer when I need the upper hand. A thing to use for my own pleasure. Nothing more."

The words do something awful to Carter, each syllable digging and digging until they reach his bare soul. Everything twists and darkens.

Nothing more.

He knew that. Of course he knew that. He's a fucking sex slave to this man.

But hearing him say it so casually... it *hurts.*

It hurts really fucking bad.

"Oh," Carter manages to whisper when he realizes sir is waiting for him to respond.

"I'm sorry this situation happened to you, and I'm sorry that I happened to you, but I am not sorry for anything I've done to you. The moment those men kidnapped you, you became a part of this world. You became a pleasure slave. If you weren't here with me, you'd be somewhere else, and I'd be jealous as fuck, and pissed that I missed out on owning you, but I'd get over it, and I'd move on, and you'd be living a very miserable life with god only knows what monster." Sir cups Carter's cheek, pushing against his face in an attempt to lift his head so they're looking at each other. Carter fights it, his eyes remaining downcast. Sir surprisingly gives up. He sighs. "But you're not somewhere else, sweetheart. You're here, and you're mine, and I'm never going to let you go. Never. You make me very happy. As much as I realize that makes me a monster, I don't care. I'm never going to care. I won't change my mind or have a flash of consciousness. This is who I am, this is what I want, *you* are what I want, and I'm not a man who lets go of the things he feels that way about."

Carter takes a minute to process all of that, his soul still aching, his heart heavy, his eyes burning. Thankfully, sir lets Carter take as much time as he needs, not saying a word as Carter runs his fingers along sir's skin as he thinks. He maps out the contours of the man's broad chest before tracing the lines of the broken birdcage. Carter touches a fingertip to each and every bird, his heartbeat feeling as frantic as a hummingbird. *Go, hurry, fly, fly, fly.*

A tear falls down Carter's cheek. He flinches when sir lifts a hand to wipe it away. Sir drops the hand before touching his face.

Carter knows he could have it worse. He truly believes that. Hell, he's seen it himself. Some of the slaves in the house are treated terribly compared to him. He's seen enough flashes of interactions to know sir treats him very differently than the rest of his men would. He's seen enough slaves walking around with ribs showing and skin bruised and bleeding. They're passed around from man to man to be fucked and tortured at whim. Their eyes are always glazed and empty. Even if sir had been lying when he said those awful things about men in this world maiming and drugging and brutalizing their slaves to the point of them forgetting their own names, their own *humanity*, Carter at least has the proof of the slaves in the house to go off of.

Sir is good to him.

All things considered, sir is very, very good to him.

Carter is lucky.

He's really fucking lucky.

Carter touches sir's tattoo again, just now noticing that there's a small black bird tucked away in the corner of the cage, permanently trapped on sir's skin despite the door being open just inches away.

It's okay, he tells the bird, his fingertip gentle on its beak. *Sometimes it's better to stay anyway.*

"I'm glad you're who bought me, sir."

Sir's breath hitches, his grip on Carter tightening before relaxing. Then he tugs Carter forward until they're flush against each other, burying his face in the crook of Carter's neck. He whispers against the sweaty skin there, pouring out a secret of his own. "I'm very glad, too."

"Because I'm Maison's brother?"

"No," sir says without hesitation. He pulls back to rest his forehead against Carter's, their gazes locking. "Because you're *you*."

Chapter Fourteen

AFTER DRYING CARTER OFF and tucking him in, it takes the boy less than a minute to pass out cold. Nathan gives himself a few minutes to sit on the bed and just watch the boy sleep. Then he tells himself to stop being a selfish bastard and heads into the bathroom for his dreaded call with Maison. He runs the water like usual, just in case Carter wakes up, then takes a seat on the steps leading to the tub and dials the number that used to be his lifeline and now feels more like a death threat.

As always, there are 3 rings, then a clipped voice. "Name?"

"Eagle 2."

"Code?"

"7134."

"Hold."

The phone connects almost instantly, Maison obviously having been waiting. "What the *fuck* do you think you're doing skipping check-ins when you have my baby brother?"

Nathan closes his eyes. "I knew Benny would call."

"Benny isn't who I'm interested in talking to."

"I know..."

"I didn't say anything when you skipped the check-in the night you had to punish him, but you can't keep doing it."

Nathan runs a hand through his hair, sighing. "Alright, Mais. No more avoiding, I promise."

"Good." There's a stretch of silence between them, Nathan staring across the bathroom at the door keeping him from Carter. Nathan wishes he could keep the boy locked in the bedroom forever. Safe. Unharmed. Maybe even happy, as far as happiness goes in situations like these.

"Should we just rip it off like a band-aid?" Maison asks, pulling Nathan back from his thoughts.

Nathan leans back against the tub, closing his eyes. "Go ahead."

"Henley. He comes tomorrow, right?"

"Yup. Dinner meeting."

"Do you feel good about it?"

"Which part of it?" Nathan asks with a huff. "The part where I make a business deal that may lead to the end of this goddamn operation once and for all, or the part where Todd Henley comes near Carter again?"

Maison hums softly. "Let's get business out of the way first."

"I'm feeling good about that part. Real good. The guy is a fucking idiot bottom feeder. Gets a kick out of being friends with the important players without being one himself. All of the benefits with none of the pressure."

"Perfect. The more important people he hangs out with, the more info he has for us. Treat him like your best fucking friend."

Nathan nods. "That's the plan. I'm rolling out the works for him."

There's a pause, and Nathan knows exactly what Maison is thinking. He can feel the tension as his best friend tries to keep the conversation professional. It takes a few seconds, but then Maison breaks. "He'll ask to use Carter, you know."

"I assume he will, yes."

"Are you going to let him?"

"I don't want to," Nathan says quietly.

Maison makes a small noise. "You said you'd be giving him as a gift now and then, right? And a reward for your men?"

"Yeah, but I was hoping to avoid those situations as much as possible."

"If we get Henley, we'll get Miller. We *need* Henley." What he's not saying is still loud and clear. They need Henley, which means they need to keep Henley happy. If Henley gets word that Nathan promised to share Carter on special occasions, he'll see it as a snub that Nathan didn't offer him as a gift for the night.

But Nathan doesn't like it.

No, more than that. Nathan fucking *hates* it.

"I talked to the boss about it." Nathan raises his eyebrows, having not expected that from Maison. Before he can question him, Maison continues. "I admitted that I'm not able to fully remove myself from this. Henley is too fucking important, you know? He's the key."

"What'd the boss say?" Nathan asks, curious about this man they rarely talk about. The man who controls their lives. The wizard behind the curtain in Oz.

When Maison answers, his voice is detached. He's reciting the words, maintaining professionalism. "Carter is the holy grail of this world right now. To withhold him from Henley is to end things before they've begun. Offering the boy is the perfect opportunity to show that you're serious. That you respect Henley enough to share this gift with him. A gift you haven't shared with anyone else yet. He'll be a fly caught in your web the minute you let him touch the bait."

Nathan closes his eyes, bile rising in his throat as he pictures Todd Henley with his hands on Carter. He swallows hard once. Then again. His voice is still strained when he forces himself to ask, "Is that an order, then? Or just his suggestion?"

"It's – uh–" Maison releases a shaky breath. "It's an order, Trav."

"Don't." Nathan pushes off the steps, standing in front of the mirror to stare at his own image. "You can't keep calling me that. I'm Nathan. If I have to do this shit, I have to do it as Nathan. I make Benny use the name too."

There's a pause, but it's not as long as Nathan would have expected. "Alright, Nate. I get it. I respect that."

"Thank you." Nathan studies his reflection. It's harder when he's in nothing but his underwear. He looks so much like Travis without Nathan's costume. Nathan touches the tattoos on his torso, tracing the trail of birds before tapping a fingertip on the bird still trapped. The bird that represents himself. Those are Nathan's tattoos. His story. "I'll offer him, then."

They sit on the phone for a while after that, neither of them speaking.

So much gets said in the silence.

Chapter Fifteen

"WE'RE HAVING A GUEST over tonight," sir says quietly, looking down at Carter where he's kneeling beneath sir's desk. His brown eyes are dark. Nearly black. "He'll be here shortly for a meal and a meeting. You'll behave for me, right, sweetheart?"

"Yes, sir."

"What are your rules?"

Carter nibbles on his bottom lip, trying to recall them. "Always call you sir, always kneel, and never hesitate to obey you. And don't leave the bed without permission unless I need to use the bathroom."

"Good boy." Sir runs the back of his hand against Carter's cheek, the knuckles trailing along his cheekbone. "I want you to focus on that third rule. You will obey me tonight, without hesitation, no matter what, or you will be punished. Understood?"

Not liking the sound of that at all, Carter can't get himself to speak. He barely even manages a nod. His eyes fall to his hands as he clasps them tightly together in his lap. He hears sir sigh, the sound heavy and frustrated, but Carter keeps his eyes lowered and his mouth shut.

Another sigh. Softer. Defeated.

"Would you like to know what your reward will be if you're a very good boy tonight?"

Reward. That sounds promising.

Carter peeks up through his eyelashes. "Yes please, sir."

"I'll give you tomorrow off."

This gets Carter to fully look up, meeting sir's eyes. "W-what?"

"A day off. No crawling around naked. No cock warming or fucking. No leaving the bedroom even. You won't have to be a slave tomorrow. Not really, at least. You get a break." Sir pauses, eyes narrowing. "If you're good, that is."

"All day?" Carter asks, still trying to wrap his mind around it. "Really, sir?"

"All day. I'll leave you be. My men will leave you be. Just you and whatever you want to do in our room – within reason, of course."

A stab of loneliness twists inside Carter's chest. He hates himself for it. He hates himself even more for asking, "Will you be in the bedroom with me, sir?"

Sir gives him a smile that Carter can't read. It's almost... *sad.* "Not if you don't want me to be. It's your day."

"And if I do?" Carter asks, his voice breaking at the end. His face burns in shame when sir tilts his head and raises an eyebrow. "If I want you there, I mean. What happens then, sir?"

"Then," sir says softly, his fingers curling beneath Carter's chin, his thumb resting on his bottom lip. "I'm all yours."

Carter shivers. He doesn't know what it means that he wants sir to be there with him. It's fucked up, he knows that. *What victim doesn't want a day away from their abuser?* But sir is... more than that. It's twisted and messy and wrong – so very wrong – but all Carter can think about is that day in sir's office when he wasn't touched or acknowledged by the man, and the awful loneliness that was gnawing at him by nightfall. He doesn't want that again.

It'd be an entire day where Carter can spend his time with sir, a shameful desire of his, without having to dread the pain and humiliation of the man's torment.

"You can decide tomorrow," sir says, pulling Carter from his thoughts. He blinks to find the man has stood up, towering over him now, the end of Carter's leash in his hand. His face is like stone. When he speaks again, his voice is rough. "Keep your reward in mind tonight. Cling to it. Don't let it go."

Carter swallows hard. "Sir?"

"And just know that I-" sir stops himself, looking away from Carter. He shakes his head. His jaw ticks. His voice is merely a whisper when he admits, "I'm not going to enjoy tonight."

Something sick twists inside Carter's stomach. The enormity of his reward tomorrow fully hits him then. This man is willing to give him an entire day where he gets to be Carter again. That's not a flippant decision. That's fucking huge. Add in the way sir can't look at him, and sir openly admitting that he's not going to enjoy what happens tonight, and Carter is worried.

No, Carter is *terrified*.

"Sir-"

"You have to be good," sir says, each word precise and urgent. His eyes find Carter's again. "You *have to be*, okay?"

Because sir doesn't want to have to punish him.

Because sir already admitted that he'd rather pleasure Carter than hurt him.

Because sir is already going to hate this night without Carter's disobedience making things worse.

"Okay, sir," Carter promises. "I'll be good."

Sir's lips part like he might speak, but then he shakes his head and clears his throat. He looks away. Carter studies him carefully, watching as sir's jaw clenches and relaxes rhythmically. As his nostrils flare. As his shoulders pull back.

When sir does eventually speak, his entire being is different, from his tone to his posture to the cold look in his eyes as he trains them on Carter. "Come. Let's greet our guest."

They go down a different hall than ever before, Carter's heart beginning to race as he realizes they're headed toward a door that has windowpanes with faint sunlight coming through them. It's the closest thing to freedom since his momentary struggle between getting carried out of the auction house and getting shoved into sir's car.

Breathe.

Keep calm.

Pay attention.

Wait for your moment.

This isn't your moment, Carter. Not yet. Not now.

Just breathe.

"Kneel here, pet."

Carter shifts from the crawling position to a kneeling one, his stomach flipping. His hands are shaking hard. He tries to get them to stop, tries to get his body to calm down, but nothing is working as it should. He settles for hiding his hands instead, hoping no one notices them.

The door opens. Fresh air bursts into the hallway. Carter sucks in a breath, his eyes frantic as he takes in every detail. He had forgotten how bright and colorful the world is outside of this place. The green grass. The bright flowers. The watercolor sky as the sun begins to set.

Carter blinks, and the view is gone. In its place is a large man, though not as large as sir. He's still intimidating as he stands before Carter in his tailored suit, his flashy watch catching the artificial light of the hallway when he reaches to shake sir's hand.

"Roarke," the man says with a smile.

That voice.

It's familiar.

Where has Carter heard that voice?

"Please, just Nathan," sir insists. "It's great to see you again, Todd."

The man seems to puff up. "The pleasure is all mine, I assure you."

"Come. I had my chefs prepare a meal for us and my small circle, but I thought we could enjoy some drinks beforehand." Sir smiles, and it makes Carter shiver. It's a smile he's never seen before. At least not on sir. It's a smile that reeks of power and confidence, but also something evil. Something dangerous. "We can speak privately in my office after that, of course."

Carter feels a set of eyes fall heavy on him. From the corner of his eye, he sees the man – Todd – turn and focus his gaze the same as sir. Carter feels itchy and raw. He fixes his eyes on his bruised knees and reminds himself of his reward.

"As beautiful as ever," Todd says. "Is he still struggling?"

"Not terribly. Enough to keep things interesting."

"Do you intend to break him?"

Sir hums as if he's considering his order at a restaurant and not the destruction of a human being. The destruction of *Carter*. "I rather like him as he is, for now. I never did quite enjoy the house slaves. Far too easy. I like the challenge. I like to watch the fight go out of him. The hope. It never gets old. You'll see tonight, I'm sure. Though he's been ordered to be on his best behavior."

I like to watch the fight go out of him. The hope. It never gets old.

The words crash over Carter in waves until he's drowning.

"Pet, say hello to Mr. Henley."

Henley.

The man from the auction.

Carter looks up, eyes wide. This is the man who spoke with sir after sir raped him on stage. That night is a haze now, probably for the best, but he remembers Henley. He remembers the cruelty in his words.

"Pet," sir warns, his eyes narrowing on Carter. "I don't repeat myself."

Trying to keep his voice steady, Carter looks Todd directly in the eye and says, "Hello."

Todd smiles wide before looking at Nathan. "A fighter indeed. Tonight just got a whole lot more entertaining."

"Here." Carter watches with a held breath as sir casually hands over the end of his leash to Todd. Todd, the man who had called him a slut just minutes after he had been raped. Todd, who had said Carter should have to beg for food. Todd, who had laughed at Carter's impending life of misery. "I thought you might like to have my little fighter for the whole evening."

Todd takes the leash like a greedy kid in a candy shop, his eyes alight. "Thank you, Nathan. I'm honored."

"Of course." Sir winks at Todd, ignoring Carter entirely. "I hope you enjoy the view as much as I do."

The view.

The view of Carter's fight going out of him.

The view of Carter losing hope.

Todd says something that makes sir laugh, but Carter doesn't register the words. He looks away from them, focusing back on his knees. He doesn't want to look at them anymore. Partly because he can't stand the sight of them.

Mostly because he doesn't want them to see him cry.

NATHAN STARES DOWN AT the ice in his scotch, his hand wrapped around the glass in a death grip. He's been studying it for a while now. It's safer. If he's looking at his scotch, he's not looking at Carter. And Nathan... Nathan can't look at Carter.

"So pretty," he hears Todd croon to his left. "What's wrong? You don't like being touched there?"

Nathan takes another gulp of the burning liquid as Carter whimpers. This is his fault, something he realized just minutes into them taking their seats. He had mentioned Carter being a fighter to give the boy some leeway to misbehave tonight. If he slips up at all, Nathan can wave it off, say something witty in an amused tone, instead of having to bend Carter over and punish him for Todd's enjoyment. What he hadn't anticipated was that by sharing this fact, he gave Todd a challenge. Todd wants to see the fighter break.

And he's having a whole lot of fun as he pursues the goal.

"That's it, slut. Get hard for me."

Nathan closes his eyes and tries to breathe.

Carter cries out in pain, his first real cry of the night. It startles Nathan enough to draw his attention despite his best efforts to refrain. His eyes land on the boy just as Todd yanks Carter's sack for what he assumes is at least the second time. The erection he had forced on the boy is quickly waning.

Nathan looks away, staring off at nothing as his eyes blur.

Maybe he'll bring Carter some books tomorrow for his day off. Nathan bets he likes books.

"Goodness, your master must have so much fun with you."

Nathan feels Todd's gaze turn on him. With a single blink, he has his shit together again. He turns to look at the man, carefully avoiding the sight of Carter as he does so, and gives him a grin that's positively evil. He can feel it seeping into his bones. He's not sure if he'll ever be rid of it now.

He's not sure if he'll ever deserve to be.

"What are his rules?" Todd asks, still looking at Nathan even as his hands roam Carter's body.

Nathan forces a laugh, hoping to hide the fact that the boy barely has any rules compared to other pleasure slaves. "You'd have to be more specific."

"Perhaps I should say, what are *my* rules?"

That's a much safer conversation. Easier. Even if the images suddenly fluttering through Nathan's mind make him sick. "His ass is mine to fuck, but you can play with it. As for his mouth, it's all yours. And you've already realized his cock and balls are free game."

There's accidentally too much bite in that last sentence. Todd freezes, slowly meeting Nathan's eyes. "I should have asked-"

"Nonsense." Nathan waves a hand, giving him an easy smile that's anything but easy. "I would have stopped you if you did something I didn't like, my friend. Honestly, as long as your cock stays out of his ass, and you don't do anything permanent, you have almost unlimited range."

"Excellent."

"Just don't break him," Nathan finds himself adding, his heart racing. "He's – he's mine to break."

If Todd notices the struggle in Nathan's voice, he doesn't show it. He just grins and returns to his new toy.

Nathan gives himself a moment to imagine what it would be like to pin Todd to the floor with a hand to his throat as he uses his other hand to pummel him into a bloody fucking pulp. Then he forces himself to let go of the fantasy, as well as any ill feelings toward the man. Todd Henley is the key to everything. Nathan can't forget that.

Remembering what he talked to Maison about, Nathan informs Todd, "You'll be the first to use him. Besides me, of course."

The look on Todd's face is unexplainable. It's an instant confirmation of his loyalty. This plan is going to work. After all this time, Nathan's finally approaching the finish line. "Thank you for that honor, Nathan."

Nathan nods once. "This alliance is very important to me. I would like you to be in my small circle. This is how I treat the men in that circle."

Todd's eyes turn to Carter again, his grin widening like a fucking sadistic clown when he catches Carter looking at him. Carter's shoulders hunch as the boy curls into himself.

"I think I'm going to like this circle," Todd says as he fists Carter's hair and tugs, seemingly for no reason other than to draw a sound from the boy.

"Master Roarke?" Nathan turns in his seat, raising an eyebrow at the slave in the doorway. The girl quickly looks away, her cheeks going pink. "Dinner is served, Master."

Without a word, Nathan pushes to his feet. He drains his glass and puts it down on the table beside his chair before turning to his guest. Todd stands as well, just letting Carter tumble to the floor. The boy hits the floor hard enough to make Nathan wince. He releases a pained sound that's tinted with fear. Nathan can feel Todd watching him, probably unsure if Nathan is upset about the lack of regard to his slave.

Todd could do much worse than letting Carter fall a foot or two. Nathan has to set his boundaries wide tonight.

With the toe of his Berluti leather shoe, Nathan gently taps Carter's left ass cheek. He makes sure it looks like a proper kick. "Shut the fuck up."

Todd relaxes instantly, his own shoe hitting Carter's other cheek. It blooms bright red. Nathan hopes Todd is too much of a dipshit to notice that the cheek Nathan supposedly kicked doesn't look the same.

"Let's go slut." Todd yanks harshly on the leash, making Carter scramble to keep from getting choked.

Including Benny, only 4 other men were invited to this dinner. As the glass doors are slid across the tracks in the openings of the dining area to close them in for privacy, Nathan makes introductions.

"Todd, you've met my second, Benny."

"Yes, of course." Benny and Todd shake hands, agreeing it's great to see each other again. Then Nathan continues. "This here is Donavan," he pauses for their handshake, "This is Chris," he pauses again, "And this is Mica."

Todd's eyes flash at Mica, his handshake slightly more enthusiastic. "I've heard of some of your work. It's excellent to meet you."

Nathan's stomach turns. Mica's job is the most hands-on of all of them, the man not only unafraid to get blood on his hands, but *eager* to do so. Literal blood. Not metaphorical. Nathan's only ever seen him in action once. He had to fake disinterest before hurrying to the nearest bathroom and spilling his guts. That was back when he was new, though. Back when he wasn't as hardened by this life. Back when he still shared equal space in his mind with Travis. There's a good chance Nathan would barely be affected by the things Mica does to people now, but he's in no hurry to find out.

After the formalities have been dealt with, Todd turns to Nathan. "Would you like your pet back?"

"No, you're our guest. Keep him. He's an excellent cock warmer."

"Are you sure?"

"Of course." Nathan smiles. "A hole is a hole. I'll use another."

Todd ducks his head respectfully and thanks him before taking the seat that Nathan gestures to. It's to Nathan's left, directly across from Benny where he sits to Nathan's right. Todd tugs Carter beneath the table. Nathan has to dig his nails into his palms to keep himself composed. He hadn't realized how much he'd hate not being able to see his boy anymore. He doesn't like it.

He doesn't fucking like it one bit.

4 naked young men and a naked young woman come into the room, all collared and timid. Donovan grabs the woman, since that's his taste, the others spreading out for the rest of the guests. Nathan curls his hand gently around his temporary slave's wrist without making eye contact, guiding him closer. "Beneath my table. Take me out. Warm me."

"Yes, Master Roarke," the slave says quietly, doing as told. He's one of the broken ones. It's why Nathan can't stand to even look at him. At any of them. They're all broken. He failed them already. They'll never be the same, even after he's set them free.

Carter is the only one left standing.

The men all exchange small talk for the first part of the meal, allowing everyone to feel each other out as they sip their drinks and eat an array of appetizers, salad, and soup. When the main course is served, Benny jumps into the more important topics of conversation. Nathan probably would have before then, but he's been far too focused on the tiny sounds coming from beneath the table to his left.

He finishes his second scotch, ignoring his best friend's pointed look.

"The party this weekend will be the perfect opportunity to study him," Benny says. "Henley, he doesn't know about you and Nathan's growing relationship. You're our best plan of attack for information retrieval, if you can get him to trust you enough."

"You'll tell him you tried talking to us," Nathan adds. "It'll get leaked that you were here, that's just fact, but he doesn't have to know the truth. You can tell him you were considering working with us, but have decided not to. You can shit talk me. Say I didn't let you use the boy. Say we fought. Say we treated you as inferior. Whatever you'd like. You just need to convince Miller that you're pissed at me and out for blood."

Todd nods. "We can solidify a story. I have no problem doing that."

"Perfect." Nathan smiles, his eyes flicking to the table in front of Todd. He swallows a wave of bile. "How's the slut?"

"He's very pretty when he cries." Todd leans back in his chair, grinning down at Carter. He does something that forces a choked sob from the boy.

Nathan wants more than anything to ask what Todd is doing to make his sweet, tough boy cry under there. Instead, he smiles. "Yes, he is. Is he satisfying you?"

"Absolutely." Todd looks down again, his smile fading as he sees something Nathan can't see. "The fuck are you lookin' at? Eyes down."

There's a soft sound, Carter in pain, but muted by the cock no doubt stuffed in his mouth. Todd spits. Nathan can't see, but he can assume it lands on Carter's face.

Nathan taps his slave's cheek. The boy pulls away so his mouth is free, keeping his gaze lowered as he asks, "How may I serve you, Master?"

"Fetch me a refill."

"The Macallan, Master?"

"Yes. 2 cubes of ice. 3 fingers."

"Yes, Master." The boy gracefully crawls from under the table, past Nathan's chair, before pushing to his feet. He disappears. Another slave shortly follows, probably fetching a drink for Chris.

Something hits the table where Todd is sitting, a sharp cry following the thud. Then Carter is being dragged out by his hair and forced to stand up. The boy stumbles a step before gaining his balance, his eyes blinking rapidly as he tries to adjust to his new surroundings. His cheeks are ruddy and covered in tears, his forehead has a glob of spit in the center, and there are deep red finger marks around his throat. His nipples are puffy and dotted with red specks. Nathan accidentally darts his eyes down to the boy's genitals. His soft cock is a muddle of reds, his poor balls nearly purple and covered in little indents that match the shape of fingernails.

"Go on!" Todd snaps, reaching out and smacking a hand against Carter's ass. "Get me a drink."

Carter sways on his feet, blinking again. "W-what would you like, sir?"

"More of this." He grabs his mostly empty glass and splashes it in Carter's face, making the boy stumble and splutter. All of Nathan's men laugh with Todd, including Benny. So, Nathan laughs too. It feels like the sound comes from somewhere else. Somewhere far away. Like Nathan is just watching the scene and hearing a laugh that resembles his own, but surely can't be his.

The slave for Chris subtly grabs Carter's fingertips and tugs at them. It's enough to get Carter to follow him out of the room, the boy trembling as he goes.

Nathan closes his eyes and breathes as Benny begins speaking again. He's getting too close to the edge. He doesn't know how much more of this he can take.

He doesn't know how much more *Carter* can take.

Nathan is determined to keep this boy from breaking, but how the fuck does he realistically do that?

What if he can't?

CARTER HATES TODD. DESPISES him. He will never doubt how grateful he is for sir again. Sir is kind if Carter is good. He praises him. Strokes his hair. Gives him pleasure. Todd doesn't give a shit if Carter is good. He scolds him and degrades him. He tugs his hair so hard Carter swears it will come out of his scalp. He plays sadistic games with Carter's cock and balls.

At some point, Carter zones out for his own self-preservation. Between the nails scraping at him, the cock choking him, the hair getting yanked, the insults, the humiliation, the spit on his face, and the leather shoe digging into his genitals until they're throbbing with white-hot bursts of pain, Carter's only chance at sanity is to disappear somewhere safe inside his head.

He chooses a field of daffodils. The air is warm and fresh like the air that had filtered in from that door earlier. The sun is setting. The grass is soft on his skin as he lays in it.

It works, until it doesn't.

Until Carter gets jostled, and his eyes skitter away from Todd, and he sees the slave between sir's legs. Then he's snapped back into the present, every pain sharp and urgent, the worst of it emanating in his chest.

Sir is being gentle with the slave, letting him rest his head on sir's thigh while petting his hair idly like he does with Carter. The slave is good, too. He isn't clumsy or hesitant. He knew exactly what sir wanted him to do. He stays still instead of fidgeting. He never chokes or makes a sound. He remembers to keep his eyes down, and he speaks to sir with nothing but subdued respect. There's no fear in him. No emotion at all. He's perfect for sir. Far better than Carter will probably ever be.

A hole is a hole. That's what sir had said.

Had Carter really believed he was special somehow? That perhaps sir liked him?

How pathetic of him. How *silly*. Carter is nothing but a hole to the man. Granted, Carter's hole has added benefits, symbolizing power, giving sir something to taunt Maison with, but that's his worth. That's all he is. And sir doesn't have to like him to wield Carter in those ways. Sir doesn't even have to use him.

A hole is a hole.

It hurts so badly, Carter's not sure he's managing to breathe around the pain. He starts crying at some point. Or maybe he's been crying the whole time and is just now noticing it.

Todd says the tears are pretty.

Sir chuckles and agrees.

By the time Carter has been pulled to his feet, steady tears falling down his cheeks, a drink tossed in his face, Carter has realized exactly how insignificant he is to sir. Sir *lied*. Sir doesn't care about him. He's clearly enjoying the night just fine. He had said those things and made those promises earlier to trick Carter into behaving for their guest. He hadn't meant them.

Carter wishes he had the energy to throw a fit and show Todd Henley exactly how misbehaved he can be, but just the thought of it is draining. It takes everything for Carter to even walk as a slave leads him away from the dinner guests who are still laughing at him. He has nothing left for rebellion.

The slave brings him to a drink cart near the kitchen where the other slaves who were ordered to get refills are standing.

"Is it your first time with someone other than the master of the house?" the slave who rescued him asks quietly as they wait in line.

Since Carter assumes that his sir is the master of the house, he nods. "Yeah..."

"I thought so. We were all wondering. None of us have seen him share you at all."

"Is that... bad?" Carter asks, looking around to make sure no one is listening to them.

"That Master Roarke doesn't like to share you?" the slave in front of Carter asks, turning halfway to look at Carter. His eyes narrow as he takes in Carter's appearance. "Don't be an idiot. You're fucking lucky."

It takes a moment for Carter to place the slave. Then he realizes he's the one sir is using tonight. Carter's replacement. He hates himself for the angry burst of jealousy he feels towards the young man. It's not like he wants to be here. He's in the same boat as Carter.

The slave beside Carter continues the conversation. "I'd give anything to be Master Roarke's. Is he nice in private? I bet he is. He's so fucking gentle, even with the others around."

"Maybe he's really fucking nasty in private," the only female slave mutters, eyeing up her glass as she considers how much vodka to pour into it.

Another slave scoffs. "So fucking true. That's how Master Mica is. He acts all relaxed and indifferent in front of the other men, almost like he doesn't know what to do with us, but in private..." the slave trails off, shaking his head with a sigh.

The slave sir is using tonight finishes the thought. "He's a sadistic fuck."

"That's an understatement," the slave beside Carter jokes.

"What do you expect?" the female asks. "He's their interrogator. Dude is fucking vicious. I heard he once disemboweled someone and then used their own intestines to strangle them to death."

The slave who had first brought up Mica rolls his eyes. "That's not even possible."

"How would you know?" the slave beside Carter asks.

"Because I was a year away from graduating medical school, assholes. I'm not saying the dude isn't a sick fuck, because he totally is, but that one is a stretch."

The female arches an eyebrow. "You haven't had anything done to your body that you previously thought was impossible? Because I fucking have. This world doesn't follow the rules of physics."

The ex-medical student looks away then, his eyes glazing. His words are quiet when he admits, "Yeah, you're right..."

"How did you even hear about that?" Carter asks, not liking how dark the conversation just got. "Did Master Mica tell you?"

They all laugh then. The female slave explains, "We pay attention. Eavesdrop. The kind of information we can overhear in our positions is fucking big. Especially you. The things you probably hear..."

"Not the time," the slave next to Carter hisses. "So not the fucking time."

"What does that mean? Not the time for what?" Carter asks.

They all look at him. Their eyes flash with rebellion.

It feels like Carter's been injected with a brand-new life, his body singing with energy and hope. They aren't broken. None of them are broken. They're all just better than him at pretending.

No. Not *all* of them. There's something different about the slave sir is using tonight as Carter studies him harder. He seems to be experiencing a sort of dry amusement, almost like he's the adult silently judging the children for having silly fantasies. There's no rebellion or hope in his expression.

Before Carter can dwell on the difference, the female changes the topic to something safer. "So, is Master Roarke nice in private or what?"

"I-" Carter pauses, looking at each of them in confusion, "Wait, none of you have been with sir – I mean, Master Roarke – in private?"

"Nope. He doesn't do that. Slaves are too beneath him. None of them are allowed in his personal wing or his office," the slave sir is currently using explains. He sneers at Carter. "That is, before *you*. Seems he's broken his own rules for you."

"Is he gentle?" the slave beside Carter asks.

"Of course he is," the slave sir is using – a slave Carter is starting to realize is very jealous – growls. "I always have such a hard time warming him. He makes me so sleepy."

"Ugh. The hair petting thing," the slave beside Carter says in agreement, sighing wistfully. "It feels sooo good."

The slave Mica is using tonight speaks next, his expression dreamy. "How are we not talking about the fact that he lets us come? Like – he doesn't even fuck us, just makes us suck his cock, and he lets us come while we do it. Hot damn. He's a *godsend*."

Carter's throat goes tight.

He really isn't special to sir. Not at all.

The female slave tosses her hair over her shoulder and teasingly flips them off. "Fuck you all. The straight guys here suck ass." Then she's off with a sway of her naked hips, leaving Carter with all the slaves his sir has enjoyed the use of.

He can't look at any of them.

There's a heavy silence as the jealous slave finishes making sir's drink. When he turns to go, the other slave by his side now, he pauses to look at Carter. His gaze travels from head to toe, then back again, his expression twisting into disgust. "You're not special. He'll get tired of you once the whole Maison's brother thing wears off. Then you'll probably be tossed into the basement like the rest of us to be communal. You should appreciate what you have before it's gone. I mean, he's already getting bored if he's letting that asshole do what he's been doing to you. Which, by the way, he's barely hurting you. Stop crying. You're not even *bleeding*."

With a final nasty look, the jealous slave walks away, leaving Carter alone with the slave that originally rescued him from Todd. The slave stays quiet for a moment before sighing. He hands Carter a bottle of scotch and an empty glass. "This is what your master for tonight has been drinking. He wanted 2 fingers last time. Safe bet to do that again."

Carter takes the items from him with shaking hands. "Thanks."

"He's right, you know. Not about the stuff he just said, but the stuff earlier, about listening. It's not just to get information for-" he pauses, looking around, then lowers his voice to continue. "-getting out of here. It's also for stuff like this. A house slave came in and got drinks for everyone when the meal first started. Your temporary master had given his order. You were right there when it happened. It's important you soak up all the information you can. These men don't like to give any leeway. They'll use whatever excuse they can find to punish you. Don't make it easy for them."

"I'll try," Carter whispers. He hasn't poured the drink yet. His hands still haven't calmed. "I thought it'd be easier to just... pretend like I'm not here."

"It's easier in the short term, but you have to play the long-game here. It'll get easier to stay in the present. It'll get easier to keep your mind active, but separate your emotions. Soon it'll be like – well, I don't know how to explain it really. It's probably different for everyone. But for me, it feels like I go to work. You don't deal with your personal shit at work, right? You don't have mental breakdowns or outbursts, unless you want to be fired. You deal with that stuff at home. It's the same for me. When I'm up here, being used, I look at it like a job. It took me a long time to get like that, though. A lot of practice." He shrugs, looking away as his eyebrows pull in. "Maybe I'm just desensitized now..."

Carter puts two cubes of ice in the scotch glass, remembering the distinct sound of Todd making them clack together as he had swirled his drink. "Thanks for the advice."

"No problem." The slave shrugs. "And don't take what that asshole said to you personally. He's been in love with Master Roarke for at least a year now. He's just jealous of you."

"In love?" Carter asks with a scoff. He ignores the tiny part of him that burns with jealousy at the thought of someone loving sir. In fact, he pretends the part doesn't even exist. "How could someone love a monster like that?"

The slave shrugs, a sad expression twisting his features. "I don't know. 3 is different. Or maybe it's me that's different. I don't know. Everyone copes in their own ways, I guess. And some just sort of... break mentally, ya know? I think that's what happened with 3. I don't really know his story, he doesn't talk a lot, but I think he's seen some serious shit. He's sort of empty. Not that he's the only one. 11 doesn't even talk anymore, hasn't in months, and 9 has been losing chunks of time. He said it's like he wakes up to find himself in the middle of something, and has no memory of how he got there or what has happened to him. I'm one of the lucky ones. I haven't lost it. At least... not yet."

Carter has to take a moment to process all the information. One thing sticks out. "3? 9? 11?"

"Yeah. We get numbers." The slave tugs at his collar where Carter sees a shiny silver 7 dangling off the front ring. He had noticed numbers before on the slaves, but he'd never allowed himself to dwell on the detail. "It's easier to just go by numbers. We don't really use names anymore, even when we're alone. When a master grabs you and asks if you've seen 7, you better fucking know who 7 is, ya know?"

"And that's you."

"Yup. Lucky number 7." The slave scoffs. Carter can't blame him. Nothing about their lives is lucky. "You don't have a number, I see. Not that it matters. Everyone knows your name."

Carter shakes his head. "Everyone seems to know everything."

"It's not your fault. I mean, I get that they're all jealous, hell I'm a little jealous too. Master Roarke is very gentle, and he never asks for anything truly bad. And he's breaking his personal rules for you, which makes you seem more special or whatever, but you've gotta be fucking *lonely* man."

Carter aches with the truth of the statement, his eyes pricking with tears. "You aren't?"

"Not really. Not like you, anyway." The slave's smile is sad. "We all have each other. If we're not being used at night, we sleep in the basement together. Sure, we get locked in, and it's cramped and dark and everyone gets on each other's fucking nerves, but we all get to talk like this. We get to remember that we're human. I don't know how you do it all by yourself. Does he at least talk to you? Like this, I mean? Openly? Does he let you talk to him?"

Focusing on the alcohol he's pouring, Carter goes with a half-truth. "Not really. He talks to me sometimes, but it's usually just like... him musing out loud. You guys are right, though. He is gentle in private. Most of the time, at least... If I'm good."

"Is it true that he-"

"7," a deep voice says from their left. Then, "Pet. What are the two of you doing?"

7 whips around, Carter following. The boy goes directly to his knees and presses his forehead to the floor, muttering an apology. When Carter begins to do the same, a large hand wraps around his bicep and keeps him on his feet. That's when Carter's mind slows enough to realize who just caught them speaking.

Sir.

The man keeps his eyes narrowed on Carter as he growls at 7, "Get back to your master before I decide to let him flog you for tonight's post-dinner entertainment."

"Yes, Master Roarke!" 7 squeaks, scrambling to his feet. "Thank you, Master Roarke!"

Sir releases Carter's arm before quickly taking it back in his hands so he can gently rub the red marks his bruising grip left behind. The man looks torn. Upset. When his eyes take in the front of Carter's body, all the way to his cock and balls, the torn expression twists into something devastated. Sir tears his gaze away long enough to check their surroundings. Then he lurches forward without warning, grabbing Carter's head in a strong grip, holding him still as he crashes their mouths together.

Carter startles for just a moment before completely melting. The kiss is violent and desperate and reflects exactly how Carter has been feeling all night. He feels sir's erection press against him and moans, hating himself for the thrill it sends through him. Maybe he isn't special, but sir still *wants* him. This is proof.

Sir shoves Carter back until he's pinned to the wall, growling as his hands make quick work of his belt and zipper. He yanks his cock out at the same time as he removes Carter's plug, then spits on himself. Carter barely has enough time to comprehend what's happening before sir is lifting him up by the back of his thighs like Carter weighs nothing and slamming his cock into him.

The sudden intrusion blurs Carter's vision, stealing his breath, but sir works his magic and chases the pain away with his lips on Carter's ear and his hard cock angling right at Carter's prostate. Carter cries out as his cock starts to harden between them, too thankful for sir's attention to be mad at his cock for the betrayal. When sir notices the erection, he pulls his head back to look into Carter's eyes. Something intense passes between them. Something Carter isn't sure there's a name for. Then the man is pressing his forehead against Carter's and growling, "*Mine.* You're fucking *mine.*"

"Yours," Carter promises, his body trembling with emotion and need. "All yours, sir."

Sir gives him another searing kiss before pulling back. "Touch yourself. Come for me."

Carter bites back a sob of relief and nods, wrapping his hand around his cock and quickly tugging. Despite all the abuse it endeared tonight, the thing is fully on board with what sir is doing right now. It's as relieved as Carter is to be feeling pleasure for a moment during a night so riddled with pain.

It can't be more than a minute before Carter's free hand is clawing at sir's shoulder, his cock spurting stripes of white cum all over the powerful man's suit jacket.

"Fuck, Car-" sir groans, cutting himself off by biting down on Carter's shoulder. Carter has a fleeting thought that sir was about to use his name for the first time, but then sir is pumping him full of hot cum and whispering praise in his ear, and Carter forgets.

Sir rests his forehead against Carter's for a few seconds as he catches his breath, their eyes locked.

"I hate his hands on you," sir admits, his voice raw.

Before Carter can tell him how much he hates it too, how much he hates sir's hands on another slave, how much he wants this night to be over so they can be together again, sir is pulling out of Carter and setting him back on his feet. "Turn around, hands on the wall, ass out."

Carter does as told, biting his lip to stave off the sudden overwhelming urge to cry. He whimpers when sir presses his plug back into his hole, but he doesn't complain. Not then, and certainly not when sir scoops up the drops of cum that had spilled out, pressing his fingers to Carter's lips in a silent order to clean his mess. Carter sucks and licks the fingers like he can somehow convey everything he wanted to say by doing this simple task perfectly.

"Good boy," sir finally says, stepping back. Despite sir only being inches away, Carter suddenly feels very alone. "Face me again."

Carter follows the order, swaying slightly on his feet. He winces when he sees the mess he made of sir's jacket. "I'm sorry, sir..."

"Don't worry about it." Sir squeezes his eyes shut before taking a deep breath and looking at Carter again. "Get back to Todd. We'll discuss the little chat you were having with 7 later."

"Sir, I didn't-"

"Sweetheart," sir says quietly, giving Carter a pained look that steals his breath. "Don't make our night worse. Please. Go back to Todd."

Tears prick the corners of Carter's eyes, but he grabs the drink he had poured earlier and skirts around sir without a word. He finds himself hoping that sir will stop him, *chase* him, but he doesn't. He lets Carter go.

Todd is thankfully busy talking when Carter returns, not bothering to acknowledge Carter or his drink. Carter crawls under the table to retake his place, even though it's the last thing he wants to do. 7 is sitting back, his master's pants zipped up. He gives Carter a worried look. Carter tries to smile at him in a way that conveys everything is okay. He has no idea if it works. He's a little rusty on non-verbal slave communication.

When Carter looks in the other direction, he finds the jealous slave glaring at him. Carter can't help but puff up a little. He knows it must be obvious sir just fucked him. He assumes that's why Henley didn't mention how long it took him. The slave is clearly pissed about the turn of events.

After a minute or two, sir returns. He apologizes as he takes his seat, undoing the button of a suit jacket that looks almost identical to the one Carter came all over just a few minutes ago. He keeps his pants closed like all of the other men, meaning the dinner is probably coming to an end. But, to Carter's devastation and to jealous slave's joy, sir still guides jealous slave's head to rest on his thigh as he returns to petting the boy's head. The jealous slave grins at Carter like he knows exactly how much watching the scene hurts him.

Carter is fucking relieved when the meal is officially declared over.

Except, sir invites Todd into his office for a private chat, and he mentions something about Todd enjoying his gift more thoroughly, and Carter suddenly realizes that *his* evening isn't done. Not by a long shot.

Todd half-leads, half-drags Carter across the floor, not giving him time to get into a proper crawling position. He's out of breath and trembling violently by the time they enter sir's office. The click of the door shutting feels like an executioner's song.

Sir sits at his desk. Todd sits across from him in one of the leather chairs. Carter kneels at Todd's feet. It feels wrong. He should be kneeling for *sir*.

At least jealous slave wasn't brought in here too. Carter's not sure he would have survived watching sir interact with him any more than simple cock warming at the table.

Todd catches Carter by surprise, picking him up and hauling him into his lap. "May I?" he asks sir.

Sir doesn't say anything, but he must nod because a moment later Carter is being laid out on sir's desk in a sick mockery of the position he was in when sir fucked him on it before. It feels so much different this time. Cold. Lonely. When Carter realizes his eyes are pointed up at sir's face, he quickly squeezes them shut. Just the momentary flash of sir looking at him in boredom was enough to bring all of the pain and emotions rushing back. A tear slips down his cheek. Carter freezes when it's licked away. He doesn't want to know who did it.

Carter isn't special - that's what the jealous slave said.
But isn't he?
Sir treats him like he is.
Or maybe he doesn't...
How is Carter supposed to know?

Todd grabs Carter's soft cock and squeezes it so hard Carter's eyes fly open as he gasps for air. A haze of pain and nausea washes over Carter, thankfully making it impossible to focus on sir's face above him.

Carter jerks when something non-human touches his sensitive skin down there. He lifts his head in a panic only for sir to grab him by the hair and pull him back down, holding him in place as the thing closes around the base of his cock and balls. Carter jerks when he hears the thing snap into place, but it doesn't hurt. It's just uncomfortable.

Then his cock is being pushed into something cold and metallic. The thing is sharp, Carter hissing as it drags against his skin. He gasps in pain and tries to buck his hips. All that happens is the men both laugh. Then, "Hold still, pet. Just let us cage your pretty cock. It won't hurt if you hold still."

Carter whines in protest and fear, squeezing his eyes shut and turning his face to the side. His cheeks nearly throb with how quickly blood rushes to fill them. He feels hot all the way down his chest with humiliation and shame.

What sir said was true, it didn't hurt anymore once he held still, but he's still humiliated, and his abused member is aching something awful.

The plug in Carter's ass is removed. He feels sir's cum gush out of him. He hears Todd groan. He thinks he might hyperventilate.

Something pokes at Carter's hole. He squeezes his hands into fists to keep from swinging them at the men. He can feel blood pooling in his palms where his nails dig into the skin. It's empowering, in a way. They can hurt him all they want, but he can make himself bleed too. They aren't special.

A sharp pain in his nipple pulls a gasp from Carter. He opens his eyes again, looking down to see what caused it. His eyes fill with tears as he watches Todd twist his nipple again.

Fingers push into his ass, and he knows that Todd is searching for his prostate. Carter turns his head, whimpering. He knows what will happen when his prostate is found. He knows what his cock will do. It won't matter that this isn't consensual. It won't matter that he's in pain. It won't matter that there is a fucking cage in the way. It's biology.

Todd is going to force Carter to get hard.

And sir is just letting it happen.

The moment the fingers graze his prostate, Carter flinches. He hates himself for not having the foresight to keep from reacting. Hates himself for giving Todd exactly what he needed to know he found his goal.

As the man doubles-down on his efforts, he and sir talk.

It's all a blur of words and phrases, punctuated by bursts of pain.

"-unlikely, but quite-"

"Miller isn't-"

Too tight, the cage is too tight.

"-kill-"

A twist of his right nipple.

"-useless-"

A twist of the other one.

"-isn't necessary-"

"That's an excellent-"

Teeth sinking into the flesh of his shoulder.

"-could be worth-"

The cage, the cage, oh god, take it off, please, take it off.

"-agree entirely."

Make it stop. Just make it stop.

"It's settled, then."

Sir looks into Carter's wide eyes, guilt etched into his expression as he gently runs his fingers through Carter's hair to soothe him. Carter jerks away, not caring that it makes what Todd is currently doing hurt even worse. Sir stares at him in stunned silence.

"You were right about him, Nate."

Eyes on Carter. Two sets. Heavy. Predatory.

"How so?"

Two hands slap down on his abused nipples. Carter cries out.

"It's quite a view, watching him lose it all."

"Mmm. Yes." Sir sits back in his seat, moving further away from Carter. "We're finished now. Might I suggest using him to handle that little issue in your pants? He's excellent with his mouth."

There's a relief that blooms in Carter's chest when he's dragged off the desk by his hair and dropped to the floor, even when his leg gets caught and twists in a way that sends pain down to his toes. He closes his eyes just as a hard cock is shoved into his mouth. Todd doesn't stop until Carter's nose is in his pubic hair, not caring when Carter chokes and gags.

Words are growled at him. Degrading things. Cruel things.

Carter manages to keep himself distanced from it all until Todd brings up Maison.

Until Todd hits him where it hurts.

"What do you think your older brother would say if he could see you now, hmmm? Think he'd be proud of how much of a cock slut you've become, or do you think he'd be fucking disgusted? He'd probably disown you after watching your useless cock trying to get hard for us. He'd see how much of a whore you are and probably fucking leave you here. You're fucking *pathetic*. Why would he even want you? We've *ruined* you."

Carter crumbles. Todd's eyes flash in triumph, his cock exploding without warning. It's a big load, and Carter is mid-sob, so he chokes on most of it. Todd just collects whatever he missed and shoves it back into his mouth, fingers reaching down his throat until Carter is gagging.

He slaps Carter across the face for good measure afterward.

With a terrifying smile, Todd wipes his cock clean on Carter's tear-soaked cheek before ordering, "Swallow all of this, or you'll fucking regret it."

Carter has no idea what the words mean, since he had already swallowed the man's disgusting cum. Before he has time to figure it out, Todd is harshly yanking his jaw down and holding it with a finger latched in his mouth, his softening cock coming to rest between Carter's parted lips.

Carter's eyes fly open at the first spurt of hot, rancid urine. He panics, trying to pull away, piss shooting all over his body, but stops immediately when it earns him a shoe to his caged cock. His eyes quickly squeeze shut before they get the chance to accidentally fall on sir. Carter can't see that man right now. He just... *can't.*

And then Carter hears a dark, cold, "No."

The piss stops, Todd apparently holding it in as he turns to look at sir. Carter looks too, his chest heaving as he tries to calm himself down. Sir's eyes meet his and something passes between them. Something Carter doesn't understand.

"No?" Todd asks.

"Do not piss in my slave's mouth."

Todd seems perplexed. He looks at Carter, frowning, then back at sir. "I'm sorry. I – most men don't care. I shouldn't have assumed."

"Most men's slaves aren't Maison Beckett's little brother. The last thing I need is the slave getting sick."

"Of course. My apologies."

"No reason to apologize." Sir smiles, but it's tight. "I assure you, it's not something I'm upset about. I realize I should have mentioned it when giving you the rules. It had slipped my mind."

Todd tucks himself away, looking less afraid now but still uncomfortable. He must not like that he's lost his power over Carter because he turns to him right then and smacks the back of his hand against Carter's wet cheek hard enough to make lights burst in his vision.

"See ya this weekend, whore."

Now that Carter's panic is pulled back, his mind coming down, all he can focus on is the physical issues he's facing. The throbbing cheek from where Carter was hit so hard that he's wondering if the skin broke. The leg that's still tingling with a numbing sort of pain that makes Carter a little nervous. The piss that had made its way into his mouth and on his body, his tongue heavy with the rancid liquid, his stomach hot, his skin slick and smelly. Carter shudders, clamping his mouth shut as he fights the urge to vomit.

"I gotta tell ya, Nate," Todd says with a dark chuckle. "If you do decide you don't want the thing when you're finished using him against Maison, I'd be willing to buy him off ya. No reason to kill something that's so pretty when it cries."

"I'll keep that in mind," sir says in amusement.

Carter wonders what it'd be like to die. *Would it hurt? Would it be a relief? Would it be better? Worse?*

This would all be over if he died.

It'd all *finally* be over.

Sir pushes to his feet as Todd walks towards the office door. Carter stares straight ahead without really seeing what's in front of him. He barely hears when sir says, "Stay. Don't move."

Carter doesn't move. He doesn't speak. He's honestly not sure if he even can.

Carter doesn't understand his life anymore. Everything was twisted and turned until he was something he never imagined being. Then, miraculously, he had started grasping his life again. He thought he was learning. Him and sir were finding a delicate balance together. He was special. Sir liked making him feel good. If he behaved, he'd be treated well. Carter was prepared to live this new existence. He was prepared for this to be his world.

Then sir gave him to Todd.

Sir let Todd abuse him.

Sir used another slave.

Sir proved that Carter isn't special.

Nothing makes sense anymore. Nothing feels even slightly okay.

Todd was right. They've *ruined* him.

Carter barely understands how to *breathe*.

He doesn't even know if he wants to anymore.

AFTER A FEW MORE minutes of speaking with Todd in the hall, Nathan escorts him to the main door and wishes him a good night. The guard hasn't even locked up before Nathan is turning on his heel, all but running to his office. Tonight went too far. Nathan let things go too far.

How the fuck was he supposed to know Todd Henley would decide to piss in Carter's mouth? The bastard didn't ask for permission. He just fucking did it.

And the awful things he had said to the poor boy...

Nathan can't stop rewatching it all unfold in his mind. Every step brings a new flash – Carter crying, a purple cock pushing against a cage, puffy red nipples, Carter's body crumpling to the floor, Carter's expression when

Todd spoke of Maison, the burst of panic when Carter first realized – Nathan closes his eyes, shaking his head.

He'll never forgive himself.

All that matters is Carter now.

Nathan has to focus on Carter.

The apology Nathan had planned dies on his tongue when he enters his office to find Carter curled in a fetal position beside a puddle of vomit.

Carter's eyes snap up to Nathan when he senses him. He pushes himself into an awful kneeling position and starts to shake his head frantically. He cries, "I'm sorry!" before dropping his head and succumbing to uncontrollable sobs. Nathan rushes forward, skirting around the vomit on the floor. There's some on Carter too – a few drops on his knees, and a splotchy coating on his hands like he had tried to catch it.

"Christ," Nathan whispers, feeling the sudden urge to join Carter in his puking and crying endeavors.

"I'm sorry!" Carter says again, though it's barely discernible with how hard he's sobbing. "I'm so sorry!"

"Shhh. No. Don't apologize. You're okay. It's okay." It doesn't seem as if Carter hears him, the boy just continuing to sob. "Sweetheart, you were so good for me. You made me so proud. This is - you're *fine*. I'm not mad, okay? I'm not mad."

Carter's crying slows, but it seems less to do with him feeling better and more to do with him going almost... *empty*. Every second that passes brings him out of his fit and into something blank. It's not long before he's gone quiet and still, his body barely trembling anymore. The boy stares straight ahead, no trace of emotion in his eyes. His breathing goes very slow and calm.

No. No. No. No. No.

This can't happen. He can't be broken. No.

Nathan quickly scoops Carter up, hating how lifeless the boy is in his arms as he carries him back to the bedroom. Carter continues staring straight ahead at nothing.

He doesn't speak or respond to Nathan, not even when he's asked questions or offered praise. When Nathan asks if he'd like to bathe or shower, Carter just breathes. When Nathan removes his cock cage, he doesn't even flinch. When Nathan tells him he's so very good, he only blinks.

"Hey!" Nathan finally snaps, his panic getting the best of him. He grabs Carter's cheeks with one hand and squeezes until their gazes lock. "You fucking answer me when I speak to you."

After one slow blink, Carter responds in a robotic version of his voice. "Sorry, Master."

Master.

What the fuck?

"Do you want a bath or a shower?"

There's a pause. Then, "Alone, Master?"

Nathan shakes his head, giving the boy what he hopes is a comforting smile. He would never leave him alone right now. He knows how much Carter craves touch and affection, especially when he's upset. "Of course not, sweetheart. I'll join you in either."

"Oh." Carter drops his gaze just as Nathan catches a glimpse of emotion in his eyes. His voice comes out raspy as he whispers, "May I just sleep, Master?"

"You're covered in piss and vomit," Nathan states dumbly, feeling like he's going crazy.

"If it bothers you, Master, I can sleep in the cage instead." Carter looks at him through his lashes. "I wouldn't want to ruin the sheets."

Nathan's heart begins to pound, his hands trembling as he carefully removes them from Carter's body. He takes a step back as realization strangles him. Carter is willing to sleep all night covered in piss and vomit inside an uncomfortable cage just to be away from Nathan.

Nathan endured a wide variety of training before being posted in this job, and he's seen a decent amount of action as Nathan Roarke. He's been shot. Stabbed. Cut. Electrocuted. Broken. Waterboarded.

But Nathan swears, he has never felt anything worse than this moment.

"You'll clean yourself if you're alone?" he asks, praying to whoever the fuck might be listening that he has it wrong.

"Yes, Master."

Nathan feels his throat close with grief. He blinks back tears. He should insist he stay. He should force the boy to accept his care. But then he remembers how he had tried to comfort Carter earlier, when Todd had him sprawled on the desk, and how Carter had jerked away from him. The boy doesn't want his comfort. Things are bad enough without Nathan bothering him too.

Feeling numb, Nathan turns his back and says in an emotionless voice he's really fucking proud of, "Fine. I'll be back, then. Get in the shower and clean yourself."

He leaves Carter, going into the bedroom so he can undress and get his shit together.

Needing to feel like himself again, needing to feel *human*, Nathan takes a risk by putting on his faded Nike shirt with his favorite sweatpants. When he returns to the bathroom to check on the boy, he finds him curled up on his side, cheek resting on the floor of the shower, eyes squeezed shut so tightly they must ache.

"Are you clean?" Nathan asks over the sound of the water.

Carter blinks his eyes a few times before forcing himself to sit up. "Yes, Master."

Nathan stands there just staring at him as water falls down his body. He can see that the body wash and shampoo have moved, so he knows the boy at least properly washed himself before deflating to the ground. There's also his toothbrush, toothpaste, and a very depleted bottle of mouthwash on one of the shelves now too. Nathan supposes that might be the best he can ask for in this scenario.

Grabbing a towel, Nathan motions for Carter to get out. He lifts the towel as if to wrap it around the boy's shoulders, but Carter very obviously pretends to misunderstand, taking the towel from Nathan to wipe himself off. His eyes remain on the floor as he methodically dries his body, not even lifting when he offers the towel back to Nathan.

Not knowing what else to do, Nathan puts the towel in the hamper and follows Carter to bed. If it bothers Carter that Nathan is suddenly wearing sleep clothes when he never has before, the boy doesn't indicate it.

Pausing, Nathan finds himself wondering if maybe clothing could help Carter feel better right now too. He needs a reminder of his humanity just like Nathan does.

Peeling his shirt off, Nathan climbs onto the bed where Carter is now sitting and offers it to him. Carter just stares at the ball of fabric.

"Sleep in this tonight. You've earned it."

Carter licks his bottom lip before tentatively taking the shirt. He slides it on with shaking hands, his small body drowning in it as it flows down to his thighs and falls off his left shoulder. The angry bite mark there taunts Nathan. He quickly looks away.

"Here," Nathan says softly, grabbing the small moose that had somehow made its way on his side of the bed and handing it to Carter. He gives the boy a smile. Carter takes the stuffed animal, curling it tight to his chest, but he doesn't smile in return. He doesn't even make eye contact with Nathan.

"You also earned your reward," Nathan adds as he dims the lights and gets beneath the blankets.

Carter slowly lowers himself until he's lying down, his body so close to the edge of the bed Nathan's afraid he'll fall off. "No thank you, Master," he whispers.

Everything in Nathan seems to screech to a halt. "Excuse me?"

"I - I'd rather not, Master. If it's okay."

"You don't want a day off tomorrow?"

The boy pauses. Then, sheepishly, he asks, "Will you be there, Master?"

"You don't want me to be." It's not a question, but a statement. A *realization*. Carter doesn't bother confirming it.

Nathan had used tomorrow as a way to survive what happened in his office. Hell, to survive all of tonight. He had thought of all the ways he was going to pamper Carter. They were going to be lazy in bed and watch movies. He was going to bring him books. He'd give Carter a massage. He'd make Carter laugh. He'd let Carter talk like a real person.

He had really thought Carter would want him there. Nathan is supposed to be the good guy. Or, at least, the best of the bad guys. But Carter is saying he'd rather spend another day miserable as a *sex slave* than be stuck in the bedroom all day, *free* but with Nathan.

Unable to grasp the enormity of that, Nathan just says, "We can speak about it in the morning. Get some rest, sweetheart."

Carter doesn't respond.

Feeling very close to heartbroken, Nathan leaves the bed again, heading into the bathroom. He locks the door and runs the water to keep Carter from eavesdropping. Then he dials.

3 rings. "Name?"

"Eagle 2."

"Code?"

"7134."

"Hold."

Maison answers immediately, clearly having been waiting. It'd be amusing how *not* nonchalant he is when he says, "Hey man, what's up?" if Nathan wasn't having the awful night he's having.

Nathan gets a glimpse of himself in the mirror on accident.

He quickly turns away.

Nathan cuts to the chase, not bothering to pretend Maison actually wants to chit-chat for a while. "Carter is okay."

There is a heavy, relieved sigh on Maison's end of the phone. "What happened? How bad-"

"Henley is going to work with us," Nathan says in a cold, even tone as he cuts his best friend off. He needs to get this out. Get this over with. "He's agreed to the plan we pitched. He'll be at the event this weekend and will approach Miller there."

After a pause that Nathan is sure Maison uses to consider whether or not he's going to allow the sudden topic shift, Maison asks, "You trust him?"

"Nope. But compared to most of the others in this world, I at least trust that he's truly on our side. He seemed eager."

"What did he do to Carter?"

Nathan looks at the door separating him from the boy, gripping the phone tight enough to hurt his hand. "Carter is okay. He's safe."

"Nate..."

"I'm sorry." Nathan squeezes his eyes shut, trying to breathe. Trying not to fucking breakdown. He *never* cries. He got this job in the first place partially because of how well he's able to compartmentalize his emotions. "I can't, Mais. Not tonight. I – I can't."

"Okay. I trust you."

"He's-" Nathan slaps a hand down on the countertop, gritting his teeth. He hates this. He fucking *hates* this. "I can't do this much longer, Mais. I can barely fucking look at him half the time. It makes me sick."

There's a long pause before Maison says, "Good."

Nathan huffs. "Good?"

"Yeah. If this wasn't hard for you, it'd mean you're not the man I thought you were, and that would fucking suck because the man I see you as is a man I trust with my brother, even if the choices you're forced to make fucking suck. But a man who doesn't feel sick at the end of a day like today? I wouldn't want that man anywhere near my baby brother. Carter is safest with you, even if it doesn't feel like it."

"No." Nathan hangs his head. "No, I'm going to break him. I can feel it. I can't save him from this world. He's so good, Mais. He's too fucking good to be here. There has to be a better way. I don't want to ruin him."

"It's going to be okay, Nathan. You've got this. You've got *him*. I know you do."

Nathan huffs. "How? How do you know?"

"Because I can hear it," Maison says with a strange amusement in his voice. "I can hear it when you talk about him."

"Hear what?"

Maison chuckles. "Get some sleep, Nate. Go hold my baby brother for the both of us. I'll talk to you tomorrow."

Before Nathan can question Maison further, the asshole has hung up on him, leaving Nathan reeling with cryptic questions thrumming in his mind. He stares at his reflection for a long time as if it holds the answers. When nothing happens beside his self-loathing deepening, he splashes water on his face and heads back into the bedroom to try and force his body to get a few hours of rest.

Carter is fast asleep, curled up on his side with the moose tucked under his chin. Nathan leans his shoulder against one of the wooden bedposts. He sticks his hands in his pockets, letting himself just appreciate the view of the boy safe in his bed, wearing his shirt, looking every bit as beautiful and innocent as he had in the first picture Nathan ever saw of him. He's thankful for the dim lighting, knowing if there was any more light in the room he'd have to see the boy's bruising cheek and puffy lips, and probably that bare shoulder with the bite mark too. He can pretend right now that Carter is okay. He can pretend that Nathan is a man who can save him.

Just seconds after Nathan has settled down on the mattress, Carter surprises him by asking in a tiny, vulnerable voice, "Was the slave you used tonight better than me, Master?"

Feeling his heart fucking shatter, Nathan turns onto his side and reaches out, touching Carter's bare wrist with his fingertips. Carter doesn't pull away. It feels like such a monumental win. "Of course not. You're the best I've ever had, sweetheart."

"Promise?" the boy asks, his voice wobbly.

"I swear. You're the only one I want."

"Oh." Carter sniffs. It takes everything in Nathan not to wrap his arms around him and hold him as close as possible. "I'm just a hole, though. And he – he knows more stuff. It's not like I'm special, not really, and – and I cry a lot. And I'm lucky for you and – and you're – and they're all so much better than me. And you're gentle, and you don't even make me bleed, and they'd be so good for you... better than me. I – I just – I can't even – he knew what to get you to drink and – and I just – I want to be good for you, but I'm not cut out for this. I'm weak, and – and I just – I – I'm not good enough for you, and –"

"Shhh." Nathan brings his hand from the boy's wrist to cup his cheek, pressing his thumb against his lips to silence him. His chest is tight. "Sweetheart-"

Before he can continue, Carter shakes his hand loose and blurts, "Please don't punish 7, Master! *Please*. He was just helping me make the drink, and I – I had no fucking idea what I was doing and I didn't want to get hurt anymore because that's – that's all that – that *man* did was hurt me and I know that it's okay that he did that because you said it's okay and I belong to you, but I was just – I was trying to be good for you sir, and 7 – he was just helping me."

"Okay. Okay, sweetheart. I won't hurt him. Calm down now, okay? Calm down for me." Nathan shifts closer, once again placing his hand on Carter's cheek. He uses his thumb to soothingly stroke his cheekbone. He decides to test his luck as he realizes that maybe Carter's sudden change in behavior tonight has to do with more than just Todd. "Can you tell me what those slaves said to you tonight? At the drink cart?"

Carter locks up, letting Nathan know he's going to lie before he even speaks. "Nothing, Master."

Master.

"Stop. Fucking stop with that shit." Nathan sits up in the bed, raking his fingers through his hair. "*Fuck.* Since when do you fucking call me Master?"

The boy fidgets. Then, softly, "The others use Master."

"I don't want the others," Nathan says in exasperation. "I want *you.*"

"But *why?* Just put me in the basement with the rest of them. Take 3. He likes you, and he'd be better at all this. He'd make you happy. It's not like Maison would know the difference. It's not like it's any worse for him even if he did know the difference. Hell, making me a communal slave would probably be worse in his mind. And then you'd be happier..."

"*Christ.*" Nathan rolls over, pinning Carter down on the mattress. He swallows the boy's gasp with a searing kiss, one that he lets linger for much longer than usual, until the biting and the tongue fucking softens into something *more* between them. Something that makes Carter whimper beneath him, the boy's hands coming up to grip Nathan's shoulders, pulling him close instead of pushing him away. Nathan is panting by the time he breaks the kiss, resting his forehead against Carter's as he tries to catch his breath. "*Fuck.* Don't you see what you do to me, sweetheart? I only want *you.* You're the only one to ever make me feel like this. Remember?"

"Yes, sir," the boys says breathlessly.

Nathan deflates in relief at being called sir again. "Good."

"Did you... enjoy tonight, sir?"

"No." Nathan releases a shaky breath that probably gives far too much away. "I fucking hated every second of it."

Carter is crying when he speaks again. Nathan can hear it in his voice. He hates that he can already recognize the slight shift in tone. "Me too, sir. It - it was *awful.*"

"I know. I know, sweetheart." Nathan rolls to lie on his back and pulls him in close, sighing in relief when Carter relaxes against him. "Get some rest. Please."

The boy doesn't speak, but he presses harder against Nathan, his body going slack after only a few minutes.

"I'm sorry," Nathan whispers once Carter is asleep in his arms. A single tear falls down his cheek. He can't remember the last time he cried. "I'm so fucking sorry."

Chapter Sixteen

I'M SORRY. I'M SO *fucking sorry.*

The words echo in Carter's mind as he lies wide awake most of the night. He hasn't been able to decide if sir actually said them, or if he had been dreaming. There's a good chance it was a dream. Carter can't imagine sir feeling sorry, let alone *admitting* that he's sorry. It's a nice idea, though. Better than nice. It's pretty much all Carter has left to cling to.

"How long have you been awake?" sir asks quietly, startling Carter. He turns his head and takes the man in. Sir looks sleepy, his blonde hair mussed and his eyes heavy. His smile is lazy, but genuine. He makes Carter's heart race. Carter wishes he could say the reaction is from fear, but it'd be a lie.

"Not sure." Carter bites his bottom lip before adding, "A while."

He waits to see if sir will make a comment about Carter not addressing him properly.

Sir doesn't.

"Did you sleep well?" sir asks instead.

Carter looks at sir's shoulder, unable to see his face any longer. "I slept okay."

Sir gently brushes Carter's hair off his forehead, fingertips ghosting over his skin. He shivers beneath the touch, eyes fluttering closed. Carter doesn't want to forgive him, he really doesn't, but it's so damn *hard*. Things feel easier when he's not hating sir. Things feel *safer*.

Except, sir let that monster hurt Carter last night. He let him say awful things. He let him strip away Carter's humanity until he felt empty and meaningless.

But then there was the way sir had kissed him last night. The way he had promised Carter he was the only person sir ever wanted like this. The way he made Carter feel so fucking special after he had convinced himself he was worthless.

Add in the possible apology, and Carter doesn't know what the fuck to think.

"Are you ready for your day off, sweetheart?"

Unsure of what he should say considering he told sir last night he didn't want the reward anymore, Carter just keeps his eyes closed and nods. He thinks it's probably smart to accept the reward. He doesn't want sir to never offer him rewards again if he's upset with Carter for rejecting the kind gesture. Also, sir has historically been much nicer to him inside the bedroom than in the rest of the house. After last night, Carter could really use some of sir's kindness, even if he has to hate himself for enjoying it.

Of course, the moment Carter decides to give in and accept his day with sir, the man says, "I'll leave you alone today, alright?"

Carter opens his eyes to look at sir. The man is smiling at him, the expression faltering when their gazes lock. He parts his lips and runs his tongue along the bottom one before taking a breath. Carter waits for him to speak, but he doesn't. Sir just closes his mouth again and shakes his head.

When sir finally speaks, he avoids looking at Carter. "I'll bring you your meals. All three today, for how good you were for me. The remote for the TV is on my bedside table, and you're welcome to read any of the books I have on my shelves, though they're fairly boring reads."

Something akin to heartbreak blooms in Carter's chest. "You aren't staying?"

"No." Sir sits up, running a hand through his hair. He laughs humorlessly. There's a sadness and an anger to him this morning, though Carter doesn't think it's directed at him, funnily enough. "If you don't want me in here today, then I'll stay away. It's your day. Your reward."

Is that what Carter wants? He's been so fucking lonely, and when sir is kind, he's not so bad to be around. In fact, Carter almost... *likes* being with sir when sir is in the mood to treat him well. It'd be nice to have someone to be lazy in bed with as he watches TV or reads a book. Maybe sir would even be open to some cuddling.

Besides, it doesn't really accomplish anything to push sir away. *Isn't the man always telling Carter to take every chance he can to get pleasure from this situation he's in?* This is the perfect example.

Carter's pulled from his thoughts when he feels sir shift on the bed to stand up. His heart races as he watches the man leave him behind, a sudden loneliness closing in on him. It almost makes it worse that Carter is wearing the man's t-shirt that smells like him, the soft fabric a taunt, just an echo of the real thing.

The shower turns on, the bathroom door only partway closed so Carter can hear it. Even the sound of the water is lonely.

Carter still isn't sure what he's doing. He doesn't know why he decides to get out of the bed. He doesn't know why he walks to the bathroom. He doesn't know why he has this aching in his chest that's begging him to go to sir.

What he does know is that, when Carter approaches the glass door of the shower that hasn't fogged yet and sir catches sight of him, sir doesn't look sad anymore, and Carter doesn't feel quite so lonely.

HEART POUNDING, NATHAN SLOWLY opens the shower door, pushing a mass of wet hair off his forehead as he tries to figure out what to say. The boy looks unsure, but not afraid. If this is Carter coming back to him, forgiving him, letting him in, the last thing Nathan wants to do is ruin it.

He treads carefully. "What's up, sweetheart?"

Carter blushes beautifully at the pet name, his teeth nibbling at his bottom lip. "Can I join you, sir?"

The weight that had settled itself firmly on Nathan's chest loses a few pounds. "I'd love that."

Stepping aside, Nathan gestures for the boy to come in. Carter fingers the hem of his shirt anxiously for just a second before grabbing it and pulling the shirt over his head. Nathan enjoys the view, even if the few marks Todd left behind are there taunting him.

Nathan closes the door behind Carter once the boy has entered the shower, taking a step back to give Carter space if he wants it. Carter chases him, though, stepping forward. His blue eyes are wide as he stares up at Nathan.

Taking a chance, Nathan reaches out to run his fingers along Carter's arm. The boy shivers before inching closer to him.

"I thought you were mad at me," Nathan admits, even though he knows he shouldn't.

"I was." Carter frowns, eyes darting to the shower floor. "I *am*."

"But?"

"But I don't get to be," Carter states matter-of-factly. "You're my master."

Something in the response doesn't sit well with Nathan. It feels as if Carter is using that as his excuse for being here when really Carter is here because he wants to be. Then again, that could easily be wishful thinking on Nathan's part.

"You're allowed to be mad at me as long as you still respect me and behave." Nathan puts a finger beneath Carter's chin and lifts his face so their eyes meet. "You can have the day off, sweetheart. You can have it without me. It's allowed."

This must be the right thing to say because Carter admits in a rush, "What if I don't want to be alone?"

Nathan smiles softly, feeling more of that weight lift. "Then I'd be happy to stay and keep you company."

"Will you... *use me*, if you stay?" Carter asks quietly, his eyes darting towards Nathan's shoulder.

"No, I won't. You'll-" Nathan stops the words from tumbling out, knowing they're a bad idea. A terrible fucking idea.

Then again, Maison said maybe he should act like he's falling for Carter. Make Carter feel safe with him. Perhaps this could be a good step in that direction, if handled properly.

If handled properly being the operative phrase.

"You'll have your consent today," Nathan says carefully. "In this room, until tomorrow morning, you can tell me no."

Carter's wide eyes snap to Nathan's face, searching for a sign that he's lying. "R-really?"

"Really."

Tears start pooling in the boy's eyes. Nathan drops his hand, releasing Carter's face so he can duck his head if he wants to. Instead, the boy steps forward and wraps his arms tight around Nathan, resting his cheek right over Nathan's pounding heart.

Nathan runs his fingers down Carter's spine, resting his chin on the top of his head.

"What are my rules, sir?" Carter asks against the warm skin of his throat.

Nathan gently guides Carter's head back so they can look into each other's eyes. He gives the boy a warm smile, cupping Carter's cheek with a hand. The boy nuzzles against his palm. It does crazy things to Nathan's cock.

To Nathan's *heart*.

"You don't have to kneel for me, and I won't be giving you orders that you need to obey without hesitation. You may roam free inside the suite, but I don't want you snooping." Nathan runs his thumb along Carter's bottom lip, wishing the boy liked him enough to use his consent for dirty things today. He doesn't regret giving it to him though. Carter earned a day where he gets to be in charge of his own body.

"Should I call you sir still?"

"No. Not if you don't want to." Nathan swallows hard, knowing how stupid what he's about to do is, yet unable to stop himself. "You're Carter today, and I'm Nathan."

"Okay." Carter smiles. "Thank you, s – Nathan. For, you know, the day off and everything."

"You more than earned it." Nathan can't help but grin. "I can't wait to pamper you today, sweetheart. I hated seeing you hurt when you were being such a good boy for me. My sweet boy. I wanted to snatch you away from him and keep you for myself."

Carter's cheeks go red, the skin warm beneath Nathan's hand. "Is that why you came and... used me? At the drink cart?"

Not Nathan's finest moment. His self-control had snapped after watching Todd throw that drink in Carter's face. He had managed to hold off for a few minutes, but his hands had been itching to get on the boy, to touch him, to comfort him. Nathan was fucking desperate to just get a moment with the boy alone. When he hadn't come back by the time Nathan found a lull in the conversation, he took the opportunity to excuse himself and go find him.

He hadn't meant to fuck Carter, but he had seen him there, so damn beautiful and perfect and *good*, and hurting despite it all, and he had to make him feel better. It was supposed to be just a kiss and some praise, but once he had the boy in his arms, Nathan was dizzy with need. He couldn't stop.

"Yes," Nathan finally says. He quirks his lips at Carter, his emotions still conflicted on the event. "It killed me to watch someone else touch you."

"You could... not do it again." Carter says the words carefully, lightly, like he's handling a bomb.

Nathan's heart races. He wants that. Oh god, he wants that so *badly*.

He had let Todd use Carter. He doesn't see himself needing to use him again for any other business arrangements. Todd is one of the final pieces, as long as things go as Nathan plans, and the only other man he'll need to influence can be swayed in other ways. There's the issue of his promise to allow his men to use Carter for rewards, but he's the one who decides if something is worth a reward in the first place. Nathan can be a hard ass. He can act like no one is impressive enough to touch his prized possession.

It's not what he and Maison agreed to.

It's not what the elusive boss ordered.

But... what they don't know won't kill them, right?

"I'm sorry, sir," Carter says in a voice that trembles. The boy steps away from him, putting his body beneath the spray of the water. His gaze is locked on his feet. He looks like he's wavering on the decision to kneel and beg for forgiveness. Nathan took too long to respond. He got lost in his head. Now the boy is afraid. "I didn't mean-"

"Shhh." Nathan wraps an arm around him, pressing a big hand to the small of the boy's naked back and gently pulling him closer. He's even more endearing now, water dripping seductively down his body, begging Nathan to lick it up. "You're not in trouble. I've decided I'm going to consider it."

Carter's chin snaps up, eyes wide. "Really?"

"Yes. I've learned I'm a very jealous and possessive man. You're mine, after all. If I don't want to share you, I don't have to." Nathan drops his hand just enough for his fingertips to brush the curve of the boy's ass cheek. "Isn't that right, sweetheart?"

Carter firmly nods. "Yes, sir. I'll be so good for you, sir. I'll make the decision worth it, I swear."

"I know." Nathan forces himself to step back, knowing he's going to do something stupid if he doesn't get at least a little bit of distance from the naked, dripping boy. "And it's Nathan, remember, sweetheart? Just Nathan."

Carter, being the death of Nathan that he apparently is, just follows Nathan to close the space. Nathan's breath hitches. His hard cock rubs against the boy's stomach. In his defense, he tried to give him space.

Those big blue eyes train on his face, damp eyelashes batting. Nathan wants to fucking devour him. "Nathan?"

"Yes?"

"May I wash you?"

Jesus Christ, this boy really is going to be the fucking death of him.

"Absolutely." Nathan reaches for the washcloth he had grabbed before getting into the shower earlier, handing it to Carter. He starts to reach for his soap next, but Carter beats him to it. The boy blushes when Nathan arches an eyebrow at him. "How'd you know that's mine?"

"It, um... I used it last night. It smells like you."

A wave of possessiveness overwhelms Nathan. This boy, even as upset as he was, had washed himself with Nathan's go-to soap, spending the night smelling of him. "Do you like how I smell, sweetheart?"

Carter focuses *very* intently on his cloth and bottle of soap. "Yes, s - Nathan."

"I like the thought of you smelling like me. I like that quite a lot, actually."

"Um," is all the boy manages to say. His cheeks go darker red. Then he shifts focus. "Why do you have multiple soaps anyway?"

The question fills Nathan with a mixture of guilt and shame, but he answers anyway. "The white bottle is pretty harsh and doesn't smell that great, but it's much better at cleaning certain... things."

"*Things.*" Carter nods to himself, squirting Nathan's usual soap onto the cloth and rubbing it into the fabric. "Like... blood and stuff?"

"Yes," Nathan admits. "Blood and stuff."

"Do I even want to know what the third bottle is for?"

Nathan grins. "Something far less dramatic. I get flare ups of dry skin in winter, and that one is great for fixing it."

Carter looks up at him then, his expression almost startled. Nathan tilts his head and asks, "What?"

"That's just so *normal.* Dry skin." The boy giggles. "Big bad mobster with dry skin."

Nathan laughs with him, trying not to get mesmerized by how insanely perfect the boy is. "I bet even the big bad wolf had a few weaknesses."

"Is that what you are?" Carter teases. "A big bad wolf?"

"Maybe I'm *your* big bad wolf." Nathan growls, snapping his teeth at the boy to make him yelp and giggle. He wants to fucking bottle that laugh. To hold it close and keep it safe until Carter has escaped this place forever.

Peering up at Nathan through his lashes, Carter starts to swipe his soapy cloth over Nathan's broad chest. "Are you going to eat me all up, Nathan?"

"Mmm." Nathan inhales deeply through his nose, trying to remind himself that fucking this boy is *rape*. "It's tempting, little red."

"Maybe I'll eat you," Carter flirts, his cloth getting closer and closer to Nathan's hard cock. He adds a cheeky, "*Sir*," as his fabric covered hand wraps around Nathan's cock.

Nathan grits his teeth, blinking a few times. *It's rape. It's rape. It's rape.*

But Christ... Carter is *not* looking up at him like it'd be rape right now.

This boy is Nathan's greatest fucking weakness.

"Is this okay?" Carter asks, his grip on Nathan's cock tightening.

Nathan's voice comes out rough. "Very."

"I like this," Carter adds, his bare hand tracing Nathan's birdcage tattoo while the other hand continues working Nathan's cock. "It's beautiful."

Thanks, Nathan wants to say. *I got it for you, and I didn't even know it.*

Cloth covered fingertips brush against his balls. Nathan groans, his hips snapping forward. Carter grins up at him like the cat who just caught the canary.

The tattoo is forgotten.

"Careful little red," Nathan growls. "I may have given you your consent today, but a man like me has limits."

Biting down on his bottom lip, Carter seems to debate what he wants to do. Nathan can't decide if he's relieved or disappointed when the boy moves the cloth elsewhere, now working on soaping Nathan's shoulder and arm.

They fall into a surprisingly comfortable silence then, Carter washing him from behind his ears all the way to his toes. Once Nathan is rinsed, he crowds Carter against the shower wall and soaps up the cloth a second time, deciding to give the boy a taste of his own medicine.

He starts innocently enough, dragging the fabric down the elegant curve of the boy's throat and across his collarbone, but then he lingers on his nipples, loving the soft, ragged sounds Carter makes when he rubs the material against them. They've seemed to have healed since yesterday, but Nathan still asks, "These feeling better today?"

Carter whimpers and nods.

"Good. I don't like you hurting." Nathan drags the cloth down his torso with a mischievous grin before wrapping it around the boy's half-hard cock. Nathan leans in, dropping his voice low. "I much prefer you feeling good."

Carter whimpers again, his hips moving to meet Nathan's touch.

"This is good, right, sweetheart?"

"Yes," Carter gasps. "Yes, sir. Nathan. Yes."

"Good." Nathan cups the boy's balls, rolling each one, then slides the cloth between his legs to rub against his hole. "How does this feel?"

The boy rests his head back against the shower wall, eyes fluttering closed. "Good."

Nathan smirks. "Good."

Before he loses his self-control for the second time in less than 24 hours, Nathan moves on to wash the rest of the boy. He thinks Carter looks a little sad about it, but he doesn't say anything, and Nathan respects the promise he gave of consent. He'll happily use Carter, but only if the boy very clearly asks.

He might have to sneak away and jack off once or twice today...

Carter is too short to wash Nathan's hair, so Nathan does it himself while Carter just watches him with a hooded gaze. He moans when Nathan's fingers make their way into his hair next, massaging his scalp. His eyes fall closed. "That feels so good."

"Good." Nathan gives in to his temptation just a little, leaning forward to press a kiss to the boy's soap-streaked forehead. He continues to work the soap into his hair before gently guiding him towards the shower spray. "Tilt your chin and close your eyes, sweetheart."

As usual, Carter does as told. The water works in tandem with Nathan's fingers until his pretty hair is all washed out.

Nathan's never wanted to stay in the shower so badly before. He'd live in there with Carter if he could. There's a chance Carter feels the same, his lips curving into a subtle pout when the water is turned off.

"Stay," Nathan orders, though he makes sure his tone stays soft since it's the boy's day off. Once he steps out and quickly dries himself off, wrapping a towel around his waist, Nathan grabs a fresh towel and gestures for Carter to step out. He carefully dries him off, lingering in the same areas as he had when he washed him. The boy shudders and sinks back against him when Nathan turns him around to dry his hair with the end of the towel.

"I really like days off," Carter sighs. "Not sure I want to do anything to earn another one, but this is nice."

Nathan's chest aches. He wishes he could give Carter days like this all the time, without the boy needing to earn them. Since that's not possible, he just tosses the towel off to the side and orders, "Brush your teeth and meet me in the bedroom."

Then he leaves the boy behind before he can do anything reckless, his heart fucking racing as a sudden realization sinks into his bones.

Maison said to *pretend* to fall in love with Carter.

What if Nathan is accidentally doing it for real?

THERE'S A PAIR OF black Armani boxer briefs that he recognizes immediately as Nathan's, along with a faded t-shirt that he assumes is the man's as well, set out on the end of the bed. Nathan – Carter isn't sure how he feels about using that name, his heart racing at the thought of allowing this man to live in his mind as something other than *sir*, but he's trying - is standing by the dresser wearing nothing but sweatpants. It's a similar pair to the ones he wore last night. Carter thinks they might be his favorite things on Earth. He could spend hours just appreciating the way the waistband slings low on the man's hips, his happy trail curling its way down to the cock Carter has become well-acquainted with. His mouth goes a little dry as he stares at the man, taking advantage of Nathan being distracted by his phone.

Except Nathan smirks and asks, "Enjoying the view, sweetheart?" without even looking up from his screen.

Damn him.

Carter feels his face flush. "I – uh – the clothes on the bed. Are they... for me?"

Still smirking, Nathan puts the phone on top of the dresser and turns to face him fully. His own gaze travels appreciatively down Carter's naked body. It's hungry and possessive. Carter shivers as he remembers the man growling at him, calling him little red. Carter had liked that.

Carter had liked that far too much.

"Those are for you, yes. I just sent a message for breakfast to be delivered."

"Awesome." Carter grins, but then he freezes. "I mean – I get to eat, right? You mentioned I get to eat all my meals today."

Something dark passes through Nathan's expression, but Nathan responds before Carter has a chance to apologize. "Yes. You can eat all you want. I'll even get you snacks."

Carter has to fight the urge to do something ridiculous like jump on the bed and cheer. He's pretty sure he's happy enough today to do so, if only Nathan hadn't gotten weird at the end of their time in the bathroom just now. He shouldn't have said that stuff about liking his day off so much. This might be the worst part of the freedom he has today. There are plenty of opportunities for Carter to fuck up when he can't rely on strict rules and orders.

"Are you going to get dressed, or are you letting me enjoy my view all day?"

Startled out of his anxious thoughts, Carter hurries to grab the briefs off the bed and tug them up his legs. He does the shirt next. It's just as big as the one from last night, going down to his thighs, sliding off his shoulder. Something flashes in Nathan's eyes when Carter turns to present himself with a ta-da gesture. It's either lust or anger. Before Carter gets the chance to inspect it further, there's a knock on the door, and Nathan is jerking his gaze away like just looking at Carter is enough to burn him.

"Kneel on the floor," Nathan orders, already walking to the door. "Opposite side of the bed. Now."

Flinching at the sudden shift of tone in their day, Carter steps around the end of the bed and sinks to his knees. Something hot and sharp twists in his gut. Nathan – *sir?* – had said he wouldn't have to kneel today. He said no following orders without hesitation either. If Carter was braver, he would have stood his ground and questioned the man, but Carter isn't brave. Or maybe bravery has nothing to do with it. Maybe it's about being smart.

Not angering his big bad, terrifying mobster wolf that fucking *owns* him and can do absolutely anything he wants to him is the definition of smart.

The man speaks with someone at the door, his words too soft for Carter to hear. Carter peeks over the edge of the bed just as he steps aside to allow a house slave to push a large metal cart on wheels into the room. The smell of food is suddenly overwhelming in the small room, making Carter's stomach growl. Carter curls in on himself and ducks his head back down as he hears him dismiss the slave.

But the door never closes, and when the man speaks again, he sounds... *angry.*

Carter peeks over again, heart in his throat. It's his best friend, Benny. He looks as pissed as sir – *Nathan?* - sounds, his own voice angry too, rising in volume as he seemingly chews Nathan – *sir?* - out. Words make their way to Carter, jagged and confusing, some from Benny, some from the man Carter can't decide the name of.

"-fucking idiot, Nate. Why-"

"-not like that-"

"You can't just-"

"-tell me what-"

"-decide to fuck around?"

"He fucking earned-"

"-through your mind that he's a sex slave, Nathan!"

And then, very quietly, almost to the point Carter isn't sure he hears it correctly, Nathan/sir says, "He's a god-damn human being, and you can go fuck off."

Then the door slams.

A tense silence drapes itself over the room, wrapping around Carter's throat like a noose. Every second that ticks by is torture. His muscles nearly jerk with panic, his mind racing as he tries to understand what all of that meant.

It isn't until a hand touches Carter's shoulder that Carter realizes sir has come around the bed to stand before him. He looks up at the man, heart pounding. He looks enraged. Carter prepares himself to be yelled at or hit. He prepares for the man to tell him the day is over and ruined.

Instead, he surprises Carter by saying, "I didn't mean to lie to you."

Carter just blinks at the man. He's clearly misunderstanding.

When the man doesn't say anything else, Carter manages to ask a shaky, "Sir?" He uses *sir* instead of *Nathan*, figuring it's safest that way. Carter thinks it's probably best to play it safe right now.

"I promised you things about today, and I already broke them." Sir offers Carter his hand, helping him stand. "You need to be able to trust my word. That's important for us. I'm sorry."

Carter blinks some more. "You're... *sorry*?"

"Yes." Sir cups his cheek, his thumb stroking Carter's skin ever so gently. Carter fights the desire to nuzzle into the man's palm. Things are far too confusing right now. He needs to be on guard. "Shall we eat?"

Carter shifts, still not exactly sure how he should act. "If you want, sir."

"If I want," sir repeats softly to himself, his eyebrows pulling in. He drops his hand and sighs before waving towards the bed. "Get comfortable. I'll bring you your tray."

Carter obeys. A sick part of him is relieved to be given orders. It's better than being confused and scared.

When sir places the wooden breakfast tray over Carter's lap, he gives Carter a brilliant smile. It causes Carter's breath to catch. He looks away quickly, trying to keep his head straight.

Everything about sir and his behavior is forgotten when sir takes the cover off Carter's tray to reveal the fucking *beautiful* buffet of food before him. Carter feels like his eyes might bulge out of his head as he takes it all in. A bowl of berries, a bowl of mixed fruit, a bowl of oatmeal, packets of brown sugar, a small plate of sausage and bacon, a plate of mini-pancakes with a little cup of syrup and a little cup of whipped cream to dip them in, and a plate of bite-sized omelet circles. There's hot tea, a water bottle dripping with condensation from how cold it is, and a little orange juice box. There are napkins, but no silverware, which Carter supposes makes sense even though he's not going to hurt sir with a damn fork if he hasn't hurt him with the guns and knives he puts on the dresser every night.

When Carter looks over to where sir is lounging in the bed beside him, a tray of his own on his lap, he sees that he has a similar array of food, the only differences being that his pancakes and omelet are normal size. He seems to have coffee instead of tea as well, which Carter is slightly jealous of, not that he'd ever complain. And, of course, sir has silverware.

"Go ahead," sir says quietly, his focus on Carter instead of his own tray. "Eat whatever you'd like. You'll get plenty more today, so don't worry about stuffing yourself either."

With a nod, Carter tentatively grabs a strawberry. It's not until he's chewed and swallowed it that he feels sir's gaze leave him. They eat in silence for a few minutes, Carter trying not to act like a complete pig. He gets tears in his eyes when he tastes the pancake dipped in syrup and whipped cream.

Carter pauses to take a sip of his orange juice, his guard dropped because of how fucking happy he is in the moment. That's how sir catches him off guard when he says, "I'm confusing you with how hot and cold I am."

It's not a question, but Carter still meekly nods.

"I figured." Sir huffs a laugh under his breath. "Want to know a secret, sweetheart?"

Carter looks up to meet sir's eyes. He nods again.

"You confuse me too."

"I do?"

"Yes."

Carter frowns, unsure how that's even possible. "But... how?"

Sir reaches over, his thumb dragging along Carter's bottom lip to wipe away a bit of whipped cream there. He brings it to his own mouth to suck it clean, eyes never leaving Carter's. Carter swallows a whimper at the action as he tries to remain focused on the important conversation they're having. Except, sir is distracting, the man just staring at Carter like he's a piece of abstract art; beautiful, but complicated.

"Sir?"

"Nathan," he says softly, his eyes squinting fondly at Carter. "Please call me Nathan, Carter."

Carter nods dumbly, feeling a bit like this man has pulled him into a trance. "Nathan."

"Good boy." Nathan's lips twitch before he tears his gaze away from Carter. "You make me doubt everything I've ever known."

Feeling as if the air has been knocked out of him, Carter is breathless when he asks, "What do you mean?"

"You-" Nathan stops, shaking his head as he laughs humorlessly. Then he grabs the remote and says, "We should put a movie on. Would you like to pick?"

The topic change is the opposite of subtle, and Carter wants to call Nathan out on that. He's too afraid, though. It's clearly a sore subject if Nathan is acting like this. He should be smart. Leave well enough alone.

Knowing he might not ever get another day like this again, Carter shoves his lingering thoughts and questions aside. "I'd like that. Thank you."

Nathan turns the TV on before handing Carter the remote. It's one of those huge fancy smart TVs, but it doesn't take long for Carter to figure it out. He pauses when he sees the assortment of apps, though, unsure if

Nathan wants him to purchase a movie or browse one of his subscriptions. Nathan seems to read his mind. "You can go to that app on the left and buy something."

Carter does so, too giddy to be nervous as he scans the familiar titles he thought he'd never get the chance to see again. His cheeks hurt from how hard he grins when he finds one movie in particular. "Can we watch this, Nathan?"

"Hmmm?" Nathan looks up from his phone, squinting at the TV in a way that Carter does *not* find endearing. Then he raises an eyebrow at Carter. "Harry Potter?"

"I love Harry Potter. Maison used to read me all the books, and then when they started coming out in theaters he'd bring me. We'd get straws from the concession stand and pretend we were wizards." Carter's eyes meet Nathan's, his smile dropping a few levels as his reality sinks in. He darts his eyes back to the screen and shakes his head. "We can watch something else."

"No, let's watch Harry Potter."

"Are you sure?" Carter asks, looking up at Nathan through his lashes.

Nathan's smile is warm and, if Carter isn't mistaken, *fond.* "I'm sure. Though I don't have any straws, so I suppose Maison is better than me in that regard."

For some reason, this makes Carter laugh. Maybe it's just the easy way Nathan talks about his brother, not making Carter feel guilty or anxious about the subject. Maybe it's just the goofy smile Nathan gives him when he says it. Maybe it's something else. It doesn't matter. What matters is that when Carter laughs, Nathan's whole face lights up, and then Carter is trapped in this moment of awe as he stares at the man who stole his whole world from him, forgetting for just a second why he hates him so much.

Carter snaps his attention back to the TV and fumbles with the remote until the movie has been purchased.

Then he stuffs his mouth with a pancake bite to make sure he doesn't say something stupid.

Within the first few minutes of the movie, Carter learns 3 very devastating facts about Nathan.

One: Nathan has never seen Harry Potter before. None of them! When asked, he also admits to having never read the books either. Carter can't decide which is a worse offense, the whole sex slave thing, or being a person who has lived a cold, lonely life without the joy of Harry Potter in it.

Okay, obviously that's dramatic as fuck, but it's still a pretty bad offense on its own.

Two: Nathan is one of those people who asks *questions* when watching a movie.

So. Many. Questions.

"You just have to watch!" Carter says with a laugh for what must be the 5th time in as many minutes. "It'll explain."

Three: Nathan is a *pouter*. The tall, muscular, dark and dangerous man fucking *pouts* when he does not get his way.

By the time the second movie is over, Nathan has come to two very important conclusions: Snape is obviously a bad guy, and everyone who doesn't see that is an idiot.

"If this kid can see it, the grown-ups should be able to," Nathan argues, shaking his head like he just can't believe the stupidity of it all.

"Looks can be deceiving."

"But his aren't! Look at the damn guy. He's a classic case of villain. Black clothing. Dark cloak. Creepy looking. And the way he treats Harry, *openly* treats him. I mean, Harry saved the fucking world, and here this asshole is, treating him like a pile of shit he stepped in."

Carter bites back a smile. "Exactly. His looks could be deceiving you. Maybe they're making him *seem* like the villain when he's not. He could really just be misunderstood."

"He's clearly the villain."

"Not every villain is a creepy looking guy in all black. Some villains are attractive rich men in fancy suits," Carter tells him without thinking. Then his gut clenches as he realizes what he just said to the man. He ducks his head and holds his breath, waiting to see what will happen. Best case, Nathan just ends their evening and leaves Carter alone. Worst case, Nathan teaches Carter a lesson about attitude.

After a longer pause than Carter would prefer, Nathan finally releases a sigh and agrees. "You're right. Looks can be deceiving." Before Carter can figure out what to say to that, Nathan pulls him in close and presses a kiss to the crown of his head. "I think it's a good time for us to take a little nap. Don't you agree?"

Carter nods carefully.

"Excellent." Nathan shifts the pillows around before lying back with Carter still in his arms, guiding Carter's head to rest on his chest. He tucks Carter's moose beneath Carter's chin before pulling the large comforter up to cover them. "Get some rest, sweetheart. We have 6 more movies to watch."

Nodding, Carter closes his eyes and tries to force himself to relax. It takes a while before he can finally let down his guard enough to sink into Nathan's warmth. Nathan releases a satisfied sigh the moment Carter's body melts into his own.

As Carter drifts to sleep, Nathan's steady heartbeat his own personal lullaby, he thinks that maybe looks can be deceiving, but maybe actions can be too.

Benny had reminded sir that Carter is a sex slave.

Nathan had reminded him that Carter is *human*.

When they're around Nathan's men, Nathan says and does terrible things to him.

When they're alone in his office or in the bedroom, Nathan pampers him and cares for him.

Nathan shared him with Todd Henley.

He told Todd to stop when he tried to piss in Carter's mouth.

Nathan said he only did that to keep from dealing with a sick slave.

He had sounded so broken when whispering his scotch-soaked apologies to Carter last night.

Nathan could be a villain that's attractive and rich, wearing a fancy suit.

Or maybe, just maybe, Nathan is misunderstood too.

Chapter Seventeen

BODIES ARE PRESSED AGAINST Carter.

Too. Many. Bodies.

They're wet. Frigid. They must have gotten the hose recently.

Though... Carter doesn't remember that happening. Not that he remembers much lately. Time in the cell is a blur, which he thinks is probably for the best.

There's an ache in him. A need. He... god, he misses someone.

Severely misses someone.

But who?

He smells scotch and spice. He knows that smell. That's – who is that?

Sir.

Carter has a sir. He shouldn't be in the cell. He should be in sir's manor. In sir's bed. He should be with sir.

It's his day off. They watched a movie. Cuddled.

Sir gave him his consent.

Sir snapped his teeth at him, growling as he called him little red. Carter had giggled.

Why is Carter in the cell if he has a sir who makes him giggle?

"It was all a dream," someone whispers. Carter whips around, but nobody is there. It's just black. A dark, empty, nothingness. "You were dreaming, Carter."

Carter turns again. "Who's there?"

Nobody.

Nothing.

Carter blinks rapidly, trying to get his vision to form something. Anything. A shadow. A vague shape. A shade of grey.

"You haven't been sold yet," the voice explains. "Nathan Roarke wasn't real. None of it was real."

That voice... Carter knows that voice, but he can't place it.

"Who are you?" Carter demands. "Fucking show yourself!"

"I can't. They won't let me see you. They took you away."

They took Carter away?

He's right. They did. They took Carter away.

They put him in the dark.

Oh god, the dark. That awful cell. Is Carter really still in there? Starving? Thirsty? Lonely beyond belief? Did Carter conjure sir as a way to cope?

No.

No way.

Sir bought Carter. He knows he did. Carter remembers. Sir bought him, and sir is keeping him. He promised. Sir doesn't get rid of the things that belong to him, and Carter belongs to him.

That wasn't a dream.

He isn't supposed to be here.

He isn't supposed to be here.

He isn't supposed to be here.

Carter isn't supposed to be here.

Looking around the darkness, Carter tries to search again. This time for the man he knows should really be here. "Sir? Where are you, sir?"

Nothing.

"Stop it." *That voice.*

Casey.

It's Casey.

"Don't call for him, Carter. Stop."

Carter ignores Casey. He's a liar. He's trying to trick Carter.

Sir is real.

Carter knows it.

"Sir?"

"You're letting the bad guys win," Casey accuses. "Why are you letting them win?"

"Shut up!"

"We said it'd be okay. We promised Elliot. But it was a lie."

"We had to," Carter argues, ending his search just in case this is real. Just in case he's really gone crazy, and sir was never a man who existed. "Casey, we had to. Don't you understand? We had to tell Elliot that. He needed to relax. He deserved to relax for just a fucking minute."

There's a low voice then. Dark. Dangerous.

It's not Casey.

"Sweetheart, what are you doing?"

"Don't answer him," Casey hisses. Carter jumps at how close the boy suddenly is. He still can't see him, but he can hear him right in his ear now. He can feel Casey's breath on his skin. The heat coming off him in waves is the only source of warmth in the darkness. "Don't, Carter."

"He'll be mad if I don't," Carter growls.

Casey scoffs. "You just don't want to disappoint him. You fucking like pleasing him, don't you?"

Carter doesn't answer that.

He doesn't want to talk about sir anymore. He doesn't want to admit to Casey that every fiber of his being wants to run to the man right now. He doesn't want to admit that the moment he heard sir's voice, he felt like he could fucking breathe again.

He doesn't want to admit that Casey is fucking right.

"You're with the bad guys. You're helping them win now."

This makes the low voice from before chuckle. "Damn right he is. That's because he's a good boy, aren't you, sweetheart?"

273

Conflict and chaos roar inside Carter's mind. He wants to be good for sir, but he doesn't want to let the bad guys win. They promised Elliot that the bad guys won't win. That was supposed to be true. They were supposed to hold onto that hope. To fucking cling to it. Until their moment. Keep calm.

Breathe.

Pay attention.

Wait for your moment.

"I'm not helping the bad guys," Carter whispers.

Casey laughs cruelly. "You're not fighting either, are you, Carter?"

"I –" *Carter has to stop, swallowing the words down as he realizes they'd be a lie. He's not fighting. Of course he's not. He's being good.*

"He's nice if I'm good." *Carter turns, trying desperately to find Casey in the dark. He needs him to understand. Casey has to understand.* "I can't be bad, or he hurts me."

"Sounds like a dog with a shock collar." *Casey scoffs.* "He has fucking weapons in the bedroom. You were in a fucking McDonald's parking lot and you didn't even try to escape. You were just by a door and all you did was stare outside like a fucking idiot!"

"You're the one who fucking told me to wait until the right moment!" *Carter growls.* "I'm just waiting!"

"No, Carter. You're not just waiting. You're enjoying. You're forgetting. Do you even want to leave him? Do you want to be free?"

"Of course I do! I – I'm just trying to survive."

"He was willing to give you the day alone, and you begged him to fucking stay with you instead. You rode him like a whore in his bed, and you got off on it. You moaned and came and loved every second of it when he fucked you over a desk. You feel comfortable and at peace when you have his cock in your mouth to warm. You begged him to use you even after he had beat you until you pissed yourself."

Carter shakes his head furiously, eyes watering. "Stop it."

"You love it when he holds you, don't you? When he kisses you. When he calls you sweetheart."

"Stop."

"You like him, don't you, Carter? You're probably falling in love with the sick fuck."

That's not true.

It's not.

But... isn't it?

He was just willingly in bed with the man, cuddling him as they fell asleep after watching a movie together. He didn't cry or try to fight sir any of the recent times sir tried to use him. He even got off on the things sir did to him, just like Casey said.

Carter squeezes his eyes shut, shaking his head. He pants under his breath, "No, no, no-"

"Admit it, Carter. Be a fucking man and admit it."

"No!"

"Sweetheart?"

Carter sobs, trying so damn hard to ignore sir. To not go to him. He wants to prove Casey wrong. He wants to show him that he doesn't want to be with sir. He'd rather stay here in the dark with Casey.

But that's a lie. It's such a goddamn lie. Things have been better since sir. Sir saved him, in a way.

"Saved you?!" Casey nearly screeches. "Better since him? Are you fucking kidding me? He raped you, Carter! More than once! He let that man piss in your mouth! He let him hurt you!"

"He – he made him stop. And he said he was sorry!"

Casey steps away from him, the cold seeping back into Carter's bones with the loss of his presence. "You're not special. You're just a hole to him."

"No." Carter tries to step toward Casey, but he can't see him in the dark. He reaches out, waving his hand, but there's nothing there. "He said I'm special. He said I'm the only one he wants."

When Casey speaks, his voice is soft. Far away. Carter's heart pounds as he realizes he's losing Casey again. "I can't believe you love him."

"I don't." Carter swallows a sob. "Casey, come back. Where are you going? Come back."

"Sweetheart?" Sir hums softly, the sound he makes when he's contemplating. Then he whispers right in Carter's ear. "Come back to me. You're safe. I've got you. Come back."

"Stay," Casey begs.

"Come, sweetheart. Come to sir."

"Please, Carter!"

"Sweetheart."

Casey shrieks, the sound sharp and violent. Carter quickly brings his hands to his ears to check if they're bleeding. "They'll kill me, Carter! They'll kill me! Please! Don't leave me! Please don't leave me!"

Sir sighs in annoyance. "If you want to stay, then fucking stay. But I'm not coming back for you. This will be your life now. The dark. The loneliness. The hunger and thirst. Is that what you want? Don't I treat you so much better than that, sweetheart? I don't ask that much of you, and I take such good care of you when you're good, don't I?"

Yes.

Yes, he does.

Being with sir has been so much better than the dark.

Carter won't survive the dark. He can't be left here. Not again.

Never again.

"Last chance, sweetheart."

"Please don't leave me, Carter!" Casey rasps. "Please don't leave me again."

Carter grabs at his hair, yanking it. "I don't know what to do! I don't know what to do!"

"Alright." Sir sighs. When he speaks again, his voice is too far away. He's leaving. "Goodbye, sweetheart."

"Wait, no!" Panic seizes Carter's body. "Sir, please. I don't want to be in the dark anymore. I don't want to be alone. Please! I'll come with you. Please!"

"Shhh." A hand touches Carter's face. Gentle. Comforting. He reaches for it, wanting to hold it there, but it vanishes. Carter sobs at the loss. "Shhh. You're okay, sweetheart. Just follow my voice. Be a good boy and follow my voice."

Carter can do that. He can be a good boy.

He stumbles through the dark, blind, falling twice, once right on his damn face, but then there's a light ahead, and he's fucking running. His lungs ache. His body begs him to stop. He needs water. Food. He's hurt.

Just a little farther.

Just a little farther.

"Car-ter," sir singsongs. "Where are you?"

"I'm coming!" Carter tries to yell, but his throat is too raw. All that comes out of him is a strangled cry that tastes metallic on his tongue.

Then he bursts forward into the light.

Sir is there, standing in his low-slung sweatpants and faded shirt, looking tousled and relaxed and so fucking sexy. He smiles at Carter, offering a hand. Happiness blooms in Carter's chest as he takes it.

They're standing in a field. There are daffodils as far as the eye can see. It's all blue sky and green grass and yellow flowers.

The air is fresh.

The wind is the perfect cool temperature as it kisses his warm skin.

He's not hungry.

He's not thirsty.

Everything is perfect.

Everything is safe.

Something moves in the daffodils, bright yellow rippling. Carter doesn't approach with caution. He just smiles and goes forward. Hopeful. Naïve. This place is too pure for something bad to happen. He's not afraid.

There's a body in the daffodils.

Naked.

Bloody.

Carter stands there for a moment, trying to figure out what he's seeing. Trying to make sense of it.

"Casey?"

"Carter!" Casey sobs, trying to look at him. Something is happening to him. Something... not right. As Carter stands there watching, Casey's body begins to bruise and break. The marks bloom angry on his flesh. A rainbow of pain.

But no one is touching him.

"C-Carter... help me."

"I can't – I – there's no–" Carter gasps for air, feeling a spin of panic. "Who's hurting you, Case? Who is it? How do I help?"

Carter sobs as he watches more injuries bloom on his friend's body. In desperation, he throws himself over Casey, trying to cover him, to protect him from whoever is attacking him. "Stop! Leave him alone!"

This can't be happening.

This can't be happening.

Carter has to save him! He failed the first time, but he can do it now. He can fix this. He can save Casey. He can. He knows it.

He just – he doesn't know how.

"Stop it!" Carter begs as Casey's body continues jerking beneath him. "Don't hurt him! Stop hurting him! Hurt me!"

Casey looks at Carter, his eyes fading, going lifeless. A tear runs down his cheek. It's bloody. "You left me, Carter. Why did you do that? Why'd you leave me?"

"I'm sorry!" Carter sobs, clinging to Casey harder. "I'm so sorry!"

Something comes around Carter's waist. An arm. Heavy. Secure. Too strong. He's pulled away from Casey, sir whispering things like, "Shhh," and, "You're alright, sweetheart," and, "Just breathe for me," as he drags Carter away from his *dying friend. Carter tries to reach out for Casey, fingertips brushing the silky soft petals of the daffodils.*

"Casey!"

"You chose me," sir whispers. "Remember?"

"But – but I – I – but-"

Sir puts him on his feet. He takes Carter's face in his hands. The smile he offers Carter is so damn soft. Genuine. Loving. He runs a thumb along the curve of Carter's cheek, eyes looking at Carter like he's never seen something so beautiful. "Stay with me, sweetheart. Please. Don't think about him. Be mine. Just mine. All mine."

Carter opens his mouth to argue, to beg, but sir is no longer in front of him. He whips around, heart pounding as he prays the man didn't leave him too.

He finds sir standing over Casey. He has his arm out-stretched, a closed fist hovering in the air above Casey's body. When Carter takes a step towards them, sir lifts his head. He grins at Carter. Then he opens his hand and pours daffodil petals over Casey's body. They cover him completely, filling his mouth, choking him, burying him alive.

"Casey!"

Carter dives for his friend, needing to help him, needing to fucking save him, but sir grabs him around the waist and keeps him out of reach. Carter keeps reaching, keeps trying, but every time he pulls back his hands, they're covered in blood-stained daffodils. "Sir, help him, please!"

He looks at sir as he begs, but sir just stares at Casey in boredom. When Carter looks back, he sees that Casey isn't alone anymore. Elliot is there now. He's kneeling beside Casey in the grass, his own body a rainbow of pain. His eyes are dead, his expression blank.

Elliot looks up at Carter, his voice monotone as he says, "He'll be okay."

"No!" Carter screams. "He's dying, Elliot. Help him. He's fucking dying!"

"It'll be okay."

"Elliot!"

"It'll be okay," the boy says again. Then he grins, a wicked, twisted thing that looks wrong and foreign among the dead features of his body. Daffodil petals begin pouring from his mouth. "It'll be okay, it'll be okay, it'll be okay."

"He's dying!" Carter sobs. "They're both dying!"

"It's okay," sir whispers, holding him close, rocking him back and forth. "It's okay, now. You're okay. I'm right here."

"I'm so sorry!" Carter sobs.

He sobs in frustration. In grief. In guilt.

He sobs for Casey. For Elliot.

He screams for them. Begs for them.

For himself.

Carter blinks, and he's no longer in the field of daffodils.

He's with sir in the dungeon, tied down to something he can't see, and he's begging sir to stop, stop, please, god, stop.

Sir just swings the toy in his hand again, hitting Carter with it. A flogger. A flogger whose leather trusses have been replaced with razor sharp daffodils.

Oh god, they fucking hurt when they hit him. Each strike draws blood.

Carter shrieks. Sobs. Begs.

"You fucking asked for this," sir reminds him. "You picked me over your own friends. You let those boys fucking die because you wanted this!"

"No!" Carter shakes his head rapidly. That's not what he wanted. That's not what he wanted. "Stop, please, stop!"

"Do you want to go back? Should I put you in the dark again?"

Carter just sobs.

Sir laughs.

He keeps beating Carter. He beats him over and over. He beats him until he's bled everything out, his veins no longer pouring red liquid. Instead, Carter is bleeding daffodil petals.

Hazy with pain, Carter lolls his head to the side. His tear-filled eyes catch sight of a man behind sir. He's standing a foot or so behind sir, but to the side, so his view isn't disrupted. He's wearing his high school football jersey and faded jeans, a worn-out blue baseball cap backwards on his head. When he sees Carter looking at him, he just lifts his chin in acknowledgement. His face remains impassive.

"Maison?" Carter gasps. "Maison, help me!"

"It's okay, baby brother. Just be good for him."

Sir hits Carter again.

Again.

Again.

The petals are pouring down his body in rivulets now, leaving black goo in their wake. "Maison! Please, please, please, oh god, please help me! Fucking help me!"

"You're not behaving, Carter," Maison chides. "Behave!"

"W-what? No. I – Maison, please. Please help me!"

Maison sighs heavily. Then, "Just hit him harder, Roarke. He obviously needs to learn."

Carter slumps in his restraints, his breath rushing from his lungs in a sob. "Why won't you save me?"

"Why the fuck would I?" Maison grunts in disgust. "You're a fucking cock slut, baby brother. You're useless. Pathetic. Why would I want you anymore? Why would I ever want a brother like you?"

"M-Maison?" Carter gasps, positive he's misunderstanding.

"You like this. You want him." Maison sneers. "You've let them ruin you."

"No!" Carter shakes his head furiously, desperate for Maison to believe him. "I don't like him. I don't. I promise."

"Don't lie, baby brother."

"All he does is lie," Casey tells Maison, suddenly standing beside his brother now, still covered in daffodils, his eyes creepily blank. "He fell in love with that sick bastard. Can't you see it? Watch. You can tell."

"I don't love him!"

"Shhh, sweetheart," sir whispers, stroking his tear-soaked cheek. The flogger is gone. The petals. The blood. The pain. "Open up for sir. Be good for me."

Carter exhales in relief, sagging back against whatever it is he's tied to. His eyes fall closed as sir presses his cock into him. It feels good. So damn good.

"That's it, sweetheart." Sir presses kisses to his shoulder. His throat. His lips. He pants against Carter's mouth. "Christ, you take my cock so well, sweetheart. You're so fucking perfect for me."

Oh god.

Oh god, they're right. Maison. Casey. Elliot. They're right.

Carter likes this.

He's fucked up.

Ruined.

Disgusting and pathetic.

"Sir," Carter sobs, shaking his head. "Sir, please, I don't know what to do..."

"You're doing it," sir coos. "Don't you see? All you have to do is please me. Be good for me. Just let everything go, let it all go, and be good for me. It's that easy, sweetheart. Nothing else for you to worry about. No reason to be upset. Just be mine. Please be mine."

Carter nods. He wants that. He wants to be sir's.

Sir shifts over Carter, and they're suddenly in sir's bedroom. Harry Potter's voice is in the background. He's talking about the sex trade. About Stockholm Syndrome. About abuse victims and PTSD. Snape is arguing with him. He's saying people sometimes love people they shouldn't, but that doesn't make their love wrong.

"Sir..."

"Shhh. Just trust me. Let go and trust me, sweetheart. It'll be okay."

"It'll be okay," Elliot echoes, now hovering strangely in the air above them, eyes white like Casey's had been in the dungeon.

Casey is beside him. He's a second echo. "It'll be okay."

Then Maison, standing there staring at Carter in betrayal and disgust. "It'll be okay."

"It'll be okay."

"It'll be okay."

"It'll be okay."

"It'll be okay," sir gasps, pushing Carter's legs harder against his chest, fucking into him faster, each movement steady and sexy and pushing Carter closer to an orgasm. "It'll be okay, it'll be okay, it'll be okay."

Casey is fading. Elliot too.

Maison already left.

"Casey!" Carter sobs. "Elliot! Stay here, stay with me!"

"You chose him," Casey says in betrayal.

"You left us," Elliot adds.

Carter tries to escape sir, needing to get to his friends. Needing to find his brother. But sir holds him too close, too tight, not letting him go.

"I don't know what to do!" Carter sobs, sagging into the mattress in defeat. "I don't know what to do! I don't know what to do!"

"Shhh, sweetheart," sir whispers, holding him close, fucking into him nice and slow. "Shhh. You don't have to do anything. You're okay. I have you now."

Carter tries to get away. Tries to fight sir. He thrashes and swings and kicks. "Casey! Elliot!" he screams as he fights, wanting the boys to see that he's trying to get to them. He's trying to help them. They just have to hold on a little longer.

But Elliot is dead, limp in Casey's arms, and Casey is wavering on his feet, eyes falling shut.

"Casey! Casey!"

Sir holds Carter too close, his arms sandwiched almost painfully between his chest and sir's. "Stop it! You're going to hurt yourself, sweetheart."

"Casey!" Carter sobs, throwing his head back in grief as he gives into sir's hold. "Casey, I'm so sorry!"

He doesn't see it, but he hears it when Casey dies. The final gasp. The muffled sound of petals hitting the floor. The heavy thump of a body following.

"I'm sorry," Carter cries. "I'm sorry, I'm sorry, I'm sorry–"

"Shhh, sweetheart," Nathan whispers again, relieved that the boy has at least stopped fighting him now. When he had first woken, Carter had been in the middle of punching and kicking at the air, screaming for someone named Casey. Someone named Elliot. He was sobbing. Pleading. "I don't know what to do!" he kept saying, thrashing his head back and forth in pure agony. "I don't know what to do!"

While Nathan had fought to get Carter under control, the boy had continued yelling, mostly just for Casey then. He was desperate to get to Casey, it seemed. It took forever before he finally gave up and went limp in Nathan's arms, but now he's finally calmed down, reduced to nothing but softly cried apologies.

"I'm sorry, I'm sorry, I'm sorry–" the boy continues whispering, his body trembling from the exertion of his fight with Nathan, as well as the overwhelming emotions he's clearly experiencing. "I'm sorry, I'm sorry–"

"Shhh," Nathan repeats. "Hush, now. Sir has you. You're okay. You're okay, sweetheart."

"I'm sorry," Carter whispers. "I'm so sorry."

"Sweetheart." Nathan shifts Carter in his arms, gently shaking him to try and pull him from the nightmare. This needs to end now. The boy has suffered in his own mind long enough. "Sweetheart, wake up now. Come back to sir. Wake up."

Carter buries his face in Nathan's neck and sobs harder, still apologizing.

And then...

Then he says something else.

Something that stops Nathan dead in his tracks.

"I'm sorry I picked him, Casey. I'm sorry I picked sir over you..."

Nathan is still trying to process what the fuck that could possibly mean when the boy finally goes quiet, his breathing evening out, his crying coming to an end. He relaxes into Nathan's hold as he begins to sleep peacefully.

It takes everything in Nathan to keep from waking Carter up. He wants to demand Carter tell him what the dream was about. He wants to know who Casey is. Who Elliot is. He wants to know what the fuck Carter meant when he apologized for picking Nathan over Casey. But all of that is selfish. It's none of his business. He's taken enough from Carter. He doesn't need to invade the privacy of his dreams, too. And he sure as hell doesn't need to steal whatever peaceful sleep he manages to get.

Nathan carefully rolls Carter onto his back, settling the boy among the pillows, putting his moose in his hand, and pulling the blankets up to tuck him in. He presses a soft kiss to his forehead, whispering an apology.

Unable to stand another minute in the room, Nathan shoves out of bed and grabs a random shirt from his dresser before leaving. He doesn't care that he gets a ton of strange looks from his men. He doesn't care that even a few house slaves double-take at him. He doesn't care that he's fucking bare foot in sweatpants and a cotton t-shirt walking through a house he usually never sets foot in except when he's in one of Nathan's suits of armor. All he cares about is the bottle of whiskey he knows is in a drawer in his office, and he wants it.

He makes it there without incident, heading to the compound's gym next. He's already taking swigs of the alcohol as he walks. Each one burns away some of the ache in his chest that's developed ever since he first set eyes on Carter Beckett.

Two of his men are in the gym when he enters, one spotting the other as they lift weights. Both pause when they see him, holding perfectly still, staring at him like he's an anomaly. Nathan usually works out early in the morning every day, at least before Carter was here, and it was made clear that he doesn't like working out with others, so everyone always avoided the gym at that time of day. Now these men clearly don't know what to do with the fact that Nathan is suddenly here in the afternoon.

Nathan takes another gulp of whiskey, raising an eyebrow at the idiots. "Well? Get the fuck out."

They scramble, nearly tripping to get away from him fast enough.

After setting the speaker system to a playlist full of music angry enough to match his own raging emotions, Nathan sets his bottle down on the sparring mat beside a heavy bag. He should wrap his hands, but he won't. He deserves the pain of the leather scraping his knuckles raw and the throb of his knuckles hitting the bag of sand. Nathan needs to bruise and bleed, just like Carter.

He pounds his fists into the bag over and over, trying to escape Carter. Trying to escape the feelings he's developing for the sweet boy, to escape the overwhelming amount of *Travis* Carter always manages to coax out of him no matter how hard Nathan tries to stay in control.

But the boy haunts him.

I'm sorry, I'm sorry, I'm sorry.

I'm sorry.

I'm sorry I picked him, Casey.

I'm sorry I picked sir over you...

Nathan doesn't even realize the music has been turned low until he stops to take a swig of whiskey. He turns, expecting to find some idiot he can take his anger out on. Turns out it's worse.

Benny.

"I don't want to talk," he growls.

"Too bad." Benny crosses his arms and frowns at him. He reminds Nathan of an angry old man. Nathan snorts at the thought, almost asking Benny if he's in trouble for walking on his lawn. Benny arches an eyebrow at him. "What's so funny?"

Nathan laughs harder, shaking his head. "My fucking life."

Benny frowns. "Nate-"

"Have you ever seen Harry Potter?"

Clearly confused, it takes Benny a moment to respond. Nathan uses the opportunity to drink more whiskey.

Finally, *carefully*, Benny says, "I've read the books."

"Of course you have, you fucking book nerd." Nathan snorts. Then he frowns at his bottle. "I should get Carter the books."

"*Nathan!*" Benny growls, walking forward quickly until they're just inches away from each other.

Eyes wide, Nathan leans towards his friend and dramatically whispers, "*Benny!*"

"Fucking hell, you're hammered, aren't you?"

"Beside the point." Nathan waves a hand, brushing the silly topic away. "Tell me what happens with Snape."

Benny squints at him. "Snape?"

"Yeah. Tall, dark, not at all handsome, asshole potions teacher." Nathan takes another drink. He doesn't like the way Benny is eyeing the bottle. Benny better not ask to share. Supply is running low. "What happens to him?"

"I'm sorry, are you asking me to spoil Harry Potter right now for you? Like the entire series?"

"Yes."

"Okay, as a *fucking book nerd* – your words, not mine – I can't in good conscience do that."

"But I need to know," Nathan says in desperation, his heart pounding. "I need to know about Snape."

Benny rubs a hand across his forehead. "Why?"

"It's *important*."

"Nate... what's going on, bud?"

Nathan takes a gulp of his whiskey, closing his eyes as he savors the burn. He sucks in a deep breath right after, the air rushing in, stoking the fire. Then he meets Benny's eyes and asks point-blank, "Am I the villain?"

Benny's expression softens. "Oh, Nathan..."

"No, no, don't – don't look at me like that." Nathan points the bottle at his friend, contemplating hitting him with it. "Just fucking tell me."

After scanning the area again, Benny looks him in the eye and says, "You're a goddamn hero, Travis."

"No. No, I'm not." Nathan shakes his head and takes another sip of the whiskey. He stumbles, but just for a second. The mat must be slippery. "Heroes don't rape the boys they love."

The words feel like a bomb.

Nathan snaps his chin up, staring wide-eyed at Benny. He suddenly feels very sober. "I-"

"You're drunk," Benny says, interrupting him. "You just need to sleep it off, alright?"

"Carter's gonna want me when he wakes up. He won't know what happened."

"I'll stop by and tell him you had something come up with work. He'll understand."

Nathan takes a wobbly step back, shaking his head. "You'll scare him."

"I'll be quick. I won't go near him."

"It's his day off."

"I know, bud. I know." Benny tentatively reaches forward. His fingers brush the whiskey bottle, but Nathan can't get himself to let go. "Don't ruin his day off, Nate. It'd be better for him to think you're working than to see you like this. If you go to him now, you'll be the one to scare him."

"But-"

"Nate." Benny ducks his head, forcing Nathan to meet his gaze. "You're drunk off your ass, rambling about Harry Potter, confessing love, and bleeding all over the place."

"I'm not-" Nathan's words stop when he sees that Benny is telling the truth. His hands are covered in blood, the skin of his knuckles bruising and split. He just stares down at them in wonder. "*Oh.*"

Benny tries to take the bottle of whiskey again. Nathan lets him this time.

"Can I trust you to keep your mouth shut until we get to my bedroom?" Nathan nods, deciding he should start now for some practice. "Okay. Let's go, then. I'll send a slave in to clean."

He lets Benny guide him out of the gym and into the main area. People keep looking at him, just as they did before. He holds his head high and glares at them to keep them in their place. They all quickly skitter away.

"Alright, bud." Benny opens his bedroom door and forces Nathan inside, not even allowing him to glance over his shoulder at his own door down the hall. He sits Nathan down on the edge of the bed before disappearing into the bathroom for a while, coming back with a bottle of Tylenol, a wet cloth, and his med-kit.

Nathan groans. "Nooo."

"Shut up." He tosses the bottle at Nathan before grabbing some water from his mini fridge and placing it on the mattress beside him. "Take the damn pills."

"You're very bossy..."

"You're very pouty."

Nathan frowns, his bottom lip curving out. When he realizes he is, in fact, pouting, he quickly straightens his expression and focuses on the pills instead. He hisses when Benny pours antiseptic over his cuts, shooting a glare at his unsympathetic friend. "Careful, asshole."

"Shut up." He dabs Nathan's hand with a piece of gauze. "I can't believe you did this. So reckless, you fucking idiot."

"I know." Nathan swallows hard, hearing the echo of Carter in his mind. "He had a nightmare."

Benny looks up at him, his hand pausing its work. "And?"

"He eventually calmed down without waking up, but he – he said some things, while having it."

"What things?"

"Confusing things." Nathan winces when Benny returns to working on his hand, but he doesn't complain this time. He deserves the pain. "He was crying, saying he didn't know what to do, apologizing over and over. He was talking to someone named Casey, it sounded like. And he – well, it sounded like he was apologizing for picking me over him."

His friend frowns as he wipes off the extra blood on Nathan's hand and wrist. "Picking you over Casey?"

"Yeah."

"You don't know who Casey is?"

"No."

"Do you know what he was picking one of you for?"

Nathan sighs. "No."

"But you must have an idea if it fucked you up this bad."

"Yeah. I – fuck, Benny." Nathan laughs humorlessly, feeling sliced open and raw. "I think he chose to stay with me. It sounded like this Casey wanted Carter to leave me, and Carter picked to stay with me instead."

Benny nods slowly without saying anything. He carefully wraps Nathan's hand before moving on to the other one. When he still hasn't said anything, Nathan asks, "Why would he ever pick me, Ben?"

His friend sighs heavily before rocking back to rest on his heels and looking up at him. "I don't know. Maybe he sees the real you. Maybe you're not as good at hiding yourself from him as you'd like to believe."

Nathan closes his eyes, picturing Carter.

How could he ever pick him?

How could Carter ever fucking pick Nathan *after Nathan...* "I took his virginity."

Benny's attention snaps to him, his eyes wide. "What?"

"The night of the auction." Nathan lifts his gaze, forcing himself to look at Benny. "When I raped him. When I raped Carter up on stage while he sobbed and begged for help, while men and women laughed at him, while they yelled awful fucking things to him, while he was starving and hurting and – and fucking breaking apart, I took his virginity."

"Fuck, Nate... I – that's – okay. Okay." Benny releases a slow, even breath. Then he straightens his back and slips into what Nathan recognizes as his professional, no bullshit mode. "Okay. This has to stop. You need to get your shit together, Nathan. Now. You'll get us all killed – or worse. Do you understand me? You will get Carter killed. The boy you love. Understand?"

Throat tight, Nathan nods.

"No, I need to hear you say it."

"I understand."

"Good." Benny wraps Nathan's knuckles, then moves on to the other hand. He sighs. "And we'll conveniently forget about that confession of yours, alright? Blame it on the whiskey. Go on as normal. No nightmare was overheard, no meltdown occurred. Alright?"

Knowing that's for the best for so many reasons, Nathan nods. "Yeah. Alright."

"Is it out of your system now? Have you worked through all this?"

"Yeah." Nathan winces as Benny finishes his other hand. He's not entirely sure if he'll ever truly be able to work all of this out of his system, but he thinks he worked enough of it out at least. "I'm on track again. I've got my shit together. Promise."

"Good." Benny squeezes his shoulder, giving him a tight smile. "I'll bring you some ice when I'm done checking on Carter. You need anything else?"

"No, I'm good." Just when Benny gets to the door, though, Nathan blurts, "Don't go to him!"

Benny turns with an eyebrow raised. "Huh?"

"Don't go to him. Please. Just – I'll explain to him in the morning. I'd rather him wake up confused than be afraid of you. You'll scare the fuck out of him, Ben. Don't ruin his good day."

"Nathan," Benny chides, giving him that disapproving dad look again. It doesn't make Nathan laugh this time. "You can't protect him from everything."

Nathan shrugs, helpless. "I have to try."

His best friend looks at him for a long time before sighing. He doesn't look defeated, per se, but he looks resigned. "You're really fucking gone for him, aren't you?"

"Yeah." Nathan gives him a tight smile. "Yeah, Ben. I am."

"Okay." Benny nods. He looks away, staring at the wall, then nods again before looking at Nathan once more. "Okay."

Benny returns to the bed, taking a seat beside Nathan. At some point, they collapse backwards, sprawled out on top of the blankets with their clothes still on. It takes a while for Benny to pass out despite their silence, the air around them remaining heavy long after he'd lost consciousness.

It's Carter's ghost that's the problem. It's hanging over Nathan, bearing down, threatening to suffocate him in guilt and shame.

Moments haunt him.

The first time their eyes met. Carter's trembling hand clutching his little moose close. That moment when Carter finally allowed his body to sink into Nathan's hold after falling apart in the bathroom his first night.

Nathan's cock nudging between Carter's cheeks, Carter's eyes squeezed shut, his quiet voice pleading *No, no, no.*

The boy riding Nathan's cock, whining, begging for more, begging to come, out of his mind with pleasure.

Carter clinging to the sheets as piss soaks the material between his legs, his ass and thighs varying shades of red and purple.

An adorable frown pulling at the boy's lips as he sleepily tries to button Nathan's shirt. Carter sleepy and warm in his arms, dozing in Nathan's lap as he warms his cock.

Carter sprawled out on Nathan's desk, looking beautifully wrecked, whispering, *Only one, sir. Only person to ever make me feel like this.*

Carter curled up in the fetal position on Nathan's office floor, soaked in Henley's piss, vomit surrounding him as he sobs.

The boy grinning, his laughter still echoing in the air, soapy hands navigating Nathan's skin as he teases, *Are you going to eat me all up, sir?*

Carter's face twisted in anguish, his head jerking back and forth, sobs catching in his chest, heartbreaking apologies spilling from him in waves of guilt and pain, *I'm sorry I picked sir over you.*

At some point, Nathan loses the battle, Carter's ghost luring him back to the bedroom. It's the dead of night. Nathan is still soaked in scotch and confusion. The boy is asleep on their bed, illuminated by the soft light they always keep on for him near the door. The little stuffed moose Carter loves so much is hooked around his thumb, resting in the palm of the boy's open hand.

He looks at peace, no trace of the nightmare from before in his expression.

Nathan startles when Carter suddenly stirs awake, his eyes locking with Nathan's. The boy pushes off the mattress with one hand, scrubbing at his face with the other. "Sir?"

"Hey, sweetheart," Nathan says softly, his voice embarrassingly rough. "Hope I didn't wake you."

"You're fine. What are you doing?" Carter looks over at the spot on the bed where Nathan should be before looking back at Nathan again. "Come to bed."

Nathan hums softly. "I'm not tired. You go back to sleep. Get some rest. You still have a few more hours."

"I'm not tired either."

"Carter..."

"Are you still Nathan?" Carter asks tentatively.

Nathan sighs. "Yes."

"Then come to bed, Nathan. Please."

This is a bad idea. Nathan is far too drunk, and coming off of a major emotional breakdown. He should not be crawling into bed with this boy. Lord only knows what idiotic things he'd do or say.

"*Please*," Carter says once more, voice so impossibly soft.

All of Nathan's self-restraint melts away. It's almost laughable that he thought he'd be able to resist at all. He'd give this boy the world if he could.

Nathan stands up, sliding his hands into the pockets of his sweatpants as if that'll keep him from reaching out and mauling Carter. He pauses at the foot of the bed to level Carter with a serious look. "If I come to bed, are you going to get some sleep for me?"

Carter nibbles on his bottom lip, forcing Nathan to swallow a moan. Then he shakes his head.

Nathan raises an eyebrow. "No?"

"No," Carter confirms. "I want to do something else."

"Oh?" Nathan leans forward, pressing his hands into the mattress on either side of Carter's legs. He smirks when he hears Carter's breath hitch. "And what is that? Watch another Harry Potter movie?"

That gets Carter to grin. It's a playful expression. Mischievous. Nathan's cock hardens, lust coursing through his veins as he considers what the boy might have in mind. His suspicions are confirmed when Carter says, "I want you to fuck me."

Nathan doesn't manage to swallow his moan this time. He reaches down to adjust himself, liking the way Carter's heated gaze locks onto his erection far too much. He tries to remind himself that this is a bad idea. A terrible one, in fact.

"I'm rather drunk, sweetheart." Part of Nathan wants to scare Carter off. The other part wants to tell the truth just so he doesn't have to be guilty when he gives in to his desire. "I'm not sure how gentle I'll be able to be with you tonight."

"That's never stopped you before."

"This wouldn't be like before." Nathan rests a knee on the mattress to bring himself closer to Carter before wrapping a hand around the back of his neck. He squeezes. "You still have your consent, Carter. It's not morning yet."

"I know." Carter shifts on the bed, leaning forward until their noses are bumping. "And I'm using it. Fuck me, Nathan. Fuck me like I'm yours. Like what we had today could be real."

The hand on the back of Carter's neck tightens without Nathan's permission. Instead of apologizing, he uses his grip to yank Carter forward, smashing their lips together. The kiss is brutal. Frantic. A sudden fear rises up in Nathan, like he's never going to get to do this again; he's never going to be lucky enough to have this again. He grabs at Carter every chance he gets, squeezing his neck, pulling his hair, shoving him onto his back, dragging him closer, pulling him this way and that. He tears Carter's shirt off of him – literally, he hears the threads rip – before hooking his fingers into his underwear and dragging them down his long legs.

Then Carter is stretched out before him like a goddamn buffet of seduction. He replaces his wandering hands with his mouth this time, licking and sucking and nipping at all of the sensitive flesh on his boy's body. His calves. His inner thighs. The subtle creases of his pelvis. He noses along his too-thin stomach. Drags the tip of his tongue teasingly around his nipples.

"Please. Please, Nate," the boy begs, his hips rolling against Nathan. "Fuck me."

"Patience." Nathan nips at Carter's shoulder. His trap. His throat. The hinge of his jaw. There's an animalistic part of himself that's demanding that he mark this boy. Claim him as Nathan's. Only Nathan's. *Always* Nathan's. "Mine. Mine, Carter. All mine. You're mine."

Nathan doesn't even realize he's saying those words out loud until Carter is panting them back to him. "Yours. Yours, Nate. All yours. I'm yours."

"I want-" Nathan stops himself, biting down on Carter's neck to keep from speaking things he knows he'll regret. He licks the mark, realizing it was a harder bite than he intended, but he doesn't apologize for it. He doesn't say a damn thing. If he speaks, he might admit to desires he's promised himself to never give into.

"What?" Carter asks. "What do you want?"

Nathan wraps his hand around Carter's cock, hoping to distract him. The boy moans and writhes and gasps, but he doesn't drop it. "What do you want, Nathan?"

Shaking his head, Nathan presses his mouth over Carter's to silence him.

It doesn't work.

"Tell me," he gasps. "Tell me, tell me, tell me."

"I want to tie you up," Nathan nearly growls. "I want to tie you to my bed frame and fuck you so hard you forget anything but me."

Carter stills beneath him, staring up at him with wide eyes. Nathan's heart stutters. "Carter, I-"

"Yes," Carter says quickly, cutting him off. "Yes. That. Do it. Tie me up."

With a shudder, Nathan pulls away from Carter and goes to his bedside table, opening the second drawer. His body is trembling with a need he's quickly losing control of. There's a steady panic rising in him, keeping his chest from fully expanding, keeping his lungs lacking in oxygen. He wants to do so many things to Carter. Things he'd never allow himself to do without the boy's consent. Things that aren't just to fulfill the expectations of his role as Nathan, but genuine desires of Travis's. His fingers are unsteady as he strokes the red rope that's looped and tied off in the drawer.

"I want to hurt you," Nathan forces himself to admit. His throat feels impossibly tight. "I'd make you feel good, too. So fucking good. But I want to hurt you."

There. He said it. Now Carter knows.

When he gets the courage to look over at Carter, he sees that the boy is watching him carefully. He's not afraid. Not even nervous. He's aroused, his cock still hard and leaking against his stomach, his lips wet and parted as he pants in anticipation. His cheeks are pink. So are the tips of his ears. His voice is merely a rasp when he speaks. "Yes. Yes, please. Nathan. *Sir.*"

Nathan grips the rope tight, heart in his throat. He forces himself to take in a deep breath and release it slowly as he sinks into the part of himself he doesn't enjoy very much. The part of himself that's still completely Travis, but looks an awful lot like Nathan. Like the *monster.*

"You have to tell me if it's too much." He approaches Carter slowly, a predator afraid to spook his prey. Nathan locks eyes with him before slowly, carefully, lifting his hand to cup Carter's right cheek. He brushes his thumb along the delicate line of the boy's chin. The boy leans into his palm. Nuzzles it. "You won't get in trouble, but you have to tell me."

"Okay."

"No, Carter. Promise. Promise me you'll tell me."

Carter raises his hand, pressing it against Nathan's. There's nothing but trust in his eyes. Well, trust and arousal. "I promise."

"Alright." Nathan clears his throat before jerking his head in a nod. "Alright."

He stands, reaching for the rope now. Carter's eyes lock onto it immediately. His breathing goes rapid. His body trembles.

"You okay?" Nathan asks, his hands worrying the red rope.

"I'm fine, Nate." Carter licks his lips before offering a shaky smile. "I trust you."

Don't. God, don't do that, Carter. I don't deserve it.

Nathan takes Carter's hands in his, hoping the boy can't feel the way his own hands are unsteady. He stays still and quiet like the perfect little slave as Nathan wraps his wrists with the soft rope. It's almost soothing to begin binding the boy, every intricate knot steadying him, every stretch of red across pale skin an echo of peace.

After guiding the rope through one of Carter's knots, Nathan brings the material up to one of the metal rings near the top of the bedframe that he never thought he'd actually use, tying off the ends and tugging at the rope twice to make sure the boy can't possibly escape. His cock is so hard it aches.

More rope around the boy's legs. Bright red securing one ankle to the intricately carved wooden bedpost on his left. The process repeated until the other ankle is secured on the right.

"Watching you do this is unfairly hot," Carter says breathlessly.

That startles a laugh out of Nathan, the pressure in his chest releasing. He grins at the boy before him, taking him in now that he's all wrapped up and ready to go.

Carter looks like a goddamn dream.

He looks like the most dangerous thing Nathan has ever encountered.

The way Carter is looking at him, eyes hooded, tongue resting on his bottom lip, cock leaking, could very easily become Nathan's new addiction. "God, you're fucking beautiful."

A deep blush spreads across the visible skin on the boy's face and down his slim throat before moving across his chest. His stomach is smooth and pale before the flush picks back up at the root of his cock. His cock grows darker as the skin stretches towards the very tip of it, a small drop of precum glistening against the nearly purple head. Nathan wants to lick it.

Then he realizes he *can*. They're alone. No one is around to judge him for putting a slave's cock in his mouth.

Pressing his hands on the mattress to frame Carter's hips, Nathan lowers his head and wraps his lips around Carter's cock. He darts his tongue out to catch the moisture that's been teasing him before pushing downward until the boy's entire cock is nestled in his mouth and brushing the beginning of his throat. The noises spilling out of Carter are fucking *obscene*. Nathan could quite possibly come just from sucking this boy's nice little cock and listening to his sounds of uninhibited pleasure.

"Sir!" Carter gasps, his hips jerking the minuscule amount allowed with the restraints. "Sir, I'm – oh *fuck*. Nathan. I'm going to come."

Nathan pulls off with a chuckle, standing back. He's unsure what he loves more – the boy's sad whimper, the sight of his spit-soaked cock helplessly bobbing in the air, or the adorably sexy pout on the boy's face. "You won't be coming until I say, but good try, sweetheart."

The boy whines. "Sir, please."

"So needy," Nathan teases.

"It's been like – like an entire fucking *day* of foreplay!" Carter tugs at the restraints, but it's a weak attempt. The ropes don't even pull taut. He whines again. It's pathetic. It's *endearing*. "This is torture. Hurry up and fuck me!"

Nathan arches his eyebrow, smirking. "Oh sweetheart, if you think this is torture, you have another thing coming."

"Ummm, no thanks!" Carter says in an adorably high voice, his blue eyes wide. "Just kidding. Not torture. Like... at all. This is great!"

"That's what I thought." Nathan chuckles darkly. "But for the complaints, you're going to have to wait an extra bit before I give you my cock."

"Sir..."

Before Carter can accidentally dig himself any further in the hole, Nathan squats down at the foot of the bed and takes advantage of the boy's position by burying his face between Carter's plump little ass cheeks. The boy squeaks. Then, as Nathan very slowly licks Carter's tight furl, the boy moans wantonly.

It's not long before Carter has dissolved into a frantic, jumbled mess of syllables and noises that make absolutely no sense apart from the very obvious one – it feels really fucking good.

"You taste damn good," Nathan growls against the boy's hole before stiffening his tongue and pressing it deep inside him. The muscles of Carter's body twitch as his cock spurts a few beads of precum onto his stomach.

A dangerous possessiveness encircles Nathan. "You smell like me. Like you. Like us. Fuck, Carter." Nathan bites at the boy's hole, unable to help himself. Carter shouts, his body jerking again, his babbling sounds growing more frantic.

It isn't until Nathan is sliding a finger into Carter's hole, lapping at the boy's tight rim as he stretches it, that Carter finally finds some semblance of his brain. Enough to slur, "Sir, please."

Nathan ignores him, continuing to open him up nice and slow, his fingers and tongue moving in tandem to systematically take this boy apart. Soft sobs begin to catch in Carter's chest when the second finger is added.

His cheeks are damp with tears by the time the third has been fully worked inside of him. The stumbling pleas escaping him transform into desperate begging when Nathan pulls at 3 fingers out to leave him gaping and empty.

"Sir, please, sir!" Nathan carefully traces around the boy's rim with the tip of his tongue. "Oh god!" Nathan pokes his entire tongue into his hole and swirls it. "Nate!" Nathan nips at his rim. "Sh-shhh-shhhiiiiitt." Nathan nips at him again. "Fuck, stop!"

Nathan rears back, heart racing, stomach heavy and acidic. His hands shake as he tries to find the knot of Carter's right ankle bindings.

"Wait, no!" Carter shouts. Nathan pulls his hands away like the rope burned him. If Carter won't even let him un-tie him... he'll have to go get Benny. His friend will fucking kill him. But if that's what Carter wants, then he'll – "I didn't mean really stop. Don't stop. Oh god, Nathan, don't you dare fucking stop! Get back to work immediately!"

Still feeling damn unsure, Nathan rests his body between Carter's spread legs and reaches up to run a hand through Carter's unruly hair. Carter blinks, more tears falling down his cheeks, but he gives Nathan a fucked-out grin when their eyes lock. "'S good, Nate. Sooo fuckin' good. Don't stop, please don't stop, never fuckin' stop."

With a shuddery sigh of relief, Nathan presses a kiss to Carter's salty lips. He licks them free of tears. Then he drags his tongue up to lick away the rest of them on his cheeks. Before he can worry that Carter is disgusted, the boy is releasing a shuddery breath beneath him, lifting his chin to press harder against Nathan's mouth.

"I want to fuck you now," Nathan rasps.

"Yes. Now. Great. Do that."

Nathan releases a shuddery breath of his own. He reaches between his legs to shove his sweatpants down to his thighs, wrapping his hand around the root of his cock and rubbing his thumb beneath the crown. It throbs and aches in his palm. His heart is pounding. "I don't want to use lube, but it'll hurt, sweetheart."

Carter licks his lips, his eyes hooded as he tries to decide if he should look at Nathan's face or his leaking cock. "You said you want to hurt me."

"I do. But not if you don't want that."

"Hurt me," Carter breathes. His lashes are still wet. His cheeks flushed. His cock hard and dripping. His gaze has finally decided what it wants to focus on. Nathan's cock. "Tear me apart, Nathan. Use me. It's okay."

"If you want to stop, you have to tell me. You have to-" Nathan pauses, his mind spinning in desperation as it fights against the urge to shove his cock into the boy in front of him and fuck him senseless. They have to come at this a different way. Just saying *stop* won't be enough. Not if it's anything like what happened just now. Nathan's eyes catch on the red rope wrapped around Carter's pretty skin. "Red. If you want to stop, you have to say red, okay?"

"Like- like a safe word?"

"Yes." *This is so far from okay, you goddamn idiot. What are you thinking?* "Red. Understand?"

"Yes, sir. Red."

With the boy's permission washing over him, Nathan presses the tip of his cock against Carter's spit-slick hole and places both hands on the mattress to frame the boy's head, leaning his entire body forward as he slowly pushes inside him. Carter whimpers, his hole fighting the intrusion, but Nathan ignores it. Ignores him.

He's a fucking monster, but Carter wants him that way tonight. It spins Nathan's whole damn world.

How did he get so lucky?

How the hell is he ever going to let this boy go?

Nathan bottoms out. He doesn't give Carter the chance to adjust. He doesn't even give him the chance to catch his breath. Nathan just grabs the knots at Carter's hips and pulls back before snapping forward hard enough to shove a wrecked sob from the boy beneath him. He does it again. Again. Again. The tight heat around his cock is agonizingly pleasurable, the sounds Carter is making drawing him towards the edge already. It's going to be tough to last long. Damn near impossible. Consensual rough sex with Carter Beckett just might be the death of him.

Grip tight on the knotted rope, Nathan uses Carter's own body against him, dragging him back and forth as he fucks into him with abandon. He can tell by the boy's reactions that Carter feels good, but he isn't where Nathan wants him to be. Not yet.

Nathan tugs at the ropes as hard as he can, pulling restraints taut, forcing Carter's body into a slight tilt. He grips the base of Carter's throat in a possessive hold that will keep the boy somewhere between choking and breathing.

The next time Nathan fucks into him, Carter screams. Actually fucking *screams*. Nathan feels his lips split into a wicked grin in victory. He focuses on that exact position, holding Carter down by his throat, nailing his prostate over and over again until the boy is wailing.

"Come for me," Nathan growls, fucking him even harder, even faster. Fucking him until he can hear the hitch of Carter's breath as his cock forces the boy to choke on air. "Come on my cock, sweetheart. Be a good boy for me."

Carter shudders in the restraints, his eyes fluttering closed. Nathan pounds into him three more times before the boy arches his back and comes. With a breathless laugh that's just shy of giddy, Nathan continues fucking into him, enjoying the mewling sounds of the boy beneath him.

Nathan eases his grip on Carter's throat, bringing the hand down to run the tips of his fingers up and down Carter's spent cock. The boy shivers. Moans. Whines. He shakes his head, bucking his hips. His cheeks are damp. His eyes wide. "Sir."

"What?" Nathan asks with a false innocence.

"Too – too sensitive," he gasps. "Too much."

Nathan leans forward to press his lips against the base of Carter's throat. He drags them up the elegant curve of his neck until he reaches that sensitive spot right below the boy's ear. He nips at it. Licks it. Sucks it. His hand wraps around Carter's cock, squeezing it just shy of too hard as he ruts against the boy's ass.

Carter sobs, shaking his head desperately. He fights the bindings hard enough to make the rope creek and stretch. "Sir, stop! Oh god. Stop, stop, stop. I can't!"

"Maybe I'll make you come again," Nathan growls. He removes his hand, chuckling at the boy's sigh of relief. The sound turns into a pained whimper when Nathan presses every available inch of his body against Carter's, pinning Carter's cock between them. "Maybe I'll make you come all fucking night long."

"No!" Carter shakes his head harder, his sobs choked. His hole squeezes Nathan's cock rhythmically. It's the best fucking thing he's ever felt. "Sir, no!"

"You can beg me to stop all you want," Nathan growls. "But this tight little hole of yours is begging for more."

"Sir!"

"Should I give it what it wants? Hmm?"

"Oh god..." Carter gasps, eyes rolling.

One hand on the boy's throat, the other on his shoulder, Nathan holds him firmly in place as he fucks him senseless.

"Yeah," Nathan says, more to himself than anything. "You're going to come again."

Carter tosses his head back, choking on his own sobs. "I caaaan't!"

"You can." Nathan separates their bodies to spit on Carter's bright red cock. The boy shouts at the stimulation, then sobs when Nathan adds a second glob. His sounds start to choke and fade when Nathan wraps his hand tight around his cock and begins to pump it. "You *will* come, Carter. Your body belongs to me. Don't forget that."

"Nathan..." the boy slurs, his head rolling on his neck as he tries to stay coherent. There's drool sliding down his chin and onto his chest. His eyes are glazed and distant.

Nathan twists his wrist, ringing a startled cry from Carter. "Your safe word is red. Use it if you need to."

With a weak, pathetic little sob, Carter's back arches, his breath catching. His wide eyes lock with Nathan's as his face flushes red. He whispers a breathy, startled, "Oh, sir!" before his cock shoots for the second time, the release hot and sticky. He sucks in a shuddery breath before going lax against the mattress, his eyes fluttering shut. Nathan stares down at him, mesmerized.

God, he's so in love with this beautiful, perfect boy.

So. Fucking. In. Love.

He's positively fucked.

One more look at Carter's blissed out expression and Nathan is finishing too, spilling his hot seed into the boy's fluttering hole.

"Fuck, Carter," Nathan gasps, his hips rolling like he might be able to fuck his cum in deeper somehow. Stake a stronger claim by marking the boy inside and out. A *permanent* claim. "Fuck, you have no idea how much I-" Nathan cuts himself off last minute, dropping his head between his shoulders as he catches his breath. The confession feels hot and heavy on his tongue. It hurts to swallow, hurts to keep in, but he manages.

Nathan carefully pulls out of Carter and tugs his sweat-pants up before immediately starting to free his boy. The knots he did were surprisingly well-done with his level of sobriety at the time. They unravel perfectly, the ropes unwinding exactly as they should, no worrying marks left behind on the revealed flesh. Nathan gently rubs the boy's arms and wrists, then his thighs, legs, and ankles. All Carter does is moan in a sleepy sort of pleasure.

The boy is out, either asleep or flying too high mentally to be present. He looks damn good in the dim lighting. Full of marks that Nathan gave him, still sticky with his release, Nathan's cum dripping out of his loose hole.

After using the bathroom and gently cleaning Carter up with a warm cloth, he tucks the boy in and returns to his seat on the lounge chair near the bed. He rests his elbows on his knees and leans forward to clasp his hands together. He's grossly sober now.

And still very much in love with Carter Beckett.

Maybe even more so than before.

Nathan stays there until morning, just watching the boy. Watching him sleep. Watching him breathe. Watching him lay there, safe from the horrors of the world outside the bedroom door.

And all that time, as he stays there unmoving, holding a silent vigil for the boy's life that he himself is destroying, the one question Nathan wants so badly to ask him, the one question he had tried to drink away, tried to punch away, tried to fuck away, the one question he'll never be selfish enough to voice, repeats itself in his mind:

Why the fuck would Carter ever pick him?

Chapter Eighteen

CARTER WAKES UP SORE and satisfied. He also wakes up alone. He frowns, pushing himself up into a sitting position. Nathan – *sir*, he has to be *sir* again – isn't in the chair like last night. For just a second, Carter worries that he made the entire thing up. That he had never woken up at all, his time with sir just another dream. Then he looks down at his body and sees that it's positively *littered* with marks from the man aggressively fucking him last night. There's no way it didn't happen. He even has some subtle rope burn on his wrists.

Wearing his marks like a warrior, Carter decides to be brave and go knock on the closed bathroom door. Maybe he can join sir in the shower again. He can call Carter little red, and Carter can offer himself up to be devoured. They could just spend all day in here, fucking and watching Harry Potter.

Of course, this is reality. Carter is a sex slave, sir is his master, and life is not as easy as Harry Potter and great sex. That's why Carter really shouldn't be surprised when sir opens the bathroom door before he can even knock and immediately snaps at him. "What are you doing?"

"I was – I just..." *shit, he looks mad.* He also looks impossibly sexy standing there with a towel loosely knotted around his waist, water dripping down his chest, pooling in his stomach muscles, his happy trail curlier than usual.

His blonde hair is damp and messy, locks falling on his forehead.

So. Fucking. Sexy.

But also *very* fucking mad.

"Were you just spying on me?" Sir squares his shoulders, chin lifting as his eyes narrow. He suddenly feels 10 feet tall and deadly. "Were you listening to me?"

"I-" Carter pauses, looking behind sir, then back at him again. "Listening to you... what? Shower?"

"Answer the fucking question, Carter," sir growls. He's backing Carter up now. Pinning him against the wall. There's nothing desirable about the position. Carter's heart isn't pounding in arousal or anticipation. It's in fear.

"I didn't hear anything! I was just going to knock and see if – if I could..."

Sir presses harder against him, making Carter perfectly aware of his size and muscle mass compared to Carter's weak, underfed body. "If you could?"

"I was going to ask to join you, like yesterday." Carter drops his chin, feeling ashamed and stupid. "But it's not yesterday, it's today, and I'm just a slave, and I'm really sorry. I forgot my place, sir. I'm so sorry."

The longest pause in the history of pauses stretches between them, though Carter's fully aware that if he subtracted his stirring panic, it was probably only a few seconds. Then sir takes a single step back and clears his throat. "I'm glad you've remembered your place. It'd be quite inconvenient to have to remind you of it this morning. We're already running late. Go wash up. Bare minimum. Then come kneel in the closet. We need to talk."

We need to talk.

That's never very good...

Not wanting to push his luck, Carter hurries through the motions of going to the bathroom and washing himself up for the day. He finds sir in his closet as expected, but before he can lower himself to his knees, he sees a flash of angry red on sir's hand. He accidentally gasps. When sir whips around to look at him, Carter immediately takes a step back. Then, like an idiot, he asks, "What happened?"

"Hmm?" Sir follows Carter's gaze to where his hand is holding his phone, his jaw ticking when he sees what's got his attention. "Oh. That."

"Are you okay?"

The look sir gives him is annoyed. "I'm fine, pet. I've had much worse."

That doesn't make Carter feel any better. At all.

His worry overpowers his self-preservation. "You should ice it."

"*Pet*," sir says warningly.

But then Carter is seeing sir's other hand, his knuckles just as bruised and cut up as the first, and his body is going cold. "Oh... *sir*."

"It's not your concern."

"Were they like that last night? I – I don't remember them being hurt when we-"

"You were rather distracted, and the room was dark." Sir levels him with a gaze that leaves no room for argument. "And you're not kneeling."

Carter bites the inside of his cheek, warring with himself. He's worried. Especially so. Sir had been in the chair instead of the bed last night. He had been drunk, smelling of scotch. And now Carter knows his hands had been injured.

"What happened?"

"Enough!" Sir snaps. He reaches forward and fists Carter's hair, pushing him down to his knees. "Is this going to be our day? Because I have to say, I'm really fucking unimpressed with how it's starting."

Carter immediately curves his shoulders forward, his gaze falling to his throbbing knees. He presses his hands against the floor hard enough to make his fingers ache.

"I'm sorry, sir. I'm sorry. I won't misbehave anymore. I'm done being bad."

Sir says nothing, but his gaze is heavy enough to speak on its own. Then he sighs. "We need to talk."

Considering sir's bad mood, Carter doesn't take any chances by speaking. He just remains quiet and still, trying not to panic as every agonizing second sends his anxiety ratcheting up to suffocating levels.

Sir sighs again. Then Carter hears the soft thud of sir's towel hitting the floor. A moment later, he's getting a spectacular view of sir's perfect ass as he walks over to the dresser at the very back of his large closet.

"We're going to an event tomorrow evening." Sir pulls on a pair of tight black boxer briefs, followed by a pair of dress socks that stop mid-calf. "It's a very important event for me."

Carter remains silent, but he lifts his chin to look at sir directly to show he's listening. Sir moves over to his rack of blue suits. "I've spoiled you, something we're both aware of, yes?"

"Yes, sir. I-" Carter pauses, swallowing hard. "I'm thankful, sir."

Sir's jaw ticks. He chooses a suit and starts to pull the pants on. "You'll be expected to be on your best behavior tomorrow."

"Yes, sir. I will be, I promise, sir."

"I know." Sir's lips twitch, almost like he's trying to fight a smile. He grabs a white dress shirt and begins to put it on. Sir turns to face him, his fingers working the buttons on his shirt. His gaze is intense as it settles on Carter. "I told you yesterday that I was going to consider no longer sharing you."

Carter goes perfectly still, his mind racing.

"I've decided to keep you to myself. You're mine. Only mine. Understood?"

"Oh," Carter whispers, his exhale shaky. His chest feels warm. His entire body does, in fact. "I – thank you. Thank you, sir."

Sir shoots him a look as he tucks his shirt into his pants. "It's not for *you*."

"Right. I – obviously, sir. I'm sorry."

"Just because I won't be sharing you doesn't mean I can't make you miserable." It dawns on Carter that he might still be in trouble. The fear only grows as he watches sir pick a belt. He doesn't put it on, running his fingers over the smooth leather instead. Carter's heart races. "If you misbehave at this event, the punishment you will receive will make what happened with Todd Henley seem like a rainy afternoon nap. Understood?"

Carter's stomach burns with acid. He won't be misbehaving. No way in hell. "Understood, sir."

Sir puts the belt on. Carter nearly cries in relief.

"Some behaviors that I usually allow to pass will not be acceptable tomorrow. I'm going to give you additional rules, which you will practice today."

"Yes, sir."

"*That*." Sir points his finger at him, eyes narrowing. "That right there is one of them. Do not speak unless asked a question. Ever. Understood?"

A *question*.

"Yes, sir."

"And you looking at me right now? Not okay. Eyes on the floor, always. Chin down as well."

Carter follows the instructions, biting his bottom lip to keep from speaking out of turn. His fingers itch when he sees sir choose a tie. It feels strange not helping him dress this morning. That's always been their thing. The last time he was denied the privilege to do so was when he was in trouble.

He realizes he's looking at sir again and quickly drops his gaze.

This is going to be hard.

"Tell me your rules, pet. All of them."

Fuck. That wasn't a question.

That wasn't a question. He said only questions.

Do not speak unless asked a question. Ever.

Is this what 7 meant when he talked about these men setting the slaves up for failure?

"Are you being disobedient right now, or are you having an issue remembering the very *few* rules I've given you?"

A *question.* Thank god.

"I'm unsure of the new speaking rule, sir. I – I didn't know if I could speak. It wasn't a question. You said only questions." Carter stops his rambling. Then, for good measure, he adds, "Sir."

Carter hates not being able to see sir right now. He can't study his expression and movements. He can't predict his mood or actions. It's unsettling. Terrifying, even.

He's relieved when sir finally speaks. "Questions *and* orders. If I give you an order to say something or tell me something, you may also speak. An oversight on my part."

No question or order.

Carter remains silent.

"Tell me your rules."

An order.

"I should always kneel for you, I should always call you sir, and I should always obey you without hesitation." Carter pauses, a flash of himself clinging to a bedpost filling his mind, sir's men watching and laughing at his turmoil. He shudders at the memory. "I should never leave the bed unless going to the bathroom, and I have to get back in right after I'm finished. I shouldn't look at you, and I should only speak when asked a question or given an order."

"Good." Not *good boy.* It hurts in a way that Carter hates himself for. "As long as you follow those rules, we'll have a successful evening."

The urge to say *yes, sir* is on the tip of Carter's tongue. He catches it between his teeth to keep the words from spilling out.

After a moment, sir sighs and walks away from Carter. He mumbles something under his breath that sounds like *fucking ridiculous* before snapping his fingers in a silent command for Carter to follow. Carter does.

The sight of his collar in sir's hands when they come to a halt at the foot of the bed again hurts Carter more than he should allow it to. Maybe this switching between Carter and slave isn't such a good idea. It's much harder than he anticipated.

Sir encircles Carter's throat with the collar, the simple accessory an overwhelming weight on his heart and soul.

"You'll have four verbal cues tomorrow night. We'll practice those as well."

Carter bites his tongue harder. It feels as if the collar constricts, threatening to suffocate him, but he reminds himself that's not the truth.

"First is *Show*." Sir's fingers brush along the curve of Carter's jaw before settling beneath his chin and guiding it upward. Carter's eyes find sir's. "Keep your eyes on the floor, pet. Show means I want to see your face. Understood?"

A *question*. Carter averts his gaze and responds. "Yes, sir."

"When I say *Eyes*, it means you may look at me. *Eyes*, pet."

Carter looks at sir.

Sir smiles, but it seems... *sad*.

"Very good. Two more, and then you've learned all your new rules, alright?"

A *question*.

"Yes, sir."

"Eyes to the floor, chin down again." Carter obeys. "Spread your knees a little wider and straighten your spine." Carter obeys. "Both hands behind your back, the right hand grabbing the left wrist." Carter obeys. "Good. This position is your resting position. The cue is *Rest*. If you've ever been taken out of this position, whether just to tilt your face for me or perhaps to crawl, you immediately get back to this exact position here and stay that way until told or moved otherwise again. This is your default setting. Understood?"

A *question.*

"Yes, sir."

"Good boy."

Carter's body practically hums with the praise. Maybe he can do this after all. It's not so hard, if he stays focused. He just has to wait for questions, orders, or one of the cues. When he's waiting, he needs to kneel a certain way. He can do that.

Carter can totally fucking do that.

Then sir says, "The last one is called *Present*," and Carter doesn't know if it's the tone of sir's voice when he says the last word, or if it's just his common sense kicking in, but his heart sinks with the realization of what this position is going to be.

He's proved right when sir places a hand on his back and pushes him forward until Carter's forehead is to the floor. Carter holds his breath, hoping this is as bad as it gets even though he knows deep down it's not. Nothing important is presented. Not yet.

Sir begins to move his body, treating Carter like a puppet. He puts Carter's elbows to the floor on each side of his head, setting them wide, then brings Carter's hands to cup the back of his neck, coaxing Carter's fingers to intertwine once there. Carter squeezes his eyes shut as he feels sir's hands move to his thighs, spreading them apart. Then the final movement, sir lifting his ass in the air, making it so anyone would be able to see Carter's hole if they desired.

"This is *Present*," sir says in a rough voice. His hands linger on Carter's hips for a moment longer before he quickly pulls them away as if he's been burned. He clears his throat. Twice. "*Rest.*"

The transition is clumsy, but Carter manages to move back into the *Rest* position.

"You need practice. *Present.*"

Carter pushes forward. Still clumsy.

"*Rest.*"

Still clumsy.

"*Present.*"

"*Rest.*"

"*Present.*"

"*Rest.*"

"*Present.*"

Smooth. Almost instinctual now. Everything settles into place as it should, no adjustments needed, no regaining of his balance required.

"Good boy," sir croons, running a hand along the curve of Carter's back. It makes him feel like a show dog.

What's worse is that he likes it.

Not the show dog part, obviously, but the part where sir pets him and praises him.

He doesn't let himself feel guilty about it. He refuses.

And if he hears Casey's voice echoing in his mind, if he sees Maison's sneer every time he blinks, well... he just does his best to ignore them. They only exist in nightmares now. This is Carter's real life. No one gets to judge him for how he survives it.

CARTER IS AMAZING WITH his new rules, only messing up once while he was alone with Nathan in his office. Nathan had asked him a question, something about lunch, and for just a moment, Carter had forgotten not to look at him when he answered. It was a single flicker of his eyes before he had remembered and quickly tucked his chin back to his chest, eyes on the ground. Nathan had pretended not to notice.

The only real issue they're having today is one Nathan hadn't expected; Carter isn't eating. He only ate a few bites of fruit at breakfast, and at lunch he had told Nathan he wasn't hungry. Now they were seated for dinner, Carter kneeling between his legs, and Carter was taking a long enough time to chew a single piece of chicken that Nathan was starting to wonder if maybe the boy had already swallowed and was merely pretending. He presses a cooked baby carrot to Carter's lips, holding it there until the boy finally opens his mouth to take it. Then there's more slow, prolonged chewing.

It doesn't help that morale isn't great at the dinner table tonight.

It's Jason.

It's always Jason, if Nathan is being honest. Jason is the only one in the organization to ever dare question Nathan. He will sometimes make faces when he thinks Nathan can't see him, or he'll comment under his breath

316

when he thinks Nathan isn't paying attention. The little shit has always been ever so slightly disobedient, challenging Nathan's authority, but never enough for him to feel justified enough to do something about it.

Nathan can tell that today's issue originated with Jason because his men keep looking in his direction, as if waiting to see if he'll say something. Instead, the little prick just stays quiet as the men bicker amongst themselves.

When Carter is mentioned, Nathan finally forces himself to care about whatever has everyone so on edge. "Someone needs to tell me what's going on right now."

Everyone goes quiet, avoiding eye contact with him. Nathan turns to Benny and raises an eyebrow. His friend sighs before gesturing to the rest of the table and explaining, "The men were all hoping to attend the party tomorrow evening."

"Oh?" Nathan scans the men. A lot of them look like they're regretting their existence at the moment. Or at least their attendance at this particular meal. "Why? None of you cared much before. I asked for volunteers weeks ago."

"That was *before*, sir," Jason explains.

"Before?"

Benny's eyes flick to Carter. "Before the boy."

Nathan looks down at Carter as well, then at the table in confusion. "Someone is going to have to explain the logic here."

Jason looks around the room before lifting his chin defiantly at Nathan. "You're letting people use him at the party."

A sharp rage spikes in Nathan's chest. He forces himself to breathe through it before responding. "Actually, I don't believe I am."

"You're putting a show on for them, at least. Rumor has it, it's going to be quite entertaining. And interactive." Jason shrugs. "We'd like to be in on that."

Nathan looks down at Carter again. The boy is in the perfect rest position, his eyes on the floor, but every muscle is locked up impossibly tight. He's practically vibrating.

If Nathan was better at his job, he'd say something like, "Sure, then. Whatever. If you want to come, talk to Benny. He'll sort out the details."

But Nathan is shit at his job lately, so he says, "Your intel is wrong. I have no intention of sharing him. If I play with him, it'll be because the host invites me too, but there is no plan in place. If I do, in fact, play with him, it will not be elaborate *or* interactive. Tomorrow night is too fucking important to risk everything just so I can show him off and share him."

They all look extremely disappointed.

Benny looks shocked and unsure.

But Nathan looks down at Carter to find the boy relaxing in relief, and that's enough to make the risk worth it.

That's enough to make it so Nathan can fucking breathe again.

At least until he tucks Carter in for the night and goes to Benny's office. Then his best friend pours him a stiff drink, double-checks that the locks on his office door are in place, and looks him directly in the eye to say, "That boy needs to be in a much deeper slave mindset tomorrow. Tell me what you're going to do to make that happen," and Nathan suddenly can't quite breathe at all.

Chapter Nineteen

CARTER IS STILL AWAKE when sir comes back to the bedroom, having been unable to sleep as his mind raced with the possibilities of what this party will be like tomorrow. He tries to pretend to be asleep, holding still and breathing evenly. He's not sure if it works or not, but sir doesn't say anything to him, which is something at least.

Something is off with sir, though. Carter can't tell exactly what because he's keeping his eyes closed, but sir is much louder than he usually is, and when he bumps into something and grunts an angry, "*Fuck*," under his breath, he laughs right after.

Is sir... drunk? Again?

The bathroom door shuts a little too hard, and Carter hears something fall in the bathroom. He opens his eyes just enough to look at the door, seeing a sliver of light coming from the crack in the bottom. Carter takes a risk by sitting up in bed, hoping to be able to hear better.

Usually, when sir is in the bathroom at night, sir takes a shower. At least, that's what Carter always assumed because the water always runs for a long time. But, sir isn't showering tonight. He's not using the sink either. There's no water running. Nothing to drown out sir's voice. He's muffled, the door getting in the way and preventing Carter from hearing any actual words, but it's clear he's talking. From the sounds of it, he's talking to someone on the phone.

Carter wonders if he talks on the phone to someone every night. He wonders if it's the same person. He wonders what they mean to sir. He wonders if they're special. Important. If sir maybe... loves them.

Not that Carter would care.

He *wouldn't*.

Sure, Carter is still thankful it was sir who bought him, one night with Todd was enough to help him realize how much worse things could be, but sir being the less of two evils doesn't erase the fact that he's still evil. Even if they did manage to have a great day together yesterday, it was just a day of playing pretend. It has to be that way. Sir has to be the villain.

It doesn't matter if sir loves someone.

It's not like Carter loves him.

He *doesn't*.

Carter hates him.

Carter *has* to hate him.

He just... has to.

Realizing the talking has stopped, Carter hurries to lay back down and close his eyes. He definitely doesn't want to be caught eavesdropping, especially after the way sir had reacted this morning when he had assumed Carter was doing just that.

The bathroom door creaks open. Carter tries to keep his breathing slow and even. Sir is quieter now. Less clumsy. From the sound of things, he's stripping, his clothes hitting the floor with soft thuds. Then the bed dips, and the blankets move. Carter accidentally tenses when the corner of the blanket slides across his ass, but he acts like he stirs in his sleep and sighs before relaxing again, hoping sir will believe that he's still asleep.

"You awake?" sir asks softly. Carter takes a slow, even breath in. Then he blows it out. Sir moves on the bed again, the rest of the blanket coming up. It's tucked gently around Carter's body.

"There you go, sweetheart," sir whispers softly once the blanket is where he wants it to be. He brushes Carter's hair off his forehead, then strokes along his temple. A soft sound comes from somewhere in sir's throat. Then his breath is fanning over Carter's face, the smell of scotch overwhelming his senses. Lips brush the corner of Carter's jaw before sir seems to deflate, pressing his forehead against Carter's shoulder without putting any actual weight on him. He must be trying not to wake Carter up. "God, Carter, I wish I could save you from this."

Carter tries his best to keep his breathing normal. He hopes sir can't hear his heartbeat because it must be erratic.

"I wish I could save you from *me*." Sir pulls away, laying back on his side of the bed. He releases a slow, soft sigh, then whispers something Carter can't even begin to understand. "You'd be so much better off with Travis. He'd be good to you. He'd know how to love you better..."

Sir goes quiet after that, eventually falling asleep. Carter stays awake for a long time. He must lay there for hours, wondering if sir meant what he had said. If he was really sorry. If he really wishes he could save Carter.

Wondering who the hell Travis is. Wondering if Travis really would be better. Wondering why there's an ache in Carter's chest at the mere thought of being with anyone but sir.

Wondering what sir meant by Travis loving him *better*, as if sir loves him too, just not as well as Travis would.

Carter finally drifts off at some point, damn near drowning in confusion.

CARTER BREAKS ONE OF his new rules within seconds of being awake the morning of the party.

Sir is shaking him, saying something about waking up, and Carter makes the mistake of blinking his eyes open to look directly at the man. He gets just a glimpse of messy hair and dangerous eyes before a hand is smacking against his cheek. It's more of a surprise than it is painful, but Carter still gasps.

"Rules haven't changed, pet," sir says in a cold voice. "It's going to be a hell of a night for you if you fuck up, remember?"

A *question*.

"Yes, sir."

"Do better."

Carter bites his tongue to keep from promising he will. It wasn't a question or an order. It feels too strange to say nothing, though. He settles for a subtle nod of his head. Sir doesn't acknowledge it.

"What are you, pet?"

"A – a slave, sir?"

"Exactly. *Eyes.*" Sir grabs his chin and forces his face into the *Show* position. Carter flicks his gaze upward, shivering when he sees the anger in sir's expression. "I've spoiled you. I've let you pretend. But every second you've been mine, you've been a slave. Correct?"

"Yes, sir."

"Anything else I allow you to pretend to be is just that – pretending. A roleplay. You are *nothing*, do you understand me?"

Carter swallows hard, trying not to cry. His voice is pathetically shaky when he responds. "I understand, sir."

"What are you?"

"A slave, sir."

"And?"

"Nothing," Carter whispers. His chest feels impossibly tight. "Nothing else, sir. Just a slave. A – a set of holes."

A hole is a hole, right?

Sir had said differently, he had said Carter was *special*, but that was roleplay. Carter was so silly for not understanding that.

"Good." Sir wraps his hand around Carter's bicep and tugs him off the bed, not giving him a chance to gain his balance before dragging him to the bathroom. "Don't fucking forget your place today. Your reminder will be something you won't even want to survive."

Carter won't forget it.

He won't ever let himself forget it.

What he does *make himself forget?* The whispered apology and kind touches when sir had thought he was asleep. How special he felt when sir would hold him close and kiss him like he's something precious. The teasing snap of teeth as sir called him little red. The bubbling laughter as sir argued about Harry Potter.

He makes himself forget it all. Every kind moment. Every gentle touch. They make him weak. They make him misunderstand things.

All that's real is *this*.

Carter is a slave.

Carter is nothing but a set of holes.

Carter is an object for sir to use and show off.

Carter doesn't even exist anymore.

All that's left is the slave. Sir's pet.

He promises himself he won't ever let himself forget that again.

THE DAY BLURS ONCE Carter has sunk into his reality as a slave. He pays attention to sir's voice, listening for orders and questions, but shuts everything else out. He's placed in the bathroom and told to use the toilet, wash up, and brush his teeth. Then he's ordered into the *Present* position, sir putting a plug in him.

Sir's cock is placed in his mouth with the order to only keep it warm. There's food pressed against his lips that he keeps on his tongue until sir instructs him to chew and swallow. The food is sweet. After only a few pieces, sir sighs angrily and stops feeding him. He's not given sir's cock either. He's a good boy and pays close attention, waiting for the next direction.

He thinks he's brought to sir's office for a while.

At some point, he's definitely given a bath. Sir says something about hair growing back and the auction before giving him orders to move this way and that. Carter obeys, a distant voice in his mind explaining to him that he's being shaved clean. He thinks the bath oil smells like honey, but he's not positive, and it's not important enough for him to try to figure it out.

He's told to get out of the bath, sir holding his hand to steady him. He's told to spread his legs as sir towels him off. He's told to turn around when sir rubs lotion into his skin. He's told to kneel in his *Rest* position at the foot of the bed.

Carter's not positive, but he thinks he's left there for a long time.

The spicy scent of sir's cologne fills his senses as a warning, preparing him just seconds before sir is finally giving him another order. "*Show.*"

Carter tilts his chin, keeping his eyes low. Certain details register in his mind without his permission. Sir is wearing black dress pants and black shoes, a simple white gold watch on his wrist flashing in the bedroom lighting. A comb is brought through Carter's hair, each stroke slow and deliberate. Sir dips his fingers in a tub of something that smells fruity before running them through Carter's hair to tame it.

Just as Carter is trying to pull his mind back into focus, remembering that details don't matter, sir does something that terrifies him.

He removes Carter's collar.

Carter chokes on a gasp, fingers scrabbling at his neck in a frantic attempt to fix the situation. He needs his collar. He's nothing but a slave – he has to be nothing but a slave – and slaves need collars. He feels raw without it. Wary. Vulnerable. He doesn't like it one bit.

Tears burn Carter's eyes as he tries to decide which is better behavior – to beg sir for his collar back, or to stay silent and obedient.

Sir makes the decision for him.

A white gold collar that matches sir's watch is brought up to his neck as a replacement collar. It's thin and intricately engraved with flowers and vines. It's almost... *pretty*.

A sudden sharp, breathtaking pain lights up Carter's right nipple without warning, drawing him out of his thoughts. He looks down just as sir moves on to his left. He's clamping Carter's nipples, the clamps the same design as the collar. There's a thin string of chain looped through the front ring of his collar, twisting elegantly before falling down to where each clamp is. His wrists are next, the cuffs sir places on him the same white gold engraved metal, but thicker and sturdier. By the time sir is done, Carter looks decorated.

It makes him unbelievably pleased.

"*Present.*"

Carter moves his body down and forward, swallowing a cry of pain when the chain swings with the movement, tugging at his nipples.

Sir is cold and clinical as he stretches Carter with two lubed fingers before inserting a plug that's slightly too big, making his hole stretch and burn.

"Rest."

When Carter returns to his Rest position, something soft brushes along his temple. He flinches but settles when sir gently hushes him. It's just sir's thumb. A gentle stroke. Nothing more.

Yet... it feels like *everything.*

The air seems to shift in the room. A long, tense silence stretches between them. Then sir grabs the sides of Carter's head and leans down, pressing their foreheads together, so Carter has no choice but to look into his eyes. Sir's inhale is shaky and labored when their gazes meet. His lips twitch into an incredulously relieved smile. "There you are, sweetheart. I thought I lost you."

Carter swears his heart catches in his throat. He doesn't know what to say.

He knows what he *wants* to say, though. He wants to remind sir that he *did* lose him. The Carter sir knew is gone. Sir might be trying to confuse him by switching back and forth, but Carter is in this now. He's a slave. It's been decided. There's no going back. He doesn't *want* to go back.

Sir presses a kiss to his lips. It's soft. Chaste. A promise of... *something*. When he pulls back enough to meet Carter's eye again, he looks unbearably sad. "Be good for me tonight. You have to be good. *Please*."

Not sure if he can speak, Carter just presses his forehead back against sir's and makes a soft noise in his throat. He doesn't know if it's the right thing to do.

Sir seems to sag in defeat before he pulls away completely and stands again.

The moment is gone.

Carter looks stunning, which fucking kills Nathan. His brown hair is brushed and gelled. His body is shaved and covered in a lotion that subtly glitters in the party lights. His lips are pretty pink, his blue eyes bright. The 14k white gold collar Nathan bought him wraps around his throat elegantly, lightweight and intricately carved, with the matching chain draped over his chest to connect with the clamps on his nipples. His ass is stuffed with a blown-glass anal plug that's laced with swirls of black.

He's the picture-perfect slave, and everyone is enjoying the view. Every weapon Nathan has on his body feels heavy and urgent against him. He wants to shoot and stab and strangle with his bare fucking hands until every fucker who looks at Carter is dead.

Instead, he sips his fucking champagne from his fancy ass champagne flute and keeps his expression bored.

"Nathan!" Nathan turns, raising an eyebrow until he sees it's the host's wife. Then he paints on his best charming smile and takes the hand she offers him, kissing her knuckles and shooting her a wink when she blushes. "It's such a pleasure to see you! We're so happy you could make it."

"Excellent to see you as well, Jamie. The party is beautiful. I wouldn't miss it."

Which is partly true. Nathan *wouldn't* miss it. Two very important things need to happen tonight; Todd Henley needs to convince Miller that he's on Miller's side and willing to go after Nathan, and Nathan has to find a way to subtly plant seeds of doubt with one of Miller's allies before extending a casual invite to his birthday celebration next month.

So much hinges on tonight. If something gets fucked up, Nathan won't get a chance to see the ally again for another 4 months. Not unless he requests a meeting, which would be far too suspicious of a move. Even sending an invite to Nathan's birthday party would be out of place if he doesn't have a conversation like the one he's planning to have tonight to support such an action. He would tip his hand, ruining everything.

"Oh good, you found your way to the champagne already," Jamie exclaims, oblivious to Nathan's plotting to take her and everyone she knows down.

"Did you doubt me?" Nathan asks, giving his tone a flirty lilt. It's harmless fun. Jamie and her husband are the types of people who enjoy playing and teasing and having a good time, but at the end of the day, they're hopelessly devoted to each other. So devoted, in fact, that Jamie helps her husband when he buys his slaves to torture them to death.

Jamie and Charles Kensington are in Nathan's top 10 on his list of people he can't wait to destroy when the operation is over.

If he has his way, their destruction will be particularly slow and brutal.

They banter for another minute before Jamie loops her arm through his and escorts him, Benny, and Carter over to their designated table. It's the second table as far as status goes, the first being just to the left where Jamie, Charles, and their four closest friends will sit. "Here we are! Can I get you anything, Nathan?"

"I believe we're good for now. Thank you."

Her eyes flick to Carter, a mischievous twitch showing in her lips. "Anything for your slave?"

Nathan flicks his hand dismissively. He wants her to leave. Now. "The slave is just fine. Go on and greet your guests. I'll come find you and Charles later."

"Promise?"

"Of course."

She winks at him before flitting off to speak to someone else. Nathan eyes the table until he finds his place card, then guides Carter over to the black silk pillow beside his designated chair. "Kneel here. *Rest* position."

The boy moves effortlessly. It hurts Nathan to watch. The true Carter is clumsy and goofy, always getting flustered and doubting himself. The confidence would be nice if it meant Carter felt secure in himself, but that's not it. This confidence is the one of a slave who knows all he has to do is follow orders and obey. It's a confidence that comes from mindlessness.

Stomach turning, Nathan turns away from the boy and tries to forget he's there. Benny takes the opportunity to sidle up to Nathan, their shoulders brushing as they survey the crowd. Nathan puts the rim of his glass to his lips to hide his mouth from anyone who might be trying to read his words. "Eyes on Miller?"

Benny tilts his chin towards him. "Not yet."

"We don't take a shot tonight." Nathan takes a drink before shifting his body in another direction. He watches as someone sets their slave up on the stage. It's a young woman. Somewhere around 18, if he had to guess. By the way her head is lolling to the side, she's either drugged out of her mind, or struggling with a head injury. Nathan slides a fascinated expression on his face to mask his disgust. "Make sure our men fucking understand. No blood. This is a recon."

"I'll make sure the idiots behave themselves, don't worry."

"Have you seen Henley?"

Benny smirks. "No. But I'm sure he's here somewhere. Kissing an ass or two."

"Hopefully he's wherever the hell Miller is."

"It sounds like he was damn happy the other night." Nathan looks over, eyebrows pulling together as he tries to figure out what Benny means. Benny's eyes flicker toward Carter for half a second before returning to the stage. Nathan forces his gaze to do the same. The woman is being flogged now. A gag in her mouth keeps her from disrupting the party.

"What are you trying to say?" Nathan asks, carefully maintaining his casually amused expression as he pretends to enjoy the show.

"I spoke to him this morning, just to check in before the party. He went on for quite a while about how... *satisfied* he was."

"Mmm."

Benny scoffs. "Mmm?"

"What would you like me to say, Ben?" Nathan tears his gaze away from the stage to glare at his best friend. "If you have something to say, say it."

"Fine." Benny squares up, glaring back at him. "He seems to be under the impression that he'll be getting some more of the boy in the future."

White-hot rage sparks through Nathan's veins. "Why the fuck would he think that?"

"I was planning to ask *you* that."

"I didn't give him that impression." Nathan pauses, his mind flitting rapidly through that night. "I didn't *mean* to give that impression. I-" *Fuck, did he give that impression?* He hadn't meant to, but maybe he did.

Nathan shakes his head. It doesn't fucking matter. "He won't be touching him again. No one will be."

"Oh god." Benny grabs Nathan's elbow, squeezing it hard enough to make Nathan hiss. "Do not fucking tell me you promised that. Don't fucking tell me you promised that to him."

"Can we not talk about this right now?" Nathan harshly whispers, eyes searching for eavesdroppers.

Benny ignores him. "Fucking hell, you did, didn't you? You fucking promised that boy-"

Whatever else Benny wanted to say is cut off by a startled, "Casey?"

It's quiet at first. Enough where only Nathan and Benny hear it. They look down at Carter in unison just as the boy grabs hold of the back of a dining chair and uses it to lift himself to his feet. Nathan darts his hand out, grabbing Carter's elbow to stop him from going anywhere.

Carter doesn't even look at him. His eyes are wide, his chest heaving. Then he gasps and yells, "Casey!"

Casey.

From his dream?

"Casey!"

"Slave!" Nathan hisses, his heart racing as he feels everyone's attention falling to them.

But Carter isn't listening. His focus is on –

"Carter?"

Nathan snaps his chin in the direction of the voice, trying to find who spoke his boy's name. His eyes land on a slave just a few feet away. He's around Carter's age, though taller and broader. An athletic frame, but a body that's seen better days. Nathan watches as the boy stares at Carter in shock. Then awe. Then overwhelming *relief*.

"Oh god, Carter!" The boy rushes forward, grabbing Carter in a hug that yanks him straight out of Nathan's grip. Nathan's too shocked to even fight it. "They told us they killed you!"

"I thought they killed *you*!" Carter sobs, clinging to the boy. "I didn't think you'd survive. I – I saw it! I saw them take you!"

And then they're talking over one another, neither probably even registering what the other is saying.

"You idiot! You fucking–"

"–didn't want them to–"

"–told you to leave it be!"

"I couldn't–"

"–believe you're okay! They–"

"–god, I'm sorry, Casey. I tried–"

"–they do to you?"

"*Nate*," Benny warns.

Nathan nods, sharp, one time. It's like a reset. Then he lunges forward and grabs Carter, fisting his hair and yanking him back. Carter reaches out for Casey, screaming his name, but he's no match for Nathan. Casey tries the same, but he's stopped by someone who must be his owner. A man Nathan recognizes, but can't place at the moment.

Not that it matters. They both have naughty slaves to deal with. And *fast* because all eyes are on them.

The man doesn't hesitate. Casey is already crumpled on the floor, the man's shoe kicking into his side.

Fuck.

Nathan turns Carter towards the table, slamming him down on it. Glass shatters, candlesticks shake, flames smoke out. A flute of champagne spills, soaking the blood red tablecloth until it's nearly black. Nathan uses his grip on the boy's hair to casually roll his head to the side so they're face to face. He ignores Carter's cry of pain.

Clinging tight to the rage he's feeling towards this entire goddamn situation, Nathan wraps it around himself like a fucking protective cloak and slips into the man these people believe him to be. "Big. Fucking. Mistake," he growls.

"Sir-" Carter whispers in what can only be described as devastation. "I'm so sor-"

Nathan grabs his pocket square and shoves it into the boy's mouth to cut off his apology. Carter begins to violently tremble then. Low keening sounds are emanating from his throat, muffled by the silk fabric stuffed in his mouth.

Casey is off the ground now, laid over a table just like Carter. His master is whipping the ever living shit out of him with a belt as his men hold the boy down. He's already bleeding from cuts on his back.

Nathan curls his free hand into a fist, thinking fast. Carter has to hurt, and hurt badly, but he can't get himself to do something like *that* to him. Never.

Jesus Christ.

The host and his wife are standing a few feet away, eyeing Nathan in anticipation. There's also a curiosity to their gazes, though. It's interesting to them that Nathan hasn't done anything yet. For now. Pretty soon it'll be less interesting and more suspicious. They'll start asking questions.

Nathan can't have them asking questions.

"My apologies," Nathan says to Jamie and Charles. He gives them his best smile. "Do you have somewhere I can straighten this one out privately? I don't want him to disrupt your party further."

His mistake, Nathan realizes too late, is that Carter being punished wouldn't be a disruption to these people. It would be *entertainment.*

Charles gives Nathan a smile that's dangerously wicked. "Why don't you take him up on the platform and let us all watch?"

"What's better than dinner and a show?" Jamie adds, giggling. "Oh, you *have* to, Nathan! Please?"

Nathan swallows hard, reminding himself of the person he's built himself into. Cold. Uncaring. Dangerous. Violent. He smiles, the thing feeling sinister on his lips. "Of course. Lead the way."

THEY'RE RAPING CASEY.

Carter can see it from where sir and Benny have him standing on the stage. They finally stopped whipping him once Casey went limp against the table, but now his master is letting anyone and everyone take turns with him. They aren't even waiting. They're using his ass, his mouth, his hands. Some are rubbing their cocks against his back, apparently not caring that it's slick with fucking blood. Others are rutting against his hair.

Carter failed him *again*. He got Casey in trouble *again*. This is his fault.

This is all his fault.

He should be down there. That should be him. *Why won't they ever fucking hurt him? Why is it always Casey?*

A metal stand is rolled up behind Carter, made of two sturdy poles that cross each other. Hands are all over him, forcing him to turn and face it, then wrenching his arms and legs to force his wrists and ankles into restraints until he looks like a sprawled-out X. The cloth was taken out of his mouth when Benny told sir that Carter was crying too hard and needed to be able to breathe. Carter hasn't said anything, though. Partly because he's afraid to be punished if he fucks up again, and partly because he hasn't seen sir yet, and sir is the only person he'd be interested in speaking to right now.

Other than Casey, of course. Not that Casey looks like he's capable of speaking right now if Carter's view over his shoulder is any indication.

Casey's awake again, at least. They've rolled him onto his back. Carter can see his eyes, wide as they stare up at the ceiling, slowly blinking. Only for a moment. Then his hair is grabbed, and a cock is getting shoved in his mouth, disrupting Carter's view.

Carter forces himself to keep watching. He deserves it. *This was his fault.*

Sir passes in front of Carter, holding something Carter doesn't recognize in his hands. Whatever it is, it looks intimidating. Sir doesn't even bother to look at Carter. He hasn't acknowledged him at all since he had slammed him into the table and growled at him.

Big. Fucking. Mistake.

Sir was right. It was exactly that. The biggest.

God, what the fuck had Carter been thinking?

His excitement and relief had made him idiotic. Reckless. He should've held his tongue and waited. Maybe later in the party, he would have had the chance to get close enough to Casey for a hurriedly whispered hello, or a quick reassuring touch in passing. Now, he's suffering the consequences. Casey is too.

Carter deserves this punishment. Not just because he misbehaved, but because he got Casey in trouble. He got Casey *hurt*.

Just like the Casey in his dreams.

It's getting harder to breathe. Carter is gasping for air, his desperation growing every second his chest burns.

Most of the crowd is watching Carter now. Their anticipation and amusement are thick in the air. Carter swears
it's fucking choking him. Filling his lungs and leaving no
room for oxygen.

Carter tries to convince himself he's okay. That he's
getting air, even if his mind is trying to make it feel
otherwise. He's getting oxygen, he *knows* he is, but his
body doesn't believe him.

They're going to kill Casey.

They're going to kill Casey, and all Carter can do is
watch.

"Sir," Carter gasps, his chest heaving. There are black
spots in his vision. "S-sir?"

A hand wraps around Carter's throat from behind him,
sir's cologne filling his nostrils. "Talking is not a good idea
right now, understood?"

"Please." Carter turns his chin the best he can with sir's
tight grip on him, trying to look up at the man. It's dumb,
he has his new rules telling him not to, but he can't help
it. He's fucking desperate. "Sir, please. Save him. Let – let
them hurt me instead."

Sir's eyes find Carter's, shock in them. Then confusion.
Then rage. "*What?*"

"Casey." Carter widens his eyes, wanting sir to see how
serious he is. "Please, sir. He won't survive it. Give them
me."

The hand on his throat squeezes until Carter gags. He
barely registers sir's mouth against his ear, the man's
voice sounding faded and distant. "You should probably
worry about your own survival right now, you fucking
idiot. Don't you remember what I told you would happen
if you did something like this? Why do you always have
to fucking ruin everything?"

Carter feels tears roll down his cheek. It's a strange
sensation considering his skin is going numb. There's a
humming in his head. He wonders if anyone else can hear
it.

The hand loosens, allowing Carter to suck in a gush of air. The fingers remain in place like a threat. A violent promise.

"My fault," Carter whispers, closing his eyes. "It's all my fault."

The fingers twitch against his skin. He expects them to tighten, but they don't. He thinks maybe they... *stroke him.*

His mind is clearly oxygen-depleted.

"No more talking. You're done talking now. Understood?"

Carter looks over his shoulder at Casey again, his chest quaking. He looks so lifeless. Like a ragdoll. "They're gonna kill him."

Sir sighs before muttering an angry, "Christ." His hand leaves Carter's skin. Just seconds later, a blindfold is wound around his head.

True, uninhibited terror overwhelms Carter. He thrashes his head, words pouring from his lips before he can stop them. "No, not the dark, not the dark, sir, *please, not the dark-*" he's cut off by something hard pressing into his mouth. He feels leathery straps on each of his cheeks, digging into the skin, and he realizes it's a ball gag.

For the first time since he was brought on stage, Carter releases a sob. There's no holding back after that. He just sobs and sobs and fucking *sobs*, barely noticing as he's pushed and pulled into position.

His plug is pulled out of his hole, something else nudging against his rim instead. Something too big. Too dry.

The hauntingly familiar sensation of a cock cage returns to Carter's genitals, cold and tight. He's not concerned about it. Not really. There's no chance he'll be getting hard tonight. Biology or not, nothing can overcome this terror.

But then Carter remembers that Todd Henley was the last person to put a cage on his cock; it had been his idea to do so at all. Todd Henley, who is in attendance tonight.

Todd Henley, who might be touching Carter right this second.

Sir had said he wouldn't share Carter anymore, but that was before this.

What if sir changed his mind?

There's a rattling sound. Metal on metal. It's sharp in his ears. Irritating.

Carter realizes after a moment that it's his cuffs against the frame. He's shaking.

He can't stop shaking.

Something warm and wet is squirted down Carter's ass crack and all over the toy threatening him. Then the toy moves away slightly and the tip of what Carter assumes is a bottle is being pushed into him. He jerks as he feels the same liquid filling his hole.

The bottle disappears.

So do all of the hands touching him.

Then Carter is alone. Left on a fucking stage strapped to a metal frame with his lubed ass facing a crowd. And he's in the dark.

All alone in the dark.

Again, again, again.

Please, not again.

He tries to tell himself that he's done this before, that it'll be okay, but this is nothing like the auction. Carter is smart enough to know that.

His shaking just gets worse.

There's the sound of a machine whirring to life. Then the thing against his hole is pushing against it, demanding entry. White dots spark in his vision behind the blindfold as he sobs into the gag. The machine moving the toy doesn't care that he's not ready for something so big. It just pushes and pushes, making room for itself where there is none.

It hurts.

God, it *hurts*.

Carter sobs and screams until his throat feels like it might start bleeding. He writhes in his restraints, bucking his body, thrashing his head.

People are laughing at him. Cheering. Catcalling.

He's not sure where sir is. He's not sure where he wants him to be either. *Is it better for him to have abandoned Carter?* At least it means he's not standing there enjoying himself like the others. That has to be better than if sir is just standing a few feet away right now, grinning, uncaring, watching Carter like he's never kissed him or held him or watched Harry Potter with him. Abandonment has to be better than that.

Carter tries to focus on other positives of his situation, trying to find the silver lining. First, it's just a toy raping him for now. That's a definite bonus. Second, the cage on his cock will most likely save it from being abused too badly. Third, no one is touching him or hurting him.

He can hear the party. Laughter. Talking. Light music, enough for an ambiance, but not so much no one can enjoy their time with friends. Glasses are clinking. Perhaps silverware as well. *Dinner and a show, isn't that what they said?*

Maybe they'll get distracted by Carter and leave Casey alone. Another silver lining.

The crowd quiets. Carter's heart lurches, knowing that can't be good. Just seconds later, something is slashing across his back. His back bows as he screams into his gag. There's laughter and applause. He's hit again. And again. And again. On his back, his ass, his thighs, his calves. The toy starts moving faster inside of him, pounding him in rhythm with the hits.

Is this sir?

Benny?

Someone else?

Oh god, what if sir gave Carter to the party? What if he handed him over to not just be raped, but to be tortured and punished until they've had enough?

339

Sir wouldn't do that.

He – he wouldn't.

He *wouldn't*.

The pain stops. Carter sucks in as much air as possible, relief rushing through his system, even as his body throbs and burns in agony.

He's hit again. This time it's the front of his body. A thigh. Then the other. His stomach.

Then his genitals. He thought the cage on his cock would protect him, but it doesn't.

Still recovering, Carter's not prepared for the pain of a brutal hit against his left nipple. It's hard enough to send the clamp there flying. Blood rushes to the abused nub too fast, sending Carter into a dizzy spell. He starts to sag in his restraints. His shoulders burn as they take the brunt of his weight, but he can't get himself to straighten out again. No fucking way.

The person hitting him is trying to get the other clamp off now, but they're struggling. Hits come fast, one after another, sharp bursts of pain until the clamp is finally snapped off. Carter chokes on air.

The dildo speeds up.

The person hits his genitals again.

Something hot and wet pours down Carter's balls and thighs, making him writhe in agony as the liquid hits his welts. He realizes distantly that he caused this. Carter pissed himself.

People are cheering.

Someone is close in front of him. He can feel the heat of their body rippling off them.

No, it's two people. They're whispering to each other. One is angry. The other is desperate.

He hears, "-can't-" and, "-shit together-" and, "-have to stop." He hears, "-a little more," and, "-please, Ben-" and, "-get us fucking killed."

It's hard to concentrate on any of it. Everything is numb and distant and much safer if he doesn't let the words or the sensations register.

The dildo slows. Then stops. Then disappears.

Something warm and heavy is being pressed against Carter's front. Things piece together in a quick jumble. His gag is removed, something wiping his chin and cheeks. Then the blindfold is gently slipped free. He blinks a few times, but his vision is too blurry. He can't get his eyes to focus.

The cuffs on his ankles are freed. Strong hands grab the backs of his thighs, twitching when Carter sobs in pain. His nipples throb as something coarse rubs against them. A thumb is stroking his cheek. The crowd is louder. Words are being whispered in his ear. A cock is sliding into his hole.

"-got you. You're safe now. Never – never again. Never again, sweetheart."

Carter blinks, and he sees a watercolor painting of sir's face in front of him. The sight of him rips Carter out of his lingering fuzziness and plunges him straight into turmoil. He hangs his head to rest on sir's shoulder and sobs freely, his chest heaving, his eyes pouring tears too fast for him to see anything even if he wanted to. Not that he wants to. He keeps his eyes closed nice and tight.

Even though Carter can taste blood on his tongue, he can't get himself to calm down enough to stop sobbing. He's convinced he'll never be able to stop. None of this will ever stop. There's no escaping it.

"I know. Fuck, I know. I'm so sorry. I'm so fucking sorry, sweetheart. I'm so proud of you. You've done so well. Taken your punishment so fucking well. Such a good boy. My good, good boy." Sir kisses his throat. His jaw. His earlobe. "Sir is almost done, okay? Almost done. Then we can go home. Sir will take you home and we'll – we'll never fucking do this again, okay? You'll be forgiven, and this will all be over, and you'll be safe. Okay?"

Carter nods rapidly, wanting that. *Needing* that. Sir is almost done. Then he gets to go home. Then he's forgiven. Then it'll be *over*.

Sir's thrusts are hard and smooth as he presses more kisses to Carter's throat and face. In between each peck is a whispered word or phrase.

Good boy.

So fucking good for me.

That's it, sweetheart.

Fuck, you take sir's cock so well.

So perfect.

No more. I promise. No more.

I'll take care of you now.

I'm so fucking sorry.

Never again.

God, Carter, I'm so in love with you.

The world spins and spins and *spins* before going blissfully black.

NATHAN GIVES UP WHEN Carter passes out. He can't come. It's not in the cards tonight, little blue pill or not. No fucking way. *How could he when his perfect boy – the boy he fucking loves – is wrecked in such a terrible way?* Nathan's not even fully hard for fuck's sake.

Faking an orgasm with a few jerks of his hips, Nathan sighs in relief and pulls out of the boy. He plugs him quickly before anyone can notice that cum isn't sliding out of him before tucking his cock away. Everything fades as he steps back to look at Carter. There's an ache in him. Something deep. Primal. It's like Nathan's body can recognize that he's done something wrong on a cosmic level.

This isn't what Nathan signed up for when he took this job.

This isn't what *Travis* signed up for.

He realizes it then, standing on the stage, faded applause in his ears, a broken boy in front of him - Travis isn't going to make it out of this alive. It was a delusion to ever think otherwise.

And after tonight... Nathan's not sure if Carter will either.

Chapter Twenty

THE TWO AMERICAN HEROES playing the roles of monsters don't say a word as they carry the boy off the stage. As they follow the directions of the hosts to a guest suite. As they lie the boy on the bed without a care for the expensive bedding.

Benny wipes Carter's body down with a warm, wet cloth. Nathan paces around the room. Benny uses a combination of toilet paper and band-aids to dress Carter's wounds. Nathan throws up in the toilet twice. Benny tries to wake Carter up in the hopes of checking on his mental status. Nathan hovers nearby with his breath held. Benny fails at waking the boy. Nathan kicks a chair over. Benny comments that being a cliche white male isn't going to solve anything. Nathan debates the merits of punching his best friend during a time like this. Benny checks Carter's vitals. Nathan decides Benny can be punched later instead.

Carter's vitals are good, all things considered.

"Okay. I'll take him home," Benny says, gesturing towards Carter's limp body. "You need to get back to the party. You have a man to schmooze."

Nathan sneers at his friend in disgust. "The fuck I do! The night is fucking over."

"No. *Carter's* night is over. *My* night is over. I'll take him home and get him settled. *You* need to seal the deal with Vasco."

"Benny, you can't possibly ask me to do that."

"I'm not asking."

The two men glare at each other, but only one is heart-broken and defeated, so the one who has his shit together wins. Nathan looks away.

"Wash up first," Benny advises. "You've got blood on your hand."

Nathan looks down at his hand, startled to find that Benny is right. His skin is streaked with angry crimson. "It's not mine," he says unnecessarily.

"I know."

"I – I made him bleed."

"I know, Nate. Don't think about it. Not right now. Just wash it off and get back to the party."

"Right." Nathan stares down at his hands, transfixed by the sight of Carter's blood slashed across his skin. His hands begin to tremble. "I should call Maison."

Before he can comprehend, Benny has Nathan by the arm and is shoving him into the bathroom. He shuts the door before pinning Nathan up against it and growling at him. "Are you a fucking idiot?"

"I–" Nathan stops himself, trying to remember what he even said. Maison. He should call Maison. He *should*. But… he shouldn't have said it in front of the boy.

Maybe it's time Carter knows.

Hell, maybe it's time all of this ends anyway. Nathan will take the hit. He'll happily die for this boy.

"He can't be here any longer, Ben. We can't keep doing this to him."

"There's no other choice!"

"We can let him go! Claim he escaped. Claim he killed himself. I'll go down for it. I don't fucking care."

"Jesus. You've fucking lost it." Benny shoves off of him, shaking his head in frustration. Then he's back against Nathan with a hand around his throat. "There are two ways this ends - that boy safe with Maison once we've finished this mission, or that boy in the hands of someone

345

like Miller or Henley or God forbid the fucking Kensington's because we failed. That's it. There's no clicking our heels and sending him home. We're *this* close, Nate. We are *this fucking close.*"

"Ben..." Nathan meets his friend's gaze, searching for the man he knew before. The man Benny really is beneath this cold persona he's always managed to maintain so much better than him. "Jake, we have to save him from this."

Benny flinches at the use of his real name. He pushes away again, maintaining his distance this time. He won't meet Nathan's eyes. "We'll figure something out, okay? We'll figure this out. We'll call Maison. But not right now. Right now, we have to do what's best for Carter and the mission. Right now, we have to stick to the fucking plan. Otherwise we'll wind up dead by morning, and he'll be even worse off. Do you understand?"

When Nathan says nothing, Benny changes tactics. "Did you see what they did to that other boy tonight? Casey?"

Nathan shudders as the memories burst through his mind. Of course he saw it. So did Carter. *God, Carter had wanted to take his place.*

As if Benny read Nathan's mind, Benny asks, "Do you want Carter to be like that? Do you want him in the hands of someone like that?"

"No."

"That boy is probably violently raped and beaten nightly. Do you want that for Carter?"

"No."

"Do you want him to be gang-raped? To be used like a sex toy for an entire group of violent, fucked up men?"

"No!" Nathan growls, snapping his gaze to his friend. He flashes his eyes in warning. "*Stop.*"

"No, Nathan. *You* stop. It's not me who is putting him in danger right now. It's you."

346

Fury bubbles inside of Nathan's chest, threatening to burst. He wants to destroy something. *Someone.* He wants to claw and break and shred all of these people until they're nothing but piles of filth and sin. Until they can't possibly hurt anyone ever again.

"Who was that piece of shit?"

Benny tosses a hand up in confusion. "Who?"

"Casey's owner. Who is he? What do we know about him?"

"Christ, you're scatter-brained today." Benny rubs at his forehead, eyes half-closed as he thinks. "Dugray. William Dugray. He's a cleaner. Works for Hanson, I think."

A cleaner isn't one of the people who launders the dirty money for people like Nathan. They're who accepts the money once it's been laundered and makes damn sure it's squeaky clean by running it through all sorts of stocks and funds. Launderers take away the obvious filth on the cash in case anyone decides to snoop around. Cleaners make it so no one ever even thinks of snooping in the first place.

They're valuable, yes, but they're not irreplaceable.

"How high up is Dugray?"

"I don't know. Up there. Not the top."

"Disposable?"

Benny's lips part, a question clearly on the tip of his tongue, but then realization relaxes his expression and he's smirking. "Oh. I see now."

"So?"

"So, I'm pretty sure we could make that work, yeah. Let me dig around a bit. Give me 24."

Nathan nods. He can do that. He can be patient.

Or he can at least *try* to be.

The idea of William Dugray getting eviscerated will certainly hold Nathan over for the night at least.

"But Casey," Nathan thinks out loud. "If he survived tonight, you make damn sure he gets taken care of. Even if we can't get rid of Dugray. I don't want that boy with him anymore. Things have to change for Casey. Understood?"

"Absolutely. I'll keep you updated." Benny reaches out and squeezes Nathan's shoulder in what he knows is meant to be a comforting gesture. It's not comforting, but nothing would be right now. Nathan appreciates the effort. "Hold it together, man. Clean yourself up, get a drink, mingle for 20 minutes, find Vasco, and get this shit over with. Then come home and be with your boy."

"Promise you'll take care of him?" Nathan asks like a pathetic idiot. He *knows* Benny will take good care of the boy. Of course he does. But... he just needs to hear it.

"Yeah, Nate. I've got him."

"Okay." Nathan takes a deep breath, steadying himself. "Okay. You go. I'll stay in here and clean up. I - I can't see him again. I need to stay focused."

Benny nods, giving him a tight smile. "He's going to be okay, Nate. I promise."

Nathan turns away from Benny before he can say what he's sure they're both thinking.

That's not a promise Benny can keep.

Carter Beckett may not ever be okay again.

CARTER WAKES SLOWLY, TAKING stock of every new thing he feels as he crawls back to awareness. A violent, burning sensation is licking across most of his skin. His hole is throbbing. His cock and balls feel raw and heavier than they should. His mouth tastes like copper and bile, the inside of it dry and tacky. His cheek aches.

The first emotion that returns to him is a deep, over-whelming sadness.

Terror isn't far behind.

Then he *remembers*.

Casey. Seeing him. Holding him. Relief. Peace. Then being torn away, kicking and screaming.

Sir smashing Carter's face against the table. Growling at him. Angry at him.

He remembers watching Casey's master whipping him bloody. The men who used him after. The way his body had gone as slack and lifeless as a sex doll.

He remembers his own whipping. The toy shoved in his hole. The pain. The pain. So much fucking pain.

The laughter.

The cheering.

The dark.

The dark, again, again, again in the dark. Alone in the dark.

He pissed himself.

He sobbed.

He screamed.

Sir fucked him.

Sir... promised him things. So many things. They're all a jumble in Carter's mind. *Something about forgiving him, maybe?* Something about being *good*. But that can't be right... because Carter wasn't good at all. He was naughty. Disappointing. Carter ruined everything. He *always* ruins everything.

Was there an apology?

Did sir apologize?

No. Certainly not. Carter must have apologized to sir. That must be what he's remembering.

There was something about love, too. A confession. A heated surge of emotions. That couldn't have been sir. No way.

Which means...

Oh god, did Carter confess his love to sir?

No.

No, no, no.

He wouldn't be that stupid. He *wouldn't*.

He doesn't even love sir. Not at all. He hates him. Despises him. The man is a fucking *monster*.

Maybe it was all just some fucked up mind game that his traumatized brain decided to play with him. It wouldn't be the first time Carter's mind has done that to him. It's never had a problem creating whispered apologies and gentle touches out of cruelty and pain. It's practically a fucking expert at it by now.

Carter startles when the bedroom door opens. He jerks into a sitting position, an agonized sound ripping its way up his throat as he immediately falls back down. Every inch of his body burns and throbs. Tears fall down his face, stinging the small cut on his cheek from where he was slammed into the table earlier.

"S-sir? 'M sor-" Carter chokes down the apology when he sees that it's not sir at the door.

It's his friend. Benny.

The instinct to toss the covers over his head and hide is overwhelming. The only reason he doesn't give in is how painful it would be to do such a thing with his body right now. Even turning his head to look at Benny fully is enough to have fresh tears springing to his eyes. His body jerks with every panicked intake of breath, pulling whimpers from him.

Carter wants to ask where sir is.

He wants to ask if Benny is going to hurt him.

If Benny is going to fuck him.

If Casey is dead.

If maybe they'd be willing to take pity on him and kill him too.

But everything hurts, and his brain is fuzzy, so he stays silent. His body continues to jerk.

He jolts when a hand touches his shoulder, a new wave of panic welling up in his chest when he realizes Benny made his way across the room without Carter even noticing.

"Shhh," Benny coos. His eyes are gentle. Warm. Kind. He looks at Carter like he cares about him. *God, Carter's mind is even more fucked up than he thought.* "Just breathe, little one. I'm not going to hurt you. I'm just here to make sure you're alright."

Carter doesn't believe him, but he doesn't say that. He thinks it's safest if he continues to say nothing at all.

"Sir is still at the party." Benny smiles softly. "He had me take you home so you could be cleaned up and put to bed."

More questions bubble along Carter's tongue, but he manages to hold them back.

"I was hoping you'd sleep longer, but that's alright. This gives me a chance to get a proper look at your wounds now."

Carter flinches at the words. They sound sincere, caring even, but he knows better. This man is a monster. They're all monsters. Even sir.

Especially sir.

The blanket is gently pulled off Carter, revealing a body littered with welts and bruises. He quickly looks away from himself before too many details can register.

"Roll onto your front." When Carter hesitates, Benny asks, "Do you need help?"

Carter squeezes his eyes shut, terror thick in his veins. "Please," he manages to choke. He feels tears spilling through the tight seam of his eyelids. "Please, it hurts so bad. Please don't fuck me."

"Shhh." Benny runs a hand through Carter's hair. It feels just like sir's. Instead of calming him, it just makes Carter feel worse. A sob catches in his chest. "Your master didn't give me permission to do anything like that to you. I'm just here to make sure you're okay."

The words *I'll never be okay again* materialize on Carter's tongue. It takes a great sacrifice to keep them inside. They burn like acid.

"Do you need help, or can you roll over on your own?"

If he's being honest, Carter probably *does* need help, but he refuses to give anyone permission to touch him if he has the chance to avoid it. So, he grits his teeth and forces his body to move.

It doesn't hurt. *Hurt* isn't a word that is even close to describing the sensation of his skin dragging against bedding, his muscles stretching and twitching, his bones weak, his mind fuzzy. There is no word. Not for Carter, at least. Not anymore. If it existed in his vocabulary once, it's been evicted. Beaten from his mind. Burned away by the acidity of words left unsaid.

Agony is the closest thing, but even that's not enough.

He wants to die.

Carter would give *anything* to die.

The bed shifts as Benny climbs onto it. Teeth of a zipper hiss as they're torn apart. A bottle softly clicks open. Something is squirted onto something else.

He's going to fuck Carter. He lied. Of course he lied. These men always lie. *Carter is about to be raped by someone other than sir for the very first time.*

Carter makes himself a promise right then. When Benny finishes with him, leaving Carter behind like he's nothing, Carter will kill himself. He'll end this once and for all. Then, maybe, if he's lucky, he'll end up with Casey in heaven. Carter has never been much of a believer, really, but he's had to have earned that at least, right? After surviving this hell, God would surely take pity on him.

He just has to die first.

Carter wonders if sir brought all of his weapons with him to the party tonight. Of course, a gun would be the best option, but a knife would do.

Otherwise, Carter can improvise. There are the sharp blades from sir's shaving kit. Or the sturdy beams of the ceiling in sir's closet and the red rope sir used to tie him up before. Or the bathtub where he can force his lungs to fill with water.

Carter begins to drift along with the safety of his new plan. So many options. It's blissful, really, to realize how easily he can escape it all when he's ready.

This is his mistake; the drifting. Carter forgets to control his mind.

He forgets to keep the acid words from bubbling past his lips.

"I made him mad..." Carter whispers, the truth of the words impossibly heavy as they pull him out of his false bliss and back to the present.

Benny tenses, the air between them suddenly heavy. Then he sighs and places a gentle hand on Carter's ankle. "I know."

"He - he *hates* me."

Carter hates *himself*.

"Hey, no. He doesn't hate-" Benny stops with a frustrated noise. "Just hold still, okay? Be a good boy and hold still. No... talking. Conserve your energy."

Carter nods, turning his face into the pillow to hide that he's crying again. God, it feels like that's all he ever does anymore. His whole life is crying.

The thought makes Carter cry even harder.

Benny sighs. "This might hurt a bit, but I need you to try to stay still and just breathe, okay?"

Try to stay still and just breathe while I rape you. If Carter had the energy, he'd scoff. But he doesn't have the energy. He doesn't have much of anything at all.

He sags in defeat. "Yes, sir..."

Carter immediately fucks up when he feels something wet touch his calf. He jerks, his head turning even though it hurts. He has to blink a few times before believing what he's seeing.

Benny is fully dressed. The bottle in his lap isn't lube. The unzipped bag beside him is full of medical supplies. His hand is covered in some sort of cool gel as it rests on Carter's red skin.

All Carter manages is a small, "Oh."

"This will make you feel better," Benny promises. He's making eye contact, looking kind again, so Carter quickly turns his face away.

It's not real. He's a monster.

He has to be a monster, because then sir is a monster.

And sir... has to be a monster.

Carter can't let himself see sir as anything but a monster.

"Just lie still now."

It's easier said than done. For the first few seconds, the pain of Benny spreading what feels like a cool gel over his calf is manageable, but the moment he comes in contact with one of the more abused spots, Carter's mind is whiting out. He comes back to himself to find that he's begun sobbing. Benny is hushing him, saying things like *I know*, and *You're okay*, and *Almost done*. The pain doesn't fade. It doesn't ease. Every time a welt is touched, Carter jerks and sobs.

"I'm sorry," Benny says after a particularly painful spot on his shoulder is assaulted by his slick hand. Then, his voice hoarse, he admits, "That's it for the salve on your backside, but... I need to treat the welts that broke now."

"B-broke?"

"He... drew blood tonight. In a few places. I need to treat them so they don't get infected." Benny rubs little circles with his thumb against the uninjured skin of Carter's ankle. "Do you want something for the pain? I have morphine. It's just a quick shot. It'll probably put you out."

Carter grips the sheets tight, swallowing a moan when his muscles disapprove. He wants that, he does, but he feels selfish for it. Casey is probably *dead* now. The least Carter can do is suck it up and take this. He deserves the pain. He deserves worse than the pain.

This is all his fault.

He ruined everything.

"Do you want the morphine, little one?" Benny asks again.

"N-no, sir."

"Okay." There's some rustling from Benny's position on the bed as he digs in his bag. Carter can feel the heavy thud of things being set down on the mattress beside his leg. "This is going to hurt like a bitch, but I'll try to do it quickly."

Carter has just enough time to register the words before something is being poured over his left thigh. He shrieks, the sound taking enough energy from him that he sags into the mattress after, struggling to keep his eyes open. White dots float inside his eyelids. His body isn't jerking anymore. Jerking would require sudden stops between the movements. It's doing something else now. Vibrating, almost. Like a part of him is trying to escape this plane of existence altogether.

Benny is speaking again, his tone low and soothing. There's the sound of paper ripping and the pressure of something being pressed hard against his thigh. A sharp antiseptic scent fills the air. When he breathes it into his lungs, it burns something fierce.

The process repeats, this time on his ass cheek. Carter bites down on the blanket this time. He doesn't want to be an annoyance to Benny. If this is the man treating his wounds with gentle kindness, he does *not* want to find out what the angry version would be like.

Carter's mind drifts eventually. It doesn't go somewhere fuzzy or safe, though. It goes to a place like his dream the other night. Somewhere cold and *dark, dark,*

dark. Casey's sobs echo in the air. Sir is nowhere to be found. Maison is disgusted with him. Carter is choking on invisible daffodils.

Will sir come for him this time? Will he save Carter? Will he forgive him?

Does Carter even deserve to be forgiven?

After a very long time, or maybe no time at all, Benny finishes. He says something about sir putting the gel on Carter's front later. Something about the skin there being less injured. He runs fingers through Carter's hair and convinces him to drink something from a straw. It's sweet and cold. His body hums with relief the moment of his first swallow.

Benny wipes the tears from his face with a cloth before pushing his hair off his sweaty forehead. He says something about going to get ice packs. Says something about Carter going to sleep. Something about him being a good boy.

But Carter's *not* a good boy.

Sir *said.*

"Are you gonna see him?" Carter suddenly asks just as Benny is about to leave. He blames the fog of pain for his loose tongue. Mostly because he can't blame himself anymore. His load of guilt is too full.

"Who?"

"Sir."

"Oh." Benny tugs at his tie. "Yes. Most likely."

"Can you tell him somethin' for me?" Carter asks, hoping his words aren't as slurred as they feel rolling off his tongue. This is too important.

Benny frowns, but he also nods. "Sure."

"Will you tell him 'm sorry? 'M real sorry."

Benny gives him a smile that seems sad, even though Carter has no idea what the man has to be sad about. "Of course. Just try to get some rest, now. I'll be back with your ice packs soon."

"Okay." Carter swallows hard, tears burning his eyes again. Unless he never stopped crying. There's a chance he never even stopped. It's just that he's now noticing the sensation again. "Sir?"

Benny sighs heavily, making Carter immediately regret his entire existence. "What do you need?"

"'M sorry," Carter murmurs into the blankets, closing his eyes like a child trying to hide from a monster. "N'ver min'."

"No, little one. Say whatever you needed to say."

Carter curls in on himself as much as he can before his body forces him to stop. "Just, um," he pauses, struggling for a lie. "Thank you. For - for the help, sir."

"Oh. Sure. Of course."

Of course. Like it's no big deal. Like Carter isn't less than human and not worthy of help.

Maybe men like Benny and Nathan take special classes. *Contradiction 101* or *Intro to Mindfucking.*

Carter closes his eyes, trying to shut the whole world out. He'll get to killing himself later. He's just... so tired right now. He needs to work up the energy.

He wishes he had his moose. He wonders where it is. He wonders if maybe it'd be worth the pain to find it.

He wonders if maybe he should find it in order to *hide* it. *What if sir takes it away as punishment?* It'd be fitting. Carter doesn't deserve something as nice as his moose. He doesn't deserve anything at all.

It should have been him instead of Casey that died.

It should still be him.

The world would be better if he wasn't around to ruin everything. Sir's life would be better. He could use that other slave instead. The jealous one. *What was his number again?* 3.

3 would be so good to sir. He'd make him happy and proud. He'd never get other slaves in trouble by being naughty.

3 would be a good boy.

Carter falls asleep, crying softly into his pillow as he grieves his own worth.

He never even notices when Benny eventually leaves the room.

ENRIQUE VASCO IS ONE of the most powerful men in the Mexican Mafia. No one ranks above him, and only 3 other men rank on the same level as him. He's also one of Miller's biggest allies. At least, he was. They've been on the outs lately. As of January, when Miller killed one of Vasco's men for a perceived slight that Vasco didn't agree warranted a killing.

It's the perfect opening. If Nate can secure Vasco as an ally, Miller loses Mexico. If Miller loses Mexico, Miller is no longer a major player. If Miller is no longer a major player, Nathan can easily take over the rest of his empire.

And once Nathan has Miller's empire in his hands, the case is done. The majority of the Northern and Central American markets will be his. Enough where, when everything is dismantled, and bursts into beautiful flames, what's left won't be able to function. They'll crumble. Implode. They'll be sitting ducks for task forces to pick off one by one.

It's always rested on Miller, but tonight, *Miller* rests on Vasco.

Nathan is on his game tonight. He has to be. If he slips for even a moment, he'll break. So, he plays his part well, drinking the finest scotch and sharing a Cuban cigar with a wink, receiving a lap dance from one of the working slaves, laughing his ass off reminiscing with a few of his branch bosses about all sorts of idiotic adventures, flirting with Jamie Kensington and lying with a grin as he extends an invite to come play with Carter that he never plans on solidifying, making subtle comments about William Dugray and agreeing wholeheartedly when people say Dugray is a disgrace, subtly asking if Dugray's slave is alive and keeping his face perfectly neutral when he gets the answer.

By the time he's able to organically make his way to Vasco, he's walking on the air that comes from being *the* Nathan Roarke. Vasco instinctually recognizes it, straightening his spine for half a second before remembering himself. Then he slumps back into a lazy stance and gives Nathan a sharp smile.

"Have you forgotten who my friends are, Roarke?" Vasco asks as he tries to play it off like he hadn't for just a second recognized Nathan as someone who deserves his respect.

Nathan lets it slide, of course. He has to allow Vasco to believe he has the upper hand after all.

"I've forgotten why I've never considered being one of them," Nathan says smoothly. He waves a service slave down, gesturing for refills on what both he and Vasco are drinking. Vasco's expression twists, but he doesn't argue. He looks mildly curious. *Good.* "Would you care for small talk? I could ask you how business is, pretending I don't have files on your numbers. You can ask me the same, pretending you don't have files of your own. I can bitch about the latest FBI task force that's been the bane of my existence this past quarter. You can bitch about that new identification policy that Border Patrol just passed. We can agree that this shit was much easier before technology advanced, and stay-at-home moms decided to start an uprising to save the children. *Or-*" Nathan pauses. Waits.

Vasco takes the bait. "Or?"

Nathan doesn't smile, but *oh how he wants to.* "Or we can cut to the chase."

"Which is?"

"Which is that I'm having a very exclusive, very extravagant birthday party in 2 weeks, and I've placed you on the guest list."

That gets Vasco's attention. "Why?"

"Because I think we'd be fantastic friends." Nathan flashes a smile then. It's controlled. Calculated. Cunning, but in an obvious way he knows Vasco will see and respect. "It's merely an invite. Come. Don't come. No harm either way."

"And how do I know I won't be walking into a trap?"

"Because your men are invited as well."

"Weapons?"

"Are expected," Nathan says casually. "Anyone not packing at my party is an idiot."

Vasco watches him carefully, considering. Then, "And your whore?"

"What about him?" Nathan asks, unfazed. He knew it was coming. "If you're concerned about his behavior, I assure you that he learned his lesson tonight."

Vasco smirks. "I wouldn't mind if he hadn't. It was a damn nice show."

"That it was." Nathan breathes once. In. Out. *You're doing this for Carter.* "Perhaps there will be an encore. It's my birthday, after all. What better way to celebrate?"

"That's awfully tempting, Roarke."

"Then come." Nathan nods at the serving slave who appears with their drinks. He takes his own from the tray and raises it in cheers towards Vasco. Surprising the hell out of him - not that he shows it at all - Vasco returns the sentiment. "We don't have to work together, Vasco. We don't even have to be friends. But we do share a border. No harm in being neutral, don't you agree?"

Vasco studies him for a long moment. Then he smiles. "Yes, Roarke. I believe I do."

Chapter Twenty-One

THE SECOND TIME CARTER wakes up, it's to the sudden feeling of his stomach lurching. He slaps a hand over his mouth and scrambles off the bed, nearly falling flat on his face when the sheets wrap around his ankle. He half-crawls, half-stumbles to the bathroom, swallowing the first wave of vomit that crawls up his throat.

He tries to open the bathroom door only to find it locked. Carter rests his palm on the wood, his other hand still covering his mouth, and closes his eyes. He tries to breathe through the nausea. Tries to calm down. He doesn't know who is on the other side - Benny or sir - but it doesn't matter. They'll both be pissed if he makes a mess.

Somehow, he manages to croak, "Sir?" at the same time as he pathetically hits the door a few times with his palm.

There's a loud sound from the other side of the door, as if the person bumped into something. Carter hears a grumbled, "Fuck," and then, "I have to go." Then the door is opening, Carter falling forward as he suddenly loses the only thing keeping him on his feet. Sir catches Carter, hands steadying him.

"*Carter*," sir breathes, his eyes going bright.

Carter flinches. He doesn't like that name anymore. That name was attached to the boy from *before*. He'll never be him again. "No. Not - not him. Jus'-" before he can explain himself, another wave of nausea ripples through his body. He quickly presses a hand to his mouth again, wavering on his feet.

Sir's grip tightens, his eyebrows pulling in as he searches Carter's face for something. Carter's not sure what. He's not sure if he has anything to give the man. There's not much left. "What's wrong, sweetheart?"

Everything.

"Don' feel s'good."

"What doesn't feel good? Is it your cuts? Your head? Your stomach?"

"E – ev – v- v- v- thin'," Carter tries to explain through chattering teeth. His body is starting to tremble. He has to lean on sir to keep from falling again.

Carter wants to tell sir that he's afraid, but he can't find the strength to form the words. The room *spins, spins, spins.* He thinks he starts to fall. If he does, he never hits the ground. He realizes then that sir has him. He carries Carter bridal style into the bathroom, setting him down on the fluffy rug by the toilet. Carter inhales, planning to thank him.

Instead, he ends up vomiting right there, his body violently lurching forward just in time for the liquid to spill into the toilet bowl. Even after the initial surge of puke, Carter clings to the edges of the toilet for dear life and suffers through a series of dry heaves, his body determined to purge its already empty stomach.

Sir pushes to his feet and walks past Carter, heading to the sink. His face is blank as he runs the water and searches in the cabinet for something. Carter wonders if he's upset that he's stuck taking care of Carter.

He wonders if he'll get in trouble for this.

He wonders if he'll even survive.

Maybe it'd be better if he didn't.

A cold, damp cloth is placed on the back of Carter's sweaty neck. Carter looks for sir, hoping to give him a thankful smile, but he can't find him. He must be nearby though because a cup of water is magically placed on the floor beside Carter a moment later.

The man finally shows himself when he leans down and presses a kiss to Carter's temple. "You stay here, okay? I'll be right back."

"No!" Carter lifts a shaking hand to cling to sir's shirt. He barely has the strength to curl his fingers around the fabric, but he uses every ounce he can muster. Sir is all he has now. Sir is... sir is all that's left. There's no Carter anymore. He doesn't *want* to be Carter anymore. It's just sir now. Only sir.

He *needs* sir.

"Ple – please don' lea'me, s–sir. P – *please*," Carter begs, not caring how whiney and pathetic he sounds. He needs sir to stay. Sir made him into something new tonight. He proved to Carter that he truly is just a slave. Just a set of holes. Worthless. An object. Entertainment. The show during dinner. Nothing more. Not even human.

Sir took Carter up on that stage and emptied him of his humanity. He can't leave Carter alone after that. Without sir, Carter doesn't have a purpose.

Without sir, Carter is... *nothing*.

Nothing at all.

ONCE NATHAN HAS CALMED his boy down, sitting beside him and promising over and over that he won't leave, he sends a 511 text to Benny to let him know he needs him for a Carter-related emergency and they need the doctor. He gets an almost instant response that he's grabbing the doc and heading their way.

Nathan puts his phone to the side and begins running his hands through Carter's hair, hating how sweaty and matted the locks are from the night's abuse. His thoughts run wild as he tries to figure out what could be happening to his boy. All he knows is he did this. *Him.* Whatever the fuck is wrong right now, it's *Nathan's* fault.

Is he sick? With what? The flu? An infection? Something he got from the traders? Something he got when he accidentally swallowed some of Henley's fucking piss? Is he just in shock? Has his body been through too much? He hasn't been eating much the past few days. He hasn't been sleeping well either.

But he was fine earlier. Benny said when they got here that Carter was *fine.* Even after getting his wounds dressed, all that was wrong was the boy being emotional. *What changed?*

A few sharp knocks on the door yank Nathan out of his panicked shame spiral. He yells for Benny to come in. His loud voice causes Carter to jump beside him, getting startled out of the foggy half-sleep he had begun to settle in.

"Shhh, sweetheart. You're okay." Nathan holds him tighter. "Just be a good boy for sir, okay? Be my good boy."

"Yes, sir," Carter whispers, sniffling. When the doc and Benny walk into the room, Carter cowers a little, pressing against Nathan as hard as he can. He's terrified, yet he trusts Nathan. Even though Nathan is the one that keeps fucking hurting him, he trusts him. Nathan doesn't know what to do with that. He doesn't *deserve* it.

The doc nods at Nathan in greeting before squatting down in front of Carter and giving him a comforting smile. "Hello, slave. How about we figure out what's going on, hmmm? Make you feel better?"

Carter ducks his head against Nathan's chest like a toddler hiding behind a parent, but he nods.

"Can you come a little forward for me, slave? Just a bit?"

Not saying anything, Carter hunches his shoulders and scoots forward a few inches. When the doctor reaches for him and announces he's going to take Carter's temperature, Carter flinches, but he doesn't pull away or argue. He just stays quiet as silent tears trail down his cheeks. He doesn't stop trembling the entire exam, even after his tears have dried up and his eyes have fallen closed.

Just as the doc finishes up, turning to Nathan to say something, Carter doubles over and chokes out bloody bile into the toilet. Once he starts, he can't stop. He goes and goes, mostly just dry heaving, the only stuff coming up watery and red.

The doc frowns, looking very concerned.

Nathan snaps. "What?"

"I'd like to draw blood. Run a few tests. If that's alright?"

Nathan says, "Absolutely," at the same time Carter whimpers out, "I hate needles."

The doctor looks at Nathan; It's clearly his call. Nathan shakes his head. "Do whatever you need to. I'll hold him down if that's what it takes."

He doesn't have to look at Carter to know the boy is staring at him in betrayal. He can feel the look hot against his skin.

This was the worst decision of his life. *Why the fuck is Nathan here? Why did Travis ever sign up for this shit?*

He should have become an astronaut like he planned when he was 7. The foster home had a space-themed bedroom with a spaceship toy, a cheap telescope, and a stuffed moon he loved to cuddle. He was determined to be an astronaut when he grew up.

Astronauts don't have to deal with this awful tangle of morals and emotions. Astronauts don't have to hold people down for needles. Astronauts don't have to rape the boy they love.

7-year-old Travis had the right idea.

Adult Travis was a fucking idiot.

Once Carter's blood has been drawn, the doc asks Nathan to bring him to the bed. The poor boy begins trembling all over again, his pretty eyes wide open in fear. It isn't until he whispers, "Please... it – it already hurt so bad," that Nathan realizes it's not normal anxiety Carter is fighting. He thinks they're going to rape him now.

Or punish him for being sick.

Or both.

Nathan's chest caves in until he can barely breathe. He looks up at the doc, who is staring at him like he's just waiting for Nathan to give him permission to - *to what? Would the doc actually rape Carter right now? Would he stand by and let Nathan rape him?* The boy is clearly fucking sick and hurting. *Has Nathan really found himself in that dark of a world that even the doctors don't see the slaves as human?* Nathan doesn't want to find out.

"No one is going to hurt you, sw-" Nathan pauses, stumbling over himself. Thankfully, he catches the slip before it gives him away. "-slave. You just need some rest, right doc?"

"Right." The doc looks over at Nathan with a frown, though. "I'd like to give him a bag of IV fluids while I run the tests on his blood."

"Of course. Whatever you think he needs."

Carter still looks terrified, the boy sunk in on himself in the center of the large mattress. It's heartbreaking to watch him try and keep his eyes on all the men in the room, needing to track where the threats are. He can't see the doc and Benny at the same time because they're on opposite sides of the room. It's obvious the boy feels trapped.

Nathan decides to help him out by decreasing the number of threats.

"Benny?"

"Yeah, boss?"

"Can you stay here with the slave and keep watch? I'd like to talk to the doc outside for a moment."

Benny's eyes narrow on him, but he doesn't ask questions, just nods.

The doc finishes putting the IV in Carter's arm, then nods at Nathan to show his acknowledgement of the plan. Nathan leads him out into the hallway and quietly shuts the door behind himself. He takes a few steps away to make sure they won't be heard before asking, "How bad is this?"

"We need to wait for the tests, but can you answer a few more questions for me?"

"Of course."

The doc pulls out a little notebook and pen, then asks, "When did this start?"

"About an hour ago, I think." Nathan stares at the ground, unable to look at the doc even though the doc won't judge. "But he had a particularly grueling night. He was entertainment at the Kensington party."

"What form of entertainment?"

"He was put on a fucking machine and flogged. He... bled."

The doc's smile is one of amusement and envy, like he's sad he didn't get to attend this particular event. It makes Nathan want to pin him up against the wall and choke the life right out of him.

"Well then, he's most definitely exhausted and also dehydrated. Rest and the IV will help with that. How much blood did he lose?"

"Not a lot. The injuries were minor."

"Good." He makes a note. "Now, has he undergone any blunt force trauma, specifically to his torso?"

"I - no?" Nathan closes his eyes, trying to think. Trying to remember. "No. I don't think so."

"Okay. I won't bother lugging an ultrasound over here to check him out, then. I'm sure he's fine."

Nathan can't stop the look of disgust that crosses his face. "No, you're going to bring the fucking ultrasound and anything else that's needed to make that boy better."

The doc raises his eyebrows, lips twitching, and Nathan realizes that probably wasn't good. He shouldn't have said any of that.

Pasting a bored, annoyed expression on his face, Nathan says, "If this slave dies on your watch, you're going to pay me back my 2 million dollars, do you understand me? That slut needs to stay alive until I can get my hands on Maison Beckett and make him watch as we tear his baby brother into pieces. Is that understood?"

"Yes, sir. Absolutely." The doc nods frantically. "Then I'll get the rest of my equipment while the tests run. I'll get back to you as soon as I can."

"Great." Nathan scratches the back of his neck. He should leave it there. He's already shown enough concern. But this is *Carter*, and Nathan *loves* him. "He had some piss in his mouth the other night. He swallowed some. Could that be the cause?"

The doc shrugs. "Possibly, but not likely. We'll be able to know more once the test results come in."

"And that will be when?"

"A few hours. I'll rush it. A buddy of mine will run the blood under the table."

"If I offer you an extra 10 grand, will you make that one hour?"

The doc blinks slowly, then grins. "I can sure as hell try."

Nathan nods once, as if to say that's final. "Anything I can do while you're gone?"

That was too suspicious. Far too suspicious. The doc looks at Nathan like he's unrecognizable for a moment. He shakes his head in confusion, frowning down at his little notebook, before saying, "Well, I - just have him rest. Drink water. Keep the IV in."

"I'm not good at this shit," Nathan says as a non-apology, shrugging a shoulder as he tries to work himself out of this hole he's dug himself. "I just don't want him to die on my hands. Then I look like a fucking idiot."

The doc chuckles. "He's not dying any time soon, sir. Don't you worry. I'm sure you'll be back to fucking him by tomorrow."

Nathan curls his lips in a mischievous grin despite how badly they want to twist in disgust. "I guess I'll survive until then. I'll just have to find one of the other slaves to fuck. I'm too wound up after the party tonight."

"Lucky bastard. I wish my house had sluts walking around all day."

Christ, how the fuck is this man a doctor?

Nathan forces a laugh. When all this shit goes down, Nathan is making sure this fucker's name is plastered on every headline in the country. He'll testify on his behalf if he fucking has to. He's officially found himself in Nathan's top 10, right there with Todd Henley, the Kensingtons, and William Dugray.

He really needs to stop giving people the opportunity to hurt his boy. Pretty soon his top 10 is going to be a little more than 10.

Carter tries to relax on the bed, picking imaginary fuzzies off his blanket. He makes sure to keep glancing over at the monster that still remains in the room. The man is quiet, almost too quiet, as he sits in the armchair in the corner and scowls at the bedroom door.

Carter risks another glance over at Benny, startling when he sees that Benny is staring right at him instead of at the door like before. Carter quickly ducks his head and looks at his hands.

"Do you need anything?" Benny asks in the same kind voice he had used earlier. Carter's memory of the man taking care of him is foggy at best, but he does remember how gentle he had been. At least until the end. Carter thinks he annoyed him at the end. He doesn't remember Benny even leaving, which is probably a bad thing.

He proceeds with caution.

"No thank you, sir."

"You're comfortable? Do you need more blankets? An extra pillow?"

Carter tries not to look at him incredulously. He might fail. It's not very believable that this man cares about his comfort. If he did, he'd save Carter from getting raped and abused all the damn time. Same thing with Nathan. They can't have things both ways. They can't pretend to be kind whenever they feel like it.

Except they can, Carter – remember? You're nothing but the toy they use for their own entertainment. You. Are. Nothing.

"I'm okay. Thank you, sir."

Benny opens his mouth as if to speak but closes it and sits back when the door to the bedroom opens. The doctor is nowhere to be found, sir the only person to enter the room. He stuffs his hands into his pants pockets and jerks his head towards the door, which must be a signal because Benny pushes to his feet and heads towards the door. He glances at Carter before meeting sir's eyes. "He should be on his front, if he can help it. Or his side, if it hurts his stomach too much."

"Alright. Thanks, Ben."

Sir closes the door behind his friend before coming to stand at the foot of the bed. He's still in his clothes from the party, his hair a wreck, his bowtie undone but still hanging around his neck, the top few buttons of his shirt popped open, and his sleeves rolled up haphazardly.

He looks thoroughly mussed and sexy, and Carter would give anything to be worthy of being kissed by him.

Sir meets Carter's eye and speaks in a low, clear voice. "You've been under a great amount of stress. You're dehydrated, malnourished, and exhausted. Your body is having a hard time adjusting. The doc is running your blood for infections and other possible issues, and he's going to bring an ultrasound to check you out, but he seems to be under the impression that this is just from the past week's treatment of your body. Nothing serious."

Carter bites the nail of his thumb, wanting to ask questions but unsure if he's allowed to. His questions don't matter. *Carter* doesn't matter.

He's entertainment. He's a set of holes to fuck. He's a punching bag for when sir is having a bad day. He's a welcome gift to visitors. He's a reward for sir's men to earn.

He's a commodity.

He's not human.

He never will be again.

It's starting to get easier to remember that.

He should be terrified, but he's not. He's *relieved.*

There's a very long stretch of silence. Long enough for Carter to start considering dozing off. He was going to try and stay awake in case sir planned on fucking him again, but if sir wants to do that, he's going to do it. So, Carter might as well get some rest until sir is ready to use him.

Just as Carter is squirming in the sheets, trying to find a happy medium between his injured backside and his upset stomach, sir clears his throat. "Look at me."

Carter follows the order immediately. He starts to cry again when he meets sir's eyes. He doesn't even know *why*. It just happens. Sir tilts his head at him with a frown. "Oh, sweetheart. You're going to be okay."

Guilt eats away at Carter. He hates the look on sir's face. The concern in his voice. He shouldn't be so upset. Carter is nothing to be upset about. "Don't worry about me, sir. I'm nothing. I'm not important."

Sir's expression twists at the same time Carter's stomach cramps. Carter hurries to sit up, feeling the urge to vomit coming on fast. With the IV in his arm and the bathroom so far away, he has no idea how he'll get there, but he has to at least try because throwing up in the bed will definitely make sir mad.

He doesn't want to bother sir by asking for help, though, so Carter slides to the edge of the bed and starts to pull at the tape on his hand to free himself from the IV.

"What are you doing?" sir asks, making Carter jump and then immediately cower.

"H-have'ta - gon'be sick."

"Fuck. Okay." Sir hurries over to his side, eyes scanning. He carefully pushes the blankets away to expose Carter's IV line, his hands slow and gentle as he makes sure it's all freed. Then he grabs the IV bag off the hook it's hanging from and holds it up in the air by his head. "Just walk slowly, and be careful. You don't want to rip that out. It'll hurt like hell."

It takes Carter three attempts to get on his feet, his muscles fighting against him. He shuffles towards the bathroom, now nearly positive that he's going to spill his guts because the room is spinning and his head feels like a bowling ball on his neck. Sir starts to help him walk halfway there. Carter sags against him in relief, letting sir take over.

Sir deposits him on the floor in the same spot he was sitting earlier, lifting the toilet lid for him. Then sir kneels in front of Carter. It seems wrong. Strange. He wants to tell sir to please get up, but that's not his place, so he just ducks his head and waits for the next round of vomit to come to him. It feels like it's right there, burning like acid, but nothing comes.

Hesitantly, sir raises his hand and runs his fingers through Carter's sweaty hair. It feels good. Really fucking good. Carter finds himself laying his cheek on the toilet seat, his eyes falling closed.

"You want me to sanitize that first or something?" sir asks in a soft, amused voice.

"No thanks, sir."

"You sure?"

Carter blinks his eyes open, frowning. "I've dealt with much worse, sir. I'm really not bothered."

He hadn't meant to upset sir with the comment. In fact, he had wanted to comfort sir. It upsets him, though. His face crumples, his eyebrows pulling in. He quickly looks away from Carter. It hides his face, but Carter still sees the way that sir swallows hard, his throat bobbing.

"Sorry, sir," Carter whispers. "I'm really sorry, sir..."

"What?" Sir whips his head back, looking at Carter incredulously. "Why are *you* sorry?"

Carter forces himself to raise his head so he can look at sir better. His eyes water again. He's given up on figuring out why that keeps happening. "It - that - it sounded sassy 'nd I didn't mean it to. Jus' didn't want you to worry. 'M sorry, sir."

Sir roughly pushes his hand through his hair, yanking at the ends of it. He adjusts so he can rest his elbow on his knee, keeping his fingers tangled in his dark blonde locks as he looks down at something on the floor between him and Carter. His voice is strangled as he asks, "Did I break you?"

"Sir?"

Sir looks Carter in the eyes, pain etched in his own. "What I did to you tonight... did I break you?"

"I – I don't-" Carter looks down at the ground, confused. Panic begins to thump inside his chest.

"Was I bad, sir? I – I tried to be good. After my – my punishment, I've been trying to be good..."

"God, no. No, no, no, sweetheart. You were so good for me tonight. So good for me."

"I *wasn't*, though. I – I hugged C – Casey," Carter whispers, tears falling down his face. He doesn't bother to wipe them away. "I – you punished me because I was *bad*!"

"Car-" Sir cuts himself off, putting his face in his hands. His fingers are trembling. "*Fuck*."

He's upset. Clearly. Carter made him upset.

It's not right.

Carter has to fix it.

It's his job to make sir happy.

Carter inches closer to sir and lifts a hand. Then he remembers he can't touch sir, dropping it at the last second before he can touch the man's skin. Sir surprises him, though, grabbing Carter's hand and putting it against his cheek. There's already a bit of stubble growing in now that they're creeping toward morning. Carter likes the way it feels against his fingers.

"Don't be sad, sir," Carter whispers, looking up at him through his lashes. Then he looks down at sir's crotch and tentatively reaches for his belt with his free hand. "C-can I help make you feel better, sir?"

"No, sweetheart. No. Don't help." Sir puts his hand over Carter's, squeezing it gently. "I just – you seem..."

When sir doesn't finish, Carter hangs his head and whispers, "I just wanted to be good for you, sir. I'm just trying to be *good*..."

It takes sir a moment, but then he sits up and gives Carter one of his warm smiles that makes Carter feel like he's on top of the world. Sir cups the side of Carter's face and leans their foreheads together. Carter hurries to pull away, but sir chases him, holding him in place with a hand to the back of Carter's head.

"Where are you going?" sir asks in a husky voice.

"My breath smells, sir. From - from throwing up."

Sir chuckles. "God, the fact that you care - you're so fucking *good*, sweet boy. I'm so happy to have you."

"Really?" Carter asks in wonder.

"Really." Sir presses a kiss to Carter's lips. It's soft. Chaste. Just like the one before the party when sir had begged him to behave tonight. Guilt crawls up Carter's throat, threatening to strangle him. He squeezes his eyes shut and hangs his head, trying not to cry.

"Do you feel sick again, sweetheart?"

Carter's heart breaks. This man is so kind to him. He doesn't deserve it. "I'm fine, sir."

"Okay, let's get you back in bed then. I'll find you a bucket so you don't have to keep going back and forth. It'll be good for you to get some rest." Carter nods, letting sir help him get to his feet. He has to lean on him to walk. He wants to apologize for the inconvenience, but he can't find the words. Everything feels awful and wrong, and he's fairly certain he's dying, even if sir said he's not.

Sir tucks Carter in when they reach the bed, taking care with his IV as he hangs the bag back on its hook. Carter sinks into the pillows and watches the man as he continues to fuss over Carter like a worried mother, putting an empty waste basket by the side of the bed, getting Carter his stuffed moose, checking Carter's IV, getting Carter a damp cloth for his forehead, getting Carter fresh water, getting Carter a straw when he can't get himself to sit up for the water, getting Carter some heavenly gel for his welts, getting Carter a new cloth for his forehead because his fever is warming it up too quickly, checking Carter's IV *again*, getting Carter-

"Sir?" Carter rasps, barely able to keep his eyes open any longer.

"Yeah, sweetheart?"

"Can you jus'... lay with me? 'N – 'n hold me?"

There's a slight pause, but then Carter feels the bed dip beside him. The next moment, sir's hand is running through his hair like earlier, each stroke slow and gentle and reassuring. Sir's lips press a kiss to his temple. Then his cheek. Then that spot behind his ear.

As Carter drifts off, he thinks he hears sir once again whispering an apology. He knows it's not real, but he still lets himself smile.

Chapter Twenty-Two

CARTER IS PRETTY IN and out for a while. He's not sure how much time passes, or what really happens to him during any of it. All he has are hazy, fragmented moments that may not even be real:

Waking up to sir frowning down at him with a thermometer in his hand, saying something about a fever. The sticky taste of medicine on his tongue. Cool water running down his throat as sir urges him to drink.

Sir's deep voice coaxing him from sleep as he reads familiar words about three mischievous friends at a wizarding school, the soft sound of pages turning lulling Carter back to sleep far too soon.

Waking up all alone, sir nowhere to be found. He tries his best to stay awake long enough for sir to come back, but Carter doesn't last.

Stirring awake to find the room dark, lit only by a muted TV. Sir is sleeping peacefully beside him, one arm bent and tucked behind his head, his large, bare chest rising and falling steadily, his dirty blonde hair a disaster, his lips slightly parted. He looks beautiful, breathtakingly so, and Carter manages to stay awake longer than usual so he can soak it in.

Then Carter wakes up feeling better. Steadier. More human. His muscles aren't aching and his skin isn't on fire anymore. Soft fingers are carding through his hair, a warm body pressed up against his side. Once he's blinked a few times to clear his vision, Carter looks up to find sir lying beside him, propped up on one elbow. Sir's smile is brilliant when their eyes meet. "Hey, sweetheart. How are you feeling?"

"Mmm." Carter shifts, trying to assess his body. He's thirsty and still pretty tired, but other than that, he feels relatively good, all things considered. "Better, sir."

"Good." Sir runs a fingertip across his forehead, then down to bop the tip of his nose. It makes Carter laugh under his breath. Sir's smile widens. "Your fever broke a few hours ago, and you haven't thrown up all day. Hopefully you're close to the end."

Carter looks away from sir's face and focuses instead on his bare chest, his fingers pressed against a tattooed bird in flight as guilt threatens to swallow him whole. *How long has he been out? How long has sir had to deal with him?* "I feel well enough to make you feel good, sir."

Sir's throat clicks as he swallows hard. "What?"

"I mean, you don't have to worry about when this will end. You can use me still. I promise I won't... I won't throw up on you or anything."

"I'll use you when I deem fit. You're not well enough yet, and you're not going to argue with me about it. Your job is to get better. That's all you should be worrying about. Okay, sweetheart?"

Carter frowns. "Okay, sir..."

"Do you think you're well enough for a bath?"

"Yes, sir."

"Perfect." Sir plants a kiss on Carter's forehead, making Carter blush. "You stay. I'll be back."

"But-"

Sir stops him with a pointed finger, his eyebrows pulled in and his gaze narrowed playfully. "No, you stay. Rest. Look cute. I'll be right back."

"Yes, sir. Staying. Resting. Looking cute."

"Good boy."

Carter tries to hold back a smile, but he fails. He just loves this version of sir so much. The version who cares. The version that's almost... *human.*

The smile slips away when he realizes how dangerous it is for him to enjoy this version of the monster. This version isn't real. It's only a matter of time before Carter gets hurt again.

Sir isn't human.

Neither is Carter.

It's best he remembers that.

Except... it's so *hard* when the man is walking around with a mischievous smile, coming in and out of the suite to bring snacks and juice and something in a small bottle that Carter can't make out before it's being placed too far away for him to see.

It's so *hard* when the man is taking Carter's hands and helping him to his feet, wrapping an arm around his waist, pressing himself against Carter's front, his lips skimming Carter's forehead as he murmurs, "Good boy."

It's so *hard* when sir scoops him up to carry him bridal style to the bathroom, the man chuckling fondly when Carter squeaks in surprise.

It's not real, Carter reminds himself. *You can enjoy it – you might as well squeeze out everything you can while he's being nice – but don't ever forget that it's not real, Carter.*

The bathwater is warm, the oil swirling in it smelling divine. Carter's healed enough for the heat not to hurt too badly. It's mostly a relieving sensation as the lingering pain and tension in his muscles begins to melt away.

Carter watches sir carefully, his heart sinking as he realizes sir might not be joining him. He wants to beg, but he's already been so bad the past few days, he doesn't want to disappoint sir again. He wants to prove he can be good. Even if it means being lonely. His feelings don't matter. All that matters is sir.

If sir has no desire to use him right now, then Carter has to just – Carter's thoughts blank when he realizes sir is pushing his sweatpants down, revealing that he's naked beneath them. His heart races as he watches sir's tall, muscular body move towards him, sir's cock half-hard as he eyes Carter up like Carter is his prey.

It should terrify Carter.

It doesn't.

Carter attempts to move over to give sir some room as he climbs in, but once sir is seated and has turned the faucet off, he's reaching over and moving Carter until Carter's left leg is hitched over sir's right one. He rests one of his arms across the lip of the tub behind Carter, his hand closing around Carter's shoulder. Sir begins stroking his skin. Carter shivers and rests his head on sir's chest, making him chuckle in a low, sexy way that sounds fond.

It's not real, Carter. It's not real.

"I've missed you," sir whispers.

Carter's world narrows, focusing down to nothing but those three words. His voice trembles when he asks, "Really, sir?"

"Really. It's very lonely and boring without you."

An awful thought comes to Carter. It catches him off guard, pouring out of his mouth before he can stop it. "Did you use other slaves, sir?"

Sir doesn't even hesitate. "No."

"But... they could have made you feel good, sir."

"I don't want them to be the ones making me feel good."

Carter's stomach flutters at that. He remembers sir's erection when he was getting into the tub. If sir has gone this long without release, Carter needs to step up. Sir's pleasure is Carter's sole purpose. He needs to show sir how seriously he takes that. He needs to show sir he was worth waiting for.

Slowly, Carter moves in the bath until he's straddling sir. The water laps around them as he reaches down for sir's cock. It's barely hard, but Carter can fix that. He starts to stroke him in what he hopes isn't too clumsy of a rhythm, planning to get him hard enough to put him in his ass. Carter isn't prepped, but that doesn't matter. All that matters is sir's-

"No, sweetheart," sir says softly, his hand encircling Carter's wrist and gently pulling him away from his cock.

Carter whimpers. "Please, sir?"

"Why?" sir asks, sounding angry and frustrated and desperate to understand. "Why do you keep trying to get me off?"

"I'm sorry, sir," Carter whispers as he hunches his shoulders and shrinks in on himself. "I just – I don't know what else to do. It's all that I am..."

"What's all that you are?"

"Holes, sir." Carter looks sir in the eyes, needing him to understand. He *should* understand. He's who taught Carter this in the first place. "I'm just holes. If you don't want to – to use me anymore, then I'm *nothing*, sir. I'm *useless...*"

Sir just stares at him, looking upset in a way Carter can't place. It's not anger or annoyance, but it's not sadness either. Panic seizes Carter's chest.

Oh god, what if sir doesn't want him anymore?

Carter shakes his head, tears burning his eyes. "Sir, *please.* I don't want to be nothing. I – I thought maybe... the other day, after everything, I thought maybe I wanted to, but I don't. I don't want to die, sir. Please. I can still be useful. I'm not nothing. My holes, they – they still work. Let me show you, sir. Let me p - prove to you that I'm not-"

"Shhh." Sir has his eyes screwed shut, his forehead wrinkled. His hands tremble where they hold Carter's hips. "Just – shhh. Okay?"

"Sorry, sir," Carter frantically whispers. He scrambles off of him and hurries to the opposite side of the tub. Unable to stop the overwhelming emotions raging inside of him, Carter curls into a ball and buries his face in his hands. He grits his teeth so hard he's worried they'll break, but it muffles most of the broken sounds he can't seem to stop, so it's worth it. He doesn't want to upset sir by being loud or annoying after the man specifically asked for silence.

Carter hears a choked, "*Christ*," before water splashes and two arms wrap around him.

"I'm sorry, sir!" Carter cries, no longer able to keep himself quiet. He frantically clings to sir. "I'm sorry I c-can't stop cry-crying. I keep messing up and – and being bad. I'm sorry for – I'm so b-bad!"

"Oh, Carter. Sweetheart. No." Sir cradles Carter's head against his chest with one hand and uses the other to rub his back in soothing circles as he slowly rocks him in the warm water. "Shhh. You're so good, Carter. So good for me. You make me so happy, sweetheart."

"B-but how?" Carter asks between shuddery breaths. "You w-won't u-use me!"

Sir holds him tighter, a sound coming from his throat that almost matches some of Carter's. "I lied, okay? I lied to you. You're not just holes. You're not nothing. Fuck, Carter, you're so much more than any of that. You're every-"

"No!" Carter blurts out, pulling away from sir and desperately shaking his head. He can't do that. He can't let sir take him back to before. Before was too hard. Before, when Carter tried to stay himself, to cling to what was left, all he felt was pain and confusion. This is easier. He wants to stay like this. "I'm not Carter. I'm nothing, sir. Please. I'm nothing. I'm just holes!"

"Carter-"

"No! I'm not him! I'm not him! I'm not-" Carter's words are cut off when sir's lips crash against his. He sobs once into sir's mouth, but sir just swallows the sound and kisses him harder.

Then sir just... keeps kissing him. He kisses him, and kisses him, and kisses him. Sometimes on Carter's lips. Sometimes on his neck. Or his chest. His ears. His nose.

His forehead. His cheeks. His eyelids. That little spot behind Carter's ear that never fails to drive him wild.

Sir kisses Carter until he feels fuzzy inside.

Panting, sir pulls back to look at Carter with brown eyes that are lighter than Carter thinks he's ever seen them before. He pushes to his feet without letting Carter go, pulling him up along with him. Carter stumbles out of the bath. He nearly slips, but sir catches him, never letting go as he leads Carter into the bedroom with a surprising urgency. They're both still dripping wet, but sir apparently doesn't care. He just lays Carter down in the middle of the bed and climbs on top of him.

Then sir is kissing him again.

And kissing him, and kissing him, and kissing him.

Carter prays he never stops.

Nathan can't stop. Every time he manages to get Carter breathless and panting, he just drags his lips elsewhere while Carter fights to catch his breath before returning to his mouth once again. When he's not kissing the boy's mouth, he's trailing his lips and tongue elsewhere. Fucking *everywhere*. He makes sure to be gentle where he's still healing, but it takes a whole lot of effort. He feels fucking feverish with his need for the boy beneath him.

Carter tastes fresh from the collarbone down, but his neck and face taste salty from his sweat that he never got a chance to wash off before Nathan dragged him to the bedroom. Nathan spends extra time in these places. He likes the taste of *Carter*.

"S-sir," Carter pants when Nathan wraps his lips around one of his nipples. He squirms, then gasps, "Oooh, shit," when Nathan nips at it.

Chuckling, Nathan moves on to Carter's other nipple. He pulled a swear out of the boy. It's a start, but it's not enough. Not nearly enough. He wants to pull *all* of Carter out of him. Make him come back to Nathan. No more mindless slave. No more believing he's nothing but holes. He wants his fire. His passion. His sassy little attitude.

Nathan licks his way up the center of Carter's chest before latching onto the side of his throat and sucking. He adds a little bit of teeth at the end, wanting to mark Carter as his - fucking *needing* to mark Carter as his - and groans when it makes Carter grind his cock up against him.

"That's it, Carter." Nathan wraps his large hand around Carter's slim hip and encourages Carter to grind against him again. It doesn't take much convincing at all before the boy is shamelessly humping him. "That's it. Good boy. Such a good boy."

"Sir!" Carter whines, his hips moving faster against Nathan.

And Nathan, maybe because of his fear at the idea of losing what makes Carter *Carter*, or because of the blood that's leaving his brain to fill his cock, or maybe even because of his need to just feel fucking *human*, drags his mouth to Carter's and whispers, "Nathan," against his lips.

"W-what?" Carter pants, pulling back to look Nathan in the eyes.

"Nathan, Carter. Call me Nathan."

"But-"

"Carter." Nathan rests on his left elbow, moving his weight so he can reach up and cup Carter's cheek with his right hand. "Right now, you're Carter and I'm Nathan, okay?"

For a moment, Nathan is terrified that Carter is going to freak out again like in the tub. His blue eyes go wide, his breath stopping, but then the boy tentatively raises a hand to cup Nathan's cheek just like Nathan is cupping his. He drags his thumb along Nathan's cheekbone, staring at Nathan like he's a work of art. The attention is intoxicating.

What's even better, though, is when Carter looks him in the eyes and whispers, "Hey, Nathan."

Nathan fucking *shudders* at the sound of his name as it rolls off Carter's tongue. "Hey, Carter."

The boy's smile is brilliant. Nathan feels like he can finally fucking breathe again.

"I want to keep kissing you." Nathan rests the pad of his thumb on Carter's bottom lip and tugs. "Can I kiss you, Carter?"

"I - it's up to me?"

"Yes."

"Because we're Carter and Nathan."

Nathan smiles. "Yes."

Carter opens and closes his mouth twice before breaking eye contact with Nathan, his gaze focusing on Nathan's chest instead. His eyelashes are wet with unshed tears. "How fucked up am I if I let you?"

"Does it matter?" Nathan asks quietly, praying it doesn't. "Because it doesn't matter to me."

"I shouldn't want to be with you."

"Probably not, no."

"But I-" Carter pauses. He licks his lips before peeking up at Nathan. The poor boy looks so afraid and confused. "I really *really* want you to kiss me..."

The confession hangs in the small pocket of air between them. Nathan isn't sure if it's consent. He wants

Carter to give him explicit permission. He's just terrified the boy will withdraw if he pushes further for it.

Then he gets an idea.

A terrible, terrible, *terrible* fucking idea.

"Why don't you kiss me instead, Carter?"

Carter's eyebrows pull in. "What?"

Rolling off him, Nathan lays on his back and throws one arm up to rest on the pillow above his head. He reaches for Carter with the other hand, stopping just before they make skin-on-skin contact. He needs Carter to close the distance.

In a soft voice, Nathan promises, "I won't touch you tonight. We can just sleep, and you won't be in trouble. There will be no punishment. I won't be upset. We'll wake up in the morning and go back to being master and slave. Or..."

"Or?" Carter asks, his voice cracking.

"Or, you can kiss me, and touch me, and do whatever you want to me tonight. You can use your power to consent, and I can show you what I'd do with you if you were mine as just Nathan, not as the boss of this place. Not as your brother's enemy."

Carter nibbles on his bottom lip, looking unsure.

"We've done it before," Nathan whispers. He shouldn't be pushing Carter, he knows that, but... Nathan needs him. It's selfish and wrong, but after what happened at that party, Nathan *needs* him. "We had a good day together, on your day off."

"And it was over when we woke up."

"Yes."

"And that's how it will be again tomorrow?"

Nathan sighs. "Yes, Carter. I'm sorry. It's - this is all I can offer. It's more than I should offer at all, if I'm being honest, but you're very talented at making me break my own rules."

"I'd say I'm sorry, but I'm not."

"I wish I could give you more," Nathan admits. "I'd give you the fucking world if I could, Carter. But even this could get us both killed."

"It's okay. Really." Carter lifts a hand, placing it on Nathan's cheek. It feels unbelievably good. Nathan presses his hand over the boy's, wanting to keep it there as long as he can. "This is enough, Nathan. Whatever you can give me is enough."

Nathan turns his face into the palm of Carter's hand, hiding the shit-eating grin he can't keep at bay. He presses a kiss there. Then another. And another. When Carter giggles, he lifts his head to look at him, deciding it's worth showing his joy if he can see Carter's too. The boy's eyes light up when their gazes meet.

"I think I'm going to kiss you, Nathan," Carter declares.

Nathan licks his lips, already feeling a little breathless. "Do your worst, Carter."

CARTER DOESN'T KNOW WHERE to start. His experience level boils down to drunken fumbling in corners at parties, and getting raped. Not much to go off. He starts to panic a little, his hands hovering above Nathan's body, his eyes scanning everywhere like they can't manage to stay in one place long enough.

"Come here," Nathan whispers, taking Carter by the hand and gently guiding him. He helps Carter settle so that he's straddling Nathan's waist, then puts one hand on the mattress beside his naked hip and tucks the other beneath his head on the pillow. It's like he's not even willing to touch Carter without consent. He's just going to lay back and literally let Carter do whatever he'd like. Let Carter *do his worst.*

A sudden wave of *need* rushes through Carter, sending him into attack mode. He's clumsy and, if Nathan's grunt is any indication, it's a little too hard, but it's also so damn *good.* Carter kisses him, and their teeth clash a little, and he bites Nathan's lip, but Nathan moans, and Carter can feel Nathan's large cock growing hard against his ass, and Carter thinks even if it's not a great kiss, it's great for *them.*

Eventually, Carter pulls back and begins to kiss Nathan like Nathan had been kissing him earlier. He kisses up his jaw and licks the shell of his ear. He kisses down one side of Nathan's neck, along his collarbone, then up the other side. He sucks on Nathan's earlobe, which earns Carter a surprisingly loud moan that makes him grin.

With a sudden burst of confidence, Carter brings his mouth down to the earlobe again and grazes his teeth against the flesh. It nearly undoes the man beneath him, a strangled noise spilling from Nathan's lips, his hand reaching for Carter. He drops the hand last second, fisting the sheets instead, but his whole body begins to tremble with the clear effort it takes for him to behave. When Carter repeats his actions to the opposite earlobe, Nathan squeezes his eyes shut and shudders.

"Fuck, Carter," Nathan growls. Carter runs the tip of his tongue along the shell of his ear, grinning when the hand beneath Nathan's head comes out to slaps against the mattress, fingers fisting the sheets. "Shit, I forgot how fucking good that feels."

Carter sits up, still grinning as he starts to map out the dips and curves of the man's sexy body. His finger traces the outline of the broken birdcage tattoo. "Forgot? You act like you've gone years without sex."

"I have."

"You have what?"

"Gone years without sex. Sex like this, at least." Nathan raises his hand from the bed again before dropping it back down. It's sort of amusing to Carter. He's wondering how long the man will last. Especially if he's telling the truth right now.

Carter really hopes he's telling the truth. It's stupid, he *knows* it's stupid, but for some reason, the idea makes him feel special.

He decides to drop it just in case it's a lie.

"Where else are you sensitive?" Carter asks instead, raising an eyebrow.

Nathan cocks an eyebrow of his own, his lips curving into a sexy smirk. "Gonna have to find out for yourself, sweetheart."

Goosebumps ripple along Carter's skin at the dirty challenge. The reaction makes Nathan's smirk widen. He decides to wipe that smirk off Nathan's face by leaning down and nipping at his earlobe one more time, laughing breathlessly when it earns him another delicious moan.

Then Carter turns his attention to Nathan's chest. He traces the tattoos with his tongue, kissing each bird he comes across. Nathan watches him the whole time with heavy-lidded eyes, his breathing labored. He doesn't find any sensitive spots like Nathan's ears, but there is one dip near his collarbone that pulls a satisfying shudder from the man, and sucking his nipples earn Carter some more moans. Nathan stays perfectly under control, though. Nothing like the desperation from before.

Carter keeps moving, determined to force this man beneath him to unravel.

He finds what he's looking for at the crease between Nathan's thigh and pelvis. The moment Carter's lips brush across the skin, Nathan's left leg jolts and he gasps. Carter feels fingertips brush his shoulder for a breath before Nathan's hand returns to the bedding. He's pretty sure he hears the sheets rip, but he's enjoying himself too much to investigate.

He sucks the spot.

Nathan's control snaps.

Within seconds, Carter has been hiked up by firm hands on his biceps, pressed tight against Nathan's chest, and rolled onto his back. Carter is breathless as he blinks up at Nathan in shock. The man stares down at him with an expression that's positively feral.

"You remember the safe word?"

Carter shivers. "Yes, sir."

"What is it?"

"Red."

"Good boy." Nathan crashes his mouth down over Carter's, the kiss violent and urgent. Carter wraps his legs around Nathan's waist and runs his hands along the strong muscles rippling in his back. A moan vibrates between them. Or two moans. They're pressed so close, Carter can't even tell which one of them moaned, or if they both did. When Nathan pulls away, his lips are wet with their combined spit. Carter can't help that he darts his tongue out to collect his own evidence. "Hands above your head. Hold the pillow if you need."

Carter nods, not sure if he's capable of words anymore. He grabs the pillow. Nathan rewards him by moving down Carter's body and wrapping a hand tight around his cock. He chuckles when he sees Carter's eyes go wide. He's still making the sound when he wraps his lips around Carter's cock, the rumbling an intoxicating vibration against him.

"Fuck." Carter lifts his head to look down at Nathan, groaning when he sees that Nathan's eyes are focused on him, his pupils blown wide. He keeps his gaze locked onto

Carter's as he pulls off and drags the flat of his tongue along the underside of Carter's cock. Carter drops his head back and closes his eyes, feeling like he's lying on a cloud that's slowly floating further and further away from the ground. It's not long before Nathan has worked him into a panting, writhing mess.

If Carter wasn't so desperate to come, he'd be ashamed.

"Fuck - Nate - I'm - *fuck*."

Nathan lifts his head, eyes narrowed dangerously even as his lips stretch into a wide, sexy smirk. "Yes?"

"I'm gonna come if you keep doin' that," Carter pants.

"Mmm." Nathan licks his lips, his eyes flicking down to Carter's cock briefly before returning to his face. "You want to come, sweetheart?"

"Please. Please, sir, can I?"

"No." Nathan sits back with an evil grin. "Not yet. You can come on my cock."

Carter pouts. He has a feeling Nathan is going to draw this out and he's not entirely sure if he'll survive.

"My poor boy," Nathan coos. He wraps his hand around Carter's cock again as he moves forward to bump his nose against Carter's. Their lips brush in a not-quite kiss. "You want to be fucked, sweetheart?"

"*Please*."

After making a satisfied noise, Nathan begins kissing his way down Carter's body again. He doesn't take his time, a man on a mission, but he does spare a few extra seconds to tease his nipples with his tongue and teeth until he has Carter whining beneath him. By the time he reaches Carter's cock, it's drooling precum. Carter shudders at the sight of Nathan licking up his mess.

Two strong hands grab the backs of Carter's thighs and push, not stopping until he's bent in half. Nathan's hot breath passes over his balls. His taint. His -

"Oh, fuck. Wha-" Carter nearly swallows his tongue as Nathan begins to lap at his hole.

Nathan flicks his gaze up at Carter for just a second, flashing him that wicked grin of his before returning to his task of completely unraveling Carter with his tongue.

It's the second time he's been eaten out - both by Nathan. Honestly, when he'd watch it in porn, he never saw the appeal of such a thing.

There's appeal.

A whole fucking lot of appeal.

"Shhhit." Carter grabs at Nathan's hair, not even sure if he wants to tug him away to get a break from the overwhelming pleasure, or pull him closer to get more of it. Either way, Nathan doesn't give him a choice.

"Put your hands where you were told before you earn a spanking," he growls against Carter's sensitive skin.

With a whimper, Carter forces himself to let go, gripping the pillow right away as tightly as he can. His muscles start to jerk with the effort it takes to keep himself under control. If this is Nathan's revenge for Carter's earlier explorations, it's excellent.

Nathan slides a finger inside of Carter to work alongside his tongue.

Carter becomes suddenly aware that he's forgotten how to speak. In fact, he's forgotten what language he speaks entirely. All he can do is watch Nathan in a trance - as he laps at his hole, as he slides in a second finger, as he nips at the sensitive skin, as he pulls away and wipes his mouth on Carter's thigh, as he looks into Carter's eyes and *grins*.

Adrenaline spikes in his system as he watches Nathan slowly climb back up his body, the man looking far too much like a wild animal stalking his prey. Carter's never wanted to be hunted and devoured before, but it's looking damn appealing right about now.

And then Nathan suddenly... *softens*. His eyes go warm. His smile relaxes. He cups Carter's cheek and bumps the tips of their noses together. The playful moment makes Carter giggle. Nathan seems to like that. Nathan seems to like that *a lot*. He pulls back to look down at Carter like he's the most incredible thing Nathan has ever seen. It does crazy, beautiful things to Carter. Dangerous things.

"I really like making you laugh."

"I really like you making me laugh," Carter admits, smiling up at him.

Nathan grins. "Well, then. We'll just have to do that more often, won't we?"

"Sounds good to me."

"Mmm." Nathan's eyes flash, his smile going dangerous again. "Though laughter isn't what I want to hear from you right now."

Carter shivers. "Oh?"

"I'd much rather hear you moan. Whimper." Nathan drags his teeth down the shell of Carter's ear, making him cry out. He bucks up at the same time, his naked cock rubbing against Nathan's. He moans. Then whimpers. Nathan's laugh is victorious. "Maybe I'll even make you scream."

"Oh god."

"Just remember, don't go screaming my name. You're a loud little thing. Gotta call me sir." Nathan's lips quirk. "Or do I need to gag you?"

Carter nibbles on his bottom lip, his cock aching. "I can remember, sir."

"I know you can. Such a good boy. My good, good boy." Nathan slides forward, resting his forearms on the mattress to frame Carter's head. The position makes Nathan look much bigger than before, as if he's encompassing Carter completely. As if he's become Carter's whole world.

Carter supposes he has.

"You still okay, sweetheart?" Nathan asks, resting his forehead against Carter's.

"Yeah. Yeah, I'm good."

"Safe word?"

"Red."

"Such a good boy." Nathan lowers his mouth until it's pressed against Carter's. He kisses Carter gently, *thoroughly*, as he slowly runs the tips of his fingers down the right side of Carter's ribcage and over his to grip his right thigh. Carter moans when Nathan hikes his leg up and around his waist. He can feel Nathan's hard cock bump against one of his ass cheeks. It's leaking precum, leaving a warm trail across Carter's skin.

Nathan shifts his hips until the tip of his cock is pressed against Carter's spit-soaked hole. Then he pauses, looking into Carter's eyes. "You want it gentle, or hard?"

"How would you do it if I was really yours?"

Looking down at him with a hooded expression, Nathan admits, "Hard."

"Then fuck me hard."

Giving Carter a devilish grin, Nathan adjusts his weight and starts to press forward. At first, Carter thinks that maybe Nathan had changed his mind, deciding to go soft instead. The way he enters him is gentle. Slow. There's no resistance, Carter's hole opening up for him easily.

But the moment Nathan bottoms out, things change. He grabs hold of Carter's throat with one hand and pushes one of his legs further back with the other, and he begins to fuck him *hard*. Each thrust is enough to knock the breath from Carter's lungs, his body jolting up the bed until Nathan wraps his fingers around a chunk of Carter's hair and holds him steady with it. Then his thrusts feel even harder, deeper, no escape or reprieve available, his body trapped as Nathan pounds him hard enough to make Carter's mind fucking scramble.

There's enough of his mind to realize one thing, though. One strange, unexpected, mind-blowing, confusing as fuck, thing.

Nathan, when being *sir*, has been holding back.

Carter is in nowhere near the right mindset to even begin to fucking analyze that.

Nathan's hips snap forward, again and again, his balls slapping against Carter's sensitive skin. It hurts Carter's bruised ass and thighs, but they're healed enough where it's not a bad kind of pain. If anything, it heightens the pleasure, making everything more intense.

"Come on, sweetheart," Nathan growls, looking down at Carter in frustration. Carter has no idea why. He doesn't know what he's doing wrong.

Sir's big, strong hands grab Carter's legs and push them together before he sits up on his knees and hooks Carter's legs over his broad right shoulder. His arms wrap around both of Carter's thighs, holding him firmly in place as he starts to slam into him. Carter screams. Actually fucking *screams*.

"There we go," Nathan practically purrs. "There we fucking go, sweetheart. That's a good boy."

"N-no." Carter shakes his head, eyes watering as his prostate is assaulted. He barely manages to choke out another desperate, "No."

"Yes, Carter." Nathan narrows his eyes, tongue darting out to lick across his bottom lip. "You have a safe word. Use it, or fucking take this."

"Oh god. I'm gonna come."

"Did I say you could?"

Carter whines. "Sir, *please*."

Nathan just chuckles darkly before shoving both of Carter's legs off to the side. He leans down and wraps an arm around Carter's back, flipping him onto his hands and knees with one simple tug, leaving him breathless with his legs spread wide and his head spinning. He collects Carter's wrists and pins them at the small of his back, not seeming to care when it causes Carter to fall forward, his face smashing against the mattress.

Keeping Carter's wrists pinned with his hand, Nathan reaches up and grabs his shoulder with the other. If Carter thought he was being held firmly in place before, he was wrong. *This* is trapped. Nathan proves it by beginning to fuck the absolute *shit* out of Carter.

Carter's vision blurs. His tongue lulls out of the corner of his mouth. His legs spread wider like he's an absolute desperate slut - which he is right now. All he can think of is Nathan's cock. It's like a needy chant in his head. Well, that, and his desperation to come.

He tries to beg. He's not positive if he succeeds. He's not sure if Nathan even responds.

Nathan collects him at some point, pulling him up until his back is pressed against Nathan's chest. He grips Carter's throat with one hand, using the other to hold him in place by the hip. Carter whines. It's about all he can do. Words are a foreign concept at the moment. Not that he has the breath to speak even if his vocabulary was in place.

"Come for me, Carter," Nathan growls in his ear, hand flexing on Carter's throat. "Come for me right now."

Carter shakes his head, not even to argue, but to - to - he doesn't even *know*. He just keeps shaking his head. He sobs too.

And then he comes.

He comes with his back bowed, tears falling down his cheeks, Nathan fucking up into him with abandon. He comes as Nathan releases him, his body turning to jelly, falling forward until he's lying limp against the mattress. He comes until he feels emptied of everything but Nathan's cock that continues brutally fucking him.

Carter finally manages to catch his breath when his orgasm tapers off. Nathan bites down on his shoulder, pulling a hoarse shout from him. Then Carter is fucking coming *again*.

Things go fuzzy then. Blissfully fuzzy.

The only thing that makes its way through his sex-induced haze are three words. "I love you."

And Carter's vocabulary returns with some words of his own. "I love you, too."

I LOVE YOU, TOO.

Nathan stands at the sink after wiping himself down, hands braced on the counter, weight leaning forward. He can't stop staring at his reflection. At the man in the mirror. The man that Carter Beckett loves.

I love you, too.

He can still taste the boy's salty-sweet skin on his tongue. He can still feel the way he shivered against him. The way he writhed beneath his hands. He can still hear his soft moans and whimpers. His gasps. His begging.

His confession.

I love you, too.

Nathan doesn't think he'll ever stop hearing that confession.

I love you, too.

Nathan splashes his face with cold water, hoping to snap himself out of this spiral Carter has suddenly plunged him into. Maybe he should blame himself. He was the one to confess his love first, after all.

But he's said it before. He had no idea the boy was going to throw his entire existence for a fucking loop by saying the words *back*. He's never said them back. He's never even remembered Nathan saying them at all.

I love you, too.

398

"Fuck." Nathan dries his face with a hand towel. "Fuck. *Fuck.*"

I love you, too.

Nathan does the responsible thing. He collects his supplies - a bowl of warm water, a fresh cloth, the med kit Benny gave him - and heads back into the bedroom. Carter is sprawled out on his back, limp but awake. He gives Nathan a sleepy smile, though his eyes hold apprehension. "Sir?"

I love you, too.

"Still Nathan," Nathan promises, knowing that's what his boy is afraid of. "I'm going to clean you up and check how you're healing, alright?"

The boy's smile widens.

I love you, too.

Nathan gently washes the boy's chest and stomach, then his soft cock and balls. He turns him over and washes between his ass cheeks. He presses kisses over the soft, pliant globes of flesh. He presses kisses over every bruise and healing cut. He presses kisses on each individual knob of his spine.

"Gonna make me fall 'sleep," the boy mumbles, his eyelids heavy as he looks at Nathan over his shoulder.

I love you, too.

"Just let me put some of the salve on. Then you can fall asleep if you'd like."

"Mmm'kay."

I love you, too.

Nathan smoothes the cool gel over the boy's wounds. Then he covers his hands with some lotion and begins to massage all of his uninjured areas, starting with his neck and working all the way down to the boy's feet.

Carter is practically purring.

I love you, too.

Nathan cleans up and climbs into bed beside Carter, pressing a kiss to his shoulder. Carter wiggles and releases a happy little sigh.

How the fuck is Nathan lucky enough for this boy to love him?

"Are you sure you're okay? After everything?" Nathan gently pushes Carter's messy hair off his forehead. "You can be honest with me. It won't do any good for us to just pretend nothing happened."

Carter frowns, his eyes blinking a little harder than they should. Nathan isn't sure if it's from exhaustion or a fight against tears. Both send waves of guilt through him.

"You put me in the dark again," Carter finally says, his voice thin and reedy.

"What? When did I do that?"

"The blindfold." Carter's eyes slide shut, his chin dipping. "I tried to tell you. I don't know if you heard me. Or - or if you even cared..."

Words, faded and buried beneath Nathan's panic and grief from the time, flit through Nathan's mind. *No, not the dark, not the dark, sir, please, not the dark.* Nathan's heart wrenches in his chest, the realization of what he's done a fucking sucker punch.

"Oh, Carter..." Nathan nudges a loose fist beneath the boy's chin, needing to look at him. Carter doesn't fight it, showing Nathan his big blue eyes. He blinks. Fat tears fall down his cheeks. "It hadn't registered. I remember you saying that, I do, but at the time - fuck, sweetheart... it hadn't registered. I didn't mean to."

"Oh..."

"You just kept looking at Casey, and I - I needed you to stop that. I couldn't let you do that to yourself."

Carter nods, looking away from him again. Nathan allows it. He even moves away from the boy to give him space. "I'm sorry, Carter."

"Yeah." Carter forces a smile, but it's weak. Thin. He lets it fall right after. "I get it. It's fine..."

With a sigh, Nathan lays back on the bed and stares up at the ceiling. He hates himself. Fucking *despises* himself. "It's not."

"No. It's not."

An awful silence stretches out between them then. That's why Nathan startles when a body suddenly presses up against him. Nathan holds his breath, the air expelling from his lungs with a single shudder when he feels Carter's lips drag across the bare skin of his chest. The boy's breath is warm as he whispers against him, "Your heart is pounding."

"I know." Nathan swallows hard, tentatively wrapping his arm around Carter. The boy melts against him. It does something dangerous to Nathan.

"Are you upset?"

"No. God no." Nathan releases a shaky little laugh. "I'm perfect. I'm right where I want to be."

Carter sighs softly at that, his body slumping a bit. "Sometimes it hurts to hear you say things like that..."

"What? Why?"

"I don't know. I feel like..." Carter presses harder against him. "I feel like I'm always a breath away from losing you, and you're not even mine to lose."

"I am, Carter. I'm 100 percent yours to lose."

Carter is quiet for a long time. Long enough for Nathan to think he's fallen asleep. Then, quietly, he asks, "Did you tell me you love me? Just now, when we finished?"

Nathan sighs. "Yes."

"This wasn't the first time, was it?"

It's phrased less like a question and more like a statement, but Nathan answers anyway. "No. I've said it before."

"Oh." Carter releases a shaky breath. "I thought I had imagined it."

"No. I've loved you for quite some time now."

"Yeah..." Carter turns then, resting his chin on Nathan's chest. His eyes are glassy. "Me too."

Something catches inside Nathan. It's akin to the sensation of falling during a training course, plunging to your death for a second before your harness' fail-safe kicks in and jerks you to a halt.

"Really?"

"Yes." Carter runs a fingertip along Nathan's lips, tracing them. "I hate myself for it, but yes."

"I'm sorry."

Carter gives Nathan a smile that is far too easy and happy for a boy that's been through as much as Nathan has put him through. "There's no point in talking about it or even apologizing. It is what it is."

"How do you do that?" Nathan asks in awe.

"Do what?"

"Be so positive. Happy."

The look Carter gives him makes him regret the question. "You don't want me to break. And - and I don't think I want to break either. So, I have to be like this. It's the only way I'll survive."

That's the difference between them, Nathan realizes. Nathan shut himself down to survive. He put Travis in a box and replaced him with a monster. Carter is hanging onto himself to survive. He's clinging to his humanity and refusing to let it be taken from him. *What does that say about Nathan?*

What does it say about Carter?

Not for the first time, Carter's strength leaves Nathan breathless. He doesn't know how he got this lucky. Meeting Carter has been like a fucking religious experience. Carter makes him question everything he's ever thought. Carter makes him want to be Travis again for the first time in years. Carter gives him fucking hope.

"This was your first time saying it," Nathan says carefully. "That you love me, I mean."

"Is it? I wasn't sure. I've... thought it before."

"Yeah?"

"Mhm." Carter nibbles on his bottom lip, not exactly meeting Nathan's eye. "Did you tell me you loved me at the party? After my punishment?"

"Yes."

"Wasn't Benny there?"

"Not close enough to hear." Nathan laughs, short and dry. "Though I'm quite certain he's figured it out."

Carter frowns at that, his gaze finally meeting Nathan's. "Isn't that dangerous?"

"No. I trust Benny with my life. With your life. But if anyone else found out, then yes, it'd be dangerous. Deadly."

The boy shudders before tucking his face against Nathan's side and relaxing again. Nathan wraps his arm around him and pulls him nice and close, being careful not to touch him in any of his majorly injured places as he slowly begins to stroke patterns onto his bare skin. Carter sighs contentedly.

"Nate?"

"Yeah, sweetheart?"

"I'm a little hungry..." the boy's voice trembles, his shoulder curling inward. It kills Nathan that Carter's instinct is still to fear him. He'd give anything to change that. "Do you think maybe I could have a little snack?"

I told you I love you, Nathan wants to say. *Why are you so afraid to ask for food when I just told you I love you?*

But Nathan doesn't say that because he knows the truth; Carter will never trust him. Not enough. Not fully. He'll always be the monster. Even if now he's the monster in love with Carter, the monster that *Carter loves,* he's still the monster.

Nathan will never get to be anything but the monster.

"I'll get us some food," Nathan says in an awfully thick voice. "How about you get the next Harry Potter movie ready for us. If you think you're awake enough?"

Carter sits up then, grinning wide at him. There's no trace of fear in his gaze. No apprehension. The boy is purely *happy.* Nathan wishes he could press pause on the feeling. He wishes he could live in it with Carter forever.

"HEY, NATHAN?" CARTER ASKS as the movie credits begin to roll.

"Yeah, sweetheart?"

Carter rolls onto his side and looks at Nathan, frowning. He's not sure how far his *Carter* freedom goes. Part of him needs to find out. Part of him is too afraid to.

As if Nathan can sense this, which he probably can because he always seems to just *know*, Nathan encourages Carter. "Go ahead. I promise you won't get in trouble."

"I was just wondering if-" Carter trails off, the memory of Nathan slamming him into a table resurfacing. It's followed closely by the memory of the man flogging him bloody.

Then the memory of Casey. All those men. Hurting him. Raping him. Maybe even... killing him.

"Hey," Nathan says softly, reaching for Carter. His hand goes up in surrender when Carter jumps at the touch. "Carter, sweetheart, are you okay?"

"Yeah." Carter clears his throat and forces a shaky smile. "I'm fine."

"Carter-"

"It was just a bad memory," Carter explains, hoping Nathan will let it go. "Just - just left the bedroom for a minute."

"And went where?"

Carter looks away and shakes his head. "I'd like to not think about it, please."

It takes Nathan a second, but then he's whispering a broken, "Oh."

Arms wrap around Carter, pulling him in close. He tucks his face in the curve of Nathan's neck and breathes him in.

"Please tell me what you wanted to say."

Carter holds onto Nathan a little tighter. "The slave from the party. The one I hugged. I was wondering if you know if he's okay?"

Nathan sighs in resignation, as if he'd been expecting that. "Casey, you mean?"

"Yes, sir."

"Casey is alive, if that's what you're asking. I'm not sure if *okay* is a word I'd use, but I have a feeling things will be changing for him soon anyway. For the better."

Carter goes still. "What does that mean?"

Nathan smirks. "Someone new will be taking care of Casey. Someone much better."

"Oh." Carter pauses, licking his lips. He meets Nathan's gaze. The man looks relaxed, his lips having softened to an easy smile, his eyes warm and kind. It's enough to give him the confidence to ask, "Do you think I'll ever see him again?"

"Yes. With his new owner, you'll see him again."

"You know who's buying him?"

Nathan's lips twitch. "In a way."

Carter really wishes he could demand Nathan stop being so fucking cryptic. He would never, though. Not just because of the punishment it'd earn him, but also because he doesn't want Nathan to stop answering his questions. He still has so much to ask.

Turns out, Nathan has questions too. "How do you know Casey?"

"We were in the cell together."

"The cell?"

"Yes." Carter focuses on the blanket beneath his fingers, not allowing his mind to drift back to that place. "The cell the man who took us kept us in until the auction. Or, well, not in my case, but I think everyone else stayed there until they were sold or whatever."

"You two were cellmates, then?"

Carter scoffs. "Well, us and, like, 15 others."

Something complicated passes through Nathan's expression before his face goes deceptively blank. "All in one cell? 15?"

"The numbers were always changing, but yeah."

"How big of a cell?"

"I guess like a jail cell? I've never been to jail, but that's what I'd assume they're like. It had metal bars like a jail cell, but we weren't at a jail. We were... I don't even know. Somewhere damp. Dark." Carter shudders. *Don't think of the dark.* "There was a light bulb that hung in the hallway, so not... *dark.*"

"Yes, I saw that cell. He kept you all in there the whole time? That wasn't just where he kept everyone during processing?"

Carter flinches. He can't help the betrayal that seeps into his voice when he asks, "What do you mean you *saw* that cell?"

When Nathan hesitates, Carter forces himself to look at the man. He wishes he hadn't. It takes a lot to make Nathan look guilty, and right now, he looks downright remorseful. "He sent pictures of you."

"Oh." Carter tries to swallow, but his throat refuses to work properly. He remembers pictures being taken of him. The bright pops of light bursting at him in between traumatizing moments. *They had sent those pictures to Nathan?* "You got them when you - when you bought me? Like a... gift?"

"No. They were a part of your advertisement."

Carter doesn't so much as flinch this time as he recoils. He can't look at Nathan. "An *advertisement*."

"You must have known something like that happened, Carter. Men didn't just show up and get the pleasant surprise of finding out you were for sale. Hell, even normal auctions have advertisements. There are encrypted websites the sellers set up. It shows each slave's profile, including background, pictures, videos -"

"Stop," Carter begs. "Please stop."

Nathan does as asked, going quiet. The heavy silence is almost worse.

Carter squeezes his eyes shut, forcing himself to focus. Casey. They're talking about Casey. If he wants more information on his friend, he has to answer Nathan's questions.

"I met Casey in the cell. We bonded over helping a little boy who missed his - his m-mom." Carter laughs dryly at himself as he digs the heels of his hands into his eyes. He's going to cry again. He's so fucking *sick* of crying. Carter growls in frustration as the tears force their way out regardless of his fruitless attempts to keep them away.

"Carter?"

"Never mind. I can't - I don't want to talk about it anymore."

"Did you say a little boy was with you?"

Carter breathes out angrily through his nose. "I just said I don't want to talk about it!"

"Hey, look at me." Nathan's voice grounds him. It's cold. Hard. It leaves no room for Carter to do or feel anything besides what Nathan allows. Carter opens his eyes, finding that Nathan's expression matches his tone. "How little was this boy?"

"Please," Carter begs. "I don't wanna talk about it, Nate."

Nathan's face and tone soften, but he continues to push. "Carter, this is *important*."

"I don't-" Carter stops himself. If he tells Nathan, maybe he can ask for more information of his own. Maybe he can ask about Elliot. Maybe he knows something like he knew something about Casey. "I don't think he ever said. Young. Too fucking young."

"That fucker."

Carter flinches at the tone of Nathan's voice. If he thought it was cold and hard before, that was nothing compared to now. "What?"

"He's not supposed to be doing that. Selling children." Nathan huffs. "That sneaky piece of shit. There weren't any at the auction. None in the group photo of the cell either. That bastard."

"Is that your moral line?" Carter asks sarcastically. "Rape adults, but no children?"

Nathan's eyes flash at him. "No. It's just not his market. He must be selling them under the table. I'm not the only one who would be pissed if they found this out. He's breaking the rules."

"There are rules?"

"Yes. Absolutely. Otherwise it's all fucking chaos." Nathan points a finger at him. "And chaos gets you caught."

"Who makes the rules?"

"Us. The major players. Me. Hanson. Miller. Saint-Pierre. Quinton."

"And you decide who gets what markets?"

"In a way. We agree amongst ourselves. It's like a social convention. No one has it written down that this market or that market belongs to a certain someone, but it's just understood. That's not to say that everything is concrete, by any means. I've been collecting markets since I took over here. There used to be 9 major players at the table. We're down to 5. I'm hoping to get it down to 4. If I have my way, I'll control almost the entire north-western hemisphere."

Carter traces a finger along the edge of one of Nathan's scars. Something is twisting in his gut. Something... he doesn't like. "Isn't that making you enemies?"

"Well, it's not like I leave them hanging around. And those who worked under them know it's best to conform."

Carter frowns. "Did you know that J.F.K. had his own elite group of men who would infiltrate governments and assassinate major leaders he didn't like?"

Nathan sounds amused for some reason when he answers. "I may have read that somewhere, yes."

"One of his staffers was interviewed way down the road, like when everything became unclassified." Carter turns in Nathan's arms, resting his chin on his chest so he can look at him. "When talking about his assassination, he pretty much said something along the lines of, *Well, what did J.F.K. expect? He started it.*"

Nathan's lips twist into a smirk. "Are you implying that I'm going to get iced, Carter?"

"If that means killed, then yes." Carter nibbles his lip, feeling his cheeks go hot. "Or, at least, I'm *worried* about it. A... bit."

The amusement in Nathan's expression suddenly softens, replaced by fondness. "Nothing will happen to you, even if that does happen. Benny will make sure of it."

"I'm not worried about me. Honestly, I'd probably be better off in the long run. It's you I don't want to see hurt..."

"What?" Nathan sits up then, turning to give Carter his full attention. "You'd be better off?"

Carter winces. "That sounds worse than I meant it to. I just... if someone else owned me, I'd be a normal slave. I'd be like the others. I get that you refuse to let me break or whatever, but that's because of how you feel about me. Whoever took me next wouldn't have the same qualms. They'd want to break me."

"And you think you'd be better off broken?" Nathan practically growls.

"I don't know, honestly. But you have to see where I'm coming from. You're a smart man. My mind is full of fire and passion. My mind was working towards one day fighting the very thing I've fallen victim to. I have the mind of a protester. An activist. An unapologetic snowflake. You've trapped that mind in a body that has to obey to survive. That has to sit back quietly while others get hurt and killed. That has to take whatever is handed to it and thank the person after. You have to see how awful that is, Nathan. I know you do."

Nathan's nostrils flare. "So, what? You'd really rather me mentally break you? Just make you empty and worthless? Truly just holes?"

Carter looks off to the side, his eyes burning. He hadn't meant for this to be a conversation. At least not tonight. Not after they've just confessed their love only hours before.

But he won't lie.

"I think I've gotten glimpses of what it'd be like, Nathan. I think you've shoved me into that mindset a few times, not enough to stick, but enough where I know what it feels like. It's a fuzzy feeling. It's... safe." Carter forces himself to look at Nathan then, filled with a sudden desperation for him to understand. "Things are so simple in that headspace. I'm *nothing*. All I have to do is obey. That's it. That's all my brain has to focus on. That's all the energy I have to expend. I don't feel hungry or thirsty. I don't feel scared or hurt. I just... float."

"Carter-"

"Do you want to know what I feel like every single day?" Nathan looks like that's the last thing he wants to know, but he nods anyway. Carter doesn't sugarcoat it. "It feels like I'm constantly walking on a tightrope. Every second, I'm always on the knives edge between the slave you want me to be and the mind you want me to keep. It's this awful, constant balancing act, and I really want to jump, Nathan. I spend every second fighting the urge to just fucking *jump*."

"I know. I know, Carter. I see it. But I - I can't let you. You have to stay with me." Nathan looks him in the eyes, his expression anguished and pleading. "You *have* to stay."

"Yeah." Carter lays back down, grabbing his moose. There's nothing to say to that. Nothing to do. His mind belongs to Nathan, just like everything else. There's no point in arguing. He shouldn't have even brought it up in the first place. It was stupid. "I'm staying, Nathan. Don't worry. I'm aware I have to. Trust me, there's nothing I'm more aware of."

"Carter–"

"But you know I'll break one day, right? Like, medically speaking, there is a point where a person's brain breaks. My stubbornness will only last so long. I'm not superhuman."

Nathan looks away from him, jaw working. "That won't happen. It *won't*. I won't let it."

"Oh, so *you're* superhuman, then?" Carter asks with a huff.

"I don't share you anymore. I told you I love you. I don't have to force you. I give you pleasure as often as I can. I take care of you. You love me back." Nathan looks at him again, his expression impossibly fierce. "You act like you have to endure what the other slaves do. You're fucking spoiled compared to all of them. You're not going to break."

"Okay, Nathan." Carter lies down, turning onto his side so his back is to the man that he's contemplating punching. "Let's just drop it."

With a frustrated sigh, Nathan switches off the TV and sets the light near the door to its lowest setting. He waits an awkwardly long time before finally laying down on his side of the bed. Carter holds his breath, waiting for the inevitable. There's no way Nathan will drop this. Carter knows him too well.

Sure enough - "Tell me how to fix this."

Carter says nothing. It's not to be stubborn, he just has no idea how to fix it. He doesn't know if fixing it is even possible.

Unless...

"Nathan?"

"Yes?"

Carter swallows hard. *Is he really going to do this? Is he really going to finally put words to the thoughts bouncing inside his head the past few days? The thoughts he's been so afraid of, he can't even look at them straight on?*

Yes.

He has to.

"You said once that you might kill me, after you're done with me." When Nathan says nothing, just holding perfectly still, Carter pushes forward. "I was wondering if maybe you'd promise me you'll do that."

"Promise to do what?"

"Kill me."

THERE ARE VERY FEW moments in his life that Nathan can point to and say, *yes, that there, that was when everything changed.* When he was orphaned. When he joined the military. When he became Nathan Roarke. When he first laid a hand on the only boy he's ever raped. When he realized he had fallen in love with Carter Beckett.

And now.

With two words.

Kill me.

"Carter." Nathan tries to swallow, but his throat is impossibly tight. He sounds choked as he forces himself to continue. "Whatever you heard, whatever I said – you have to know that's not the case. I love you. I'd never kill you. Never sell you. *Never*, Carter."

Carter doesn't relax at that. He tenses up, then jerks around in Nathan's hold so he can look at him. His eyes are wide and panicked. His nostrils flare. "No, please."

"Please?"

"Please kill me, Nate. When it's all over. When I'm not needed anymore. *Please*."

"Carter-" Nathan breathes, unsure how he's managing to breathe at all.

"If you really love me, you'll do it." A tear falls down Carter's cheek. His fingers scrabble as they grip desperately at Nathan's arm. "Please, Nate. Promise you'll kill me. Promise you'll set me free. I'll be so good until then, so fucking good. I won't break. I'll stay Carter for you. I won't jump off the tightrope, not ever, but you have to give me this. You have to put a light at the end of the tunnel. Please just make it quick and finally put an end to it all."

Biles crawls along the back of Nathan's throat. Oxygen sets fire to his lungs. "No."

The boy sobs. It sounds eerily similar to the way he had cried when Nathan had beaten him at the party.

"Please," he begs, the word slurred by his sobs. "Please, sir. Nathan. *Please*. I can't stick around forever. Love me or not, I'll be used up eventually. I'll get old. You'll get bored. I - just - god, Nate, please. Just say you'll do it. Promise me you'll do it."

"Carter, that's enough."

"I'll do it myself!" the boy warns.

For a moment, Nathan almost scoffs.

Then he sees the look in Carter's eyes. He's fucking serious. He'll do it.

Carter refuses to live this life any longer than he has to. He's made up his mind. *When did that happen? When did Carter come to the conclusion that death would be better than this?*

"If you don't promise," the boy says carefully, having managed to get his crying under control enough for him to have a rational conversation. He must have sensed Nathan's wavering. *Is Nathan wavering?* "I'll do it before you catch Maison. I'll ruin your plans."

"Sweetheart..."

"I almost did it once already."

Nathan's world tilts. He lurches into a sitting position, his heart pounding hard enough for the beat to echo in his throat. "*What?*"

"After the party. I had it planned, but then..." Carter looks away from him, shrugging. "God, I was so *tired*. I couldn't get myself to do it."

That's it.

It's the final straw.

Nathan can't protect this boy. Not from himself. Carter said it already - he's not fucking superhuman.

This isn't working anymore. Things have to change.

Nathan tells his best lie yet. He takes Carter's face in his hands, presses their foreheads together, and whispers, "If you promise to stay with me until I'm done with you, if you promise to remain unbroken, then yes, I'll kill you. I promise I'll kill you. I'll make it quick. Painless. And when we rape you, when it's time to hurt you in front of Maison, I'll drug you so you're too out of your mind to even feel it."

Carter shudders as a sob of relief racks his body. He falls forward, burying his face in Nathan's neck and wrapping his arms and legs around him.

"Thank you!" he sobs. Once he's started, he can't seem to stop. "Thank you, thank you, thank you."

It takes forever for him to cry himself out. Even then, he keeps whispering breathy little *thank you*'s.

By the time the boy finally passes out in Nathan's arms, Nathan has come to a decision. One he's willing to die for if necessary.

He carefully extracts himself from Carter, pulling a blanket over the boy. Then he grabs his phone and heads into the bathroom.

He locks the door.

He turns on the sink.

He dials.

3 rings.

A clipped voice.

"Name?"

"Eagle 2."

"Code?"

"7134."

"Hold."

A soft crackle.

"Nate, hey man. Everything good?"

"Yeah." Nathan laughs. "No, actually. No. Not at all, Maison. Nothing is good at all."

Maison's tone sharpens. "What's wrong?"

Nathan closes his eyes, memories assaulting his brain like needles.

A *naked, trembling boy on a spanking bench, blindfold soaked in tears. Nathan placing his hand on the boy's pink ass cheek, running a thumb along the edge of a welt from that damn riding crop Quinton allowed his men to use. The soft, "Please don't." The gasps. The whimpers. The fear so thick Nathan could taste it on the back of his tongue. The wrecked, awful sob as Nathan began to rape his virgin hole.*

A *naked, trembling boy hoisting himself up to straddle Nathan's lap. Big blue eyes avoiding Nathan's gaze. The boy struggling to breathe. His cheeks burning red as Nathan slides fingers into his hole to prep him. The soft, "Oh,"* when Nathan finds his prostate. The roll of his hips. The tears of shame building. The squelch of lube. Nathan's own voice, foreign and awful as he orders, "Up." Carter's head shaking frantically, "No, no, no, no, no," falling from his lips in desperation. Someone spanking Carter to hurry him along. The sobs muffled against the skin of Nathan's throat. The uncontrollable shivers. The soft cock the boy is trying desperately to get to cooperate. Nathan forcing himself to shift gears to get this shit over with.

A naked, trembling boy tossed over the arm of a chair, sobbing so loud Nathan can feel the sounds rattling inside his chest. Nathan fucking the boy like he's nothing but a hole. The boy going quiet. Pliant. Lifeless. Just empty blue eyes and dried tear tracks on ruddy cheeks.

A naked, trembling boy spread out on the bed in the dungeon, ass in the air, face twisted in pain. The harsh thud of a paddle on skin. The mocking laughter of Nathan's men. The sharp slice of the cane. The boy sobbing. Screaming. Writhing. The desperate apologies. A cock rubbing against sheets in search of relief. Nathan's awful, "Look at this fucking slut." Nathan putting hands on his poor body, forcing him to humiliate himself some more as his men enjoy the show. Piss soaking the sheets. A boy's voice, distant and cold as he apologizes yet again. Nathan calling him sweetheart. The pet name making him cry even harder. A deflated boy who looks... empty.

A naked, trembling boy at the feet of Todd Henley.

"How's the slut?"

"He's very pretty when he cries."

A naked, trembling boy flushing with arousal and excitement.

"Are you going to eat me all up, Nathan?"

"It's tempting, little red."

A naked, trembling boy desperate to be used.

"I want to fuck you now."

"Yes. Now. Great. Do that."

A naked, trembling boy terrified as he watches his best friend inch towards the brink of death.

"Casey. Please, sir. He won't survive it. Give them me."

"You should probably worry about your own survival right now, you fucking idiot. Don't you remember what I told you would happen if you did something like this? Why do you always have to fucking ruin everything?"

A naked, trembling boy feeling sick and helpless.

"I hate needles."

"Do whatever you need to. I'll hold him down if that's what it takes."

A naked, trembling boy–

"Nathan!" Maison yells. The tone of his voice indicates this isn't the first time he's said his name. "Nathan!"

Nathan pushes to his feet. He looks at his reflection in the mirror. The same one he stared at earlier. The image of the man Carter Beckett loves.

He takes a very deep breath.

Then, "It's time, Maison."

"Time?"

And Nathan has never felt so sure of anything.

"It's time we tell Carter the truth."

Made in the USA
Columbia, SC
02 July 2025

60246475R00255